13
17

When He Found Her, Kita Nekai
Was Nea
Now She's V

I hissed at the vampire. "Do you usually make friends with shapeshifters by holding them hostage, chained up in a basement, naked?"

Nathanial shrugged. "I rescued you on the street. Most people would be appreciative."

"I don't need anyone's protection, especially if it involves making me a prisoner."

"You do not understand. I saved your life. Unfortunately, there are side effects." He let ̶ ̶ ̶ ̶ ̶ realize I was free.

I lunged to my fe̶ ̶ ̶ ̶ standing was better than ̶ ̶ ̶ ̶ a hand toward me and I ̶ ̶

I saw it then, a singl̶ the cement floor. I stare̶ up, my eyes slid to Nat̶ sluggish blood to escape.

Pressure built in the̶ longer able to close over ̶ ̶ crept closer. His blood-f̶ pulled me forward. I coul̶

"What have you don̶ my mouth closed over t̶ taste onto my tongue.

The Haven Series

Once Bitten

Twice Dead

Third Blood (Coming in 2011)

❧ • ❧

No. 1 Bestsellers at Amazon Kindle and Fictionwise!

"Urban fantasy readers who enjoy the works of Kelly Armstrong and V.K.   Forrest will have a great time reading this exhilarating story." —*Harriet Klausner, Amazon Top Reviewer*

"I had a hard time putting this book down." —*Literary Escapism*

"Different and fresh." —*SciFiGuy*

"Thoroughly entertaining." —*Patricia's Vampire Notes*

"An exciting new series." —*Darque Reviews*

"Readers will be left begging for more. —J. *Kaye's Book Blog*

"A perfect adventure" —*Paranormal Romance*

"For all urban fantasy fans out there, Once Bitten is a must read. Kalayna Price has created a tantalizing masterpiece of adventure and intrigue." —*Abibliophile*

Kalayna Price

HER NINE LIVES JUST GOT LONGER

Meow. Purr.

Die. Repeat

Once Bitten

BELL BRIDGE BOOKS * MEMPHIS, TENNESSEE

Bell Bridge Books
PO BOX 300921
Memphis, TN 38130
ISBN: 978-0-9802453-9-4

Bell Bridge Books is an Imprint of BelleBooks, Inc.

We at BelleBooks enjoy hearing from readers. You can contact us at the address above or at BelleBooks@BelleBooks.com

Visit our websites – www.BelleBooks.com and www.BellBridgeBooks.com.

10 9 8 7 6 5 4 3

Cover design: Deborah Dixon
Interior design: Hank Smith
Art Credits: Woman "© Martin Valigursky | Dreamstime.com"
                  Light © silvano audisio - Fotolia.com
                  City©: Dmitry Pistrov - istockphoto.com
:Ll.01.

Dedication

To Mom, who believed me when I said
I would be a writer.
Thanks for encouraging me.

Chapter 1

In the last ten minutes I'd gone from miserable to totally screwed.

An hour ago I'd thought a city named Haven would be good luck. Now I wondered who it was supposed to be a haven for—polar bears and penguins? Next time I snuck aboard a train, I would remember to check whether it was headed north or south. The snow-laden streets were the miserable bit; "screwed" began two blocks back when I picked up the scent of something never meant to exist in the human world. Well, a something other than me.

A woman cut a beeline through my path, her attention on a curbing taxi. I stopped, the man behind me didn't. He shouldered by with a grunt, his briefcase slamming into my thigh. I scowled after him, but he didn't look back, let alone apologize.

I hated crowds. Any one of the bundled-up people trudging down the street could be hunting me. Of course, that same anonymity protected me. Shivering inside my over-large coat, I resisted the urge to glance over my shoulder as I matched pace with the pedestrian traffic. Remaining inconspicuous was key.

A *Do Not Walk* sign flashed, and the crowd stopped on the corner of Fifth and Harden. Horns blared and drivers shouted, but despite the green light, there wasn't much room for the cars to move. Some of the more impatient foot traffic wove through the vehicles, earning a one-fingered wave from a cabbie as another car slid into the space that opened in front of him. I debated crossing, but decided keeping a low profile among the suits on the corner was safer. Shifting my weight from foot to foot, I held my breath as a city bus covered us in a dirty cloud of exhaust.

A hand landed on my shoulder.

"Kita Nekai," a deep voice whispered. "Come with me."

I froze, unable to turn for fear any movement would betray me into running. *Breathe.* I needed to breathe, an impossible task around the lump in my throat. My first gasp of air brought the hunter's scent to me, and the skin along my spine prickled in a response more primal than fear. *Damn. Wolf.* The blood rushing through my ears drowned out the street sounds so the crowd moved silently, in slow motion.

The fingers digging into my shoulder tightened, and my eyes darted to them. The manicured nails and white cuff peeking out under his brown coat sleeve marked the hunter as a suit. He'd blend in nicely with this crowd.

"Let go of me." I didn't bother whispering, and the woman beside me coughed as she glanced at us.

A half-turn put me eye level with the hunter's red-silk tie. I grabbed his wrist, a weak illusion that I was the one doing the restraining, and cleared my throat.

"Thief! Pickpocket! He stole my purse!"

People turned, their eyes taking in the hunter's pristine pinstriped suit and my Salvation Army duster with its patched elbows and frayed hem. The suits closest to us shuffled further away, casting leery glances from the corners of their eyes. But they watched. They all watched, and the hunter couldn't just drag me off the street with so many human witnesses. I saw that realization burn across his amber eyes.

The light changed, and the crowd surged forward, filling the small gap that had opened when I created my scene. The hunter clung to my shoulder, but the push of bodies dislodged his hand, and I let myself be carried away. The businessmen in tailored suits and women in pumps towered over me. I never thought I'd be grateful for being short, but with any luck, that would hide me from the hunter's view—if only I could cover my scent that easily.

The crowd flowed down a set of cement stairs to the subway. The voices of hundreds of commuters bounced off the underground walls, a symphony of impatience accented by flickering fluorescent tubes. As they pushed into lines in front of the turnstiles, I realized the flaw in this plan: money, or really, my lack thereof.

Okay, no time to panic.

A weathered sign advertising public restrooms hung on my side of the turnstile, and I hurried through the door. The hunter wasn't likely polite enough to obey the little girls' room sign, but I was willing to bet the line of women waiting inside would give him pause.

I bypassed the line, ducking inside the first open stall and locking the thin door against the angry murmurs of protest. The cramped space boasted dingy walls covered in scrawled insults and just enough room to stand in front of a rust-rimmed toilet. *What a lovely hiding place.*

The need to pace itched my heels, and I rocked back and forth on my toes, hugging my arms around my chest.

Someone pounded on my door.

"Stall's taken," I said.

"Hurry up," an agitated, but clearly female, voice said.

I ignored her. There were two other stalls she could use.

I rocked on my heels again. I needed a plan. The bladder-heavy humans aside, if I tried to out-wait the hunter the after-work crowd would thin, and I needed human observers to protect me. The bathroom had only one door, and if the hunter saw me enter, all he had to do was watch for me to exit. Of course, if I could slip out without him recognizing me . . .

How much did he know about me? He knew my name and clan, but did he know anything else? It was a chance I had to take.

Balancing on the toilet seat, I tucked my knees to my chest so I wasn't visible under the stall walls. Around me, agitated voices complained about everything from the wait to the gray weather. I closed my eyes and tuned them out. I needed to center myself. Mentally I stroked the coiled energy inside me. It boiled. Spread. I anticipated the pain but still drew a ragged breath as the energy burst to the surface.

A sharp sting shot down my back, and the skin split open. My clothes vanished as they always had for my change. A whimper trembled in my throat, and I choked it back, but it escaped as my skin slipped off and reversed itself. My joints popped loudly as they reformed.

Someone banged on my door again. Could they hear the fleshy sound of my muscles and organs rearranging? I hoped they were just impatient. Then I passed into the seconds of the change in which I had no awareness of my surroundings.

My skin sealed around my body again, and the dingy stall snapped back into focus. My right foot slipped, and I fell up to my hips into the toilet bowl. Hissing, I scrambled over the seat and landed with a wet plop on the tiled floor.

Great, now I resembled a half-drowned rat.

Twitching my tail, I shook my back legs and tried to dislodge as much of the water as possible. I only accomplished further soaking the gritty tile. My back paw slipped, leaving gray streaks in its wake across the brown tile.

Disgusting.

I craned my neck, then hesitated. Did I really want to give my fur a quick bath? That was toilet water. It was better for it to be on my fur than my tongue, right? I struggled with that thought a moment, my instincts demanding the offensive substance be removed.

"Anybody in there?" Someone shook the stall door.

My attention snapped back to more important matters—time was of the essence, a bath would have to wait. I was taking a risk by shapeshifting into my second form. If the hunter found me, I wouldn't be able to defend myself—at least not in any way that would matter, and no one would question him chasing down a cat. But, I had to get out of this subway station.

A child pointed as I crawled under the bathroom stall.

"Look Mommy, a calico!"

I sauntered closer to the girl, staying just out of reach—children had the tendency to pull tails.

"Stay away from it," her mother said, jerking the child back. "It might be rabid."

My lips curled to hiss at the insult, but I curbed the desire. Hostility wouldn't get me anywhere.

Purring, I wound around the legs of the next lady in line. She pressed a tissue to her nose and backed away. Great.

Who was my most likely ticket out? My gaze landed on a woman washing her hands. She'd been shopping, and several large department store bags stood staunchly at her feet. Slinking over, I dove into a fancy white bag and curled up beside a hat box and hoped she wouldn't notice the extra weight.

I repositioned myself to balance the load as she claimed her belongings and bustled out of the bathroom. The bag swung in her grip, propelling me into something hard. The turnstile was a nightmare. She pushed through it, and one of the packages squeezed all the air out of me. I thought the worst must be over as the bags swung free again, but the swaying made my stomach threaten to rebel.

No, I won't be sick. I refuse to.

I got sick all over her hatbox.

Shaking, I eased away from the box. The swish of the train doors opening initiated another barrage of attacks as people crowded into the car. The train lurched into motion, but the movement of the bag settled.

I peeked out and found myself at eye level with a startled brunette. She screamed, dumping the contents of her lap to the floor. I guess the cat was out of the bag—well, not yet, but I needed to be. Dashing through a forest of legs, I hid under the seat of a man in mud-caked construction boots.

From the limited shelter, I sniffed the recycled, train-car air. Not a hint of the hunter's scent.

Thank the moon.

In the past five years I'd caught a hunter's scent maybe half-a-dozen times. Most cities had at least one hunter stationed somewhere to watch for rogues and strays, but I'd never before had any reason to believe they were hunting me specifically. This wolf obviously was.

Closing my eyes, I mentally touched the tight coil inside me. It would be awhile before I could return to human form. Well, chances were good that the station where I ended up would be far from the hunter. Tucking my tail around my body, I resigned myself to a long ride.

꩜ • ꩜

Night had fallen during my subway ride, transforming the city of Haven from the dull gray of evening to inky darkness. That darkness framed the welcoming glow of storefronts and streetlights glistening in the snow. Tomorrow, when Amtrak began running again, I would need to find a way back to the train yard. Tonight, I just needed a place to lay low and protection from the cold.

The streets lacked the hurried commuters that had been present in the business district, so they were easily navigated on four legs. I could only hope there was an animal lover among the varied shoppers. I stopped in front of a high-end clothing store and perched on the cleared steps in a pool of light, better to see and be seen.

I scanned the crowd, searching for friendly faces sympathetic to a stray cat. No one looked my way. Finally, a couple turned toward me. *Show time.* The woman leaned down and scratched under my chin. I purred encouragingly and nudged her hand, but the man tugged her arm. With the swish of her coat tails, she was gone. Pressing my ears back, I huddled into a ball for warmth and glared at the shoppers as they scurried from one pool of light to another.

Ten more minutes. If no one took me home or offered me food in the next ten minutes, I was giving up and shifting back to my human form. Of course, if I wanted someone to take pity on me, I probably shouldn't glare at them like I'd claw out their eyes.

I left my dry perch and moved to the center of the sidewalk to circle the legs of the first passing person. He shoved me aside with his boot without pausing.

Jerk.

I called to a gaggle of teenagers with my most pathetic *meow*, but though one of the girls glanced at me, they didn't stop.

What was wrong with these people? I didn't look mangy, anymore. I had broken down on the subway and washed my fur. I still wasn't sure the bath made me feel any cleaner, but it did make me look more presentable.

I paced. Clumps of snow stuck between my paw pads, and ice clung to my tail. This wasn't working. Time for Plan B—whatever that was, but it definitely included two legs that could walk me into somewhere warm.

I ducked into the alley behind a clothing shop. A large dumpster took up most of the space, but a quick sniff told me everything I needed to know about it—nothing edible there. Weren't there restaurants in this part of town?

Twitching my tail in annoyance, I crouched in the deep shadows and made quick work of shifting back to human form. The snow chilled me to my core in the seconds between my bare flesh forming and my clothes appearing. *Stupid city.* Maybe I'd been too optimistic before—even polar bears would freeze here. I huddled inside my coat and hurried back to the street.

Now that I was five feet taller and walking on two feet again, the city changed for me. Colors were richer with my human eyes, but the shadows hid more from my sight, making the darkness far more oppressive. I trudged past the teenagers I had begged to take me home earlier. Now, I kept my gaze down, avoiding drawing attention to myself. The teenagers, absorbed in divvying out a street vendor's Styrofoam cups filled with hot chocolate, ignored my presence even more as a human than they had as a cat.

I turned on Magnolia Boulevard and then onto Primrose. Shop after shop displayed brightly dressed mannequins. How many clothing stores did this city have? I could understand if the people here needed more clothing than most to stay warm, but the fashions I was seeing would never have been worn on the street. I stopped to stare at a window featuring a live mannequin decked in an elaborate evening gown. It must have been deliciously warm inside for her to flash that much skin, but with my battered coat and blue jeans there wasn't a chance I could blend in to their clientele.

I trudged on. The happy glow of a bookstore greeted me a few blocks later. That I could handle.

I stomped the snow off my sneakers and watched it puddle on the welcome mat. The aroma of fresh coffee and hot cinnamon buns drew me toward the café in a corner of the bookstore. My stomach rumbled. Shifting was hungry business, and I'd done it twice today without a meal in-between. But I still had exactly no money, so after a quick glance around confirmed the café's lack of free samples, I wove my way through aisles of bookcases, further from the inviting smells.

I hadn't caught hint of a hunter's presence since leaving the subway, so this was about as safe as I could get without leaving town. I shucked my coat and hat, and left them in a vacant chair. Then I went in search of a book.

❧ • ❧

Several hours passed before the soft background music turned off and a crisp voice announced that in fifteen minutes the store would be closing. I shut the book in my lap and added it to the growing stack around me. The overly defined man on the cover stared out hungrily at me. I frowned at him.

Purposeful footsteps headed straight for me, and my head snapped up. *Had the hunter...?* My gaze landed on a teenage girl fidgeting idly with her green-and-yellow name tag. She popped a pink bubble between her teeth before looking at the top book on my stack.

"You know," she said, plastering an artificial smile on her face. "That's a great book, very sexy and hot. She's one of my favorite authors. Did you know she released a new book two weeks ago? It's hot. Really hot. I think we still have a couple in stock. Let me find you a copy." She scanned the shelf of books behind her, popping her gum again. "Ah, here it is. You should definitely read it. Speaking of hot, another steamy book is—"

"That's okay. This really isn't my flavor of reading material."

"Oh, that's too bad. Well, are there any other books I can help you find?" The smile never slid off her face. I wondered if her cheeks hurt after a full day of working.

"I'm actually on my way out," I said, freeing myself from the overstuffed chair.

It took effort to keep from scowling at the sales girl, who was still watching me after I'd donned my coat. Instead, I ignored her and walked away. I must have blipped on her radar as more interesting than the other customers, because she fell in step beside me.

"I like your hair. It's really crazy and alternative. Must take forever to do."

The look on my face knocked the plastic smile off hers. No one actually liked my hair. It was a random mismatch of black, orange-red and white streaks—not silver like aging people, but true white. It looked like the highlighting job from Hell. Unfortunately, it was natural. I tried to imagine the sales girl willingly doing something similar, but couldn't. The soft-looking girl in front of me had a heart-shaped face people probably considered cute. A word no one ever applied to me, at least not while I stood on two feet. Though the same height, which meant the sales girl was on the short side, we were polar opposites in every other way. With my sharp features and unusual coloring, people tended to call me *striking*, but never *cute*. If I could have traded my calico mess of hair for her finely permed blond, I would have. But I couldn't. My hair was a side effect of what I was.

"Here, take this." She reached into the front pocket of her apron and pulled out a red slip of paper the size of a postcard. "A friend of mine is spinning tonight. To get another gig he needs the place to be jumping, so I'm spreading the word to anyone likely to go, and with your hair . . . I thought you might be interested. There's a map on the back."

"Thanks." I shoved the flyer in my coat pocket without looking at it. We reached the door and I jerked it open. Brisk winter air rushed in, bringing with it city smells and something the sales girl couldn't detect. The hunter.

Damn. I let the door swing shut and searched for another exit. There was one on the far side of the building, but it had an "Emergency Only" sign posted above it. Well, this counted as an emergency, didn't it? Something waited for me outside the main door. However, walking out the emergency exit would set off an alarm, and I didn't need that kind of attention.

"Do you have a bathroom?" I asked, groping for a plan. If I could stay in the bookstore overnight or leave the way I had the subway station . . .

"Nope, sorry. Bathrooms are closed for cleaning. Didn't you hear the announcement? The whole store is closed."

I stared at her, trying not to let panic show on my face. I glanced around. The only other customer, a middle-aged woman with a young child, waited at the cash-wrap. Everyone else wandered around straightening books.

The sales girl tugged at the pockets of her apron. The popping of her gum escalated, sounding like a small machine gun firing from her mouth. "Um . . . the store is closed. If there's nothing else I can help you find . . ."

The customer from the cash-wrap walked to the door, child on one hand, bag in the other. As she bustled by, I followed her out. A sharp click cut through the night as the clerk bolted the door behind us. At the sound, an extra stab of tension locked onto my spine and stuck there. I could feel eyes boring into me. *He* was out there, but I couldn't pin down where.

I kept my head down and fell in step a couple yards behind the mother and child. Earlier people had been walking much closer together on the street, but now it was only them and me. The woman glanced over her shoulder and pulled the child nearer to her.

The final car left at the metered parking flashed its lights as she approached, the locks disengaging. The woman herded the child into the passenger seat and then slid behind the wheel. She didn't worry about seatbelts. I hadn't fully crossed the street when the engine roared to life. The car door slammed, and I was left not quite alone on the empty sidewalk

I watched the car speed away. The air swirling around me was tainted with the inhuman scent of another shapeshifter.

The hunter had found me.

I breathed deeply, the frigid air burning my nose. No, not hunter. *Hunters*. There was more than one scent. Cursing, I tried to pick up a trail or some indication of where my hunters waited, but the scent was dispersed. They were circling. *Like vultures. Or canids outmaneuvering prey.*

I shivered. I'd never heard of hunters traveling in packs. The mingled scents were too jumbled for me to guess how many hunters were out there, or from which families. Wolf clans were the most numerous, so if I had to put money on it, I'd guess they were the ones hunting me.

I looked around. Nothing in the darkness moved. I needed to find a new place to hide. I didn't know the area, so I left the decision of which direction to go to the wind. A bone-chilling breeze swept up the street. If I walked against it, I would be able to scent what was ahead of me, but anyone following my scent would have an easy time. If I went with the wind, I would know what was behind me, but any hunters ahead of me would know I was coming. I'd rather deal with hunters coming at me from the front than sneaking up behind me. I went with the wind.

All the shops on the street were dark and still. With buildings looming on either side, the only thing I could look forward to was the spill of the next street light to chase away the creeping dark of the alleyways. Someone digging through a trashcan crouched as I passed. I couldn't tell if it was a man or woman bundled under the mismatched clothing, but whoever it was eyed me as warily as I watched him or her. I hurried on. A solitary car threw strange shadows as it rolled down the street.

I passed another block of dark buildings. If the hunters were still out there, I should have caught hint of them following me by now. Maybe they had missed my scent and it was a coincidence more than one had passed the bookstore. But I couldn't convince myself of that.

A thrum of bass thundered in the air, vibrating off the surrounding buildings. It had to be coming from a club. If I could find the club, it would be full of people who'd provide me with anonymity and safety.

I stopped and listened. It didn't sound too far away.

After several blocks I realized I'd passed it. Now the music was diagonally behind me. Backtracking lost me the wind advantage, and I couldn't find a street leading closer to the music. Alleys cut between most of the buildings, so I turned down the nearest. A fence topped with barbed wire stopped it from being a thru-way. Nope. I wasn't going over *that*. I headed back toward the street.

Something crashed behind me, and I whirled around. A cat dashed from a toppled crate and disappeared through a hole in the fence. I took a deep breath. Jumping at shadows wasn't going to help. I needed to get off the street. I spared one last glance at the crate, then left the alley behind.

Three steps onto the street, a hand captured the back of my neck.

I swallowed a scream as my heart lodged in my throat. I tried to turn, but the hand tightened, preventing me from moving my head. My captor gave a small shove, and I stumbled forward. *Crap*. He shoved again. My muscles tensed, ready to run. The fingers only dug in harder. With little other choice, I let the hand guide me back into the alley.

We passed the crate the stray had toppled, and my captor's grip slackened. I wrenched free, spinning on my heels. I ducked, throwing my arms up to guard my face, but the blow I anticipated didn't come. I scurried back a few steps. My captor didn't try to stop me.

Focusing through the haze of fear and adrenaline took a moment. He should have just hit me—it couldn't have been any more painful than recognizing him.

"Did they send you to hunt me, Bobby? Or did you volunteer?"

Bobby straightened, his face taut. "I missed you, Kitten," he finally said, his hand reaching for my face.

"Kita, not Kitten." I took another step back, out of his reach.

His hand fell to his side then started forward again, only to be drawn back like he hadn't meant to move it in the first place. His other hand caught the first as if wrestling for control. I watched the skirmish, until I realized I was performing a very similar dance. Clenching my fists, I shoved them into the pockets of my coat. My eyes focused past him, watching the headlights of a car slide across the dumpsters in the alley. It was an effort to ignore the battle of his hands, but it wasn't his hands that had the most potential to hurt me.

"What's your plan, Bobby? Chains? Rope? Or do you intend to lock me in the basement of a safe house until the gate opens?"

"I'm not hunting you. Sebastian wants you home. It isn't safe here."

"Tell my father—"

"He isn't calling you home as a father." Bobby's fingers clenched so tight the leather of his gloves looked ready to tear over his knuckles. "I'm trying to help you. To get you home. Do you know how many hunters are after you?"

I was starting to get an idea, but I only shrugged, the movement lost under my coat. "He sent that many?" Maybe I'd been holding onto the hope that my father would be easier on me, but being the daughter of the *Torin*, the clan leader, had never helped me before. "So, what did my dear father say he planned to do after I'm hauled back to Firth?"

"Don't you know what's going on? Your being here *implicates* you. Hunters are all over this city, and they aren't playing nice right now. Too much is at stake; I have to get you out of the city until the gate home reopens."

"Implicates me for what? Not that it matters. We can't leave without a train, and they're down until morning. Sneaking aboard isn't easy, but at least it's free. Anything else is going to take money."

"I have money."

"Must be nice to be here legally."

"Kita—"

"I'm not leaving. I've hidden out this long. I'll stay a bit longer."

Bobby turned and stalked across the mouth of the alley like a predator caged in a zoo. "You don't understand," he yelled, voice bouncing off the narrow walls. He paused, turning toward me and looking lost as to what to say next.

Five years hadn't aged Bobby much. He'd cropped his tawny hair at the shoulders, and lines crinkled the edges of his eyes, but otherwise he looked the same to me now as he had looked to the nineteen-year-old shifter who ran from her clan. The torrent of emotions that had gripped me the last time I'd seen him bubbled to the surface again and threatened to choke me. Taking a mental step back, I asked the question I wasn't sure I wanted answered.

"How is Lynn?"

"She . . . she's resting," he said, his hands finally dropping to his sides. "We're expecting soon."

"Oh." I kicked at a snow-covered soda can and let the news soak through me. I couldn't think of anything else to say, so the silence stretched on. No, it didn't stretch. It opened like a three-mile trench between us.

Bobby crossed the silence first. Both with words and a hand that cupped my face so unexpectedly I jumped.

"I didn't . . . I'm sor—"

"No." I pushed his arm away. "You weren't the reason I left."

His face shut down, becoming unreadable, and he straightened to his full, looming height. He would be an intimidating figure if I hadn't known him since childhood.

"Your clan needs its *Dyre*," he said, and I looked away.

"The Nekai clan boasts lions and tigers. It doesn't need a five-pound nothing of a calico cat."

"Kitten . . . "

A box falling to my left caught our attention. A rat as long as my forearm foolishly wandered out from the warm place it had been hiding. *Perfect. A distraction.* I fell into a crouch, and my gaze darted to Bobby. His eyes flashed, and he nodded over his shoulder at a dark corner of the alley. We both slinked backwards, eyes on the rat.

Bobby shucked his clothes before dropping to his knees. In Firth, he and I had spent most our lives as the smallest of our clan, and so we had paired up often to hunt. Bobby took my suggestion like no time had passed and we were still back home. But time *had* passed, and we had changed.

I hesitated, eyes flicking to Bobby's kneeling form.

His spine appeared to spring from his back as his skin split and slipped down. I heard the bones and joints popping, breaking, reshaping, and shrinking down from the shape of a man. His body twisted itself toward his first form, a bobcat, and his change progressed faster than I remembered him of being capable. I watched—only a single heartbeat—until the change was unstoppable. Then I ran.

I shouldn't have glanced back, but I did. The betrayed look on Bobby's face I would carry until my death.

Chapter 2

I adjusted my coat, still in a dead run. With any luck it would be a full hour before Bobby could shift back into human form. I could only hope he would hide in the alley and not trail me as a bobcat. He wouldn't risk humans spotting him on the street, would he? Surely he would want his clothes when he changed back. He wasn't like me, able to shift with clothing. I sped up, turning corners at random. There was really no telling what Bobby would do.

Shoving my hands into my pockets, I felt the piece of paper with the map the girl at the bookstore had given me. I pulled it out and stopped at an intersection to compare the street names. If the map were remotely accurate, I might survive the night. The club was probably the same one I'd heard music coming from earlier. My heartbeat drowned out all other sounds too completely to confirm my idea, but I followed the directions on the crude map and said a silent prayer.

The darkened storefronts gave way to sprawling warehouses, and I forced myself to walk as the rambunctious noise of the club grew louder. The streetlights were spaced further apart than they had been in the shopping district, the empty area thick with shadows, but the louder the music became, the more cars lined the street. At the corner of Ravin and Sloan, I stopped in front of a brick building pulsing with dance music.

This had to be the place.

I circled to the back and found exactly what I expected: two bouncers with a line of people waiting anxiously to enter. Well, maybe not exactly what I expected. To-a-one, the crowd was male, dressed in everything from torn jeans to tight plastic pants. I needed to get off the street, but the all-male clientele made me pause. I glanced at the red scrap of map; this was definitely the right address. Surely the bookseller wouldn't have suggested I show up at an all-male club?

As I deliberated, two overly made-up girls in their early twenties rounded the corner of the opposite street. They walked right past the line of waiting guys and up to one of the bouncers. The girls shed their coats as they approached, and a sympathetic shiver ran across my arms for all the bare flesh they exposed to the cold night air. The pair struck a pose, and the bouncer's eyes roved over them appreciatively before he nodded to his partner, who opened the club door and let them pass. Well, that settled it. Girls could get in.

In the shadows, I did a mental check of my appearance. My scarf and gloves would have to go, as would my bulky gray coat and sweater. Under that I had on a spaghetti-string camisole, which would be acceptable. My jeans were a little faded, but flattering, and my dark blue sneakers were in fair shape. I stripped off my warm clothes and shivered in the snow.

Spinning my hair into a bun at the top of my head, I pulled my hat on and tucked up the wisps of hair that tried to escape. My hair attracted too much attention when left visible. I didn't have any makeup to put on. Honestly, I didn't own any. My sharp cheekbones didn't play nicely with blush, my eyes were vibrant enough on their own, and lipstick alone would look silly. At one point I'd owned some lip gloss, which would have at least given my lips a little shimmer, but after searching through my coat pockets, I determined I must have lost it. Well, I looked as good as I was going to.

The scarf and gloves made my coat pockets bulge, but they fit. The sweater—not so much on the fitting front. *Great.* I only owned the one sweater. I didn't want to lose it. I glanced around. There was a stack of crates along the wall of the ally. After poking around the crates, I stowed the sweater in a dry niche between two. I'd come back for it later. By the time I had everything situated, my hands stung from the cold.

It was now or never.

I tossed my coat over one arm, and giving it all I had, walked with my head up and the best roll in my gait I could summon. Strolling up to the first bouncer, I gave him a beaming smile that hopefully cried 'I'm the best thing here tonight!' He looked me over twice, obviously not impressed, but he nodded to his companion, and the door opened for me.

I took a deep breath and stepped inside.

The assault on my senses began immediately. I'd thought the music was loud outside, but inside it was an overwhelming roar that vibrated through my skin and into my bones. Cigarette smoke thickened the air and mixed with the stench of alcohol being processed and sweated out of bodies. I looked around, desperately trying to get my bearings, but everywhere my eyes tried to focus, strobes and spinning colored lights flashed wildly.

My mind reeled. Heightened senses were a mixed blessing. Too much stimulation could trigger the fight-or-flight response of my cat. Disoriented, I fell, my back slamming against the brick wall. Burning pain ran along my spine. Fur slid roughly against the inside of my skin, promising reprieve.

No. Not here. I was in public. There were humans everywhere. The pain spread, the skin on my back peeling open.

Sweaty hands on my bare shoulders brought me back to myself. Shaking my head to clear it, I made out a pair of brown eyes inches from mine. Blinking, I managed to focus on the man's whole face but couldn't catch his words. His mouth kept moving, but all I heard was a dull roar. When his mouth stopped moving, he gave me a firm shake.

I squinted, concentrating. The point of focus helped me push my cat deeper inside, and I finally figured out he was asking if I was all right. I nodded wearily and pressed a hand over my eyes.

"Do you want to sit down?"

This time it was easier to pick out his voice. I nodded again, and he slid a hand around my waist before steering me to the back of the club. As we moved away from the entrance, and consequently, the dance floor, the lighting became steadier. Couches were tucked in a corner beyond massive machinery I couldn't guess the purpose of. The ancient industrial equipment muffled the sound a bit, and I gratefully collapsed onto a threadbare brown couch.

"Stay here, I'll be right back," the guy said after depositing me on the couch.

I rubbed my eyes, and then slowly expanded my focus from the couches to the areas beyond. Not far from where I sat, stacks of liquor crates with sheets of plywood on top comprised the bar. Next to the makeshift bar, a couple of kegs sat in garbage cans filled with ice; one was already floating. The overhead lights were not attached to the building itself but to poles, with extension cords running like giant earthworms off the dance floor. Beyond the grinding bodies and flashing lights I couldn't make out the DJ's station, but I imagined it was constructed in equally haphazard style. Based on the set up, I appeared to be at a massive party, not a club, the location probably illegally acquired. Well, that might be best. A club would have a closing time, but a party could run until dawn, assuming the police didn't break it up.

"Here," a male voice said beside me. "You need to eat something and drink some water." He placed a glass and some chips and dip in front of me. "Are you feeling any better?"

I looked up, shocked that the man who helped me earlier had actually returned. I must have stared at him a few seconds too long, because his smile dropped for a moment before he recovered it. Finally I registered that I'd been asked a question and nodded. He gestured to the chips in a 'Help yourself,' kind of motion. My mouth watered just thinking about food. Right on cue, my stomach released a pitiful growl that I felt more than heard, and I obligingly loaded a chip with the creamy artichoke spinach dip.

"How much have you had to drink tonight?" He looked embarrassed. I guess there wasn't a polite way to ask someone if they were excessively drunk, but I think he tried.

"Nothing. The lights and music overwhelmed me."

"No chance you're epileptic, is there?"

I shook my head as I munched down more chips.

"Pretty hungry, aren't you?"

"I haven't eaten yet today." And I couldn't remember if I had eaten the day before or if it had been the day before that, but I didn't tell him.

"It's after midnight, and you haven't eaten? No wonder you almost collapsed." He shook his head and laughed. "I'm Bryant, Bryant McManus."

Swallowing a chip, I reluctantly accepted his outstretched hand. "I'm Kita."

"A great pleasure to meet you, Kita," he said, and then catching me by surprise, pulled my hand to his lips.

When he lowered my hand, he didn't let go. I wanted to feel flattered. The heroine in the book I'd read earlier would have swooned, but all I really wanted to do was pull my hand away from his sweaty grasp. He must have been expecting some response I didn't give because, after an awkward moment, he released my hand and ran his fingers through his disheveled brown hair. I resisted the urge to wipe my hand on my jeans.

"You have the most unique eyes, Kita. They look almost yellow."

"Must be this light," I said. "They're light green." But in truth, in any light, they were too yellow to actually be green, another mark of what I was.

"So, since we've gotten some food in you, can I buy you a drink?"

"I was kind of planning on—"

"Come on. One drink, so we can get to know each other."

I hesitated. The party posed a great place to hide. No hunter would be able to process the sensory overload and single me out. But socializing wasn't one of my strengths. I glanced around. The place was packed, and the percentage of guys huge. If I blew off Bryant's advances, someone else would try to take his place. Forcing a smile, I nodded, and he hurried to the bar.

While he was gone, two other guys approached me, one to see if I wanted to dance and the other to offer me a drink. I declined both and almost felt relieved when Bryant returned. He handed me a plastic cup—definitely an illegal party.

We exchanged small talk. Well, in all honesty, he talked and I pretended to listen. As the sweet and sour in my drink started to lose its punch, a man in his late twenties walked up and leaned in close enough for me to smell the cheep beer on his breath.

"You lookin' to roll tonight?" He obviously anticipated a positive answer. When I continued to stare at him blankly he bumped the bill of his cap back so I could see his eyes and added, "I have it cheaper but stronger than anyone else here. You know you want some."

Like I even knew what that meant. I shook my head and turned back to Bryant. Whatever the man had, he was selling, and I had exactly no money. The guy shot a glance at Bryant, who shook his head.

"McManus-man, you know where to find me if you change your mind," he said, then stalked away.

"I used to do that stuff," Bryant said after the man disappeared to bother someone else. "Crazy junk. You can literally *feel* colors, taste the music, and the slightest touch will put you over the edge." He paused, clearly wondering if he should be sharing these particular thoughts.

"Sounds unusual," I said to fill my part of the conversation. I didn't much care what he talked about. He was going to talk about something anyway, why not this?

"Yeah, very. For a long time it was lots of fun, but this one night, several months ago, some weird shit happened. I haven't used it since."

I plucked an ice cube out of my cup and popped it in my mouth. "What happened?"

"I went to an underground party with some friends, way bigger than this one. A big-name DJ was spinning, and we drove a couple states to get there. Of course we were all rolling, we did at every party, most the people there were on something. They say the full moon brings out the crazies. It certainly did that night. About the time the party was at its height and everyone was out on the floor, some guy totally wigged out.

"I'm still not sure exactly what happened, but he must have had knives or something, because a couple of people got pretty sliced up. The thing is, there was so much drug use, the violence triggered some sort of nightmarish hallucination. I was there, and I still can't tell you what the guy looked like. I thought I saw his bones jump out of his skin before he tore into the crowd. He was like a twisted demon."

The ice cube slid out of my mouth.

He chuckled. "Yeah, pretty wicked, huh?"

"But your friends, they saw a normal guy with weapons, right?"

"No, it was like a mass hallucination. They saw a monster too, but the details were a little different. So that was it, cold turkey, no more drugs for me."

"What did the uh . . . monster look like? Did he look like an animal, you know, claws, fur, that kind of thing? Or um . . . mechanical maybe?"

"You're making fun of me."

"No, I'm not. I'm interested in . . . unexplainable events."

His posture turned rigid. "Oh, are you taking that paranormal research class at the university?" When I shook my head, he looked relieved and leaned closer. "They have a strange guy teaching that class, and when they got word I'd been at the party, one of his students pestered me for an interview. Girl bugged me for a week before finally realizing my *No* was how it was going to be. Creepy, what they can get away with teaching and call it 'academics.'"

I tried to keep a patient expression on my face as he rambled on, but I was anxious to hear a description of the hallucination-monster. "So what did he look like? Was the guy caught?"

"Nope. He cut up one guy real bad, but there weren't any reliable witnesses."

"And he looked like . . . "

"What I saw was a thing with massive claws instead of hands, covered in fur, and a twisted body. His joints moved backwards. Weird." He stood up. "I need another drink, how 'bout you?"

Walking to the makeshift bar, Bryant effectively ended the conversation. From what he'd said, the "monster" sounded far too much like a shifter who stopped his change midway between forms. If a shifter had attacked humans in such a public way, hunters really would be everywhere and any shifter here illegally would be suspect. Maybe Bobby *had* left Firth to protect me.

I pushed Bobby from my thoughts. Whether a shifter had lost control or not, didn't change anything. I wasn't going back. I just needed to be more careful than before.

A pair of hands grasped my elbows and pulled me, quite literally, out of my thoughts and toward the dance floor.

"Dance with me, beautiful," the man attached to the hands said.

He wasn't anyone I recognized, and I dug my heels in, refusing to be dragged.

"Let go." I had absolutely no intention of going out on the dance floor. With all those writhing bodies, it looked more like an orgy than dancing.

Bryant appeared at my side. "This guy bothering you, Kita?"

The man released my arms, and Bryant shoved the drinks at me. He stepped between me and the interloper, who backed away, putting his hands up.

"Hey, nothing meant by it. She looked lonely sitting there is all." The man kept backing away until the crowd swallowed him.

Bryant led me back to the couch with his arm around my shoulders. Since I needed no help walking this time, the gesture came off as creepily possessive. I probably shouldn't have accepted any drinks. Now I'd have to slip out before he expected me to work off the tab. Well, he'd already bought this one, might as well drink it and buy some time where I had safety in numbers. After all, it wasn't like I could get drunk, given how efficiently a shifter's body processed liquor, and extra calories are always welcome to a moocher.

I'd no sooner sat down, when someone landed in my lap.

The sight of a young woman resting her head and shoulders on my thighs made me cringe. Blue hair with bright pink streaks framed her face like a psychedelic halo.

"Your lap is hard," she said, lifting her head a couple inches and then dropping it again. She let out a peel of giggles. "You have kitty-cat eyes. *Meeoow.*" She made a hideous imitation of a cat's paw and pretended to claw at me.

One of her companions hauled her out of my lap. "Sorry about her. A little too much bourbon tonight."

"She's on more than bourbon," Bryant whispered.

I glanced sideways to make sure the girl wouldn't fall on me again, but she was already splayed across the lap of the guy on the other side of her.

My drink ran out too quickly; even the early train wouldn't run for several more hours. If I left now, I'd be on the street until then. It was time for a new approach. If I drank Bryant under the table, he'd be too drunk to demand repayment. I let him buy another round.

He told me stories about what his office companions did and said, wild vacations he'd taken, and finally offered a drunken spiel about his hopes and dreams for the future. I tried to listen, but mostly just nodded a lot and laughed when he did. With each drink, Bryant invaded more of my personal space: first his thigh brushing mine, then his hand resting on my knee, next his fingers running up and down my arms, and finally his thumb stroking my face. I batted his hand away and pressed myself further into the couch. He was too drunk to sit up straight, not drunk enough to step over—how long before I could safely leave? I glanced at Bryant's watch.

As I leaned in for a better view of the digital numbers, he moved to meet me and smashed his lips against mine. Stunned, I shoved him away, but that didn't discourage him.

"Come home with me, Kita?"

"I should go, now."

"Don't go. Have one last drink." He sprang up and staggered to the bar.

One more hour. I just needed to hide one more hour. I crossed my legs and tugged the brim of my hat further down. Maybe this last round would be the drink that would put him on the floor.

"Here we go," Bryant said as he settled on the couch again. He handed me a cup. "To new friends."

I obligingly tapped the rim of my plastic cup against his and took a sip of the fruity drink. Bryant leaned back, watching me. His shoulder brushed mine, but otherwise he respected my personal space. As I sipped my drink, he told me a long rambling story I didn't follow. Maybe the walk to the bar had done him some good. More sober was good in that he was no longer trying to slobber all over me, but it also meant I'd have a harder time slipping away.

As he spoke, I found myself staring at the way light played in the ice cubes in my cup. Little sparkling colors trapped in frozen glass.

"Did you hear me Kita?"

I tore my attention away from the ice and looked at Bryant. "Is it hotter in here than it was?" I asked, rubbing a hand over the thin material of my camisole.

Bryant only smiled at me. His arm fell around my shoulders. The weight of it felt strange, but not bad as he scooted closer to me. Hadn't he asked me a question? I tried to remember, but Bryant's fingers drawing shapes over my collar bone distracted me.

The cup with its melting ice slipped from my grasp and dumped down the front of my jeans. I jumped up, surprised. The room spun around me and not because of the lights. I blinked. Alcohol shouldn't have affected me, but something had. I looked in Bryant's direction and his smile danced in my vision. My mouth went dry. I expected to have to fight to keep from shifting into my second form, but my cat stayed quiet. That made my fear sharper.

Bryant handed me my coat and his other hand slipped around mine, our fingers interlocking. "Let's go home, Kita."

I stared at my hand, at our touching skin. I could *see* it, but I couldn't *feel* it. I had to get out of here.

Wrenching my arm away, I ran while I still could. People were a blur as I barreled by them. The doors were in front of me, and then I was in the snow. The cold felt good compared to the alien heat rushing through my veins and churning in my stomach. I didn't know if I was being followed. In that moment, hunters didn't matter and Bryant didn't matter. All that mattered was outrunning the fog settling in my mind.

❦ • ❧

I ran until my knees gave out. Hot vomit burned at my throat, and my stomach heaved. I retched.

Gasping for clean air, I dragged myself away from the area I'd defiled.

The street lights quivered, becoming uncertain stars in my darkening vision. Leaning against a doorjamb, I closed my eyes and tried to block out the dizzying way the buildings swam around me. I shrugged into my coat, but snow was already melting into my jeans. The bitter cold soaked through my clothes, making my body painful and stiff. My mind felt like it was floating in warm water.

Snow crunched under heavy boots and my eyes snapped open. I immediately regretted it as my stomach tried to leap out of my mouth again. With nothing left inside me, I coughed and felt no better for it.

Whoever was behind me hesitated. *Please, let it be a bum.* Pushing myself up, I concentrated on seeing past the static in my brain.

A broad man in a coat that had seen better days stood two yards away. A grin caught one side of his lips as he studied me. Casually, he tipped his head in the pantomime of lifting a nonexistent hat.

Wolf musk met my nose.

Another hunter? I was in so much trouble. *Think.* My hand slid across the door behind me, but there was no outside handle. *Damn it, think of something.* No bright plans emerged from the syrup my brain sloughed through.

"A stray *Dyre?*" His tone made it apparent it wasn't a question.

Yeah, a stray *Dyre.* The heir to the *Torin*, the future leader of my clan, run away to hide among the humans.

"Hard to believe, huh?" I was going for bravado, but the words came out slurred. I gulped. *Crap.*

His lopsided grin widened. "I'll take it you're at fault for filling my city with hunters? So much trouble for such a small feline."

His city? Not a hunter. A stray? No. We strays avoided each other.

He stalked forward, and I pressed my back against the door. *Apparently not this stray.*

"Stay away from me!"

He didn't listen.

I swung hard, my fist connecting with his shoulder. He grunted, but I hadn't scored a solid hit. Before I could pull back and swing again, his fist landed in my abdomen. The world spun, and I doubled over, gasping. There wasn't enough air, and as I tried to drag some into my screaming lungs, he caught my wrist and jerked me upright.

I stumbled.

Faking a second stumble, I lunged forward, throwing my weight against him. The stray hadn't expected that. I wrenched my wrist free, but he immediately snagged me by my coat collar. I wiggled out of it, pulling my arms free of the sleeves as I ducked.

Damn, and I really loved that coat.

Skittering sideways, my foot landed badly on the edge of the stoop, and I tumbled into a snow drift. My reactions were too slow to brace my fall, and my head slammed into the brick wall. Gray fog filled my already sketchy vision.

Large hands hauled me out of the snow. I kicked wildly, but my foot passed through empty air. Thrown off center by the failed kick, my back slammed into the wall. The stray caught the front of my camisole, and bunching it in his fist, dragged me forward. A fuzzy outline of his shoulders filled my vision.

"Thanks for the dance, sweetheart." He pulled something shiny from his pocket.

Frantic, I squirmed, and the thin material of my camisole ripped in his grasp. Backpedaling, I turned to run, but the drug in my system made the street lurch. I fell into the wall again, my cheek scraping hard against the brick.

A large hand slammed between my shoulder blades, pinning me to the wall. His other hand wrenched my arm behind my back, and a cold chain snapped around my left wrist. My arm went numb.

I screamed and thrashed in his grip. He grasped my arm harder, jerking up until my shoulder cried in agony. I went still.

I still had one arm free. One chance left. I spiraled my attention inward. I needed just a little energy and a narrow focus—I didn't want to fully shift. At first, nothing happened, and panic made me reach deeper, draw more of my cat. I'd only done this twice before, and only intentionally once. I poured energy into my free hand. Pain blossomed in my palm, spreading toward my knuckles. The joints popped, bent backward. Blood streamed down my fingers as the skin over the tips split and my claws extended.

I'd only get one shot at this.

Moving as quickly as my drug-addled brain would allow, I reached back, raking my claws over my opponent's thigh. Cloth and flesh split. Cursing, the stray shoved away from me.

I whirled around. There were less than two yards between us, but he didn't press forward. Instead, he eyed me warily, one hand clamped against his leg. Dark liquid seeped into his pants, but not a lot, and not quickly. I'd been aiming to rip muscle, at least enough to slow him down, but I'd only scored a superficial wound.

My left wrist burned. I had to get the chain away from my skin. I clawed at the thin metal, and he took advantage of my distraction. He lunged, grabbing for me. I raised my claws, ready for him.

He hesitated.

Movement at the side of my vision alerted me to a newcomer. *Great, and just when it looked like the tide might turn.* With a violent shake of my arm, I dislodged the chain and sent it flying into the snow drift.

The newcomer moved toward us. I spun to face him, but that proved disastrous, as my vision swam again. The stray obviously saw his opportunity. His foot slammed into my knee. A sickening pop heralded waves of pain, and I went down.

The double combo of pain and drug were too much. I struggled to focus. A blackness behind my eyes grew denser. I lost seconds of time with each heartbeat. The broken sounds of a fight raging around me made no sense.

A hand landed on my shoulder, and I struck out with all the strength I had left. My claws sank into flesh. The darkness withdrew long enough for me to see surprised gray eyes studying me.

"You are not human," the stranger whispered. He didn't smell like a shifter.

Alarm penetrated the deep water where my brain floated, but new panic didn't have time to set in. Blackness swept over me again, and this time, it didn't let go.

Chapter 3

The lumpy mattress under me smelled of mold and rat droppings. Rolling over, I blinked into the darkness. Something wasn't right. Where was I? The Davidson's? No, I'd moved on and jumped a train to a new city. Haven. Memory rushed over me: the hunters, Bobby, the party, being drugged, and the stray. The Stranger.

I jolted fully awake. The stranger on the street—he wasn't a hunter, and he knew I wasn't human. Who was he—rescuer or captor?

I made a quick scan of the unfamiliar room. There were no windows, only four cement walls and a heavy-looking door. No furnishing, no lighting fixtures, and no people. Not reassuring. Where the hell was I?

A *wrongness* clung to me, my body disconnected like a puppet with slack strings. How long had I been unconscious? Slowly I moved my arm and realized for the first time that I was shackled with a wrist manacle large enough to anchor a barge. I pushed away from the bare mattress. Sitting up made me lightheaded, and I had to wait for my vision to clear. My eyes followed the chain to where it disappeared into the cement floor.

So . . . the stranger was definitely not a rescuer.

I pulled hard, but aside from making an awful racket, nothing happened. *Where am I?* I dropped the chain. The rough metal scraped down my bare thigh as it fell. *And where the hell are my clothes?* The only scrap left on me was the woven cord of my necklace. I fingered one of the small bones bound in the leather as I glanced around the room; not even my shoes had been left.

I bit my lip hard. Was I wrong? Had the stranger been a hunter? Able to hide his scent somehow? All I could remember were those cold eyes. He hadn't smelled like a shifter, but where else could I be but in the holding cell of a hunter's safe house, imprisoned until the gate reopened and they hauled me back to Firth?

The latch on the door snapped loudly. I fell back on the mattress and pretended to be unconscious.

"Up, up little chicky! The sun is down, time to look alive," a voice beside my ear said, and my eyes flew open. I hadn't heard her approach, but the most bizarre old woman I'd ever seen leaned over me. She smiled at me once she noticed she had my attention, and I flinched. "Good, good," she said, standing up straight. "And, how are you feeling, chicky?"

I said nothing as she turned her back on me and pushed her frizzy white hair into what might've passed for a bun.

"Oh, all right, don't answer that," she said, glancing at me over her shoulder. "I've heard it all before, anyway. You feel like you were hit by a car and buried over a week ago, not to mention the burning in your throat." She turned and smiled again. Her teeth were a sick yellow framed by pale, bloodless lips.

I grimaced, and she laughed. "What? Did you think you were the first little lost chick left on Mama Neda's doorstep? It's always the same story. Things get too hot and someone loses control, and next thing you know, they call Mama Neda to fix the problem. Does anyone call her when there's *not* a problem? Nooo, of course not. Leave the crazy old bat to putter away her time unless someone needs her." She paused and then said, "I never thought it would be the Hermit calling, though. Are you special, chicky?"

Her words pounded in my ears like she'd yelled over a megaphone. My brain spun. Who was this old woman? She didn't smell like a hunter, not that the elders would have let a woman, let alone such an old one, leave Firth. What happened to the stranger on the street? Had he brought me here, or left me to the hunter? Neither of those possibilities explained the old woman's presence, nor gave a hint of what she was talking about.

My voice crackled into nothing the first time I tried to speak, but finally I asked, "Who is Mama Neda?"

"Why me, of course." She leaned over me again. Spots of white flashed at the corners of her dark eyes; either her pupils were over-dilated or her irises were black. "Perhaps not the brightest chicky in the pen, no? I always thought brains should be a requirement, but I guess you've got a pretty face, and that's enough for most." She tugged a strand of my hair. "Would have waited for this color to grow out though. Might like streaks for awhile, but it'll drive you crazy for an eternity." She leaned closer. I anticipated terrible breath to waft out of that gruesome mouth, but the air around me didn't shift. "Not very talkative, are you, chicky?"

I didn't think that deserved an answer.

"Oh, dear me. The chicky's throat. They'll say Mama Neda forgot her task." She scampered away, but paused before reaching the door. She considered me over her shoulder. "Stay here a minute. Mama Neda will fix that throat of yours. Better than new you'll be, chicky."

As the chain had not been removed, I stayed where I was. What else could I have done? The old woman had mentioned being called by a hermit. The man from last night? But if he wasn't a hunter, why would he bring me to this jail cell of Mama Neda's?

Mama Neda was crazy, no doubt about it, but if she was my only jail warden, he couldn't expect to keep me here. The chain would hardly be an issue when I shifted; my hand would slide out as it changed into a paw. Shifting would also heal my wounds from the fight with the stray. Remembering the sickening snap my knee had made before I passed out, I glanced down and realized I'd been moving it without pain.

Strange. I didn't have a scrape on me. Not that being in better condition than I expected was something to fret over. I could figure it out later, once I was out of this basement and away from this cursed city.

I listened for Mama Neda's retreating footsteps, but the only sound I could hear was car traffic in the distance. She hadn't closed the door behind her, and the stairway beyond was visible. A single panel of light illuminated a door at the top of the stairs. Mama Neda had been wearing a summer dress, which was ridiculous in this weather, so the stairway must lead up to a heated building. She might have left that door unlocked as well. Careless of her, but good news for me.

Well, no telling how long she would be gone, so no time to waste. Reaching deep inside, I called for my cat to shift forms, and found . . . nothing.

Not a rub of fur emerging nor a sense of waking, nothing but growing panic answered my call. Part of me embraced the panic with an edge of relief; if I got worked up enough I would shift instinctively. Still, my body remained whole. I had failed to shift on command in the past, but I'd always felt *something* while trying.

I searched harder and finally sensed the energy inside me, but it was hard, cold. *Not possible.* I pushed harder, but all I found was a dead coil where my cat should have been. A chill crawled down my spine. It had to be the effect of another drug or this place, somehow. I slid off the mattress, placed my feet on either side of the chain, gripped it with both hands, and heaved with all my might. It didn't give an inch. Okay,

I needed a tool or . . . my eyes searched the room frantically, but saw nothing that could break the chain. Working spit around the manacle proved useless, it wasn't coming off. At least, not with my hand still attached.

I stopped and stared at my wrist.

If I could get out of this basement, I could figure out what was stopping me from finding my cat. Biting my lip, I tried to think clearly. I wouldn't actually have to rip off my hand, just crush it so it could slide free. My hand would heal when I shifted. My stomach clinched at the thought, but I reminded myself I had no idea what my captors planned for me. Getting away with only a crushed hand might be a small price compared to what might happen if I stayed. I closed my left hand around my right and shut my eyes. A big, deep breath.

"What're you doing, chicky?"

I nearly jumped out of my skin. Unfortunately, not literally.

Mama Neda peered down at me with colorless black eyes. I got the distinct impression she knew exactly what I'd planned. Letting my hands fall to my sides, I tried to look unruffled. That this old woman could hold me prisoner was one thing, that she had snuck up on me twice was unsettling. I looked through her, the blank look any cat worth her salt could summon at will.

Mama Neda appeared unimpressed.

"Drink this, chicky." She held out an orange, plastic mug.

When I didn't reach for it, her smile vanished. She didn't move, or change her expression, but suddenly my stomach twisted. A wave of fear crashed over me. I grabbed the mug. Lifting it to my lips before the next thud of my racing heart, I swallowed the viscous liquid. My throat immediately felt better; my stomach calmed; my body registered relief, as if one sip had been a whole meal after several days' fast. I swallowed another mouthful. *That taste . . . metallic. And the smell. No, why would she . . .*

I stared at the mug's cooling contents.

"This has blood in it."

"Not blood in it. That *is* blood. Mama Neda would never dilute it, not even for mad little chickies abandoned at her doorstep." She smiled, more to herself than at me. "Of course, it's not the best to be had, short notice and all. But a stray cat will do to fix your throat."

The mug fell from my hand and splattered blood everywhere. I stared at it in shock. A cat? I spent more than half my time as a cat. This made me a cannibal. My stomach heaved. I coughed and hacked, but not so much as bile came up. Mama Neda sat down crosslegged on the mattress, watching. I thought I heard her laughing once or twice.

"Is she all right?"

I spun toward the new voice, but the chain wasn't long enough, and my own momentum pulled me off my feet. I landed in the spilled blood and screamed. Backpedaling away from it put me on the mattress and too close to Mama Neda. She reached out a stick-thin hand and stroked the top of my head. I jerked away, and she laughed again.

"What happened?" the voice asked.

Hissing my displeasure, I watched the stranger glide across the room. His height wasn't impressive, only a head or so taller than me, and he didn't look like much of a threat in his khaki pants and collared shirt. A pair of wire-framed glasses perched on his nose. The outfit should have made him look like a geeky librarian or professor, but no stereotypical geek wore such a look of arrogance on a face that could have been carved by a Renaissance master.

He paused, studying me. "Is she all right?"

"About time you joined us, Hermit. Mama Neda was quite worried you were abandoning." She reached out and stroked my hair again. "Physically this little chicky is fine. She turned completely. Mentally . . . " She shrugged.

"Let me go," I said, surprising myself with how steady my voice came out.

They exchanged glances, then turned to study me. Mama Neda's eyes even had a gleam of sanity in them. The man she called Hermit took a step closer, and I pushed myself as far back as the chain would allow.

"Do not be afraid. I mean you no harm."

"That's why I'm chained to the floor? To show your good intentions?" I couldn't bite back the words, even though I knew it wasn't smart to antagonize the people imprisoning me.

He frowned. "I am Nathanial. You are Kita, correct?"

How did he know my name? He wasn't a hunter. I gave him a minute nod, and he smiled. Was he in league with a hunter? While my consciousness was fading in and out I'd thought I had heard a scuffle, but Nathanial didn't look like anyone who would, or even could, fight off a serious foe. He appeared, while still masculine, rather delicate under his pressed clothing. Maybe he wasn't the stranger from the street? I would have expected to remember the black hair pulled back at the nape of his neck—a man with hair down to his waist was unusual. But the eyes were the same, a strange crystal gray, though they weren't as cold as I remembered.

"What do you want from me?" I asked, and his smile faded.

He looked down at the bags in his hand. "I brought you clothes." He thrust a bag toward me, but I kept staring at him. I'd forgotten I was still quite naked.

Mama Neda sighed. "Well, if you aren't going to take them, chicky, I will. No one ever buys Mama Neda nothin'." She pulled a red knit sweater out of the bag and pressed it against her sagging breasts. It clashed badly with her floral sundress.

"I did get something for you, Mama Neda, to thank you." Nathanial held out a small cardboard box.

She grabbed it and threw off the lid. Inside was the most horrible bracelet with large, bright-orange and light-blue plastic gems. Snaking it on her wrist, Mama Neda examined it.

"Oh, I like it! Mama Neda was quite afraid the Hermit wouldn't know he should reward her for her help."

While Mama Neda was distracted, I grabbed the clothes she had forgotten on the mattress. No underwear in the bag, but I wasn't about to be picky. The jeans slid on quickly enough, and surprisingly, fit well. The sweater presented more of a problem. I had it over my head and one arm through before I realized the chain prevented me from sliding it on the rest of the way.

A hand closed on my arm, and I jumped. I tried in vain to jerk away from Nathanial's grasp. He frowned at me, and I realized he was trying to unlock the manacle. It took effort to still myself. Relief washed over me as the chain clattered to the floor.

Mama Neda looked up. "Trusting her already, Hermit?"

"She needs to put on clothing."

Mama Neda stood between me and the door, which hung open. I wondered if I could make a run for it without either of them stopping me. Nathanial was too close. If I bolted, he'd only have to reach out a hand to stop me.

I stared at the floor. "What happens now?"

"That depends entirely on you, chicky. Mama Neda has done her part." She moved the obnoxious bracelet to her other wrist. "Hermit, you may use this room as long as you need, but I suggest as soon as she's ready you get her in front of the council." She moved closer to Nathanial, putting a hand on the side of his face.

He flinched at the uncomfortably intimate gesture. Apparently I wasn't the only one afraid of the old woman.

"A little advice from Mama Neda, share a little of your own before taking her out. Ta-ta now." With that she sauntered out of the room and shut the door.

I listened for the bolt to latch, but only silence followed. Backing away from Nathanial, I tried to keep one eye on him and one on the door. "What's going on? What do you want from me?"

He said nothing at first, and then held out the second bag he carried. "Here. The shoes you were wearing when I found you. The coat that was nearby too." His lips twisted into a frown. "Dry cleaning did very little to help the coat, but I thought you might want it back, anyway. Something familiar. I threw the other clothes away. They were ruined."

I looked at the bag, but didn't reach for it. I wasn't fool enough to grab it. That would be like inviting him to try to catch me and put the chain back on. He set the bag down, moving slowly, as if he was afraid he would frighten me. Way too late for that.

Nathanial took a step forward, his hands flat in front of him. *Surrender, or an indication of harmlessness?* I didn't believe either for a second. I jumped backward, and the rough stone of the wall pressed against my back. With nowhere left to go, and Nathanial still walking toward me, I glanced from him to the door, and bolted.

He caught me before my second step. I hit him as hard as I could, but despite his slight build, he didn't flinch. Okay, he was considerably stronger than he looked. With cool efficiency, he captured my wrists, one in each hand. I tried to wrench away. As if I was little more than a rag doll he turned me, my own arms crossing over my chest. He pinned me to him, my back against his chest.

"Let go!"

"Kita, you have to calm down." His lips brushed against my ear, and a shiver ran through me. I sagged in his arms, hoping gravity would be my friend. He sat down, and I found myself still trapped against him, but now also in his lap. "Kita, listen to me. You have to calm down. You will injure yourself."

The position was too intimate, the words too soft and kind for someone I didn't know, who had thus far shown me very little reason to trust him. I kicked and thrashed, but he held onto me.

"Let me go!"

"I did not want it to be this way. Please, calm down."

I continued to struggle and he pulled me tighter against his chest.

"There was an accident," he said, not even sounding winded. "I never meant to harm you."

I stilled. I was getting nowhere but exhausted. "All right then, *Hermit*. What do you—"

"Nathanial, if you please."

I gritted my teeth. "Fine, Nathanial. What do you want?"

"For my mistake not to cost you your life."

"How very noble of you, and I suppose you're going to tell me what I have to do to stay alive."

"I am not threatening you, Kita. Honestly, I am worried about you. I want us to be friends, all right?"

The laugh that escaped my throat wasn't a happy sound. The memory of his astonished voice whispering that I wasn't human echoed in my head. Did he think I was something he could keep in a cage? Domesticate?

"Do you usually make friends by holding them hostage and chaining them in a basement with a mad woman who forces them to drink blood?"

"I rescued you on the street. Most people would be appreciative. As for the rest, Mama Neda helped you. She saved your life earlier today, and you were down here for your own protection."

"Were you expecting a 'Thank you?' Forget it. I don't need anyone's protection, especially if it involves making me a prisoner."

"You do not understand." He let go of my wrists so fast it took me a second to realize I was free.

I lunged to my feet and pivoted to face him. That put my back against the wall again, but standing was better than the disturbing intimacy of his lap. His face looked more tired than his voice had sounded, his gray eyes pinched around the edges. He reached a hand up to me, and I pressed myself harder against the wall.

Hesitating a heartbeat, he rolled to his knees, and I realized the outstretched arm wasn't in a position to grab me; he held it up for my scrutiny. I saw a single dark drop falling free to land shapelessly on the cement floor. I stared, fascinated, not understanding why. My eyes slid to Nathanial's wrist, where two dark holes allowed sluggish blood to escape.

Pressure built in the roof of my mouth, and my lips parted, no longer able to close over my teeth. Nathanial slowly rose to his feet.

His other hand slid into my hair, his fingers cradling the back of my head. He gently tugged me forward.

I couldn't look away from his wrist.

As though in a dream, my mouth closed over those two little holes, welcoming the coppery taste onto my tongue. Strange teeth I knew I hadn't had earlier sank into his flesh, and he drew in a breath. Then the world slid away. Time pressed down on me, and I saw and felt things that couldn't possibly have been happening. It was wrong, all wrong, especially since it felt so right.

I reeled backward. Nathanial's face was peaceful and clearly dazed. I glanced down at his wrist, which now sported *four* small holes. My tongue tasted blood. I pressed my hand to my mouth. Sharp fangs pressed into my palm. They weren't remotely like the canines I sprouted in my cat form.

"What have you done to me?" I whispered. Nathanial blinked, but his eyes didn't focus. "What have you done to me!"

I darted out of the room, barely noticing that the steep stairwell led up to a narrow alley instead of the building interior I expected. I ran outside blindly, not caring where I went or who was on the street around me. I'd forgotten my coat and shoes. Snow crunched under my feet, but the cold didn't affect me. Perhaps adrenaline made me oblivious. I didn't pause to consider it.

A scent on the wind caught my attention. Dearly familiar and thick with Firth, it was close, but I lost it. I ran down the next street and stumbled over the scent again. A moment later, I saw Bobby standing in the shadows of an alley. He hadn't seen me yet, but more surprisingly, he hadn't picked up my scent. I ran for him, scarcely missing a taxi that sped by, the driver yelling a string of obscenities.

Bobby's eyes grew wide as he recognized me. He rushed forward, and we collided near the mouth of the alley. I collapsed into his arms. Tears that had been carefully in check poured from my eyes.

"Kita, Kitten, what happened? Are you all right?" He cradled me against his chest, pulling me deeper into the shadows. "Did a hunter find you?"

I kept crying. Slowly a deep rumbling drifted from his chest. I had been away from Firth so long, it took a moment for me to realize he was *purring* in his human form. I knew he was trying to comfort me, but I pushed away and sat down in the snow. Wrapping my arms around my legs, I cried into my knees.

"You must be freezing." He wrapped his coat around me, his fingers lingering on my shoulders. "Talk to me, little kitten."

"I'm not cold. I don't feel it at all. I don't think I'm alive."

His fingers worked at my neck and shoulders, looking for knots of tension. It was an old and familiar gesture, but I shrugged him off. He stood beside me for a long time before finally sitting down.

"I don't know what's got you thinking like this, but you're alive. For one thing, dead cats don't *cry*. Want to talk about it?"

What could I say? That a stranger had turned me into something I couldn't understand? I looked over at him, and he sucked in a breath. "Your eyes are bleeding."

Scrubbing my cheeks with my hands, I found my tears were, in fact, tinted with blood. "I'm a monster! Look at my teeth."

"There's nothing wrong with your teeth. What's going on, Kita? How did you change your scent? You don't even smell like Firth. Yesterday you did."

"Yesterday? Was that yesterday?" Everything that had happened since I ran away from him spilled from my mouth in a barely coherent jumble. My tears found fresh fuel in the retelling. He watched their blood-tinged trickle suspiciously, but didn't interrupt me. "And now I'm a monster, and I can't shift forms, and I don't know if I'll ever be able to again, and I'm scared, really, really scared, Bobby."

He tried to wrap his arms around me, but I curled tighter in on myself.

"Then let's get out of here. We'll hide out until the gate opens, and I can take you home. No hunters, and no trial. Just you going back to the clan, where you belong."

"I can't go back to Firth! I was a constant embarrassment to my father before. What will he do if he finds out I can't shift?"

"You would rather stay in the human world? What if this . . . this condition . . . is only temporary, and you'll be able to shift—" Bobby fell silent. He tensed, and I followed his gaze to the end of the alleyway. The shadows stirred then parted, as Nathanial strolled toward us.

"He smells like you," Bobby said. "What you used to smell like. That's him, isn't it?" Bobby took a step forward.

I leapt up and grabbed his wrist. "Don't. Whatever he is, he isn't human."

An awful sound leaked from Bobby's throat as energy danced over his skin. Things were going to get worse if he shifted.

"Run," he whispered at me, taking another step forward. He would make sure Nathanial didn't follow me, or at least try to, but I didn't want him hurt. I squeezed his wrist harder, my nails biting into his skin, but he didn't pay any attention.

Nathanial tossed a bag, not to me, but at Bobby. "Kita, you left your coat and shoes. I thought you might need them." Perhaps he expected Bobby to try and catch the tote, but animals don't catch, they dodge. Bobby was charging before the bag landed.

I hesitated, glancing at the mouth of the alley. The need to hide my kind's existence from humans was firmly ingrained in me. I'd forgotten while drugged, and I'd extended my claws against the stray, but I was thinking clearly now, and even a secluded street was not a safe place to fight. At the same time, I couldn't let Bobby tackle my battle alone.

I raced forward to join the fight.

I circled the two men, letting Bobby's full-out attack cover my actions. Nathanial glanced my way as I reached his side, but he didn't divide his attention or even seem to care I had gained a flanking position. My foot shot out, fast, but Nathanial simply wasn't in the space where the kick landed.

He *had* been there, the moment before. I gaped and realized none of Bobby's attacks were landing, either. Nathanial wasn't blocking or even dodging the blows, he simply wasn't there when they landed. Sweat broke over Bobby's brow, but Nathanial didn't even appear winded. *What was he?*

Nathanial grabbed two handfuls of Bobby's sweater and lifted him a foot in the air. Bobby was the taller and broader man, but Nathanial hurled him down the alley. Bobby rolled as he hit the ground, the shock on his face mirroring what I felt.

Nathanial moved to continue the attack, leaving me his unguarded back. I lashed out, the kick fast and clean. In less than a racing heartbeat, Nathanial whirled to face me, my foot caught effortlessly between his hands. He pushed, just pushed like it was no effort, and tipped me off my center of balance. I landed on my butt in the snow and stared at his retreating back as he stalked toward Bobby, who hadn't straightened from his tumble yet.

The bag Nathanial had tossed earlier was within reach. I grabbed it, hurling it at his back. He turned, batting the bag aside. A sneaker escaped and fell to the ground in slow motion.

Suddenly, sickly green light flashed through the air.

The putrid smell of decay met my nose, and I found myself surrounded by three purple shrouded . . . *things*. They held up taloned, three-fingered hands, and the light returned, creating a green haze between them and me. I jumped to my feet and tried to back up, but the thin haze of light was behind me, as well. A solid barrier forming a cage.

What kind of monster was I dealing with?

I couldn't take anything else bizarre. A scream bubbled up from my throat and ricocheted off the brick walls.

"None of that, now," said a voice near the front of the alley.

I turned.

A man in a tight, tailored suit walked toward me, his face a picture of disdain. "Have some dignity and don't draw attention to yourself," he said, pulling a thick book out of thin air. He stood there a moment, flipping pages.

I glanced over my shoulder. Bobby was up now, his attention shifting from Nathanial to the shrouded things and then to the book-conjuring stranger. Nathanial, for his part, appeared to have forgotten the fight and looked just as baffled by the stranger's appearance.

I turned back to the stranger in the expensive suit. "Who are you?"

"I am your judge, and you . . . " He ran a finger down a page in the book, stopping halfway. "Ah, here, you are, Kita of the clan Nekai, Shifter of Firth. You are found guilty of attacking and wounding a human, thus turning said human into a rogue shifter who menaces his fellow humans, *thus* endangering and exposing the whole nonhuman community. You are also held responsible for the deaths caused by that rogue. For those crimes, your life will be forfeit." He snapped the book shut.

My jaw fell slack, but no words emerged. *No, I couldn't have . . .* I shook my head. *Forfeit?*

Bobby rushed forward. "That's not the way of our kind!"

The judge flicked his wrist, and Bobby slammed into the wall a few feet away. "This does not concern you."

Bobby's limp form slid down the wall to land in a heap.

I stifled another scream.

"Kill her," the stranger commanded. The creatures surrounding me slid through the barrier.

"Wait! Don't I get a defense, or last request, or anything?"

"*We could make a deal*," one of the creatures offered. Its voice crashed through my brain like a jackhammer.

I wasn't sure which of the three had spoken. I glanced between them. Cowls covered their faces, and I was glad for that. I had the feeling I didn't want to see what they actually looked like.

"What kind of deal?" I asked.

"No! No deals," the judge yelled. Under his breath he added, "I hate working with demons."

"*Your soul*," said the demon and then made an awful sound that might have been a laugh, "*or in your case, souls. We will even grant you immortality.*"

I stared. Demons wanting souls, how original. I had never been sure there was such a thing as a soul, but now that I knew, I didn't want to give mine to these things. Life couldn't be worth whatever they planned.

The judge's cheeks flushed, his knuckles whitening around the book. "You will kill her. No deals with this one. I have been tracking her for months. No deals."

"One young woman that hard to find?" Nathanial emerged from the shadows "Do you have any evidence of this alleged crime she committed?"

The judge's eyes narrowed as he studied Nathanial. "What business do you have here, vampire?"

"None at all, but I have perused her mind. I personally saw no evidence she attacked a human and turned him into a rogue shifter." Nathanial paused. "But, if her claims of innocence are unimportant to you, at least let her be of service. Surely your biggest concern is finding the rogue who is causing the problem? Let *her* find him. She can deliver him to you."

I glared at Nathanial. Was he crazy? Yes, obviously. But the judge looked thoughtful.

"Do you agree to this, Kita, Shifter of Firth?"

I bit my lower lip. Find a crazed murderer or die right this moment? Hesitantly, I nodded.

"Say that you accept," he snapped.

My voice didn't want to work at first, but I finally got out my acceptance. The judge's lips carved a smile across his face, and he turned to the demons.

"I banish you," he said, and waved his well-manicured hand in a dismissive gesture.

A flash of light and the three demons were gone, as well as the barrier holding me. I ran toward Bobby's crumpled form, but the judge intercepted me halfway. With a hand twisted in my hair, he pulled me backward. His other hand fumbled with my sweater. He pressed his palm into the small of my back, and torrents of pain washed through me.

"You will mention this to no one." He let me go, and I fell on my hands and knees in the snow. "You have two nights, Kita, Shifter of Firth. Bring me the one responsible for these murders, or you, and your two friends here, belong to me and my justice." He turned and took a step back as I tried to focus past the pain. "Do not think you can run or hide. I can find you anywhere now. Two nights."

Then he vanished.

Chapter 4

I looked around to see if anyone else was waiting in line to threaten me and utterly turn my world upside down. Vampires, demons, and psychos with wicked magic, so far. Perhaps Frankenstein's monster would show up next and demand my head for his bride. My quick search turned up only Nathanial and Bobby, the latter disturbingly still. I crawled through the snow to him.

His crumpled body leaned against the brick wall a few yards away, but I seemed to take forever to reach his side. He didn't stir. *Don't you dare be dead.* His chest finally rose, not much, the shallow breath rattling, but he was breathing. Movement behind me reminded me that it might not be time to stop and lick our wounds yet. I whirled around, growling a feline warning. Nathanial raised a single eyebrow and squatted in the snow beside me.

I backpedaled. "Get away from us."

"I saved your life . . . again. Do you think you could try to trust me a little?"

"You didn't save my life, you postponed my death. There's a difference. Besides, I haven't forgotten you attacked us."

Nathanial made a sound of protest and waved a long-fingered hand in Bobby's direction. "Actually, he attacked *me.*"

I ignored that, because I couldn't dispute the charge. Well, I could, but I was currently more concerned with Bobby's laborious breaths. I settled my weight into a more defensive position, watching Nathanial's body language for signs he would attack. But he didn't move. He only watched me. The rattling sounded in Bobby's chest again, and still Nathanial remained perfectly still. *Like a well-dressed statue.*

Angling my body, I kept one eye on Nathanial as I examined the extent of Bobby's injuries. I tipped Bobby's head to the side. Blood matted his tawny hair, and as soon as I caught sight of it, pressure built in my mouth. I spun away from him and covered my mouth with my hands. Sharp fangs pressed against my fingers.

I rounded on Nathanial. "What have you done to me?"

"There was an accident and . . . " Nathanial trailed off.

"I'm a monster!"

"Technically, 'monster' is a human concept, and by it you already were one."

"I hate you." I swung, open handed and blind.

I must have looked as surprised as Nathanial when my palm connected with his face. Color rushed to his chiseled cheekbone in the rough shape of my hand. Okay, so he could be hurt. *Good to know.*

He touched his cheek lightly with three fingers. "Feel better?"

I did, actually, but I wasn't sure voicing that opinion was the best plan. I waited, but he just watched me, his gray eyes touched with amusement. *This was funny?* I turned away from him. Since he obviously wasn't leaving anytime soon, I ignored his presence and concentrated on Bobby. My hand still stung, and I rubbed it against my pants. I'd slapped a creature stronger than me and now was giving him full access to my unprotected back, but instinct told me he wouldn't retaliate. I didn't have any reason to believe that, but I also didn't know how much time Bobby had, so I trusted my gut.

Tilting Bobby's head to a more natural position, I averted my eyes from his wound. Not seeing the blood helped, but I could still smell it. I groped his neck for a pulse, but regretted the decision the moment the first beat danced hypnotically under my fingertips. The hunger rose in me, again.

I jerked back, my hands shaking. *Oh crap.* I buried my face in my hands, dragging in a deep breath meant to be cleansing, but the tantalizing scent of blood filled my senses. A half-scream, half-growl caught in my throat, and I turned to glare at Nathanial. He watched me, but the expression on his face was so blank it had to be intentionally neutral.

Swallowing the sound, I held my breath and returned to studying Bobby's prone body. Apparently my instincts weren't exactly trustworthy, because they were definitely telling me he was food. The fangs worrying my bottom lip agreed.

I pushed that thought away. I didn't know much about head wounds, but I was pretty sure Bobby should have regained consciousness by now, if his injury weren't serious. I reached a trembling hand toward his face, moving slowly so my blood thirst wouldn't betray me. If I could just get him conscious enough to shift . . .

I saw the movement in my peripheral, but didn't have time to process it as a threat before Nathanial grabbed my shoulders and jerked me to my feet. I stumbled as he dragged me. We halted several feet from Bobby. Nathanial shoved me behind his back.

"What the—" The words died on my tongue.

Not a foot behind where I'd been kneeling stood a woman in a floppy yellow hat and oversized pink coat. Her eyes were a little too wide as they followed the path Nathanial had carved as he dragged me away from Bobby. The edges of her smile wavered like she was concentrating hard on holding it in place. I tried to step around Nathanial, but he moved to block me with one arm, clearly more worried about the woman than I was. Peering under his arm, I reassessed her. Threats don't typically come in pastel or wear plastic rain boots, but, she *had* appeared out of nowhere.

She held out her hand, and the hat slipped over her eyes. "Um, sorry. Didn't mean to startle you. My name is Gil." She pushed the hat back up quickly, but her fingers caught in her curly hair. Frowning, she fought with the hair before tugging free.

Okay, surely not a threat.

When she held her hand out again, her fingers trembled, betraying nerves hidden from her chirpy voice. She winced as Nathanial stepped forward, but pumped his hand enthusiastically.

"I am—" Nathanial started, but she interrupted.

"The hermit Nathanial. Vampire. I know. I read up on you before I came. And on *you*." She tried to peek around him to see me, but he shifted his body again, ever so slightly, barricading me.

Goody, my very own vampire meat shield.

I slipped under his arm and circled to the side of the woman. She was between Bobby and me, and I hadn't heard or seen him breathe since she arrived.

I met her eyes. "What do you want?"

She winced at my harsh tone, but the smile grew across her face. "Ah, yes, you must be Kita, the kitten shifter from Firth, fugitive. I have read that you are one of the very smallest of your kind. That must be fun." She didn't offer me her hand—not that I would have taken it. Her brown eyes widened as her gaze fixated on my mouth. "Mab's tears. You're a vampire. You can't be a shifter!"

I'd had enough of this. Bobby still wasn't moving.

"Are you here to kill me?"

The question startled her, but with the day I was having, I thought it was justified.

Still staring, she shook her head. "I was sent to—"

"Then get out of my way."

Panic flashed across her face as I stepped forward. She thrust her arms forward, fingers spread wide, and purple light danced in front of her hands. The blinding flash left yellow dots in my vision. I blinked rapidly, trying to force my eyes to readjust to the darkness. Around the spots, I saw her bounce off the wall next to Bobby, her butt hitting the snow.

Was that what she meant to do?

She jumped to her feet, her cheeks flame-red. "Stay away," she warned, sidling along the wall. She tripped over Bobby's leg, and she shrieked, her eyes going wide. "Mab's tears." The color drained from her face. "Is he human? What did you do to him?"

Her gaze accused me as she crossed her arms over her chest. *Oh hell. I don't need this—not now or ever.* I glanced over my shoulder at Nathanial, but his face was completely empty again. He could have vouched for me; could have told her it was the psycho judge-mage who slung Bobby against the wall. A sting of betrayal twisted in my stomach, though I didn't know why I expected him to defend me— obviously my instincts were *way* off tonight.

Crossing the alley without a word, I crouched at Bobby's side. Gil scuttled out of my way, but I felt her hovering around me, the scent of her fear and suspicion pressing against my back. I tried to ignore her. Bobby's face had taken on an ashen shade, his cheeks cool under my fingers.

"Step away from that human," Gil said, her voice trembling. "Feed your monstrous craving elsewhere."

Bobby was running out of time. *If it isn't already too late.* I brushed that thought aside.

"She is going to force him to shift," Nathanial whispered.

I flinched. Nathanial was crouched beside me again, and I hadn't heard him approach. I frowned at him. *How the hell did he know what I planned to do?* I didn't ask. I needed to concentrate. Reaching deep inside myself, I strained to find the coiled energy that would bring my shape-change. If my energy could call to Bobby's beast . . .

The cold and quiet lump in my center was all I found.

"Force him to shift?" Gil's voice was uncertain, then turned excited. "Ooooh, you know, I've read that the fastest way to coax a shifter's beast out is through food or sex."

Heat crept to my cheeks, leaving me a little light-headed "Your books don't know everything," I said, the edge of a growl in my voice.

"Now shut up. You're distracting me." But she wasn't entirely wrong . . . it might be worth trying.

I put my hands on either side of Bobby's face, avoiding the blood trailing down his neck. It took me a second to remember how—it'd been years since I'd tried in human form—but slowly, a low purr rumbled up out of my chest. I moved closer until I could cradle Bobby's head. After a moment, muscles in his face began to twitch.

Sex or food . . . not entirely inaccurate. Purring in human form was an intimate act, typically reserved for comforting mates or children. I cursed myself for resorting to it, since Bobby was mated to someone else, but it was working. Bobby's fingers twitched at his sides as he took a deep breath.

Come on, wake up.

Still not fully conscious, Bobby's body jerked away from me.

Crap, I'd forgotten I didn't smell like myself. Or, perhaps he'd expected Lynn, his mate. I didn't let that thought stay with me long, but glanced over my shoulder at Nathanial. He was watching me with unabashed interest. I *so* didn't want to ask his help. Bobby struggled against my arms again, still not conscious enough to shift.

Swallowing the sour taste in my mouth, I motioned Nathanial closer. "Earlier Bobby told me you smell the way I usually do."

Nathanial waited, either not understanding my unasked request or wanting me to voice it.

Gritting my teeth, I whispered, "If you could touch his face, so he can pick up my . . . your scent."

Nathanial nodded and moved closer. I started purring again, and as soon as Nathanial touched him, Bobby calmed. Energy built in him, spilling heat over my arms. By the time his skin slipped, I was standing and pulling Nathanial up with me.

"Wow, reading about it is nothing like seeing it in person," Gil said, her mouth hanging open.

I frowned at her but said nothing. Bobby's cat form solidified. The scent of fresh blood vanished as his fur sealed around his body, and I breathed easier, both because he'd healed and because the tainted need constricting my chest loosened. Bobby scanned the alley, bewilderment masking his eyes.

I felt for him. Being forced into a shift was disorienting at best, and being unconscious beforehand probably hadn't helped. He stood on four shaky legs, tripping over his first step. He blinked, shaking his head like he could expel the fog in his brain with motion. As he stared,

I could almost see memories sliding back in place behind his eyes. Arching his back, his gaze darted around the alley. His green eyes narrowed, and he lunged for Nathanial. I barely caught him by the scruff of the neck.

Bobby's surprised protest was more of a brawny squeak than any sound a muscular bobcat should make. I shook my head and slowly released him. His tufted ears flattened against his head, but he watched stoically as I gathered his discarded clothing.

Picking up the bag Nathanial brought earlier, I dumped out my coat and one shoe—the other shoe had sailed who-knew-where when the bag was thrown—and put Bobby's clothes in it. Task complete, I set the bag beside him and grabbed my coat from the snow. I still wasn't cold, but I should have been. Besides, walking around coatless and barefoot would draw human attention I didn't want.

I shrugged on my coat, shoving my hands in my pockets to ascertain I still had all my belongings. The coat's deep pockets were stuffed with the rolled-up scarf and gloves I'd removed outside the music club plus other odds and ends, like a toothbrush and comb. I had at least most of my stuff. I crammed my foot, clinging snow and all, into my sneaker. My toes squished against the wet sole as I hobbled across the alley looking for the other shoe.

Nathanial found it before I did. He held up the sneaker but pulled it out of reach when I moved to take it. The smile that touched his lips was playful, but I glared at him. Grabbing the shoe, I shoved it on my foot without bothering to tie the laces. The sneakers squeaked as I stomped toward the street. Bobby trailed me, growling.

"Kita," Nathanial said at the same time Gil yelled, "Wait."

The sound of rain boots clomping in the snow bounced off the alley walls as Gil ran to catch up with me. I whirled around.

Nathanial had moved silently—not surprising—so he was considerably closer than expected, but Gil ground to a stop several feet away, well out of arms' distance.

I wasn't sure whether to be flattered or irritated. No one had ever been afraid of me before. *What does she think I'm going to do?*

"You can't leave," she said, her face flushed. She hadn't run that far, so I guessed it wasn't from exertion.

Who was she to tell me what I could and couldn't do? Actually, for that matter, who was she? It was a valid question, so I repeated it aloud.

She fidgeted with her overlong coat sleeves. "I thought we covered this pretty extensively. I am Gil."

"Got that part. Your name means nothing to me."

"I think," Nathanial clarified, "Kita is asking, what are you and how do you know so much about us?"

That was what I meant, but I rounded on him anyway. "And why are *you* still following me?"

"I helped, did I not?" He motioned to Bobby.

"And I kept him from mauling you. I'd say we're equal."

Nathanial didn't act impressed. Of course, Bobby hadn't landed a single hit on him as a man, though Bobby was head-and-shoulders taller than Nathanial. So Bobby probably didn't scare him much as a bobcat. But still . . .

"Don't underestimate him because bobcats are small," I said. "I've seen him take down full-grown deer."

Nathanial smiled. "I am not a deer."

Gil cleared her throat. "You asked me a question," she said, her voice laced with impatience.

I nodded, but now that everyone's attention had turned to her again, she wasn't in any hurry to answer.

She cocked her head to the side, her eyes assessing me. "Are you really Kita of Firth?"

I nodded again, and she waved a hand. A scroll materialized out of thin air. She jotted something down and, hopefully, missed my flinch. The "pulling things out of nowhere" was a nice trick. If I'd had any doubts about what she was, after the whole purple-flashing-light incident, it was crystal clear now—the judge had used the same trick.

The scroll vanished again, and she looked back up. "All right then. I'm a scholar-trainee from Sabin. A couple of days ago my headmaster announced a potential accomplice had been identified in the rogue murders. A shifter who'd made a deal with the judge to find the rogue she created; she would make an excellent study subject. He asked for a volunteer, and I won the assignment." She smiled brightly, pushing at her frumpy hat. "I'm getting fieldwork credit for this."

"Nice to know my life being destroyed is helping someone out."

"Wait." Nathanial tapped under his eye with one finger. "The judge left here no more than five minutes before you arrived. How could your headmaster have given you the assignment days ago unless he—and the judge—knew even before the judge approached Kita that he would make a deal with her?"

"Well, it might have only been five minutes here, but who says time has to move the same everywhere?" Gil crossed her arms over her chest.

I sighed. *Right. That made as little sense as everything else happening tonight, so why not?* I looked out at the street. It promised freedom, if I could just lose my present company. Okay, maybe not complete freedom, since the judge planned to fulfill my death sentence in two days. Of course, he had to find me first.

I turned back and studied Gil. *Where the hell was "Sabin" and what exactly was a scholar-trainee?* Flaring my nostrils, I searched for a scent betraying her nature. If I ran across any more of these Sabinites, I wanted to be able to identify them *before* they started using magic on me. The demons had smelled like decay, an easy enough scent to identify, and one I wanted to avoid, but the judge had had no discernible scent, and all I caught from Gil's direction were hints of lavender and vanilla—scents much too common in a world full of perfume and shower gel.

Sighing again, I wondered why I bothered trying to log her scent in my memory. The judge hadn't accidentally run across me on the street. He had appeared out of nowhere.

Nathanial moved closer, his hands sliding over my shoulders as he positioned himself behind me. "You look on the verge of running," he whispered, drawing me against him.

The movement had the grace of familiarity to it, like it was an everyday occurrence for him to draw me into his arms. Heat from his skin soaked through my coat. I hadn't realized I was cold until he touched me, but now a shiver crawled down my spine. The temptation to wrap myself in his warmth caught me off guard, and quite frankly, pissed me off. My cheeks flushed, and I shrugged him away.

"Don't touch me," I warned, sidestepping further from him.

Bobby, crouching near my feet, arched his back. His hackles rose. He growled at the vampire.

Unchecked menace slid across Nathanial's face, but disappeared quickly as the neutral expression I'd seen him wear earlier fell into place like a mask. He smiled, tight-lipped, and it didn't come close to reaching his eyes.

"We should get moving," he said. "There is much to do and very little time."

We? We my ass.

He must have read my thoughts from my face, because he continued, "The judge said 'you *and* your friends belong to his justice.' That means the bobcat here, and, of course, myself, will be thrown to the demons if you do not succeed in tracking the rogue. Did you not think I would assist you?"

"I don't want or need your help."

"Then you are confident you can hunt the rogue on your own?"

"Of course I am." Not. There wasn't a chance. I wasn't a hunter, I was a runaway, no doubt labeled a hopeless stray by my clan. How would I find an insane human-turned-shifter, and in only two days? Even if I did find him, what was I supposed to do with him? Tie him to a chair and wait for the judge to appear? I kicked at a pile of snow and concentrated on the burrow my shoe made.

I could feel Nathanial and Gil's stares boring into me, but looking down let me avoid meeting all but Bobby's gaze. He studied me, unable to voice anything in the conversation. The weak light from the streetlamp caught in his eyes, turning them into green, glowing orbs. I had the distinct impression he knew I was lying—they probably all did.

Without breaking eye contact, Bobby planted one of his front paws on my tennis shoe. His claws extended, not enough to pierce the fabric, but enough to convey the fact he didn't plan to let me leave without him. He hadn't been conscious when the judge and I made our deal, but apparently he'd pieced together the details from the current conversation. I tried to nudge Bobby loose, but stopped as I felt the top of my shoe tearing—good sneakers were hard to come by. Of course, I might not have to worry about that too much longer. *Okay, that's a morbidly depressing thought.*

Well, a little help couldn't hurt. Cats can't actually grin; their facial structure wasn't made to, but when I stopped trying to shake him off, Bobby expressed his triumph with the angle of his eyes. I'd snatched him back from death's claws, so we might as well go down trying to find the rogue. Either way, we were demon food. Nathanial too, though I tried not to care. After all, he'd chosen to get involved, not to mention being responsible for whatever he'd done to me.

I ran my tongue over my teeth. They were flat again, the fangs retracted and hiding.

With the fangs gone, I could almost convince myself the last few hours hadn't happened. Except that Gil was standing across from me, her scroll in hand again, and Nathanial's cool gray eyes were watching me, waiting, not a movement betraying he was animate. Yesterday I would have claimed shifters were the only supernaturals; tonight, I was apparently a vampire. *Was I even alive anymore?* Maybe I didn't need to worry about being executed by the judge. A cold shiver of panic crawled over my skin as I thought back to the demons. They wanted my soul, no matter what I'd become.

Tugging the front of my coat tighter around me, I met Nathanial's eyes. "How will you help?"

"Any way I can."

He smiled. I didn't.

That wasn't an answer, but then I doubted he knew what it took to hunt a rogue. Hell, I didn't know, either. But he was fast and strong, which might come in handy. And if he got in the way it would be easier to lose him later, when he didn't expect it.

I nodded at Nathanial and then down at Bobby. "Let's go."

"Wait!" Gil jolted forward like she would grab my shoulder, but her hand fell short of touching me. She shuffled from foot to foot, her gaze meeting mine and then flickering past my head. "I'll assist you, as well," she finally muttered.

"I don't need a spy for the judge keeping tabs on me."

"Spy?" Her jaw dropped and she shook her head a little too vigorously. "I'm here to study, not spy, and I'll gather a lot more data working beside you than tailing you. Besides," she said, glancing at her hands and tugging her sleeves again. "If my hypothesis is correct, the judge can find you anywhere. He doesn't need my help. Did he . . . " She peered at me, her gaze searching. "Did he mark you?"

"The only thing he did was hand down a death sentence."

Her eyes continued studying me. "He would have had to press it directly into your flesh."

Nathanial took a step forward, reaching for my waist. I stepped away. "Don't come near me."

Nathanial stopped, but didn't back off. He gestured toward my middle. "The judge touched your back. If he marked you, it would have been there. Turn around."

I glared at him, but he waited, his face patient. I glanced at Gil. The fear in her face had given way to excitement. *How had I gotten tied up in being this chick's class project?*

I turned reluctantly and dropped my coat in the snow. I expected the cold air to attack me, but the chill emanated from inside my skin; my lack of coat made little difference. As I lifted the back of my shirt,

Nathanial sucked in his breath. At the same time, Bobby made an ugly hiss. Gil gave a delighted cry.

"Amazing! It's even more remarkable than I've heard. Don't worry, I won't tell anyone I saw it." She clapped her hands together.

Straining to twist around, I learned it was impossible to look at my own back. That, of course, didn't stop me from trying. I explored my lower back with my fingers, but my skin felt as smooth and unchanged as ever.

"Stop that." Nathanial brushed my hands away. "The mark is a group of snakes twisting around each other like a Celtic knot. Two swords bisect the mass of serpents. It is quite lovely. You could probably pass it off as a tattoo, if the snakes were not actively slithering around."

Spinning on my heel, I gaped at him. "You're kidding, right?"

He shook his head.

I turned to Gil. "What is this thing?"

"The judge's mark, of course." She beamed at me. "I can hardly believe it. Marking is so rare. I'm working on my own but—"

"What does it do?"

"Oh, lots of things. The reason he gave it to you is so he doesn't have to be bothered with tracking you down again. Your existence is like a ghost in his mind now. All he has to do is follow that psychic track and find you. Of course, there are drawbacks. You mark someone and you tie a bit of your life to them. That's probably why I was told to be sure you don't die before he returns. That's how I guessed about the mark. I mean, why else would anyone care if a fugitive shifter died?"

I glared at her, but Nathanial spoke before I could. "And if she dies?"

She studied the plastic of her boots. "It would be inconvenient for the judge."

My glare deepened. "Wonderful, but my death would be a little more than a minor inconvenience to *me*. By the way, does this judge guy have a name?"

"Yes, but I wouldn't want to draw his attention by saying it. You know, I've read that he wiped out an entire race single-handedly in one of the great wars. Aside from the members of the High Assembly of Mages, he's one of the most powerful beings in Sabin's history."

I rubbed my forehead. Until tonight I'd only feared the hunters. If they'd have caught me, I would have been dragged back to Firth in chains and presented to the elders for punishment. Not pleasant, but the punishment for running stray in the human world wouldn't have lasted forever. I would have been returned to my clan eventually, and I would have survived. But no, I couldn't let myself get captured by hunters. Instead, I had to stumble into a city controlled by some kind of mage mob boss and get stamped with a death sentence. *Brilliant.*

"Fascinating, really. If he's so powerful, why does he need demons to kill me? Why can't he just do it himself?"

"Well . . ." She danced from one foot to the other. "I'm told he's trying to repair his karma, so he doesn't want to get his hands dirty by killing anyone else, even criminals." Pulling at her coat sleeves, she mumbled, "Like working with demons will keep his karma all squeaky clean."

"Bobby almost died from the judge slamming him into the wall. The judge didn't seem too concerned about karma *then.*"

Gil shrugged, not looking surprised to learn the judge had caused Bobby's injuries. She didn't even apologize for accusing me of hurting him.

I tossed up my hands. "Okay, fine, I'm stuck with you, so you can make sure I survive until he can remove the mark and execute me." I looked at the awkward woman. What could she possibly do to help?

I reclaimed my coat from the snow and shook it hard before shrugging back into it. "Now can we go?"

"Go where?" Gil asked.

I didn't answer. Right now my only plan was to prowl the streets until I either found the rogue's scent or came up with a better plan.

"Before we do anything else, I need to take Kita to the vampiric council," Nathanial said.

I shook my head. "Veto. I've had enough of vampires and weird creepies tonight."

"Kita, this is not a suggestion, it is a requirement."

"No way. You're supposed to help find the rogue, not boss me around."

"If the council finds you on the streets without their permission, they will kill you."

"They'll have to get in line." I showed some teeth, and he started another warning about the council. I cut him off. "Any ideas that don't involve the supernatural underbelly of the city? Because I'm pretty sure the rogue isn't there. Should we talk with the human police? Find out what they know about the murders?"

Nathanial shook his head quickly, his eyes perhaps a little too wide for the calm look on his face. "I know someone in the loop with the police. I will contact him and see what information he can give us. You should not go near any police stations."

"The police won't have found usable evidence," Gil said. "We had people go through and destroy any trace as soon as we found out about the crimes."

I raised my eyebrow. "Why?"

"That's part of our job."

"Your job is to help cover the tracks of murderers?"

"No, no. It's the job of my kind to hide the evidence of supernaturals from humans."

"Says who?"

Gil looked surprised. "Us, I guess. It's been our primary occupation for five hundred years. We are, after all, the most intelligent of the supernaturals. Someone has to clean up after your mess."

Bobby growled and I gaped at her. Only then did Gil's mouth snap shut like she'd thought about what she'd said.

She cleared her throat. "What's relevant is that the human authorities can't help us."

"Well, then what am I supposed to do? I'm no investigator, or hunter, or anything. I'm just a runaway who can't shift and has a brand new fixation with blood. I mean really, where do we even start? Are you sure there's nowhere I can hide from this judge guy? Some place out of range of this mark?"

"Nope, hiding won't do you any good, but I do know a place to start gathering information on the murderer." Gil walked toward the mouth of the alley. "The last girl attacked, survived. She's at Saint Mary's hospital."

I looked at Nathanial, who shrugged, but his eyes narrowed at the corners. Not that I could fault him. I wasn't thrilled with the idea of a hospital, but it was a better plan than wandering the streets. As I turned to follow Gil, Bobby made a pathetic, mewling sound. He circled his bag of clothes, then sat down and stared at me.

"I can't wait that long," I told him.

"What does he want?" Nathanial asked.

"He can't leave the alley until he shifts back to human form."

"Why can't he leave the alley?"

I rolled my eyes, but it was Gil who said, "Do you often see bobcats wandering around the city?"

Nathanial arched a brow. "Humans see what they expect to see. He does not look so different from a large house cat. As long as people do not look too close, no one will notice."

"He weighs over thirty pounds, has tufted ears and a bobbed tail. That would garner a second glance from even the least observant."

Nathanial tapped a finger under his eye. "Why not carry him? Humans carry pets all the time."

I frowned at him. But Bobby apparently thought that was a great plan, because he brushed against my legs. Reluctantly, I lifted him under the arms, holding him as far away as possible. Bobby slapped my hand with one big paw, not breaking skin. Nathanial laughed and reached for Bobby, but it was obvious within two quick slashes that Bobby would never agree to Nathanial carrying him.

Gil wound up with Bobby balancing precariously in her arms. She staggered. Whatever she was, she didn't have the strength of a shifter or vampire.

"You know," Nathanial said to me, a lazy smile at the tips of his mouth, "for someone who spent the better part of five years pretending to be a lost kitten, you know painfully little about pets."

"Just because I didn't want to carry...Wait a minute." The blood drained from my face as I stared at Nathanial. "How did you know about that?"

"Like I told the judge, I took a look inside your mind. Relax. You need to stop letting your blood rush around your body like that. You are wasting it and your supply is low currently."

Hiding my embarrassment, I looked away from Nathanial and focused on Bobby. "Do you think that's pathetic—a pureblood shifter passing herself around as a pet to lonely old women and children in order to survive?"

Bobby blinked his almond-shaped eyes, and I looked away. I didn't want to know the answer. I thought I was pathetic enough for both of us.

"I think it was resourceful," Nathanial said.

"Yeah, well, you're not my kind."

"You are *my* kind, now."

I turned from him and headed to the street. "How do we get to the hospital?"

Nathanial pointed to a set of stairs leading underground. "I suggest the subway."

The station smelled of decades of sweaty bodies, trash, and disgustingly enough, urine. I tried not to think about it. There was only one other person on the platform with us, but he got on the next train, leaving us alone. When the trains arrived, the station was uncomfortably noisy, but in between, it was eerily silent.

Gil had hidden Bobby in his clothing bag. Judging by the slit-eyed way he regarded us through the bag's opening, I guessed he wasn't too thrilled with the situation.

Nathanial quizzed Gil about the school she attended in Sabin, but I couldn't concentrate on the conversation. How could he engage in casual chitchat, given our circumstances?

"What does any of this have to do with me?" I blurted out, and they both looked surprised to be interrupted.

Bobby continued to look disgruntled in his bag.

"What?" Nathanial asked, removing his glasses and tapping the frame against his palm.

"Why me? Why does the judge think I'm responsible for the rogue shifter?" I'd been wondering about it since we reached the subway. It wasn't just the judge who thought I'd created the rogue, the hunters from Firth were also looking for me.

Aside from the events of the last two nights, nothing unusual had happened recently, and I hadn't shifted to my mid-form since I left Firth. I kept thinking about the story I'd heard at the rave. About the "hallucination" that turned out to be deadly. *Someone* had shifted into mid-form in front of humans, but it wasn't me.

Gil looked away before answering. "I gathered as much information from the investigators in Sabin as I could before I left. The earliest related incident they uncovered happened about three months ago in a city named Demur."

"Demur?"

"Have you been there?"

"No." Well, probably. The name was familiar, but that didn't make the city special. I'd been to hundreds of cities over the last few years. Admitting Demur was one of them wasn't in my best interest. "What does and incident in Demur have to do with a rogue in Haven?"

"I'm getting there." She crossed her arms over her chest. "As I was saying, three months ago four human males were admitted to the hospital with claw marks from a very large cat. When asked to explain what happened, they said, in very unkind language, that a woman with a strange dye job had attacked them. The incident was marked as suspicious, but not closely examined. Shortly after that, the rogue's first two victims were found in Demur, then he apparently moved to Haven. According to Sabin's records, you were the only known female feline shifter outside Firth three months ago."

"A *woman* with a strange dye job? That doesn't prove it was me. Do you have proof any of the guys actually changed after the attack?"

Gil shrugged. "We don't know anything for certain. When our investigators tried to track the men, all the names and addresses turned up fake. We believe they falsely identified themselves at the hospital."

"So you don't even know who they really were." I paced the edge of the platform. "If they said a *woman* attacked them, not a cat, then they wouldn't have turned into shifters. A human has to be attacked by a shifter in mid-form in order for the change to occur. It doesn't sound like whoever it was shifted. Maybe it was a human with really healthy nails."

"Kita, you do have claws." Nathanial touched his shoulder.

I'd forgotten I had dug my claws into him. "But I don't shift to use them."

Gil eyed me. "How do you have claws without shifting?" Her voice held a heavy note of curiosity.

Because she's found something new for her study, or because she thinks she'll unearth my guilt? I paced faster.

"I'm a cat. I have retractable claws, even in my human form."

"Really? I would like to see that." Gil stepped into my path, forcing me to stop. A popping sound came from the clothing bag by her feet.

I ignored the sound, frowning first at her and then at Nathanial. "I *was* a cat. He killed me."

Nathanial frowned. "You are not dead."

"Undead. Whatever."

Beside me, the popping sounds became more frequent as Bobby's human form slowly put itself together. I stared in disbelief. It had been maybe thirty minutes since he'd changed to his bobcat form. I hadn't thought him powerful enough to shift so often. The small bag buckled, threatening to rip around his expanding form. He slid free of the encumbering paper, landing on the platform as his bones lengthened.

"Wow, that hurt a little," he said, once his form stabilized. He stood, human again, and totally naked.

I averted my eyes, not confident of my expression. "Put some clothes on. The next train could be here any minute."

Thankfully, he listened to me. The sound of him digging through the bag echoed around the station.

"Kitten," he said, his voice breathy from the exertion of the change, "if you can manifest claws in your human form, you have a powerful talent. Doesn't that prove you *are* worthy of your clan? Doesn't it prove your clan needs you back home?"

My head snapped up. Bobby had his pants on, but was still naked from the waist up. The tawny hair sprinkling his chest and arms stood on end, goosebumps covering his richly tanned flesh. His muscles flexed as he pulled his shirt over his head and tugged it over his abs. Nathanial touched my shoulder, and I realized I'd been staring. I cleared my throat. *What had we been talking about? Right, my claws.*

"You're forgetting one key problem, Bobby. I can't shift anymore."

"It might not be permanent." He sounded pleading, like he needed to believe vampirism was temporary even more than I did.

I looked at Nathanial for confirmation. His face showed me nothing, his empty mask perfectly in place. I glanced at Gil.

She shrugged. "I don't think there are any documented cases of shifters turning into vampires. It could be an interesting subject to study."

"See, it might not be permanent," Bobby said again.

I frowned at him. Gil hadn't indicated that at all, but Bobby heard what he wanted—he always had.

He pulled his coat on and paced a small line in front of me. "Neither of your brothers have developed the ability to unsheathe their claws while in human form. You fight against being *Dyre*, but the *Torin* knew what he was doing when he named you as his successor. Your clan needs you."

"We are getting off topic." I hugged my arms across my chest and concentrated on a colorful bit of graffiti on the wall. "We are supposed to be proving how I couldn't be the shifter who created a rogue—or maybe rogues, plural. If we can prove I'm innocent, we can summon the judge back and get my death sentence revoked."

Gil tsk-tsked. "Oh, the judge doesn't listen to a defense once he's made a decision, and you've already bargained with him." Her eyebrows squeezed together. Could she think hard enough to hurt herself? "Your file didn't mention you are descended from a *Torin's* line. That might explain some things. But if you have the ability to use your claws while in human form, couldn't you infect someone?"

Infect?

Bobby went still, his last step slamming on the platform hard enough to echo around the station. For my part, my lips twisted in a grimace I couldn't hide.

"We are not diseased," I said, my voice barely breaking a whisper. "Humans are not *infected*. They are tagged, which is more like attaching a homing beacon for a new soul to follow than any kind of contagion."

"Fine, tagged. So 'tagging' is something that can only happen when a shifter is in mid-form—somewhere between pure-human and pure-animal? When your claws are out, aren't you in mid-form?"

"One, I didn't attack anyone. And two, I don't—didn't shift to use my claws." I crossed my arms over my chest. I wasn't pouty, really. Or at least, not much. "My claws extended while I was in human form. That's not the same as being in mid-form."

"Still," Gil said, wringing her hands together. "That ability puts you at the top of the suspects list. Is there anyone else besides Nathanial that you've used your claws on?"

I opened my mouth and closed it again. I did not want to answer that question. The first time my claws extended I'd needed and used them. But it was self defense. I hadn't shifted, so I couldn't have tagged the street thugs who'd jumped me. Still, it was probably best not to mention the incident. I was supposed to be proving my innocence, not incriminating myself.

Nathanial moved closer to me, and his hand brushed against mine. "Is that all it takes to turn someone into a shifter? Clawing them while you are in mid-form?"

Gil studied him. "I thought you pleaded in her defense. You said you had a look in her mind and hadn't seen anything indicating she'd tagged a human."

"I was unaware creating a shifter was so simplistic. Creating a vampire requires intent. I assumed creating a shifter would as well."

Gil pulled a scroll out of the air and jotted down a note. Not a good sign.

Nathanial frowned at her. "Tell me, have there been any reports of the rogue shifting into a specific type of cat? A house cat? If the rogue is not a house cat, would that not prove her innocence?"

I frowned at him. "Why would you think my animal would have to be his?" My mouth snapped shut. *Because he isn't a shifter.* "Tagging doesn't work that way. The rogue's beast could be anything—no matter who tagged him."

Nathanial started to ask something else, but a rapidly approaching train screeched to a stop, hiding his words. It was the train we were waiting for, and since other passengers were scattered around the car, none of us felt safe resuming our conversation. I was happy for that. Nathanial might have been trying to help, but so far he'd only dug my hole deeper.

Chapter 5

Saint Mary's Hospital was a couple blocks from the subway line, and the tension in the air as we walked down the street was almost tangible. I shoved my hands deep in my pockets and fidgeted with a loose button I'd found. It had been firmly ingrained in me that, when in the human world, one should stay away from doctors and scientists. Gil tugged on her sleeves again and I wondered if our presence or our destination made her nervous. Perhaps all supernaturals avoided hospitals.

Hugging my arms across my chest, I pulled my coat tighter. "It's colder than it was."

Nathanial turned to me and in one swift movement caught my chin in his hand. Scanning my face, he pressed his lips into a tight line. "Your blood supply is low. You need to feed."

"I'm fine." I jerked away.

I expected him to press the subject, but he let it drop. That surprised me, and I wasn't sure why. He was a relative stranger, but I felt like I'd known him a long time. It must have been a vampire trick, or maybe it had just been a very long night. Trudging ahead, I tried to put as much space as possible between me and my companions. Really, we were each alone in our little company. Well, that was how I wanted to see it, but both Bobby and Nathanial stubbornly kept pace with me, one on either side. They tossed less-than-friendly looks at each other over my head.

Bobby halted abruptly and grabbed my shoulder. I started to pull away, but stopped when I saw his face. He wasn't paying attention to me. He was scenting the wind, which had changed direction.

I tilted my head back, searching but the sense of smell on which I'd relied all my life was suddenly no longer sharp. "Hunter?"

He nodded.

With a rogue on the loose, no stray like me would be left unmolested. The hunter I'd evaded yesterday would have alerted the rest to my presence. If hunters caught me, they would detain me until the next full moon, when the gate to Firth opened and they could drag me in front of the elders. There was no way I could find the rogue from a hunter's safe-house. I'd be a sitting duck when the judge returned.

"Plans?" I asked.

Bobby frowned. He didn't think fast.

"What's wrong?" Gil asked, catching up to us.

"Hunter," Bobby said, still scenting the air. "He isn't too close, but the wind keeps shifting, so I don't know if he's caught our scent or not."

"We are not far from the hospital. Is he that close?" Nathanial pointed to a large building towering over the buildings surrounding it. It wasn't more than a block or two away.

Bobby's forehead creased, but he shook his head. After a moment he said, "If he is tracking us, he's not actually following Kita. Her scent has changed. But *your* scent is what hers should be. You have to leave. You'll draw them right to us."

Nathanial raised an eyebrow and Bobby stood straighter, interpreting the response as a challenge. Nathanial ignored him. "Which direction is the hunter?"

After consulting the wind again, Bobby pointed to our right. Nathanial nodded, then turned and gave me a small smile.

He ran two fingers down my cheek. "I will meet you in the hospital lobby."

I startled, pulling back, and his smile turned smaller. He stepped out of the circle of light from the streetlamp, and then vanished. I gaped, scanning the darkness. Shadows hid nothing from my newly acquired vampire eyes, but I couldn't see him anywhere. Gil made a surprised sound before pulling out her scroll and jotting something down.

"He plans to divert the hunter's attention?" Bobby asked, scanning the street, wide-eyed.

I shrugged.

He frowned at me. "The hunter could still track *my* scent. You and Gil go ahead. I'll catch up."

Gil started forward.

I looked between her retreating back and Bobby. He nodded me forward, then turned and backtracked the way we'd come. I frowned after him.

Wasn't I supposed to be in charge of this group?

Grumbling under my breath, I ran to catch up with Gil. "Let's get this over with. Do you know where the survivor is in there?" I nodded at the looming glass-and-brick building in front of us.

"I think I have a pretty good idea."

The harsh fluorescent lights bleached the color from the lobby; not that the cold, white walls and soft, pastel paintings had much color to spare. The astringent smell of antiseptic burned my nose. *This is where sick humans go to recover?* On the odd occasion a shifter fell sick, we—they—needed sunlight, fresh air, trees.

A pair of orderlies passed us, speaking in hushed tones, and a man dragged in a screaming child, a woman following with red-rimmed eyes. *How could anyone improve in such a morbid place?*

Bobby joined us a few minutes after we arrived, but Nathanial was nowhere to be seen. Of course, we hadn't exactly 'seen' him leave, but shouldn't he have made it back by now? I wandered into the small gift shop.

Only the lights around the coffee bar were on; the rest of the store was dark and deserted. A sleepy-looking woman sat behind the counter reading a book, drinking her wares, and paying no attention to me at all. She didn't say anything as I walked past her into the darkened store. Small stuffed animals and large flower bouquets lined the shelves. Somber 'In Sympathy' cards sat next to bright colored 'It's a Girl' cards, the contrast cruel. As I rounded a display case labeled 'For Long-term Illness,' Nathanial cruised through the sliding glass doors of the lobby. *About time.*

The sales clerk glanced up as I rushed past. "You have to pay for that, Miss."

She rounded her counter, hands on her hips.

Pay for . . . crap. I stared at the pink bear wearing a 'Keep Fighting' shirt. I didn't even remember picking it up.

"Sorry," I mumbled, handing the bear to her. Her eyes flared, but she grabbed the bear and stormed back into her shop.

As I hurried into the lobby Gil shook her head, her lips pursed, and jotted another note in her scroll. This night got better and better.

Bobby studied Nathanial through narrowed eyes as I approached the two of them. As soon as I drew closer, I realized why.

"You smell different," I whispered to Nathanial, tilting my head back, my nostrils flaring. This close a scent was unmistakable. He hadn't had a scent earlier, or at least not to me, since he had stolen mine. But now he smelled of cinnamon and cotton, which couldn't be me. I stepped closer. It was *under* his skin, not on it. How was that possible?

Bobby was leaning toward him too, sniffing and frowning. I lost the scent, sniffed harder, moving within arm's length of him. My olfactory failed me—another thing that shouldn't happen. *Further proof I'll never shift again?* I stepped close enough to feel the heat rising from Nathanial's body, but I couldn't catch the new scent again.

Nathanial cleared his throat, and I realized Bobby and I had moved closer to him than social norms allowed. Humans typically didn't stand around sniffing each other. I stepped back, glancing at the other people in the nearly deserted lobby. No one was staring at the three of us—yet.

"This isn't possible." Bobby circled to Nathanial's back, his nostrils still flaring, his steps taking him closer to the vampire.

I shuffled my feet as heat from Bobby's beast radiated off him. Agitation? Fear? I wasn't sure, but it felt like he was gearing up for a fight. He rounded back in front of Nathanial, the space between them too close to be anything but intimate or violent.

Unbothered, Nathanial removed his glasses and cleaned them with a cloth from his pocket.

"Did you want that bear?" He nodded at the gift shop.

Warmth rushed to my cheeks, and I shook my head. I swayed as I felt the blood drain from my face again, and Nathanial caught my shoulders to keep me standing.

Bobby pulled Nathanial's hands off me. "Don't touch her!"

Nathanial glanced at Bobby's grip around his wrists, and the first glint of anger cut into his gray eyes. *Oh, this will go downhill fast.*

I stepped between them, knocking their arms apart. "Enough, both of you." I met each man's eyes in turn. This was ridiculous. And people were starting to stare now, drawn to the rising tension like flies to a corpse. "Are we going to hang out in the lobby all night?"

They frowned. Nathanial shook his head, but neither moved back. Bobby's anger mixed with his energy and spilled off his skin like electrified needles brushing along the left side of my body. Nathanial went into statue mode, his cold glare unwavering. *Idiots.*

I looked at Gil for help. She shrugged, apparently the only one immune to the thick tension, and headed down a hallway leading deeper into the hospital. I followed. If the guys wanted to have a pissing contest in the lobby, they could do it alone.

Neither Bobby nor Nathanial backed down. They simply turned to follow and ignored each other. It was like having two cobras at my heels. I waited for one to land the first strike.

Gil led us into the stairwell. I lost count of how many identical flights of stairs we climbed before she finally indicated we'd reached the right level. She navigated through the bright corridors following signs with strange medical words and small arrows.

At each corner, Nathanial put out a hand, stopping me. He scanned the halls before dropping his arm and letting me pass. Apparently he wasn't concerned for Gil and Bobby, who were ahead of us, but despite my protests and trying to get around him, Nathanial managed to be in front of me at every turn.

With all his skulking caution, I was surprised when hospital security guards stopped us, not once but twice—clearly human authorities weren't who Nathanial was watching for. Both guards chastised us about being on the floor between visiting hours, but both times Gil talked for awhile, and the guards smiled and let us continue.

After the second walked away, Bobby let out a low whistle. "If I ever need to sneak in someplace, I know who to call."

"Thanks," she said, stopping to read another sign. "But don't even think about it."

We wove around several more passages, and I jumped as elevator doors opened a couple yards behind me. Two women in blue scrubs stepped into the hall. They walked in the other direction, and I let out the breath I'd been holding. I almost cheered when Gil finally led us into a waiting room. But when I saw the occupants of the room, I decided cheering would be in poor taste.

In the far corner, stationed in uncushioned chairs, a middle-aged couple leaned on each other. Streaks of mascara had dried under the woman's eyes, and the man's hands were clenched tight even in sleep. Not terribly surprising, considering the sign on the door said we'd entered the ICU waiting room.

A red-headed woman sat behind a desk at the front of the room. She peeled bored eyes off her computer screen as we approached. "I'm sorry, but visiting hours are at nine a.m., noon, and six p.m. Only direct family members are allowed to visit patients in this section of the ICU. If you'd like to wait until the next visiting hour, take a seat."

Her nasal voice was loud enough to wake the sleeping couple. They immediately became distraught, fresh tears creating new runnels through the woman's dried mascara and the man looking torn between the need to comfort his wife and the desire to burn off his emotions through movement. I shot an unfriendly look at the receptionist—not that she cared, if her apathetic expression was any hint.

"Allow me to introduce myself," Gil said brightly, holding out a hand. The woman took it limply. "I'm Gil and these are my colleagues. One of your patients was the victim in a series of crimes we're investigating. I know it's outside of hours, but it's imperative we see the young woman tonight."

I rolled my eyes. No way were we getting in with an excuse like that, true or not.

The receptionist smiled blankly and nodded. She hit something under the counter, and the doors to the unit unlocked with a loud click. Gil marched into the ICU like she owned the place.

The rest of us followed, wide-eyed.

Nathanial stared at her. "That was . . . unexpected. What did you do to her?" Nathanial might have plucked the question right out of my mind.

Gil grinned over her shoulder and smiled, but said nothing as we walked past cubicles. She paused outside of each room and examined the charts. At the fifth room, her smile nearly broke her face in two.

"Here we are. Lorna Stixon." She opened the door, and we filed in behind her.

Gil pulled a canary-yellow curtain back. At first, I didn't see the patient for all the IV's on poles and beeping machines clustered around her.

As we crowded around the bed, I did a double take. "I know this girl."

Gil's head shot up. "What, how?"

"Well, I don't actually know her. But I saw her last night." I looked at the tangled, pink-and- blue-streaked hair. "She was at a party I went to. By the way, notice that I'm not the only woman with oddly streaked hair in this city."

Nathanial touched my shoulder, expectant. "Did you see who she was with?"

If only it were that easy.

"I only noticed her because she fell in my lap, literally." I frowned, trying to remember anything useful. The party was a blur in my memory. Not so much from the drug I'd been slipped, but because I hadn't been paying attention.

The door opened behind me, and I jumped, my eyes darting around the small room for a place to hide. *Behind the bed?* But the quick squeak of sneakers on the floor meant they were already in the room. I whirled around, my eyes wide.

A woman with salt and pepper hair walked in, studying her clipboard. She looked up and gasped, pressing her hand over her chest. "My God, you guys scared me. How'd you get in here? I'm sorry, but the next visiting hour isn't until morning."

The nursed turned to hit a call button by the door, and Gil surged forward. She laid her hand on the nurse's shoulder, and the smallest touch of energy charged the air.

"We'll be out of your way shortly. We're trying to find the monster who did this to Lorna," Gil said in a sweet voice.

The nurse smiled, her eyes turning vacant. *Magic?* Probably. But, if I'd have blinked, I would have missed it. Magic would explain the guards compliance, and the waiting-room receptionist. I'd have to ask Gil later.

"Have you been tending to Lorna long?" Gil asked.

The nurse nodded. "Since she got out of surgery eleven hours ago."

"Has she regained consciousness at any point?" Nathanial asked, but the nurse didn't answer.

Gil repeated the question.

"For a little while. She's sedated now. She screams about monsters when she's conscious." The nurse paused, her smile failing. "Are you police? Some officers questioned her earlier."

"We're investigators. Were you present when the police questioned her? Was she able to name her attacker?"

"She couldn't remember who did this to her. She said she remembered being at a party, but not leaving, and then she went on about a 'monster.' She was on a lot of hallucinogens. Aside from the obvious, it's hard to say what really happened."

"What's the obvious?" Gil asked, leading the nurse closer to the bed. The woman followed like a sleepwalker, each step heavy and blind.

At the edge of the bed she stopped and pointed. "Her left arm has a spiral break, her right, two fractures. Her neck is broken, and it's unlikely she'll ever have movement below her shoulders. Three ribs were broken, and a chunk of her right thigh is missing. She also has multiple deep lacerations. The doctors think she has stabilized, but it's a miracle she survived."

I looked at Lorna's sleeping form. Her eyes were swollen shut, her lips busted, and she was in a cast or covered in gauze from the neck down. The rogue had played with her, tortured her. If she survived until the gate opened, and if the rogue's harsh game had tagged her and she became a shifter, she would heal the physical injuries. If not, she would spend the rest of her life paralyzed. Either way the attack would leave her emotionally damaged. Humans ended up on courses of therapy and drugs for something like rape. But if Lorna shifted . . . the odds of her retaining her humanity, her sanity after something like this were slim, and insanity in a shifter was a quick recipe for death.

Shaking my head, I walked closer to the nurse. I thought I caught a hint of demon-like decay, but it faded to the menthol scent of cigarettes. I tried to pick the first scent out again, but the more I searched, the more she smelled like an ashtray. I'd had no idea how much I relied on my sense of smell until it'd gone on the fritz.

Wrinkling my nose, I asked, "Did you hear anything else? Did she say what the monster looked like? Where was she found?"

Gil repeated my questions, and the nurse shrugged. "She must've been seeing things. A man did this to her, maybe with the help of others, but not an animal. The police had a sexual assault test done, it came back positive. They found bodily fluids. You'll catch this guy?"

Gil smiled. "We'll try our best. You should check on your other patients now."

The nurse nodded and sleepwalked out the door.

"She didn't tell us where Lorna was found," Bobby said.

Gil shrugged. "If she'd known, she would have answered. We were lucky she was nosy and listened in on the police interview, or we wouldn't know all we do."

I frowned. I certainly hadn't learned much—except that the rogue was a sadistic bastard, but that wasn't surprising. Rogues and insanity went hand-in-hand. At least, the one and only rogue I'd ever met had been certifiable. I shivered and wrapped my arms across my chest. I almost thought I could feel the old scars from that meeting through my clothing. "Now what?"

"Let's see if we can find out anything more." Gil reached forward to grab unconscious Lorna's hand, then hesitated before touching the cast. Her eyes slid over the prone body, and she laid a hand on the girl's face. "Wake up Lorna."

Once again, I felt a small change in the air around us. The muscles twitched in Lorna's face, and her eyes swam behind their swollen lids. After a few moments, her face calmed again, and Gil made an agitated sound in the back of her throat.

Nathanial shook his head. "She has a lot of drugs pumping through her. Combined with being half-dead, I do not think you will be able to wake her."

Gil gave him a less-than-friendly look. "How can you tell she is full of drugs?"

"I can smell them. And, the nurse said as much. Besides, anyone in her condition would be seriously medicated."

"Smell? You can smell the drugs? That's unusual." Her eyes went distant as she made a mental note. When she refocused, she glanced at me. "Do you remember anything else about her?"

I shook my head and took a step closer to the bed. Lorna's bruised and broken face did nothing to jog details in my memory, though it did make the roof of my mouth tingle with hunger. I took another step closer, my thighs brushing against the blanket hanging off the side of the bed. Lorna smelled like raw meat, maybe slightly cold and sterile. I had the feeling her blood would taste sour. Regardless, pressure built in my mouth as my fangs lengthened.

Nathanial pulled me away from the bed.

"The sour smell is from the drugs," he whispered.

I froze, the reality of what had been going through my mind sinking in. Jerking away from him, I fled the room. In the hall, a man in blue scrubs let me know in no uncertain terms that visiting hours were over. I walked away from him. Gil could deal with it. She was good at that.

Nathanial caught up with me before I made it to the waiting room.

"Why do I want to take a bite out of everyone I meet?" I glared at him, angry tears threatening to spill into my eyes. "It's vile."

"If you would feed, you would not be tempted every time the opportunity arose." He leaned down until our faces were inches apart. "Think about it, Kitten, if you are starving, everything on a menu looks good. Not quite so hungry, and you are more willing to be picky."

"Don't call me Kitten. Only Bobby calls me that, and I hate it."

"You didn't used to." Bobby's voice was a deep rumble behind me.

I crossed my arms, hugging myself hard, and stepped away. Bobby looked from Nathanial to me, and then made a point of placing himself between the two of us. I hit a metal panel on the wall, and the doors slid open. Gil had to run to catch up as I stormed into the waiting room. The red-headed receptionist looked surprised to see us, but then went back to her computer like we weren't really there. The couple in the back of the room jumped up as I entered.

"You're investigating my Lorna's case?" The woman grabbed hold of Bobby's coat and clung to him. "When will the monster who did this be put behind bars?"

Bobby shot a helpless glance at me.

How was I supposed to know what to do? I looked at Gil. She frowned and pulled on her coat sleeves. Where had her take-charge personality gone?

Nathanial finally spoke. "Finding him is our top priority."

The man soothed his wife until she released Bobby's coat, and she collapsed against her husband, sobbing. He looked back at us. "You're very young to be investigators. What are you, police? FBI?"

Gil stepped forward and patted the distraught couple on their shoulders. "We're sorry for what happened to Lorna. What she must have gone through, no one should ever have to face."

The woman visibly relaxed, but the skepticism on the man's face grew.

Gil hurried on, "We're private investigators, yes. We were given the case by someone who felt the police wouldn't be able to solve it."

The magical charge touched the air again, and the man's puzzled look vanished as he smiled the smallest bit and nodded. "So, someone high up paid for the best? Good."

We left before they could snap out of whatever spell Gil had put on them.

"Why not tell him we were from the FBI?" Nathanial asked as we wove our way back through the halls of the hospital.

Gil balled her hands on her waist. "Because we aren't."

"But they didn't know that," Bobby said.

"The spell doesn't work that way. That would have been a bald-faced lie."

"So, you can't magically hypnotize people if you lie," I asked slowly. "Or, you're incapable of lying?"

"It's not magical hypnosis." Gil sounded defensive, but she waited until we'd crossed the lobby and the exterior doors slid closed behind us before continuing, "It's a simple compulsion spell. I'm a scholar. I have to be able to collect information. But the spell works on a trading system. I have to give the target true information and a plausible reason to cooperate. Luckily, creative truths work quite well. Where to next?"

Nathanial looked up at the sky. "I have to take Kita home soon. There is—"

"I'm not going anywhere with you," I snapped, "and I don't know anything about this home place."

"She can come with me," Bobby said, his arm wrapping protectively around my shoulders.

I shrugged him off. "I don't need either one of you to take care of me. I've been on my own for the past five years, and I'm doing fine." I started down the street, so I didn't have to look at Bobby's hurt expression.

"Kita, you have a couple of new sunlight restrictions now," Nathanial said, catching up to me. "You cannot wander around hoping to find a place to sleep. If a single ray of sunlight falls on you, you could be hurt, possibly killed."

Bobby was only a step behind him. "There is a basement where I'm taking her."

Great, a basement, probably in a safe house where rogues and strays were kept until the gate opened and they could be hauled back to Firth. If I went to a safe house, I'd never come back out. Bobby's pissing contest with Nathanial was going to get me captured. That realization finally made it through Bobby's jealous haze, and he actually looked at *me* instead of Nathanial.

"We'll get a hotel room," he said. "We will make it light-tight. I'll keep you safe."

"I doubt you know how," Nathanial scoffed, and Bobby's step faltered. I hesitated, the air on the street too thick to breathe as Bobby's anger poured off him.

"Shut up, both of you." I didn't need anyone to keep me safe. What I really needed was a solid lead so I could find the rogue.

Nathanial smiled, a haughty tilting of his lips, but he changed the subject. "We need to determine our next move, and I would suggest somewhere quiet. That twenty-four-hour diner over there might work." Without waiting for anyone to agree, he steered us toward the restaurant.

He opened the door to the restaurant for me, and I stood aside to let Bobby and Gil enter first. Once they were inside, Nathanial and I stared at each other, neither saying a word. His smile melted away, but he waited, his stillness accenting my impatience as I shuffled from foot to foot.

He shook his head, but conceded and walked inside. Halfway through the door, he turned. "You are safer with me."

Chapter 6

From the outside, the diner had looked like an oasis in the predawn night. Inside, the light failed to make the dingy area inviting. I blamed the mustard-colored tables. The only customer slept beside a cup of cold coffee. His head jerked up as the bells attached to the door handle jingled, but his eyes fluttered closed a moment later. The waitress and the cook chatted at the first table. They frowned as our small group trudged in, and, with obvious reluctance, stood and retreated to the open kitchen while we situated ourselves in a corner booth.

Bobby sat down first, and to my disappointment, Gil plopped down beside him, leaving me next to Nathanial. By the look on Bobby's face, he disliked the arrangement as much as I did. Nathanial insisted I take the inside seat.

What, does he think I'll run off?

Given my history, that wasn't a completely unfair assumption, but I still sulked as I slid across the seat.

The waitress handed out menus. "This all on one check?"

I glanced around the table. "Who has money?"

"I do," Bobby and Nathanial said in unison.

Good, one of them could pick up my tab. "Same check. I'll have a double waffle, hash browns with onions, bacon, and two eggs scrambled with cheese. Oh, and a hot chocolate."

Nathanial reached over and took the menu from my hands. "No, you won't. She will have only the hot chocolate, and I would like a cup of hot tea. Thank you." He smiled at the waitress.

She glanced from him to me. Then I watched, horrified, as she scratched my order off the ticket. The waitress looked at Gil, whose face was buried in the menu.

"Um, I'm not ready yet."

"I am," Bobby said. "I'll have what she ordered, originally." He pointed at me.

Gil looked up. "I'm still not ready." She looked around the table, "What would be best?"

Nathanial ordered for her, and lucky Gil got more than just a drink.

After the waitress left, I rounded on him. "What, can't I eat food?"

"You could. Probably five or six whole bites before you had to purge it. Your digestive tract has been altered. Pretend to drink your hot chocolate."

I slouched lower in the booth, my arms over my chest. "But I really like food. It's the best part about being here in this world."

Nathanial ignored me as the waitress returned with our drinks. I picked up the hot chocolate and cupped it in my hands. I'd been feeling progressively colder as time passed, and I hoped the hot chocolate would help, but it felt neutral, neither warm nor cold. Steam rose out of the mug, but heat didn't pass into my hands. *Irritating.* I tipped the mug up slowly, testing the liquid against my lips. I expected it to burn me, but it only felt wet. *What kind of place served lukewarm hot chocolate?* I took a sip anyway. It tasted weak, watery, the bittersweet flavor of chocolate only an aftertaste. I glared at the dark-cream colored liquid, but took another sip. My mug was half empty when I put it down. Nathanial glanced at it, then at me.

"You do not listen, do you?" he asked, and my stomach clinched.

I hunched in the booth, wrapping my arms around my middle. My breath caught as pain twisted in my gut. The sting of nausea burned the back of my throat. *Oh crap.*

Nathanial stood and took my hand. "Come on, then."

He led me away from the table. He pushed me into the single-occupancy bathroom, and the metal door slammed behind us then locked with a click. I collapsed in front of the squat toilet, Nathanial holding my hair back as the hot chocolate left my body in a series of violent surges.

After my stomach stopped trying to commit mutiny, I wiped my mouth with the back of my hand. "This is the girl's bathroom, you know."

"I told you to pretend to drink."

I tugged my hair away from him and walked over to the sink. Rinsing my mouth out with water, I made sure not to swallow any. It wasn't that the hot chocolate had tasted any different coming back up, but I didn't want to have the taste lingering in my mouth. Turning to Nathanial, I found he had a very sympathetic look on his face. That did nothing to make me feel better.

The single-occupancy bathroom was crowded with only the toilet and sink. With both Nathanial and me in it too, it was downright claustrophobic. I tried to move around Nathanial, but he leaned against the door, blocking it.

"You need to feed," he said, pulling a small cloth from his pocket. He removed his glasses and wiped the lenses.

"I won't kill people to eat."

"Good, the council would be upset if you did. You need only a pint or two of blood a night, nothing more. People have quarts of blood."

"And will everyone I bite become a monster?"

"The world would be crawling with vampires if that were so. The worst your donor will experience is a little dizziness and exhaustion, not much different from giving at a blood drive."

"Vampirism's not a side effect of giving blood, then," I paused. "You said earlier that creating a vampire is intentional, so . . . there's a process. You did this to me, made me this way on purpose?"

Nathanial's face fell. "Not entirely. My curiosity got the best of me. I have been studying myths and legends for years, looking for shreds of truth that would lead me to other supernaturals. And then I found you. I took blood along with your memories. I was overly absorbed in what I found in your mind, by what you were, and the drug in your system confused me more than I expected . . . suddenly I had taken too much blood. I had to choose between letting you die and making you a vampire."

"I'd rather be dead."

"Then why did you bargain with the judge?"

I looked at the floor.

He straightened and ran a hand down my cheek. "You will adjust, give yourself time."

I backed away, my butt pressing against the sink. "I don't want to adjust. I want things to go back to normal."

"What, life on the street? Starving half the time? When you were desperate enough, pretending to be a stray kitten so people took you home and fed you before you deserted them a couple weeks later. You want to go back to that?"

I glared at him. "Stay out of my mind. I don't know a thing about you, so you shouldn't know so much about me."

"Well," He leaned against the door again and slipped his glasses back on. "I am a professor at the local university. I teach a class—"

"That wasn't a request for your life story, because I don't care. I hate you. And by the way, normal people use contractions."

He sighed and tugged the door open. "Come on. We will be missed. There is much to discuss before dawn." He held out an arm, but I walked past it.

Back at the table, the food had arrived. Bobby was quickly clearing his many plates, but Gil picked at her waffle with strawberries rather unsurely. I gave them both evil glares, but honestly, the food didn't make my mouth water. It wasn't what my body wanted, anymore.

"So what did we learn tonight?" I asked, building a tower with creamer containers the waitress set down for Bobby's coffee.

"Well, I learned a whole lot. I had no idea vamps could smell drugs in a body," Gil said, nibbling on a strawberry. She must have decided she liked it, because she then popped the whole thing in her mouth.

"Yeah, sour smell equals drugs." I knocked the tower back down. "Did anyone notice that the nurse smelled, I don't know, rotten or something?"

Bobby picked up the creamer container that landed in his hash browns and tossed it back to me. "She smelled like cigarettes to me."

"No, Kita is right." Nathanial glanced over his shoulder to check that no one else was in earshot before continuing. "The nurse is dying. She probably does not know it yet, but from the way she smelled, I would say she has cancer."

"You can smell disease? That's weird," Bobby said around a bit of bacon.

Nathanial frowned like he was being pressed by a toddler who had recently learned the word *Why*. Leaning down so his whisper was only for me, he said, "Drugs, alcohol, disease, or anything else that contaminates blood is information a vampire needs to be aware of. We can not die from such things, but it can make for an interesting night. If someone's smell does not appeal to you, it would be best to look for a meal elsewhere."

Heat crept to my cheeks. "I told you, I'm not biting innocent people."

"Who said anything about innocents?" Gil asked, her chirpy voice much too loud for the conversation. Nathanial tensed and motioned her to be quieter, but Gil continued without noticing, "I read that Nathanial feeds only from criminals. Haven's very own vampire vigilante. I think it might be the reason the judge listened to his opinion of you."

I turned and stared at Nathanial. *A vigilante.* That might actually explain some things. Like why he was out on the streets when the stray attacked me, and why he fought him off. Nathanial had planned to feed on a man he'd assumed was a mugger.

Nathanial's frown deepened, his eyes sharp as he studied Gil. Finally looking away, he pressed his palm against his forehead, bumping his glasses. "Do your people document *everything?*"

Gil shrugged. "Only the supernaturals who stand out. I didn't read anything on Bobby, but Kita is in our files because she defied the laws of Firth, which don't allow female shifters to enter the human world. It stands to reason that since she is willing to violate Firth's laws she can't be trusted to uphold secrecy laws regarding life among the humans. Nathanial, you're in our records because of the bodies you leave behind. But you cover the cause of death well, so currently you are only monitored."

I glared at him. "Bodies? I thought you—"

Nathanial cut me off. "I indicated that our kind does not have to kill to feed, not that no one did." The dark look I'd glimpsed earlier bubbled to the surface of his face again, aimed directly at Gil, but it disappeared in the blink of an eye, a pleasant but empty expression taking its place. "I am sure this conversation is fascinating, but it does not further our investigation into the rogue. Determining when and how the rogue found Lorna would be helpful. We know she was at the party before she was attacked, the same as Kita." Nathanial turned and took the creamers away from me before I could knock down my newest tower. "When was the last time you saw her?"

"Errr." I tried to think back. I'd glanced at Bryant's watch not long before leaving the rave, and it had been nearly five a.m., but I couldn't remember if Lorna had still been on the couch then. It had been hours earlier when she'd fallen in my lap. She could have left the party earlier in the night, and I wouldn't have noticed. Had I seen her at any other point in the night? The party as a whole was a blur, especially my mad dash away from Bryant after I'd been drugged. Finally I shook my head. "The last time I know I saw her was around two a.m. When I left the rave at five, she could have been anywhere with anyone."

Gil pulled her scroll out and flipped through her notes. "For simplicity's sake, let's assume that whenever she left the rave, sometime after two a.m., it was with the rogue. Judging by the news reports about her case, she wasn't found by the police until about twelve hours later, early afternoon. Think she could have survived her injuries for twelve hours, if the rogue had nearly beaten her to death immediately after she left the rave?"

Nathanial and I looked at each other, and I shook my head. Nathanial mirrored me, grimacing. "Then she was tortured later," he said. "The rave might be unconnected. She could have gone anywhere after leaving."

I rubbed my eyes, which were becoming excessively heavy. "She could barely sit up, the last time I saw her. She didn't leave the club without help. Either the rogue took her, or someone dropped her off where the rogue could find her." If a shifter was at the party, surely I would have noticed him Of course, I had gone there to disguise my own scent, so it would have been easy to miss someone else's. "I talked to someone who said he'd gone to a rave several months ago where some guy freaked out. Said it was deemed a mass hallucination because everyone saw a monster. If it really was a rogue shifter attack, the two events could be connected."

Nathanial shook his head. "Rape and torture of a girl is different from attacking a crowd. The two are not likely to be connected," he said. "What we really need to know is why and how he is picking his victims."

"Rogues are insane," I said. "It could be the same person."

Bobby nodded.

"You should not generalize something we have no proof of," Nathanial said, frowning. "Are you not considered a rogue yourself, Kita?"

I went still. "I may have left my clan, but I did not turn rogue. I didn't turn my back on everything we believe. I haven't abandoned my humanity or depraved my cat. I'm a stray, a fugitive. Not a rogue."

Bobby bristled. "You're neither," he said, his eyes capturing mine before moving on to sear into Nathanial. "She is *Dyre*, the future *Torin* of the Nekai clan. You will not insult her," His voice was a hoarse whisper, but the heat in it was enough to burn across my skin.

I took a deep breath, fighting to keep Bobby's anger from infecting mine—my outrage alone was enough. Of course, Nathanial had never met our kind before, so he couldn't possibly realize the depth of his insult. Rogues were insane. Always. *Rogue* was what we called a shifter who lost his or her mind and did things like . . . oh, attack, torture and kill people. It happened most often with tagged shifters, those shifters who had been born fully human or fully animal, but gained the ability to shapeshift after an encounter with a shifter in mid-form. Tagged shifters' minds tended to break if they couldn't reconcile what had happened to them, turning them rogue. In fact, it happened so often among the tagged that there were strict rules about when, how, and under what circumstance someone could be tagged.

Among natural-born and pureblood shifters, rogues were rare, but they did occur on occasion. There was no rehabilitation for a rogue, so accusing a shifter of *turning rogue* was serious. Serious enough that most shifter children ended up black and blue if they used the name even lightly against other children in their clan. Nathanial might be unintentionally right, though in calling me a rogue now—for feeding off human blood, the elders of Firth might deem me insane.

Forcing my fists to unclench, I stared at the half-moon impressions my nails had made on my palms. As I watched, the pale indentions slowly filled with thin streams of red. The urge to lick the blood off my palms made me shove my hands under the table.

Pushing all my frustrated anger to my eyes, I met Nathanial's gaze evenly. "We are dealing with a rogue. Whether he is natural or tagged, his mind must be broken or he wouldn't commit these deranged crimes. We will assume Lorna's attack and the attack on the crowd at the earlier party are related."

Nathanial's arched brow indicated he was inclined to argue, but Gil's fork clattered against her plate as she pulled another scroll out of nowhere. She unrolled it and scanned it furiously, nodding to herself. "You might be on to something," she said, glancing at me. "The body of an earlier victim was found in a closet at a rave."

"How many victims have there been?"

Gil's eyes went distant as she made a mental tally. "Eleven. The first two victims were found in Demur, but since then, the rogue's activities have been concentrated in Haven."

My jaw dropped. *Eleven? How had the hunters not caught the rogue yet? Or the mages who watched this world like hawks? Or even the vampire vigilante beside me?* Gil had said the attacks started three months ago. Eleven victims in three months was huge. The human authorities must have been losing their minds. How had I not heard of this before? Of course, I had only arrived in the city of Haven two nights ago, and as a pretend pet I didn't spend a lot of time watching the news.

"Bobby, are any of the hunters stationed in Haven as members of the humans' police force?" I asked.

He frowned, nodding.

"Good. See if there is anything they can tell you that might not be available to the public."

He nodded again.

Gil cleared her throat. "I told you already, the police wouldn't have found anything betraying supernaturals."

I frowned at her. "Yes, but the hunters are spread through the social structure of the city so they can clean up after rogues and strays. They might have found something useful before the mages went through and tampered with evidence. Or something specific to shifters the mages wouldn't know to destroy."

Nathanial held up a finger. "Obviously, all supernaturals have their own clean-up crews. A lack of communication among us might be hindering the investigation." He turned to face me. "We need to find out when the next rave is. How did you learn about the rave last night?"

"Some kooky girl at a bookstore gave me a flyer, but the party was hardly a secret. You could hear the music from blocks away. She might know about another one, but I'm not sure how to find her or the bookstore again."

"The one you were hiding out at last night?" Bobby asked, and I nodded. "I remember." He gave not an address, but a better description of the area than I could have.

"Let's meet there an hour after dark then?" Nathanial suggested.

I wanted to protest starting out so late—I was still operating on non-vampire time—but suddenly my head felt far too heavy to care. Exhaustion had been crawling over me, but now it hit fast, like all my energy went on vacation at once.

The table and I got to know each other rather well as I slumped over it, face first. At the same time, I knocked my now-cold cup of hot chocolate into Bobby's lap. He let out an exclamation, and the waitress waddled over.

"Everything all right here?"

Concentrating hard, I pulled my head up and blinked dumbly at her.

"Everything is fine. She is a little drunk," Nathanial said.

I tried to throw a hard look at him, but ended up falling into his shoulder. He wrapped an arm around me and dragged me out of the booth. He threw cash on the table and told the waitress to keep the change before helping me stumble outside.

"Is she really okay?" Bobby asked once we were out of the restaurant.

"It is almost dawn," Nathanial said as way of explanation.

I tried to wrench away from him to stand on my own, but the world dropped out from under me.

Chapter 7

The street was gone.

I stared up at the velvety darkness. Okay, I was pretty sure the darkness wasn't velvety, it was probably velvet curtains. I reached out a hand. *Yep, curtains.* The bed was surrounded by them. Black satin sheets spilled off me as I sat up. The street wasn't the only thing missing; my clothes were gone again.

Now where was I?

Probably Nathanial's house. *Stupid vampire.* I kicked the rest of the sheets off, and the large fur throw at the end of the bed lifted its head.

The largest dog I'd ever seen yawned, flashing a mouthful of sharp white teeth. A hiss escaped my throat, and I flung myself backward, away from the massive dog and right off the side of the bed. My scream died a quick death as I landed on my back, all the air knocked from my lungs. With the sheets twisted around my legs and the heavy curtains tangled around my arms, a quick retreat was impossible. *Oh crap.* As I struggled, something above me made a ripping sound. *Double crap.* The thick material fought me. There had to be an opening in the curtain somewhere.

The dog watched, his dark eyes apathetic. He stood, stretching, and lumbered halfway off the bed, his back feet still on the mattress and his front feet on the floor. His massive muzzle was only inches from my face, his nose twitching, mouth open, and tongue out. His panting breath felt damp against my checks.

Turning, I grabbed two handfuls of the curtain and yanked hard. The material tore with a nasty this-is-going-to-be-expensive sound. A series of smaller *pops* rat-a-tatted as a jagged section of curtain toppled down. Covered in sections of the ripped curtain, I scuttled backward through the opening I'd made.

I crossed several feet of carpeted floor in the blink of an eye, stopping only when my shoulders pressed against a dresser. The dog didn't move, just cocked his head to the side, still only half off the bed. I breathed for the first time in what felt like ages. The dog must be well over two hundred pounds, his shaggy black hair covering a bear-sized body. I tried to match a breed to him, but I was sure I'd never seen any breed of dog like him before. I wasn't a dog lover, nothing personal against dogs, but I'd been chased up one-too-many trees to trust *any* dog.

We stared at each other, his black eyes dull in the complete darkness. He hopped the rest of the way off the bed, and the solid oak dresser behind me creaked. The dog cocked his head at the sound but then plodded around the side of the bed and disappeared. *Thank the stars.* I tilted my head back and pressed the heels of my hands against my eyes.

"What I wouldn't give to wake up in the same place I fell asleep," I told the darkness.

"You wanted me to leave you on the street?" Nathanial's voice came from the other side of the room. I twisted around. He sat in a chair by the door with a book in his lap and his glasses twirling between his fingers. He smiled at me, amusement clear in his eyes. "Did you have to destroy the canopy?"

I didn't even glance at the material tangled around me. "Do you actually need those glasses?"

"I think they make me look older, do you not agree?" He slipped them on, pushing them high on his nose. When I only raised an eyebrow, he closed the book in his lap. "We have a lot to do. I only bought you one pair of clothes yesterday, an oversight on my part, so I am afraid you will have to wear the same outfit again."

"You had no right to bring me here, and you sure as hell had no right to undress me."

"You were unavailable for consultation. Besides, I washed your clothes. They were soggy. Try not to sit in the snow as much tonight." He held out a neat pile of clothing.

I looked at it without moving. "I want to take a bath."

"You do not sweat or shed skin cells, and your body repairs itself during the day. There is no reason to take a bath. I did not think cats liked water. Have you ever had a bath before?"

"No, but I don't hate water. Cats are good swimmers, you know." My glare dared him to disagree. Honestly I'd never taken a bath strictly for the purpose of getting clean. Shifting cleansed the body, but it had been over forty-eight hours since I shifted. *Dirty* didn't actually describe how I felt. It was more a sense of *wrongness* that clung to me. I wasn't sure a bath would help, but it had to be better than nothing. I jutted out my chin. "I would like a bath."

Nathanial dropped the clothes in a pile and knelt beside me. In a movement almost too fast to see, he caught my chin in his hand and tilted it up further. I squirmed, but his grip was impossible to break as he examined my face.

"You do not need a bath, you need to feed."

"I would like to take a bath," I repeated.

He released my chin with a sigh. "How about a shower?"

Shiny black tile covered the bathroom from wall to wall. An enormous black tub sprawled across the room, sparing only enough space for a walkway between it, the door, and a freestanding shower tucked in the front corner. There wasn't even a toilet. As I tried to imagine how many people would fit in the tub, Nathanial turned on the shower.

When he gestured that the water was ready, I started unwrapping the torn curtain I'd gathered around myself like a tattered velvet toga. I hesitated before dropping it to the ground. I'd never been shy about nudity before, but I suddenly felt uncomfortable at the thought of stepping into the shower naked in front of Nathanial. My instincts were clearly on the fritz. Of course, I didn't want him around, clothed or not.

"Can I get a little privacy here?"

"I have seen your body before."

As if on its own accord, my hand shot out and slapped him. Despite the fact he deserved it, I felt more surprised than he looked. Without my hand holding it up, the curtain fell to my ankles, but I wasn't feeling shy anymore—just pissed. My instincts were *so* broken, and apparently they were in a permanent bad mood. And why shouldn't they be? I was. It had been a bad couple of days. Looking away from Nathanial, I stepped under the showerhead and pulled the frosted-glass door closed hard enough it rattled.

There was gel soap, a real sponge, shampoo, and conditioner on a little inset wall rack in the shower. I popped open the bottles, smelling the liquids inside. They were all scents I'd smelled on Nathanial's skin. The sponge was wet. *That hypocrite, telling me not to worry about bathing, when he obviously did.*

I didn't hear Nathanial leave, but by the time I finished washing, the bathroom was empty. A fluffy towel had been left on the rack. I dried off, wringing my hair out on the tiles before toweling it as dry as I could. The curtain was now absent, but my clothes were piled by the door. I dressed quickly. Showering hadn't made me feel any better, just damp. Next time, I would insist on a bath.

I found Nathanial reading in the same chair as earlier. He looked up as I entered the room, but I stopped dead in my tracks when I noticed his hand idly scratching the massive dog's ears. I backed up a step, my fingers curling around the door jamb. My next breath was too loud as it trembled out.

Nathanial frowned at me. "Do not mind Regan. He is a big baby."

"Sure. Can we go, now?"

Nathanial nodded, but the frown deepened around his mouth. As he stood, the dog moved with him, and the wood moulding under my bloodless fingers cracked. Nathanial made a small motion with his hand, and the dog sat again. Regan didn't move as I backed out of the room. Nathanial grabbed my coat from where it hung on the arm of the chair then walked out of the room without a word. He left the door ajar as he turned away from it.

He held out my coat in a peculiar fashion, which I realized was meant to help me get into it. Reluctantly, I accepted his assistance. It was too small a thing to fight over, and besides, I was cold. He slipped into his own coat, a gray duster similar to mine, except that his rustled as he pulled it closed over his dress clothes.

Without a word, he strolled to the end of the windowless hall and unlocked a door secured with two deadbolts. The door opened slowly; the *slurp* of breaking suction sounding as it separated from the frame. Nathanial gave me no time to examine the plastic seals, but herded me into another hallway and through a pair of wooden swinging doors.

I paused just beyond the doors and gaped at the giant kitchen. There was enough counter space and gleaming chrome appliances for any busy homemaker's wet dream. The massive birch table in the center of the room would fit at least eight, though it only had four places set around it, one with an empty drinking glass and the chair knocked crooked like it had recently been vacated. A bay window dominated one corner; its cushioned seats the perfect place to curl up on a sunny afternoon. A pale blue teapot sat on the back burner of the stove, matching oven mitts hanging on the wall beside it. The room didn't fit Nathanial at all, especially compared to the dark wood and black furnishing in the back of the house. Not to mention the fact he couldn't eat food. Of course, I'd been assuming Nathanial lived alone. For all I knew, he might keep blood donors around like his own private harem. Gil had said Nathanial only fed from criminals. It didn't seem likely they'd make a great harem, but she'd been wrong on other things.

Dying with curiosity—no pun intended—I opened the fridge and peeked inside: crackers, peanut butter, and a box of cereal. Nope, no humans lived here, not with a selection like that. Okay, first of all, who stored cereal in the fridge? The cereal was expired. How often did that happen? Cereal was always stamped as edible for *years* in the future. I closed the door and turned to face the room again.

It was all a lie. The plates and silverware carefully arranged in the drying rack, the herbs sprouting from terra cotta pots in the window over the sink, even the delivery flyers stuck to the fridge with magnets, all of them were just decorative props. Nathanial watched me with an amused expression, but when I frowned at him, the amusement faded into a neutral mask.

"Come on." He held out a hand.

I didn't take it, but I did follow him out of the fake kitchen and onto the porch. My eyes followed the glistening plain of snow in the darkness to where the tree line of a forest broke it in the distance. We were so not in the city anymore. The porch was cleared of snow down to the second step, and I looked around for a path or a driveway. Zilch. There was evidence of two people trudging through the snow and around the side of the house. I started down the steps, but Nathanial touched my shoulder and shook his head.

I pointed to the tracks in the snow. "Isn't your car this way?"

"I do not own a car. Those are from humans employed by Mama Neda. I brought you here the other night, before I accidentally took too much blood from you. Mama Neda was able to explain how to stabilize you over the phone, but we had to be transported back to Haven after the sun rose, for her to show me how to finish turning you."

"You said daylight would kill us."

"Yes. We need wood, stone, or earth between us and the sun."

I stared at the tracks in the snow. Then how did we travel . . . my mind flashed back to every bad vampire movie I'd ever seen. "You took me to Mama Neda's in a *coffin?*"

He nodded. "Mama Neda owns a funeral home. She uses it as a front for a daytime transport service for vampires."

"I don't have to sleep in a coffin from now on, do I?"

"Did you wake up in one?" He waited, and I shook my head. "Now, you need to trust me."

That was something I wasn't willing to do, and I'd have thought him smart enough to realize it. When he reached for me, I took a step back.

He let his arms drop and sighed. "I need you to wrap your arms around my shoulders."

"Why?" I took another step back, bumping into the railing. A clump of snow fell to the ground with a wet thump.

"To meet Bobby and Gil on time, we need to leave now."

I stared at him like he was speaking Greek.

He continued, "We are going to fly, Kita. I need to carry you."

I shook my head.

He sighed. "It is the quickest way to Haven. Walking there would take until dawn."

"Eventually I'm going to wake up, curled in a fluffy ball, basking in a pool of sunlight, and discover this is all a nightmare."

"Not likely. Now come here. I promise not to bite this time."

I caught my hand before it slapped him again. *Stupid vampire.* But I needed to get back to Haven. I wasn't going to learn anything about the rogue out here in the wilderness. With a resolute sigh, I crept closer. *Fly? Had he really said fly?* If for no reason more than curiosity's sake, I would see this one through. After all, who didn't want to know what it was like to fly?

I placed my hands on his shoulders, his scent wrapping around me before his arms. He didn't smell of cinnamon and cotton like last night, but some spicy scent I couldn't quite identify. The familiarity of that scent, like something I'd always known but forgot, called to me. *Was this his real scent?*

I had the urge to explore his body and sniff out what was shower products and what was the deliciously masculine scent underneath them. His arms circled around my waist, drawing me closer. My cheek pressed into his chest, and I tried to push away, but my feet weren't on the ground. Wind roared around me, my coat slapping against my ankles. I clung to his shoulders.

Below us, the ground fell away and rushed by at an unbelievable speed—first in large plains of empty snow, occasionally broken by small forests of trees, then by dots of isolated houses, then obvious suburban areas. Finally we soared above the city. We slowed, the city lights blinking by less quickly. The black-tar roofs and concrete buildings far below looked like pieces of a maze designed for rats, and I wondered how Nathanial, or even birds, could navigate from up here.

Our progress continued to slow, until we stopped and hung suspended in the air, then the ground leapt toward us. I squeezed my eyes shut, clinging tight to Nathanial. Through the wind buffeting my ears, I heard him chuckle as his finger drew small circles along my back. I expected the wild descent to stop with a jolt, like the snap of a rubber band, but one minute the hem of my coat was swirling around my shoulders, and the next Nathanial made a movement like stepping down off a last stair, and the ground was under my feet. I pushed away from him, breathing hard as my coat hem resettled around my ankles.

"That was amazing. Can I fly, too?" Maybe being a vampire actually had some perks.

Nathanial smiled, his fingers moving to smooth my hair. "Not yet. If you learn how, it will be after you are older and stronger."

I frowned at him and turned away, which he took as an invitation to continue finger-combing my hair. His own hair was secured in a low ponytail and covered from the wind by his coat. I'd have to remember that next time. *Next time?* Over the years I'd learned not to expect anything out of the future I couldn't provide myself, but my guts told me I would fly with Nathanial again. His fingers followed my hair down the curve of my spine, a shiver crawled across my flesh. I stepped away, jerking handfuls of my hair over my shoulder. Pulling at the tangles, I tried to figure out where we were.

"The bookstore is that way." Nathanial pointed to the left. "But you need to feed first."

"Not happening." I didn't wait for him to protest, but joined the crowd on the sidewalk. Being among a crowd of humans kept hunters from pulling me off the street, and I was willing to bet the same would prevent Nathanial from forcing me to chomp on someone's neck.

I darted around shoppers, more than once catching muttered curses floating up in my wake. The street was only vaguely familiar, but I found the bookstore within a block.

The bookstore was brighter than it had been two nights ago, and I squinted as I entered, my hands flying up to shield my eyes. A warm body pressed against my back, and I jumped.

"Light sensitivity is a sign of starvation." Nathanial whispered, his hands on my shoulders, guiding me deeper into the store.

The light stung my eyes like a dozen angry ants, but I could focus through it. Bobby and Gil were seated in the little coffee shop tucked in one corner of the bookstore, which was where Nathanial was leading me. I shrugged away from him, straining to scan the book stacks through my watery vision.

"There's our girl." I pointed at the young blond who had given me the flyer advertising the rave. She was pushing a book on a very pregnant woman, managing to look both helpful and bored at the same time. I stepped further from Nathanial. "You let Bobby and Gil know we're here. I'll ask her about any other parties happening in the area."

Nathanial nodded, but pressed his lips into a worried line. I didn't give him a chance to change his mind, but walked off without another word. Remembering how I'd cried blood-tinged tears the night before, I whipped my watery eyes with the cuff of my coat. The smallest hint of pink decorated the wet streak in the gray material, and I shoved my hands in my pockets so I wouldn't have to look at it.

As I wove through the stacks of books, I shivered under my coat and wished the bookstore was warmer. Was my coat even trapping my body heat? As I approached, the sales girl's customer shook her head and walked off.

The girl rolled her eyes and put the book back. Her gum popped between her teeth as she looked at me. "Hey, I remember you. You were in here a couple of nights ago. Decide what flavor book you want?" She glanced at the shelf beside us and shook her head. "Look at this." She pulled a backward book off the shelf. "I understand the people who leave a book on the floor, they're lazy, but if they go through all the effort of putting the book back, why put it back with the spine facing in?"

"Uh, yeah, people are strange." I frowned at her, I didn't have time for idle chatter. "I went to that rave the other night, the one you said your friend was spinning at."

"Really? That's awesome. I'm a pretty good judge of personality. I knew you would be one to go." She popped her gum again.

"Yeah. So, I had lots of fun . . . and I was kind of hoping you knew about another party close by?"

"Oh, quick, act like I'm convincing you to buy this book. My boss is looking." She pressed a book in my hands. It was a child's book on counting. I raised an eyebrow, and she gave me an apologetic smile. "Okay, my boss isn't looking anymore. What were you wanting to know, again?" She popped her gum, then lifted a hand and waved it in front of her face before I could answer. "Oh right, about parties. I go to a couple, but mostly only the ones I know the DJ. I haven't heard about anything big happening in the next few weeks." Her eyes went past me.

I'd lost her attention, again. I'd chased butterflies with longer attention spans.

"Oh my gawd, look at those hunks, " she said, her eager gaze traveling over my shoulder.

I could barely see over the tops of the bookcases, but Bobby and Nathanial were both a head or more taller than the shelves and easy to spot. They looked around, and I realized the bookshelves completely hid me. I stepped into the aisle, and Bobby's eyes landed on me.

The girl grabbed my arm. "Oh, they're headed this way. Quick, do I have anything in my teeth?" She tilted her head back slightly, smiling. I stared at her. "Is that a yes?" Her lips slipped down.

"You don't have anything in your teeth."

"Ok, and my makeup's okay? My mascara isn't running?" She wiped under her eyes.

"You look fine."

"Good," she said, letting out a breath. "Why do you think they're coming over here? Do you think they need help finding a book?" She pasted her 'professional' smile on.

I almost laughed. "I was supposed to meet them here."

"You're with those two sex gods? I'm so jealous. You're going to share, right?" When I blinked at her, she giggled. "Come on, you have the two extremes of sexiness over there: one blond, large and wild-looking and the other with that long black hair, almost *beautiful*, yet masculine. You don't need both."

Bobby and Nathanial were within earshot now, though she didn't realize it.

Color crept to Bobby's cheeks.

I frowned. "I don't think—"

"You wanna know about parties? No problem, I'll find out. Just introduce me to the eye candy."

"I don't know your name," I said, as the boys rounded the last bookcase between us.

"Candice," she whispered between her teeth.

I sighed. "Bobby, Nathanial, this is Candice. And vice versa."

Bobby looked at his feet, but Nathanial lightly kissed her hand. I thought she might float away. Her smile stretching across her face to the point it had to be painful.

I scowled at Nathanial, and realized we were missing someone. "Where's Gil?"

"We're in a bookstore. Guess," Bobby said. Of course, our little scholar would have run away to read.

"So," Nathanial said slowly, "Were you able to find out about another party?"

Candice's smile widened.

I arched a brow at the sight. *How is that even possible?*

She pulled a phone out of her pants and flipped it open. "I need to talk to my friend, Jace. He would know. I get off work at midnight, and I know a great little bar where we could meet him. Let me make a quick call and set it up." She gazed at Nathanial, her eyes shiny with invitation.

He glanced at me, and I shrugged.

She started dialing then looked around, startled. Maybe she'd forgotten she was at work.

I tried not to notice all the blood gathering in her cheeks as she blushed. The roof of my mouth tingled, and I glanced away.

Candice crouched low between the bookshelves, her eyes sweeping the aisles as she finished dialing the number. "Hey Jace, you busy? Could you meet me after work, I'm with some people who want to talk to you about a party." She paused, listening to the guy on the other end. "No, I don't think any of them own a club or a studio." She glanced at us, then turned her back. "I will owe you *so* big time. *Please* do this for me." She whispered the last, and if she hadn't been in a group of supernaturals, that might have worked. But, as it was, I saw Nathanial suppress a smile. She snapped the phone shut and straightened. "It's all set. You want to meet about twelve thirty?"

Chapter 8

"Plans?" I asked, the light from the bookstore fading to a distant glow behind us. We had four hours to kill before meeting Candice. I wanted to spend them productively, and, preferably, somewhere warm. I was shivering so hard I could barely walk.

Gil pulled three scrolls out of the air. "I made lists of all the victims' residences and where their bodies were found. We should split up and search for clues as to how they met the rogue." She handed one scroll to Bobby and one to Nathanial. Bobby squinted at his, frowning. Gil unrolled hers and traced her finger down the list. "Most of the girls were found at their own homes, though a couple were found in public places. I've divided the lists up by areas of town. You guys work on your locations, and Kita and I will meet you at—"

"Kita will accompany me," Nathanial said, looking up from his list.

Gil's hands moved to her hips, elbows out, the remaining scroll scrunched against her waist. "I'm supposed to study her. I have to stay with her."

"She needs me to . . ."

I stopped listening as I buried my face in my hands. *Had I ever been this cold before?* Thick fingers curled around my shoulders, dragging me further from the argument. I almost tugged away, but I knew that scent of fur and wind. I glared at Bobby, willing him to stop pulling me before I stumbled over my own unsteady feet.

He dropped my arms. "Are you all right, Kitten? You don't look good."

Of course I wasn't all right, I probably wouldn't be all right ever again.

"I'm fine."

"I've been worried sick about you all day. Last night after we left the diner you collapsed. Stopped moving. Stopped breathing. I thought you were dead. Then Nathanial pulled shadows or something around you. You vanished."

I blinked at him, and then back at Nathanial. He and Gil had stopped arguing. Gil's face was beet red, but Nathanial's expression was, as always, carefully neutral, though the edges of his eyes were pinched.

I glared at him, and he waltzed closer. "I thought you said I'm not dead!"

"You are not dead." His face and voice were equally empty, betraying nothing.

"I stopped breathing."

Nathanial sighed. "True. But it does not mean you are dead. It means you do not need to breathe. Oxygen is poisonous. It causes aging."

"Yeah, it also causes living."

He shook his head. "You need to draw air to speak and pick up scents. Otherwise you breathe only out of habit. Stop, if you like." He turned away.

I didn't have to breathe? Yeah right. I didn't think about breathing, I just did it. In fact, I couldn't concentrate hard enough to hold my breath. I shivered, hugging my arms around me. The wind whistled through the tall buildings, lifting my hair from my face, but the chill making me tremble was under my skin, and huddling closed the chill in, not out.

Undeath sucked. I wanted a refund.

I kicked a pile of snow, sending chunks of slush and ice skittering across the sidewalk. A clump of slush exploded into a spray of wet film across Bobby's boot as he stepped closer. He reached out a hand like he would touch my face but then hesitated, his hand hanging in the air between us.

"Are you sure you're okay? You reek of his scent." Bobby nodded at Nathanial.

I laughed, but it was a bitter sound. He was jealous. *He* was jealous . . . when *he* was the mated one. To an outsider. And *he* was the one who was jealous? My laugh cracked, turning jagged.

Bobby's brow furrowed, and his fingers alighted on my cheek. The touch was tentative, ready to fall away at the slightest provocation.

As a child, whenever I wasn't occupied with my various tutors, Bobby and I spent all our time together. We had learned every nook of the clan's land and made our own secret paths through it. We made trips to a non-shifter village, wandered the outskirts of the clanless lands, and journeyed to the Elders' mountain. Too many lazy days to count, we slept off a good hunt curled together in a furry pile. It wasn't until my last few years in Firth that things changed. I couldn't remember the first time his touch had filled my stomach with butterflies, or when the affection of children had changed to something giddy and new, but I remembered the fight I'd had with my father after he forbade Bobby to take me as mate. Lynn had joined our clan shortly after that. Like a good little clan member, Bobby did as he was told. He mated with Lynn.

I meant to tug away from Bobby's touch, but the warmth from his fingers seeped into my skin, and I so desperately wanted to be warm. As I nuzzled his palm, the roof of my mouth tingled, then burned. The pressure built as my fangs extended, and I froze, fighting my new instincts.

Encouraged by my initial response, Bobby slid closer. His other hand moved to frame my face, destroying my concentration. I gritted my teeth together, my fully extended fangs pressing against my lower lip. I could feel his heart beating through his skin, hear it pounding between us. My stomach twisted, burning cold and empty. Without intending to, I turned in to his cradling hands, my lips sliding over the thin skin of his wrist.

My feet left the ground, and all that delicious heat vanished. I opened my eyes in time to see Bobby's stunned face before the side of a building obscured it. The darkness of an alley closed around me before I realized I was being dragged backwards.

No! I needed Bobby's warmth.

I twisted, struggling against the arms encircling my waist. They released me only long enough for Nathanial to step around me, cornering me against a brick wall. He used his entire body to pin me to the building's façade. His heat pressed into me, but my instincts knew he wasn't food. He was competition.

"Kita," he whispered.

I hissed at him through my fangs, my fingernails tearing at his hands where they pinned my wrists over my head. He didn't blink, his cold eyes holding mine. Reflected in those icy gray depths was a crazed creature with glowing yellow eyes and fangs. Its gaunt features were desperate, dangerous. Slowly I recognized my sharp chin line, the arch of my eyebrows, my nose. The reflected yellow eyes dimmed, and I sagged in Nathanial's arms, staring at the reflection of a creature who could consider feeding from her oldest friend. My chest stung, my breath catching in my throat. A sob choked me.

Nathanial released my arms, his body holding me to the wall. He examined the gouges in his hand, jagged pink lines left my by nails.

The wounds weren't bleeding, but they smelled fleshy, and I squeezed my eyes shut. Nathanial's thumb brushed my lower lip, then he lifted his wrist to my lips like an offering.

"If you will not feed from humans, then take from me," he whispered.

"Get away from me!" I shoved him, hard, and he fell back a step. I collapsed to my knees, hugging myself in the snow.

Bobby rounded the corner of the building, Gil only steps behind him, her face set in a disapproving scowl. Time wasn't moving right; Bobby's clipped gait was too slow. Or perhaps it was only slow compared to how fast my pulse was racing.

I threw up my arms, barricading my face from Bobby's gaze, but his eyes weren't angry. They should have been.

Nathanial pulled me to my feet, his grip tight around my elbow. *Holding me up? Holding me back?* I didn't fight against the pinching grip, but stared at my feet. My hair hung over my face like a curtain of tangles.

"You have to feed," Nathanial whispered.

I shook my head.

"Kitten, maybe you should do as he says." Bobby stepped closer, and I shuffled back. He paused and his next words were a whisper. "You look like you've been sick for a long time. Your skin is as thin as paper and your eyes are sunken in."

My stomach twisted, from guilt this time, not hunger. Bobby was supposed to be on my side. Or at least the side that didn't consider people food. He crept closer again. Nathanial released my arm and stepped in front of me. Bobby glared, moving into Nathanial's space like he wasn't there, or like the vampire was a wall he had to talk through.

"There's a park not far from here. Might have deer. It will have rabbits, if nothing else. We can go hunting. Just you and me. I'll shift to mid-form so we can work for the same-size prey, and you can make the kill, take the blood."

I straightened, pulling my hair out of my face. The park was an idea I hadn't considered.

Nathanial shook his head. "It would keep you alive, but not sustain you."

Alive sounded good enough. I crossed my arms over my chest. "Which would be worse, deer blood or no blood?"

Gil cleared her throat. She'd kept what she probably considered a safe distance several feet from us, but now she stepped closer, pulling out one of her scrolls. "The rogue's fourth victim, the second killed in Haven, was found in Sydney Park. If we go there we can check off one of our locations while Kita catches a snack."

Nathanial sighed, shaking his head again. "There are no deer in that park, but we might find rabbits, yes."

I smiled. I was an excellent rabbit hunter.

In silence, we rejoined humanity on the streets. The sidewalks were not crowded, but they were far from empty. At first I watched the people we passed, but pressure built to the point of pain in my mouth, worsening every time I looked at someone. I silently repeated a mantra about how 'People are not food,' over and over in my mind. My chant must have become less silent at some point, because Bobby, Nathanial, and Gil all stopped and stared at me.

I shoved my hands deep in my coat pockets and looked away. By necessity, I stuck close to Nathanial—he, at least, didn't register as food. I was okay around Bobby now that we weren't touching, but glancing at humans brought predatory instincts to the front of my mind. I noted vital striking zones. Even with the *flap* of Gil's plastic boots filling my ears, I could hear the humans around us. What if a human noticed the ravenous vampire with fangs extended?

I had a 'duh' moment as I remembered that the reason my hands barely fit in my coat pockets was because I'd stuffed my scarf and gloves in them. Pulling out the scarf, I wrapped it around my face. It did nothing to stop my shivering, but at least if my fangs slid out, they weren't visible.

We turned another corner onto a street lined with more shops and more shoppers.

"Shouldn't we be taking the subway?" I asked, pointing to an entrance up a side street.

Nathanial shook his head.

"I think I need to get to the park ASAP."

"It is still early enough for commuter traffic." Nathanial gestured to the other people on the sidewalk. "Do you think you could handle the press of people that will cram into a train at this hour?"

I glanced at a rotund business man as he bustled past. *An easy catch.* I cringed, realizing I'd taken a step to follow him. I glued my gaze back on my shoes and shook my head. *Definitely no crowded subway rides.*

I vaguely noticed the brightly lit storefronts fading into darker buildings, many with thick iron grating and "Closed" signs, others with boarded-up facades. Those fell away behind us as the buildings grew taller. No shops or signs now, but rugged stoops leading into worn apartment buildings. Here and there the sidewalks hadn't been cleared, and we trudged through snowy slush.

The route Nathanial led us down followed no particular street but cut through alleys and behind buildings. I stepped around a man sleeping in a box by a dumpster. The dumpster smelled better than him, so at least I wasn't tempted to bite him. The tall buildings stopped abruptly, ending in an empty gravel parking pit and scattered vacant lots. Passed that, rows of squat duplexes nestled closely together. Several roofs sagged under the weight of the snow, the dark windows looking over small yards broken by the scars of skeletal fences. Beer cans and piles of black garbage bags were the only indication of life at several of the residences.

As we hurried up the street, it became obvious some of the homes had been painted recently—or at least in the last decade. A jungle gym stood in one yard, the black of the tire swing peeking out from under the snow. The cars lining the streets gradually became shinier, their boxy frames giving way to the sleeker lines of newer models.

Nathanial's choice of streets had few people on them, probably intentionally, but I kept my gaze down, just in case. The purple of Gil's rain boots leeched away, leaving the boots a murky gray. Frowning, I rubbed my eyes and glanced around the street. *Everything* was some shade of gray. Nathanial met my eyes, and I glanced back down. I didn't bother commenting on my sudden color-blindness. He'd only tell me it was another sign of starvation. *Stupid vampire.*

After a couple turns, the duplexes vanished in favor of old brownstone townhouses, with tall, wrought iron gates marking modest front yards. Over the top of the townhouses, I could make out the rough outline of trees. We were almost there.

Bobby stopped short at a corner only blocks from the park. He tilted his head, his nostrils flaring, and his gaze darted along the street and over dark shadows between buildings. "We don't need this right now."

I tipped my head back, but all I could smell were the warm bodies of my companions. Neither my nose nor eyes could be trusted at the moment. My fangs lengthened and I cursed under my breath. The damn things had minds of their own. Of course, I had a pretty good idea what Bobby was talking about.

"Hunter?" I asked, and Bobby nodded.

I should have realized the park would be monitored by hunters. My former second shape being the rare exception, most shifters would be noticed if they walked the streets on four legs. The park would be one of the few places in the city a shifter could run as his beast without drawing too much human attention.

"Let's get out of here." I started back the way we'd come.

Nathanial grabbed my arm, stopping me. "Who will you feed from if we do not reach the park?"

I shook my head and the movement triggered a shiver that reverberated though my body. I wrapped my arms around myself to still the quaking, to keep myself from shaking apart. I couldn't just bite someone. I had to reach the park, but the hunter...

Gil tugged on her coat sleeves. "Why are you sure every shifter's scent we cross must be a hunter?"

Bobby's attention was on the street, so I answered—after all, I wasn't good for much else currently. "There are two types of shifters in the human world, the illegals and the hunters. Shifters here illegally run away from the scent of other shifters, not toward it." Or at least, that's what I'd done. The memory of the stray I'd been fighting the night Nathanial had found me popped into my head. He hadn't avoided my scent—he'd tracked me. He'd referred to Haven as *his city* and seemed damned determined to dispose of me for trespassing. How many other strays had claimed territory in the human world? I'd never heard of it happening before, but if he was the example of a territorial stray, the safest course was still to avoid any encounter with other shifters.

Bobby's nostrils flared again, his gaze sweeping the street. "The hunter's trail smells recent, and the wind's in his favor, so he might have already picked up my scent."

His scent, right. I'd forgotten I didn't smell like a shifter anymore. Bobby was the only one the hunter would track.

I blinked. Without a scent, I could, theoretically, walk into the park as unnoticed as a human. Just not with Bobby by my side. I looked up at him. "We need to separate."

His shoulders hunched, his head dropping, but Gil cleared her throat. "I think it's too late."

A man in a long trench coat rounded the corner several blocks up. He strode toward us, his eyes locked on our huddled group. His path never wavered, his steps picking up speed. The trench coat struggled to cover his long gait, gaping to reveal flashes of a tailored suit, an expensive tie.

I stumbled back a step. *Oh crap.* The world was still washed in gray, but I didn't have to see the color to know his tie was red and his eyes wolf-amber.

I had to get out of here. The street of brownstones offered little cover, unless I wanted to break into one of them, which might not be such a bad idea right now. The wrought-iron gate surrounding the nearest house reached almost to the sidewalk, and I grabbed hold of it, ready to hoist myself over it if my shivering arms would agree to hold my weight.

Bobby grabbed my shoulder, pulling me off the gate. "What are you doing? He can't smell you!"

I glanced over my shoulder. The hunter was sprinting now, he'd be on top of us in moments.

"I've run across him before. He was the hunter I crossed when I first arrived in the city," I whispered and then looked at Nathanial. "He'll recognize me, even if he can't smell me. Do the shadow thing."

"Shadow thing?" he repeated, his eyebrow lifting. I didn't have time to explain, but he apparently realized what I meant, because he shouldered Bobby aside and stepped into my space. "Too suspicious. I have a better plan. Trust me."

I didn't have much choice with the iron gate pressed against my back and the hunter only yards away. Nathanial leaned close, his heat filling the breath of space between us. I put my hands up to push him away, but his heat pulsed through my palms. It was all I could do to keep myself from pulling him closer, wrapping him around me.

He tugged my scarf away, his fingers dancing along my jaw and leaving trails of warmth in their wake. Those long fingers moved to my hair next, brushing the tangled strands away from my face and deftly twisting them into a bun. His hands glided down to my waist, and my stomach flipped in a way that had nothing to do with hunger. He moved without hesitation, each motion efficient, like this was a dance he'd practiced. His hands slipped into the pockets of my coat, pulling out my hat. He tugged it over my hair, then spun us around so we were both facing Bobby and Gil, my back nuzzled along the front line of his body.

"It might be the perfect yard for a snowman, love, but what would the owners think?" He announced the question loudly, ending it with a chuckle.

I gaped at him. *He's lost his mind.*

Bobby was staring at me, his brow knotting as his clenched fists fell to his sides. He didn't glance away from me, even as the hunter stopped directly beside him.

"Excuse me. Do you have the time?" The hunter asked, his eyes sweeping over us. "I seem to have left my watch at home." To prove that fact, he lifted his left coat sleeve, flashing his watchless wrist. But his wrist wasn't empty. The silhouette of a swooping hawk marred the skin over his pulse. The mark of a hunter.

Bobby blinked, ripping his gaze off me. "Uh . . . sure." He pulled up his coat sleeve. "Oh, I must of lost my watch, too." An identical hawk marked Bobby's wrist.

I tried not to stare, not to make it overly obvious I'd caught the significance of the exchange, but I'd never seen a hunter mark before. I'd heard of them—every shifter had heard of them, but the mark was pressed into a hunter's skin only moments before he crossed the gate and removed every month when he returned. No ink tattoo could mimic the mark—shifting would purge ink from the body. The hunter mark was something only the elders could give. In the back of my mind I'd realized Bobby would have one, since he was here legally, but seeing it still surprised me.

The hunter nodded after he'd had a good look at the hawk. "Anyone know the time?" His nostrils flared as he glanced over Gil, who was completely absorbed in jotting something in her scroll. Then the full weight of the hunter's attention fell on me. I squirmed under the scrutiny, and Nathanial held me tighter.

"It is a little after nine," Nathanial said.

The hunter thanked him with a tilt of his head before his gaze returned to me.

I didn't meet his eyes, but stared at his shiny black loafers. He stepped closer, and his gaze focused on my neck, hesitating there several heartbeats too long. I chanced a glance up in time to see the edge of his mouth quirk, and then he turned, walking back the way he'd come.

"Thank you for the time," he called over his shoulder before turning down the next street.

As soon as he was out of sight, I wrenched out of Nathanial's arms. The loss of his body heat sent a shiver wracking through me hard enough to make me stumble. He caught my arms, keeping me standing.

I rounded on him. "What the hell kind of plan was that? He recognized me!"

Nathanial only smiled, shaking his head.

"Kita?" Bobby's fingers hesitated inches from my face. "You look . . . how . . . ?"

I frowned at him. 'How' was the wrong question. 'Why' was much more pertinent. Like why hadn't the hunter pulled me off the street? Did he think Bobby, as a fellow hunter, had the situation under control?

Gil moved closer, her quill scribbling fiercely as she examined me. "This is highly irregular. How did you do that to her?" She glanced at Nathanial. He didn't answer with any more than his continued enigmatic smile. At my puzzled look Gil said, "Your appearance is different. It is—"

"It's not you." Bobby bent to look at my face at another angle. "Not you at all."

I lifted my hands to my face. It felt like it always had, nothing altered as far as my fingers could tell. I stepped further away from Nathanial and his smile slipped.

"If you move too far away you will . . . " He shook his head. "Break the illusion."

Gil gave a little gasp, and Bobby's shoulders relaxed like a great weight had been removed. Nathanial looked less pleased.

"We should move on." He pointed the opposite direction the hunter had gone.

I nodded, but as my steps dragged down the sidewalk, I couldn't help thinking of the small smirk I'd seen catch on the hunter's mouth. Had he simply been satisfied we weren't strays, or . . .? My hand crawled to my throat. Between the loose ends of my scarf, my fingers traced over the corded black leather of my necklace.

Crap.

I must have said it aloud because everyone stopped. I curled my finger around the cord and lifted it away from my skin. "During whatever you did a minute ago, was my necklace visible?"

Nathanial's gaze dropped to my throat. Gil didn't say anything, and I looked at Bobby. His eyes told me what no one else said—it *had* been visible.

Double crap.

Nathanial reached to touch the necklace, and I stepped back, letting it fall against my skin. The small bones woven into the cord clattered.

"Someone important gave that to you. Someone from Firth," Nathanial said, his voice distant, as if he were trying to remember a dream.

"Yeah, someone important. Now stay out of my mind." I wrapped my arms around my chest and tried to still my shivering. At this point, I wasn't sure if I was shaking from the cold or fear or, as Nathanial would probably insist, from needing blood. It wouldn't matter that my scent and face were different. If the hunter saw my necklace—he'd never believe I wasn't from Firth. My hand crawled to my throat again, my finger tracing the ten small bones, careful of the small hooked claw on half of them. Ten bones, a number worn only by the clan's *Dyre.* Bobby's necklace only had two bones.

Crap, Bobby.

If the hunter realized we were *both* from the Nekai clan . . . what was the punishment these days for helping a stray avoid capture? I glanced at Bobby. He looked worried, but not worried enough. As a child, I'd met a stray who'd been dragged back to Firth, and he'd never spoken about the months he'd spent at the elders' mountain following his capture and return. But he hadn't been a hunter, hadn't taken their oaths—or broken them. Bobby should have been terrified.

My fist closed around the necklace. The five small claws pricked my flesh. We had to get away from here. "Are we waiting for the hunter to pounce out at us? Let's go."

I trudged up the sidewalk, trying to focus through the haze settling over me. Maybe I was only being paranoid and the hunter hadn't noticed anything. Maybe Nathanial's playful ruse had worked and I'd only thought the hunter had focused on me because my near-constant shivering had jarred my senses. Yeah right, and maybe I'd wake up and discover the last few nights had been nothing more than a bad dream.

Nathanial's hand landed on my shoulder, and I jumped. *What did he—?* I turned, but his hand slid to the center of my back, forcing me to keep pace with him.

"I think you should know, we are being followed," he whispered loud enough for Bobby and Gil to hear. "The hunter has circled and is approaching from a side street."

"Because of a necklace?" Gil balled her hands on her hips, but her stride didn't slow. "Why are you still wearing it if it's such a blatant signal of what you are? It's not even pretty—just leather and tiny bones."

I glared at her, an effect ruined as I tripped over my own feet.

"Do you see any clasps or knots? It doesn't come off over my head, and it can't be cut, either." I stopped at an intersection. The park was just ahead, the open gate as inviting as the gapping jaws of a giant iron beast. More brownstones lined the streets leading up to it. We needed a plan. If Nathanial said the hunter had followed us, he was probably right. I hated having to rely on the senses of others. A plan wavered at the edge of my mind, but the more I trembled, the more elusive it became.

Gil stepped closer to me, leaning forward to stare at my necklace. She almost reached out like she would touch it, but apparently her caution won over her curiosity. "Why is it so special? What kind of animal are the bones from?"

I frowned at her. "They're finger bones. Five from a kitten, five from a baby girl, all of them mine."

"That's disgusting." Her lips twisted into a grimace, but her scroll appeared in her hand. "Why was it done?"

"Your books didn't teach you as much about shifters as you thought, did they?" I turned away as gray blotches gathered on her cheeks. I glanced at the side street Nathanial had indicated. Flits of plans slipped into focus before sliding away again, leaving me with conflicting ideas.

How could I divert the hunter's attention from Bobby? *If I could make him believe* . . . The thought faded without blooming into a fully fledged plan.

I pressed my palms against my eyes. "Why the hell did you sign on with the hunters anyway?"

Bobby didn't answer and I peeled my hands back so I could see him. When he noticed me watching, he shrugged but didn't meet my gaze. "Getting the mark was the only way the elders would let me cross the gate. Sebastian thought I'd be able to convince you to come home. He didn't want hunters involved."

As in my father didn't want the embarrassment of having his *Dyre* publicly denounced by the elders. I'd have gritted my teeth but they were chattering too much.

Bobby glanced at me from the corner of his eye. His shoulders were angled away from me, but his face was open, the regret tugging at his features clear. "Sebastian was wrong."

The twisting feeling in my chest was either from the trembling finally shaking organs loose, or the sinking realization Bobby hadn't come after me because my father told him to—he'd come because my father finally let him. Damn Bobby. Why couldn't he have just stayed in Firth and with his mate and cubs?

I frowned at the side street. There was no movement, no indication the hunter was watching, but I had no doubt he was. If we survived the judge, I couldn't let Bobby return to Firth as an oath breaker. What could I do to convince the hunter Bobby wasn't helping me?

I could let Bobby capture me

I shivered. Then what? If he captured me, it would clear his name but sign his death certificate when the judge returned and the rogue was still free. I could escape, but how much time would we waste? Of course, the hunter only had to *believe* Bobby was dragging me to a safe house. We didn't have to complete the charade. Once we were far enough away, we'd be safe.

It might just work. I turned to the others. "We're splitting up. Nathanial, Gil go to the park. Bobby, once they round the gate, do the hunter thing on me."

Bobby's jaw dropped. "What?"

"Trust me," I said, trying to keep my voice from trembling in time with my clattering teeth. "I think I have a plan."

Gil crossed her arms over her chest. "You think?"

Bobby turned to her. "Can you magic the hunter the way you did the people at the hospital?"

Why hadn't I thought of that? Simpler, safer; it was the perfect plan. I shot Gil a hopeful look, but her arms dropped and she concentrated on tugging wrinkles out of her coat.

"Well?" I asked as seconds ticked by.

"The spell doesn't work on supernaturals," she mumbled, her gaze on her rain boots.

Great. That settled it then. I scanned the street. It was deserted—the perfect place for a hunter to strike.

"Go," I whispered, looking at Nathanial and Gil.

She opened her mouth to protest, but Nathanial wrapped an arm around her shoulders. Her eyes flew wide, but in one efficient movement, Nathanial had her turned and walking toward the park entrance, leaving Bobby and me alone on the corner.

"Kitten, I don't like whatever plan you've cooked up," Bobby said, watching their retreating backs. They rounded the gate. "You're sure about this?"

"Trust me." I managed a weak smile. "Now, attack me."

Bobby hesitated, then lunged forward without warning. I yelped, the response only half faked. Ducking under Bobby's arm, I let his momentum take him a step past me. Then I slammed my palm into his back, shoving him forward.

He stumbled, and I skittered back. This had to look real. I needed another opening to throw a punch, one that wouldn't hurt him. He whirled around. I crouched, waiting and conserving what little energy I had left. Adrenaline zinged through my body, making my focus better than it had been all night. I centered my weight between my legs, flexed my fingers. The grim lines of Bobby's face betrayed his distaste, but however unhappy he was, his feelings didn't slow his movements.

His fist swung. I jumped back and the leather of his gloves connected with the front of my coat. A shiver wracked my body, making my muscles tighten. *Crap.* I squeezed my eyes shut. Pain shot across my ribs, and the ground fell away beneath me. Okay, so Bobby wasn't pulling his punches. I climbed to my knees. *At least it looked real.*

His hand shot out, and I couldn't roll away in time. He snagged my arm, dragging me off my knees. *Moment of truth.* I flailed in his grip, but not enough to tug free.

Then Nathanial joined the fight.

He jerked Bobby back. Bobby's hand on my arm fell away giving me the freedom I needed. I jumped to my feet and whirled around.

A growl leaked from Bobby's throat, real anger bleeding into the sound. Nathanial dragged him further from me, thrusting him against the park gate.

I glanced around. Movement caught my eye from the side street.

Crap. Showtime.

I ran.

Chapter 9

I turned the next corner, veering away from the park. I ran as fast as my legs would carry me, but I was losing speed with every step. I glanced over my shoulder. The street was empty, no sign of the hunter. *Had he followed?* I pushed my muscles for more speed, and they stung in protest. Maybe the hunter had stayed behind to help Bobby?

I couldn't rely on him not following. My teeth chattered loudly, drowning out any sounds of pursuit. I knew I was using up whatever reserves I had. Even my nose was useless, picking up and losing scents before I could properly identify them. I was as exposed as a blind rat in a mousetrap factory. How was I supposed to circle back to Nathanial and Bobby without leaving a trail?

I turned at the next corner, my gaze over my shoulder. I'd run two yards when I glanced forward and realized what I'd taken for a side street was nothing more than a nook between buildings, bricked in on all sides.

"The hunt ends here, Kita Nekai."

I whirled around. Well, that answered that—the hunter had followed. He stood in the center of the alley, blocking the exit. I crouched, scanning the brownstones around me. The bottom level of the townhouses was a garage, so there were no windows. The brick wall between them probably enclosed a courtyard, but the wall was nine feet high. I'd never scramble over it before the hunter reached me. *Great.*

I crept backward. I was going to have to run for it. The hunter would give chase—predators always did, but it was the best chance I had.

The hunter stalked closer, driving me back until my coat brushed the brick. His energy danced over my skin, the prickly musk of wolf reaching my nose. He was ready to shift any moment, but he was containing it, for now. Maybe if I didn't give him any indication I was going to change, he wouldn't shift either. I did not want to face one of his stronger forms.

The line between non-threatening and submissive could be very thin at times, but as the smallest *Dyre* in my clan's history, it was a role with which I was familiar. Straightening from my crouch, I leaned against the wall and hooked my thumbs in my jean pockets.

"The necklace gave me away, didn't it?" I asked, giving the hunter a smile, but careful not to flash teeth—a toothy smile he might take as a threat. "You're keener than the other one."

"The traitor will be dealt with later," he said, and the bottom fell out of my stomach.

He hadn't believed the fight. He knew. He knew Bobby was helping me evade them.

I had to get out of here. I had to warn Bobby. First I had to get past the hunter.

He stared at my face, his nostrils flaring. The level of energy pouring out of him kicked up a notch.

Right, my appearance had changed since he'd seen me with Nathanial.

His distress over that little detail didn't stop him from tugging a thin chain from his pocket and gripping it in his gloved hand. The light from the streetlamps glinted along the metal. Okay, casual wasn't working. I had to find a way to distract him.

Focusing on his tie, I said, "I went through all the trouble of masking my scent, and then I forgot about the necklace."

He twisted the thin chain, but paused. "How did you change your scent?"

"I don't recommend it." I pushed away from the wall, and my smile broadened, flashing the smallest amount of teeth. "I had to die."

I leaped straight toward him, and as expected, he sidestepped. *Perfect.* I hit the ground running, but my surge of triumph was cut short as his hand snaked out, snatching the back of my coat and yanking me to the pavement.

My breath whooshed out of me. A massive fist angled toward my face, and I rolled.

The blow glanced across my shoulder, but I was already in motion. I twisted to get my feet under me, and clenching my fists, I sprang upward. Adding the leverage of the leap and all my weight, I planted both fists in the hunter's abdomen.

He had a hundred pounds on me, but he toppled backward, his back slamming into the brick wall. As he fell, his foot shot out, catching me in the jaw.

Pain exploded in my face. My head snapped back, my lip bursting. I stumbled, falling to my knees. The hunter pushed off the wall, then doubled over, a coughing spasm wracking his body.

I tried to climb to my feet, but my head spun, spots filling my vision. My attempt to stand left me face down in the snow, inches from where the hunter's hacking cough had spattered it in red dots.

Red? I stared. The vivid color stood out against the otherwise gray washed world.

My mouth hurt, a burning heat oozing down my chin. My tongue traced my split bottom lip and the coppery taste of blood filled my senses.

So sweet.

My tongue dug into the wound, not caring it was my own blood. I needed more. My eyes darted to the blood spattered snow, and then to the still coughing hunter. My legs moved effortlessly under me, and the hunter straightened as I stood. His wary eyes watched me as he wiped his gloved hand over his mouth, smearing a trail of crimson across his chin.

The energy of his beast rushed from his skin, so close to shifting. I stalked closer. He wasn't the one hunting now.

Prey to be taken down or a human-shaped form of catnip to be rolled around in? Nothing protected his throat, it would be easy enough to take him down.

He didn't move as I slid into his space. His body heat warmed the air between us, but only the fabric of our coats touched. Standing on tiptoes, I flicked out my tongue and captured the pool of blood in the crease of his lips.

He tasted husky and woodsy. A shaky breath escaped him, filling me with the taste of his fear, but overriding that fear was his excitement. The energy pouring out of him changed, his beast no longer ready to spill over his skin. Something moved in my peripheral. Someone had entered the alley. I started to look up, to step back, but the hunter closed the space between us, his arms sliding under my coat to drag me against him.

Warmth washed over my body, the pulse under his skin beating against me through our clothes. My hands moved to his shoulders, and my fangs sank into his neck. Heat filled my mouth, rushed down my throat. He grunted, his body grinding against mine.

Catnip.

His movements were frantic as he dragged my hips closer to him. His fingernails dug through my sweater, a sensation approaching the brink of pain, but I quickly forgot about that as I lost my sense of myself. People I didn't know and places I'd never seen filled my mind.

A woman with wavy brown hair laughed as she pressed my hand to her round belly. Below my fingers, something moved and pride surged though me.

I stared at the cloudy sky, waiting for a shaft of moonlight to break through and open the gate to Firth. Others grumbled at my side, a stray bound in chains babbled incessantly, everyone waited for a glimpse of the full moon, and again I was tempted to turn around and go home. Marinna never understood my monthly trips. Would the elders really mark me stray for missing one check-in?

Next the apartment was empty; a note in Marinna's tight script on the counter.

"Kita, that is enough," someone said very far off. "Kita, stop. Now."

Fingers pressed against my eyelids, more closed around my throat, preventing me from swallowing. My fangs retracted, and I jerked back.

Disoriented, I blinked at Nathanial.

"Lick the wound to close it."

I frowned at him. I understood each word, but put together they weren't making any sense.

He pointed and I looked at the bared and bloody neck of the hunter. Stifling a scream, I jumped back. The hunter slid down the wall. His eyes were blank, happy, but empty, and a small wet stain soaked through the front of his pants. Blood trickled out of the two small puncture wounds on his neck. Nathanial looked between the two of us and then bent over the hunter. When he straightened, the blood and the wounds were gone.

I stared at the—now unbloody—hunter. His rich tan floated over paler skin. Panic twisted in the pit of my stomach, fighting the contented warmth spreading through my limbs.

"Is he dead?"

Nathanial shook his head. "Only dazed."

The hunter's heart finally beat, thudding loudly in my ears. I held my breath as I waited to hear it beat again, but it was a long time coming.

I stared at my hands. They weren't shaking, but shouldn't they have been? They looked too smooth, all the fine lines and pores missing. From where I stood, I could see every pore in the hunter's face, every imperfect crease around his eyes, but my skin was as smooth as poured plastic. *Was this shock?*

As if a veil had been pulled aside, the world flooded with color. The vivid hues were dizzying, even the darkest shadows highlighted with shades of deep violet. The sound of distant traffic buzzed in my ears, and a TV audience laughed in one of the nearby houses. The scents wafting from the hunter were revoltingly poignant: the citrus of his cologne battling, and failing, to cover the acrid musk of wolf; the smell of drying sweat and blood. His heart beat again—loud, too loud. For the first time since waking up a vampire, there was no magic in hearing a heartbeat or smelling blood. No hunger stirred in my stomach, only a slightly queasy feeling.

I sank to my knees and put my hands on the ground. "I'm going to be sick."

"Don't you dare!" Nathanial hauled me up with a hard grip on my upper arm. "That is his life blood, which you have already taken. A person's blood is precious. Never waste it."

"I didn't mean to . . . I wasn't trying . . . "

"I know, but you needed it."

I stared at him. His skin was like mine, poreless. How had I never noticed that before? And his irises, I'd always thought they were gray, but they were flecked with dozens of shades of gray, like a faceted diamond. I squeezed my eyes shut. My senses were overloading. I needed to stay focused on what was happening. On what had already happened. He'd been there. In the alley. I'd seen him in my peripheral, but he hadn't stopped me. He hadn't even tried until after the fact.

I shook my head. "You let me do this."

He didn't deny it, and a strangled scream surged out my throat.

"You stopped me from biting Bobby. We were almost to the park, why didn't you stop me now?"

He looked away and shrugged, but the movement wasn't smooth. "You needed to feed. I could tell you I stopped you earlier because you would carry more guilt over biting Bobby, but . . . " He trailed off, and then turned to meet my eyes. "The hunter was convenient and not an ally."

"He's a person, Nathanial! His name is Evan. He is a wolf from the Renfrew clan. He is not of an important enough family to be eligible for a mate, so he was trained to be a hunter from the time he was a child. He likes the human world. It is more a home to him, more fair, in his opinion, than Firth. He has a girlfriend here. She is pregnant, but she left him." The details spilled out of me, bubbling up from a shadow in my mind. "Why do I know all this?"

"Shhh," Nathanial pulled me into his arms.

I pushed away and hugged myself tight.

His face shut down. "You will carry a piece of everyone you bite, but their memories will fade with time."

"Their blood and their thoughts? Is nothing sacred?"

"If it makes you feel any better, donating to one of us is probably the most euphoric experience in their lives."

I looked at Evan's dazed figure. "Donating makes it sound like he had a choice."

Nathanial frowned at me, and then crouched beside Evan. He snapped his fingers in front of the hunter's nose but Evan didn't blink. Nathanial's frown faded as he motioned for me to move. Still hugging myself, I shuffled over a couple steps. Evan's eyes tracked my movement, but didn't become any more focused. A small smile broke over Nathanial's face.

"Before you bit him, did you feel his emotions or notice anything strange?"

I cringed at the word 'bite' and started to say 'no' but then remembered the touch of fear and excitement I felt a moment before my teeth sank in. Well, *felt* was really the wrong word. It was more like I tasted it, or maybe saw it, but that didn't make sense. After a moment, I nodded.

Nathanial pulled his glasses off and tapped the frames against his palm. "Very interesting."

I stamped my feet, waiting, but Nathanial was lost in his own thoughts. Hugging myself tighter, I asked, "What?"

"Did you know the most common vampiric ability is a type of hypnotism, either with the eyes or voice?" I shook my head and he continued, "I assumed that was what you did to him, albeit unintentionally. But, he would have snapped out of it by now. I think you mesmerized him."

I blinked. *Mesmerized?*

"That is good news, Kita. You can erase his memories."

My hands fell to my side. Erase his memories? I shook my head—that couldn't be possible. But, if I could make him forget seeing me, make him forget Bobby . . . I moved to Evan's side and dropped to my knees. As I knelt, some of the blankness in his features turned to anticipation. I'd seen that look on junkies before, right before they inserted the needle.

Cringing, I looked away from the raw need in his face.

"How do I do the memory thing?" I didn't look at Nathanial as I asked, but studied the trampled snow separating Evan and me. When Nathanial didn't answer, I glanced up and frowned at him. "Well?"

"I think contact is required, as that is how you enthralled him in the first place."

"Think? You think?" My voice bounced off the brick walls, an edge of hysteria touching it. I clamped my teeth shut. Evan had called Bobby a traitor. If I could do this, could make him forget me, it wouldn't matter that he hadn't believed the ruse we'd put on at the park gate.

I had to do this.

I took a deep breath and allowed the thought to add steel to my will. I had to do it. Now to figure out how.

I scanned Evan's face. His pallor had worsened. A thin stream of crimson trailed from his mouth, accenting his ashen color. He'd coughed blood after I punched him—had he ruptured something? He needed to shift and heal himself. I stared into his blank, amber eyes. He couldn't shift. He would sit there until he bled to death if I couldn't undo whatever I'd done. While that might solve our problem, the idea settled like a brick in my stomach. I choked back a frustrated scream. How had I gotten myself into this?

"This is your power." Nathanial crouched beside me, his hand moving to my shoulder as he watched my face. "Your hunger drove you, made you stronger both physically and psychically than you are, but this is what you can do. Something you must learn to control."

My fists clenched, my nails digging into my palm. I hadn't asked for this. Didn't I have enough to worry about without trying to control a scary ability I hadn't even known existed? Heat flooded to my face, my eyes stinging. "I hate this. I hate you," I whispered.

Nathanial's hand tightened on my shoulder. A quick spasm he probably wasn't aware of, and I shivered, feeling the contained strength in his grip. Somehow during all this, I'd forgotten the vampire at my side was the biggest predator in the alley.

"What is done is done. You will not die from lack of blood, Kitten. You will lose control and feed on whatever warm body you can find. No thoughts, no compassion. You will feed and you will kill until you have gorged your body enough for your mind to return. And you will remember everything." He looked away. "Feed when you first feel the need and hunger will not control your actions. Now release him.

You are wasting both your and his strength by keeping him enthralled."

Nathanial let go of my shoulder and stood. I hated that his withdrawal left me feeling utterly alone.

I stared at the hunter. *How could I undo something I didn't understand?* Nathanial had mentioned I'd need contact, so that was a start. Forcing my fists to unclench, I reached for the hunter's hand.

When I touched him, the sharp need in his face softened, his lips parting, and his pupils dilating as open adoration took over his features. I jerked back, dropping his hand. *What the—*

"It is not love," Nathanial whispered. "It is lust. Mezmers typically manipulate either fear or lust. You must have grabbed hold of his lust and magnified it."

I shook my head, not disagreeing, but trying to shake away the memory pressing down on me of those moments before my fangs pierced Evan's throat. I'd tasted his fear and excitement, and I'd thought of him, for a moment, as prey. Prey fleeing predators always reeked of fear. Would I really have ripped out his throat if his fear had been what this vamp power had latched onto? A shiver crawled down my spine. I hadn't been thinking clearly, but the memory was all too vivid.

"Now what?" I asked, not trusting my voice louder than a whisper.

"It is not a power I have, Kita, so I cannot guide you. Command him. Send him away. That is the best you can do."

The best I could do? Surely I could do better than sending him out of sight to die. I reached for his hand again, and managed not to flinch this time as adoration bled into his face. I was definitely nothing to be adored.

Somewhere up the street, two pairs of fast approaching footfalls echoed off the townhouses. *Bobby.* He was supposed to be at the park. How come no one listened to me? I so did not want him to see this.

I met Evan's amber eyes. Aside from the look of rapture that crossed his face, nothing changed. I tried mentally reaching between us, the way I would call to my own beast, but I felt nothing. *Great.* It was just my luck that being hungry enough to lose my mind would make vamp powers stronger, but not being crazy cut me off from using them.

Closing my eyes, I dove my awareness inside myself, searching. I found the dead coil where my cat should have been, but nothing else.

Bobby and Gil's footfalls drew nearer. I glanced at the empty opening between the buildings, and in the edge of my vision saw a splash of crimson twisting around Evan. When I looked directly at him, it disappeared again, but I caught a glimpse through my peripheral of something deep red contorting around the level of his navel. Well, either I was losing my mind—entirely possible presently—or that had something to do with the mesmerizing thing. I couldn't touch it or feel it, but knowing it was there, I managed to keep it in sight as I met Evan's eyes again—I only hoped that was enough.

"You never saw me. Never found me. You saw only a hunter on the street. One doing a damn fine job."

The rapture left his face, his eyes fogging to blank.

Was that all it took to erase memories? I thought of Marinna, his human girlfriend, and my mouth went dry with the taste of her betrayal. Tears threatened to spill to my eyes as I remembered the carefully penned lines of her letter. I was all too familiar with the emotional cocktail—I'd fled Firth feeling much the same way. They say time heals all wounds, but I could end his pain now. I could make him forget he ever loved her, that he knew her name. Wouldn't that pay him back in some way for the blood I'd stolen? But the pain didn't go back and taint his older memories, where his love for her swelled without reserve, and if I erased her, that happiness would be gone too. To save those, all I could do was make him forget she left. Then he would go home, expecting her to be there and hurt all over again. I shook my head. "Go somewhere safe. Shift. Heal yourself."

I dropped his hand, and his eyes glazed over. He looked through me like I wasn't there. I jumped to my feet, moving out of his way.

He stood slowly, his knees buckling under him.

I backed away as he hobbled off, his attention straight ahead.

Bobby burst around the corner, but Evan stumbled past him. Apparently my command to go somewhere safe was something he couldn't ignore. Did he realize it wasn't his own idea? How long would it take him to be *him* again?

A shiver ran through me and I held myself as tight as I could. Evan's blood kept me warm, but something deep inside me was cold. I had the feeling no amount of heat would warm that chill—it was a new part of my soul.

"What happened?" Bobby asked as Evan disappeared around the corner.

I ignored the question. "You were supposed to go to the park."

He jutted out his chin. "And you—" He stopped, his nostrils flaring. A dark look passed over his face. "Your scent changed." He stalked closer, leaning until his nose was inches from my skin. The air moved under my ear as he inhaled. "If I didn't know, I'd swear you were a wolf."

I felt my newly-acquired blood drain from my face. Bobby leaned lower, sniffing along my collar. I shoved him back.

"I want you to leave." The words came out low, gruff, as if my throat were trying to choke them back as I spoke.

Bobby's head snapped up, his jaw clenching.

I looked away. If I smelled like a wolf, illusions weren't going to cut it. Hunters would track me again. I'd find the rogue without Bobby, and I'd avoid placing him in extra danger. And maybe, if he wasn't here, he wouldn't realize what I'd done.

Staring at the wall behind his head, I whispered. "Go away, Bobby."

He didn't. With his nostrils flaring, his gaze swept over the snow, taking in the scuffed tracks from my fight. The impression where I'd rolled to avoid a hit. The scent of blood and sweat. The melted patch by the wall where Evan had slumped in his daze. His nose and eyes told him the story I wasn't willing to tell.

He stepped into my space again. "What happened with the hunter?"

I hissed, my hands clenching at my sides, and stormed past him. As I rounded the side of the building, I narrowly avoided slamming into Gil. She'd been running hard, and she flung herself out of my path and onto a porch stoop.

"Let's go," I snapped over my shoulder.

She gulped down air, her black curls plastered to her beet-red face. "Back to the park?"

I shook my head. I didn't need to hunt anymore, obviously, but there was the crime scene to consider. There were also sentries patrolling the park—I knew that for a fact from Evan's memories— and taking that into consideration made the park extremely unappealing. Because of the rogue's activities, most of the hunters in the North Central Region were gathered in Haven. It was a dangerous place for a stray. And now that I smelled like a shifter again, the hunters would be on me faster than dogs gathered fleas. "Where else do you have on those lists of yours?"

Gil frowned, and tugged her scroll from the air. Nathanial strolled around the corner. Bobby was right behind him. His face was flushed, and I was surprised the angry energy around him wasn't melting the snow in his path.

I rounded on him. "I told you to leave. I—"

"Shut it, Kita."

I blinked, but he wasn't done yet.

"I'm staying. You're dealing with it. End of discussion. Unless you want to command me as my *Dyre*."

His eyes were hard, challenging. I opened my mouth to claim my birth title, to tell him to leave and stop looking at me with eyes that guessed what I'd done, but the words soured my tongue. I wasn't a shifter anymore, and I'd given up my place in the clan long before I'd lost my cat. Besides, there was no guarantee he would listen now, but he'd sure as hell remember I claimed *Dyre* if we lived long enough to see the next gate to Firth open.

I glanced down, studying the rock salt scattered over the sidewalk. "Where are we going, Gil?"

She was still breathing hard, gasping as she scanned the list. She looked up, her bottom lip between her teeth. "We should start with Lorna's place. We aren't far. This is the right part of town."

Chapter 10

The 'right' part of town turned out to be what most people considered the wrong part, and it was much further away than I would have liked. We passed an abandoned gas station, its windows raggedly boarded over. Maybe it was my imagination, but I thought I caught eyes watching from the gaping slats. The acrid scent of smoke permeated the street. Dozens of rotting carnations lay forgotten on the blackened stoop of a charred, skeletal building. Apartment buildings that would be condemned in the next few years lined the street. Clotheslines, bare in this cold season, crisscrossed the upper levels between the closely snuggled buildings.

I tried to keep my distance from Bobby as we walked. He hadn't said anything more about the hunter, but several times I caught him studying me out of the corner of his eye. The sidewalk was only wide enough for two people to walk side by side, so the most efficient way to stay away from him was to walk beside someone else. Unfortunately my choices were Nathanial, who had made me into a blood-sucking monster, and Gil, who made it clear she was afraid of said monster. I spent a lot of time changing my pace to make sure I had the sidewalk to myself.

On Hampton Street, Gil pointed to a rundown building nestled in a row of equally dilapidated complexes. "That's it."

We were almost to the front steps when a flicker of orange light caught my attention. Two men sat in a parked car outside the building, the one in the driver's seat fumbling to light a cigarette. I noted they were watching the entrance, but my mental alarms didn't go off until one cracked the window and the wind carried trace scents of menthol and something more exotic than wolf.

I froze. *Hyena?*

Bobby stopped beside me, his nostrils flaring. He made a quick jerk of a nod, and the shadow in the seat beside the smoker nodded back.

I dropped my gaze. "You know him?"

"Yeah. Keep walking." He motioned us on with a tilt of his head. "It will look worse if we turn around."

I forced my dragging feet to follow. He headed toward the building and the hunter watching it. *So not a good plan. What the hell was he thinking?*

"Hunters or cops?" Nathanial asked without breaking stride.

"Both." Bobby took the front steps two at a time.

Bad plan . . . really bad. "Uh . . . "

Bobby didn't stop. "We share a safe house. He's one of the few who knows I'm looking for a cat, and you smell like a wolf. A male wolf who is local." He cut a glance at Nathanial. "That trick you did to Kita's face earlier, can you do it to yourself?"

Nathanial nodded.

"Then I suggest you look like the hunter Kita smells like." Bobby wrenched open the front door, stepping inside without pause. I followed, trying to act natural, but what's natural about walking into the building of a rogue's latest victim? My knees shook as I clamored up the steps, and I had that creepy feeling at the base of my spine. The one that tells you eyes are boring into your back.

By the time I reached Nathanial beyond the door, he looked like some bizarre blend of himself and Evan. The change was subtle, mostly small things like a squaring of his chin, the color of his eyes, and a tan impossible for someone who couldn't be touched by the sun. It wasn't perfect, but if another hunter gave him only a passing glance, it would probably do the trick. When he saw me staring, he smiled, just a slight lifting of his lips, which was all Nathanial, and then he lifted his sleeve. A hawk swooped across his wrist. *Creepy.*

The apartment building boasted a small lobby, just enough room for a double row of mailboxes and a small bench. A man in torn jeans sat on the bench. Though his nose was buried in a hot rod magazine, his eyes gleamed through his lashes as he watched us enter. His concealed radio transmitter gave off a high-pitched buzz that caught in my ears. I winced and concentrated on not glaring at him.

Lorna's apartment was on the first floor. Gil led the way, though she needn't have. Lorna's door was clearly marked by yellow crime scene tape and a seal we'd have to break to enter.

"Do they usually tape off the home?" I looked at Nathanial and he shook his head. *Well, now we knew where she was found.*

We were close enough to touch the crime tape when I heard the muffled voice behind the door across the hall.

"We have a visual. They don't meet any of the resident's descriptions."

I hesitated. *More cops?*

Nathanial's fingers brushed the back of my hand, then entwined with mine.

Had he heard?

He didn't look at me, but with our hands locked together, he walked past Lorna's door. Gil stopped, oblivious, and Nathanial gave her a small shove to get her moving again. She turned to glare at him, and he stepped around her. Walking up to the apartment one down from Lorna's, he rapped on the door.

What would he do if someone answered?

No one did.

He glanced at his watch, and then up at me. He knocked again, and I stopped watching his play act. He was buying us time. Closing my eyes, I made good use of the senses that had awakened since I fed. I sifted through the scents in the hall: sweet cigar smoke, a large bird, simmering stew with a healthy dose of garlic—which vampire or not, smelled good to me—and people. So many people had been through the hall recently, including the hyena cop-hunter. Under all that was the acidic rust smell of blood—old blood, rotted blood. Something else too. Animal, but different. The scent tickled something in my memory, but I couldn't pin it down.

Nathanial squeezed my fingers, and my eyes flew open. I glanced at Bobby. He shrugged, shaking his head. Well, so much for that. No rogue.

Conscious of the police listening from across the hall, I tugged Nathanial's hand. "He's not here."

He nodded, abandoning the stranger's door, and led us out of the building. Gil acted like she might protest as we passed the crime tape again, but after puffing out her cheeks, she followed without a word.

When we stepped out the front door, the hyena-shifter was leaning against the stair railing, a hoagie in one hand, while his partner stood across from him with his cigarette dangling between his lips. My mouth turned dry, my breath catching in my throat. We were going to pass within a yard of him. Nathanial still had my hand in his, and for once I was glad. I wrapped my other hand around his arm, pressing our sides together, mingling our scents. If Evan was any example, hunters kept human girlfriends. I could only hope this hunter took me as such.

As we reached the bottom step, the hunter-cop looked straight at Nathanial. Would he ask for the time like Evan had? Crap, I was wrapped around the arm with the illusion mark. Nathanial seemed to realize that too, because he released my hand and lightly tugged free of my grip. Then he slid his arm around my shoulder, dragging me closer. In the process, his sleeve crawled up, flashing the swooping hawk on his wrist.

The hunter nodded minutely, turning back to his partner. We continued without a word.

Once we rounded the corner, I let out the breath I'd been holding. That had been way too close. I shrugged away from Nathanial. His fingers traced over my shoulders, but he didn't restrain me.

I stopped under a faded 'No Standing' sign. "Now what?"

"We need to get in the apartment," Gil said, glancing back the way we'd come.

Nathanial shook his head and slipped off his glasses. "I doubt that is a smart plan while the police are watching it so closely."

I turned to Bobby. "Did the hyena give you any information we can use?"

His eyes turned stony again, his jaw clenching. Looking away, he shook his head.

Why did I get the feeling he didn't get along with the other hunters?

At the top of the street, a couple turned the corner and stopped in front of a telephone pole with a yellow strip proclaiming the word 'Bus.' A third person crossed the street and joined the couple.

Nathanial lowered his voice. "I know someone with contacts to the police, but he would want an explanation. Kita has not been presented to the council yet, so I cannot risk using him."

He met my eye and I frowned at him. We didn't have time to waste seeing the vampire council. He knew that.

After a moment, he sighed and turned to Gil. "Are you aware of the rogue ever returning to a scene?"

She twisted a strand of her dark curls between two fingers and squinted like she could read notes on the back of her eyes. "I don't think so." She unrolled her list. "Should we go to the next most recent location?"

I shook my head. "The closest." We were running short on time.

She scanned the scroll. "The home of one of the early victims shouldn't be too far from here. I think she was the fifth, maybe sixth victim." She started toward a small side street. "I'm pretty sure it's this way."

Nathanial stopped her. We'd all experienced Gil's concept of *near*. I decided Sabin must not have public transportation, because she was pretty comfortable with long treks. So was I, but we were in a hurry.

"What is the street address?" Nathanial asked, and Gil rattled it off. He thought about it a moment then pointed up the street, where a small throng of people had now gathered. "Let's take the bus."

∽ • ∾

I didn't like the bus.

To the driver's—very verbal—annoyance, I kept standing and pacing between the back seats. The only other time I'd been in a motorized vehicle some old lady was attempting to drive me to the vet to be spayed. That trip had *not* gone well.

Nathanial pulled me into the seat next to him. "Sit still, or I will hold you down."

I tried.

Graffiti-sprayed walls became less common and working streetlamps more prevalent as the tenements gave way to wealthier residences. Small trees appeared at regular intervals in the sidewalk, their skeletal limbs trembling in the breeze. Dark-eyed picture windows gazed over the street, and spacious balconies blocked out the sky.

I was the first one off the bus when we finally reached our stop.

"Which way?" I asked before anyone else's feet hit the pavement.

Nathanial pointed to a highrise condominium across the street. The building was the least impressive on the block, but still a palace compared to any of the residences in the area we'd just left. Even the brownstones around the park didn't compare. A stylized cornice framed the tall building. The arched windows and marble columns were reminiscent of neo-gothic architecture, but, despite the historic accents, the building probably hadn't been erected more than ten years ago.

I tugged the curved door handle. The door shook on its frame, but didn't open. I frowned. A large, metal, call box gleamed to the left of the glass door, a list of neatly printed names and numbers beside it. *Crap. A restricted-entry building.*

Bobby moved to my side and jerked the handle. The door rattled, but held. "It's locked. How do we get in?"

119

I frowned at him. *What, did he think I hadn't tugged hard enough on the door?* Crossing my arms over my chest, I glanced at Gil. "Can you magic someone into letting us into the building?"

She shook her head. "I have to touch them for it to work."

Just peachy. I reexamined the door. The security bolt would be tricky to pick, but not impossible to get around, but the building entry was well lit and facing the street. There wasn't much traffic in this area, but even a little was too much. A man walking a Yorkie glanced at us as the dog hiked his leg on a tree. I grimaced, edging closer to the door.

"I can pick the lock, but we are kind of exposed," I whispered. "Think there's a back door?"

Gil's eyebrows flew up. I ignored her.

Bobby grunted and nodded at an alley wrapping around the side of the building. It opened to a small, private, parking lot. I mentally upped the value of the condos.

A midnight-blue SUV was parked only feet from the back steps, the cargo area brimming with cardboard boxes. One of the boxes hadn't made it all the way inside the upscale vehicle, but was being used to prop open the building's back door. Well, that simplified things.

With the problem of getting inside solved, we followed a hallway until it fed into the main lobby. The motif from the exterior had carried over into the lobby, with large marble columns breaking up the space, accompanied by fake plants in ornamental planters. Nathanial pressed the button for the elevator, and the thick metal doors slid apart.

I eyed the interior warily. "We'll take the stairs."

"This is faster." Nathanial stepped inside as the doors began to shut. He held up his hand. The doors jerked, stopped, and then opened fully again. He motioned everyone to enter.

I didn't move. Bobby stepped inside. Gil hesitated at the edge of the opening.

She crossed her arms and stared at the thin crevasse of empty darkness between the floor and elevator. "I second the stairs."

Bobby shrugged, joining us in the hall again. Nathanial shook his head, but he helped us search for the stairwell.

The stairs were tucked away discreetly on the far side of the lobby. The stairwell itself was tight and dingy, and not at all what I expected considering the grandeur of the building. But the stairs were still a far cry better than being locked in a moving box.

Gil opened the door to the fourth floor and then stopped, scanning her list. She pressed her lips into a tight line as her eyes swept the length of the long hall.

"Whose home are we looking for?" Nathanial, like me, was watching Gil and not looking at the hall.

"The fourth victim, killed around a month ago." She poured over her list again. "Mab's tears! I could have sworn I wrote it down."

A ping sounded from the center of the hall, and the elevator doors slid open. *How were we supposed to explain wandering the halls in a locked building?* I backed toward the stairwell entrance, ready to duck inside. Bobby was half-a-step ahead of me, wrenching the door open as a middle-aged man stepped out of the elevator.

The man jumped when he saw us, nearly dropping the stack of folded boxes and packing tape he was balancing. His pace slowed as he peered around the tower of cardboard boxes. "Something I can help you folks with?"

Gil smiled, and I realized what she planned before she walked over and held out her hand. Poor guy, getting his mind all muddled up with magic. Not that I had any right to feel superior. What I'd done to Evan was worse.

"Hi, I'm investigating the murder of Phyllis Lamar." Gil had enough confidence in her voice to inspire a generation, but the man looked skeptical.

Slowly, he adjusted the weight of the boxes so he could shake Gil's hand. As soon as they touched, the confusion melted from his face.

Her smiled widened. "I forgot which number her home was. I'm sure it's in my notes somewhere, but you could help out a lot if you told us."

"Number forty two. She was my next-door neighbor."

Gil's smile widened, "Thanks so much. Those boxes look pretty heavy. I'll get out of your way so you can continue about your business."

The skin on my arms tingled a second time—funny how the air changed when she used magic. The man smiled at her and nodded. He walked past me, awkwardly juggling his load and keys.

No one moved until his door closed behind him, then Nathanial made his way down the hall. The very last door had a shiny brass *42* above the entry.

He jiggled the doorknob silently. Locked, obviously. "Looks like you will need to show us your cat-burgling skills after all, Kitten."

"Not funny." But I dug through my pockets.

My small lock-picking kit usually ended up buried at the bottom of the last pocket checked. I pulled out the winter gear I'd shoved in the pockets, and shifted through the knickknacks I'd collected. I'd forgotten about the green hair tie I'd found earlier in the week and the two blue marbles I'd found shortly after crossing the gate from Firth into the human world. I'd thought they were natural rocks at the time, and though I knew better now, I still liked them. I pulled out a tube of lip gloss which I apparently hadn't lost and a couple mismatched buttons. One of the marbles slipped from my fingers and rolled across the floor. I scrambled after it and managed to drop the other.

Nathanial scooped up the marbles, and his eyebrow quirked in a ruse of seriousness spoiled by the smile tipping the side of his mouth. "I ensure all of these . . . treasures are returned to your coat after cleaning, and you throw them on the floor?"

When my only response was a frown, his almost smile tugged his lips into a true smile. He held out the marbles, but slightly beyond my reach.

I wasn't about to amuse him by stretching for the colored stones.

Bobby pulled at one of my pockets and glanced inside. "What is all this?"

I stepped around Bobby, jerking my coat away from him. "I'm a bit of a pack rat, okay?"

"More like a pack *mule*."

Well, I was just entertaining everyone today, wasn't I? Gritting my teeth, I lunged forward, and swiped the marbles from Nathanial's palm. In the process, I nearly dropped a small, embarrassing, plastic tiger. Growling under my breath, I shoved my hand deep in my pocket and felt the smooth leather casing of the lock-picking kit.

Finally.

Turning my back on both men, I concentrated on the door. I was a little out of practice, but this lock was definitely my friend. I could feel the tinniest click as the pins caught on the edge of the locking mechanism, and my timing was perfect. The last pin slid into place, and a twist of the tension wrench unlocked the door almost as quickly as if I'd had a key.

A buzz of approval came from behind me, and I smiled as I turned the knob, letting the door swing open. There was something about succeeding at what you tried, especially when people needed your talent. Okay, so that talent happened to be illegal breaking and entering, but hey, there wasn't much I was good at, so success felt good nonetheless.

Chapter 11

Inside, the apartment appeared to be waiting for its tenant to return from a long vacation. If this woman had been the third or fourth victim, as Gil claimed, she must have died over a month ago, but the family obviously hadn't moved anything out yet. The living room was in good order, with several sleek electronics along one wall, a pale cream couch along another, and a glass-topped coffee table off to one side with a handful of magazines scattered across it.

Bobby walked in first, Gil following him.

I hesitated. "Isn't there some sort of rule about vampires entering a home without an invitation?"

"You watch too many movies," Nathanial said, and stepped around me. "The owner of this condo is deceased. It is no longer a private residence."

"Maybe someone else moved in." I took a tentative step forward. There was something wrong about the doorway. I could feel it.

Nathanial grabbed my wrist and half-dragged me into the room. As I passed through the threshold, it felt like someone doused me in cold water. Then the doorway was behind me and the sensation passed.

Disturbing. I shook my head and pointedly ignored Bobby and Gil's stares.

As the door swung shut, only the street lights bleeding through the blinds illuminated the room. Gil clucked under her breath, held up her palm, and magic coursed through the air, skittering across my skin like a dozen spiders. Above her open palm, a violet orb formed, pulsing like a small, round heart. It started no larger than a jelly bean, but with each pulse the orb grew until it was roughly the diameter of a tennis ball. The surface was a deep swirl of purples, ever-changing like oil sliding over water, and, though the orb looked dark, it cast pale, lavender light over the room. A smile creased Gil's face as the orb floated away from her palm to hover over her shoulder.

Show off.

I flicked the switch beside the door, and the room filled with yellow electric light, drowning out the purple glow. Gil frowned at me, then swiveled on her heel, and she and her floating orb disappeared into the adjoining kitchen. Nathanial shook his head, but didn't say anything as he moved through the room.

Bobby waited by the door, his hands shoved deep in his pockets. "What are we looking for?"

"I don't know. Clues, I guess." I shrugged. "Something that gives us a hint of who this woman was and how the rogue found her."

Bobby nodded, but didn't venture any further. I didn't blame him. After all, what would a clue look like? It would be nice if the clue had blinking lights and a big arrow drawn above it.

I walked a slow circuit around the room. I wasn't exactly unaccustomed to exploring strangers' houses, but normally I did it on four feet and without anything more than curiosity or hunger driving me.

All the magazines on the coffee table were addressed to Phyllis Lamar, so I guessed this really was her condo. Everything seemed to be neatly in place, but a thin layer of dust had settled on the top of every surface. If someone else lived here, they didn't dust, but kept their living room otherwise spotless.

Bobby followed in my wake, edging closer whenever I stopped to examine anything. By the time I reached the bookshelves Nathanial was scanning, I could all but feel Bobby's breath on my neck. Cringing, I rounded on him.

"Back off," I warned.

His lips parted like he would say something, but then his jaw clenched. His eyes were a little too wide, too much white showing around the green irises, and his nostrils flared as he scented the air.

Was he still prying into what I'd done to Evan? I crossed my arms over my chest. Well, it wasn't like it was hard to figure out. I'd been a trembling mess before I'd . . . I'd *fed*. I lifted my chin, meeting his eyes.

"Yes, I took his blood." There, I said it. I waited for Bobby's face to show his repulsion. For him to back away from me, finally seeing the monster I'd become.

He didn't. He cupped the back of my neck with his palm. "If that is your nature now, so be it. You look healthy again. I'd give you every drop of my own blood to keep you that way."

His touch was an old and familiar gesture. A sign of affection he'd often used when we'd been young and foolish enough to entertain the idea of being together forever. Before Lynn had joined our clan. Before my father had pressed into me the reality that I'd never mate for love. That I'd be as good as signing Bobby's death warrant if I took him as mate. My mate would share the title of *Torin* of the Nekai clan with me. The purebloods would never accept a natural shifter, a shifter born to non-shifter parents, as *Torin*, and a bobcat wasn't a strong enough form to face off all challengers.

My throat constricted. Bobby had never cared about the danger. The night after I'd fought with my father, Bobby and I had talked until dawn, sitting on a forgotten rock face in the neutral lands outside the clan's holding. The warmth of his palm on my neck had been my touch point to reality, the only thing keeping me from spiraling into self-pity. I'd wanted to run away that night, to abandon my clan and my title, and he'd talked me out of it. Even if it meant we would never be together, he wanted me to be *Torin*.

He believed in me. He always had.

He was an idiot.

"Have you lost your mind?" I asked, the words a shaky whisper. "I'm a monster. What I did was barbaric."

His fingers flexed on my neck, a gentle pressure like he would pull me forward. Which would be too much, too intimate. Shifters weren't completely human and didn't show affection with the same kinds of touch humans did. Touching foreheads together or rubbing cheeks was the shifter equivalency to a kiss, and for a moment, I thought Bobby would lean into me. For a moment, he obviously did too. Then his eyes narrowed and his fingers trembled, loosening but not dropping away.

"*Barbaric* would not be my choice description," Nathanial said, idly scanning a book. "I find it barbaric mortals kill animals to nourish their bodies for a few hours. Vampires need only a pint or two of blood for an entire night. We need not kill anything."

Though he didn't look up, I had no doubt Nathanial was watching us. I could feel it in the tension filling the room. Bobby's hand suddenly felt like a great weight on my neck, and I shrugged him away. He didn't protest, but shoved his fists into his pockets.

Gil walked back in the room and paused in the doorway. Her eyes swept over the three of us, and she screwed her mouth tight. "We're supposed to be investigating, not chit-chatting," she snapped, crossing her arms over her chest. "Can any of you scent the rogue?"

Bobby's nostrils flared again before he shook his head. I breathed in deep, working to identify the tangle of scents in the air. My senses were no longer as overwhelmingly acute as when I'd first fed from Evan, but it was hard to determine if they were back to pre-vamp normal or a little sharper. Harder still to determine how much more and how quickly they would decline.

For now I could detect the salty scent of sweat clinging to Bobby. The bitter quality to the smell betrayed his nerves, which was odd because whatever was bothering him was new, and based on his calm acceptance when I admitted to feeding from Evan, his unease had nothing to do with me. Under the nerves and sweat were the familiar scents of wind, fur, and cat that were part of his personal base scent. Beside me, Nathanial smelled of his shower products, and under those, the spicy scent I was coming to identify as his base scent. Across the room, Gil still smelled faintly of vanilla, but also dried sweat. The unlit candles spread around the room each had a hint of cinnamon to them, and wafting in from the outside hall were various scents of cooked food. The room itself smelled dusty and stale—evidence it had been empty and closed off for several weeks. Not the faintest hint betrayed a shifter had been in the room anytime before Bobby and I walked in.

With a sigh, I shook my head. Gil frowned, but gave me a curt nod. Then she turned and headed down the hall toward the bedroom.

Nathanial stuck his nose back in a book, and I glanced at it around his shoulder. It was a weathered copy of *The Canterbury Tales*. Boring.

"Learning anything useful?" I asked.

"Phyllis was likely well-educated." Nathanial made a vague hand gesture to encompass the bookcases. "Classics, histories, biographies, and psychology books."

I glanced at the books. "What fun is that?"

An oversized book with a black felt binding and no writing caught my attention. I pulled it off the shelf and blew the dust off the cover. Bobby was still hovering, his tension radiating off him in waves. I took a step back, frowning at him. "What are you so nervous about?"

"I'm not nervous about anything," he said, but jumped as the pipes in the walls roared.

"Someone flushed a toilet. Relax."

He didn't, but continued to scan the room like the walls might mutiny and crash down on him.

I suppressed a smile. Bobby had been in the human world, what, ten days? No wonder he was uncomfortable. He'd been sent here to drag me back home, so he probably hadn't received much training on what to expect. A building with people living on top, below, and both sides took time to get used to. I'd been living with humans for five years now, and had ample time to explore strange smells and sounds. Bobby hadn't had that adjustment time. Well, served him right for thinking he could show up here and drag me back to Firth.

Taking another step away from him, I opened the oversized book. An attractive, brown- haired woman of about twenty-eight smiled at me from a photo stuck to the first page. She was the recurrent theme in the album, sometimes appearing before a fountain or on the deck of a ship, and other times smiling at the camera from more mundane and unremarkable locations. Occasionally a pretty blond with hair cropped around her ears appeared in the picture, and once or twice they were together with a large group of people. "Look at this."

Nathanial turned and glanced over my shoulder.

"This one." I turned a few pages back, and showed him a picture that had been ripped so that half was missing. "And these" I flipped near the back of the album, where several more pictures had pieces torn from them, and the brown-haired woman looked a couple of years younger.

"She ripped someone out of her life. Probably an ex-boyfriend. I have seen it done before." Nathanial turned to continue perusing the bookshelf.

Okay, so apparently I hadn't found a clue. I glanced at a couple more photos before shutting the book and sliding it back on the shelf.

I finished my circuit of the room, stopping at the stereo to check the last station played. Classical. The dead woman's video collection didn't shed much light on her either, a couple of chick flicks and some exercise videos. She wasn't very interesting, and far too tidy for my liking. If she'd been the type to consider having a pet, I could tell she'd have been one of those owners who wouldn't let the animal on any of the furniture and would always worry about pet hair. I'd never been fond of staying with such people.

"Hey, check this out," Gil called from the back of the condo.

I headed in her direction. Gil's voice came from the door at the end of the hall, but I passed another door on the way and peeked in at an utterly bland bathroom with black-and-white fixtures. I missed kids; children always had interesting bathrooms.

The second I entered the bedroom, I knew it was the room where Phyllis had died. The rest of the house looked pristine, this room was in shambles: the bed was stripped and knocked crooked; the closet door was torn off the hinges; a lamp and a second TV were turned over, the pieces shattered across the floor; and patches of the carpet had been cut and removed. The carpet damage was most likely created by the police when collecting evidence. The area missing was roughly big enough for a body with a fair amount of blood pooling around it.

Something pulled at the edge of my attention, and I froze. It was that same "animal-but-different" scent I'd caught at Lorna's. Not shifter, but . . . similar.

"There's something here I can't put my finger on," I whispered as Bobby and Nathanial walked in.

They stopped and stared at me.

"Can you smell the shifter?" Gil asked.

Bobby breathed deeply. "There are lots of smells here. Death mostly; they didn't manage to clean that out, but I can't pick up the rogue."

No, there was something . . . something in the room tickled the inside of my mind. I closed my eyes and let the sounds and smells wash over me. It hit me like I'd dug up a distant memory.

"I smell the rogue." But the scent wasn't right. It wasn't like a regular shifter. I searched my mind on why I was so sure the animal-but-different scent belonged to the rogue, or a shifter at all. Slowly the reasoning filled in. "He's never been to Firth, never shifted there, so he doesn't smell like it. The rogue is definitely a city shifter." How did I know that? As I realized the source of the knowledge, I looked at Nathanial with absolute horror holding me. It wasn't my memory, or anything I'd ever heard. I was using the knowledge of the hunter I'd fed from. Knowledge he'd earned in training and years of experience. He would have known how to identify a city-shifter's scent and known why the scent was different. I'd apparently stolen the information when I ran through his memories.

"We already knew that." Bobby said.

I paled, and then realized that he meant we knew the rogue was a city shifter—not about my stealing memories. The others didn't know about the mind voyeurism, well, aside from Nathanial, who looked at me with far too much understanding in his eyes, but Gil and Bobby were in the dark. I intended to keep them that way.

"You didn't think a real shifter would do this?" Bobby asked, watching me.

"If the rogue had been from Firth, I would have been cleared of any connection in tagging the bastard." A feeble hope, but it had been hiding in the back of my mind nonetheless.

"True," Gil said, turning to study a set of framed photos on the wall. "But *now* you have confirmed yourself as a prime suspect for responsibility. The shifter is a tagged human, just as we always assumed."

I gave her a dirty look she didn't see.

"Can you track the rogue?"

I shook my head then realized she couldn't see that either. "No, it's faint here, and I couldn't pick it up in the rest of the condo." Maybe if we returned to Lorna's . . . but no, the scent there wouldn't help us track him. I hadn't picked it up on the street, only in the hall near her door.

She nodded absently, and I walked over to where Nathanial poked through things on the dresser. He opened a small, wooden box and sifted through the contents.

"We can safely assume theft was not a motive in the crime," he mused quietly.

I frowned at him. "I think that's a given, but what makes you sure now?"

"The electronics in the front room, and the fact she owned some very impressive jewelry." He held something out to me.

I reached over, and he dropped it in my palm. Immediately my hand went numb. Yelping, I recoiled, dropping the object.

"Jerk!" I jumped away from the glinting necklace. "That was silver."

"And it had an interesting effect on you," he said, reaching for my hand.

I backpedaled out of reach and cradled my hand against my chest. Pins and needles attacked my palm, now that feeling was returning.

Bobby stepped closer, his expression conflicted as his eyes darted from Nathanial to me. A growl rose in his chest, but he turned his back on Nathanial and tugged my hand into his. Gently, he coaxed me into uncurling my fingers and hissed under his breath—the necklace had left a snaking white welt with pink edges across my palm. As I watched, the pink faded and color filled-in the necklace's outline.

Bobby met my eyes. "It wouldn't burn you if you weren't still a shifter, right?"

I didn't answer. Not only did I not know, but I didn't want to put any weight in Bobby's hope. I stared at my palm until Gil poked her head out of the closet.

"Kita, come in here and tell me what you think of this. Nathanial, too. He knows more about human fashion than the rest of us."

Everyone walked into the closet. The right side stood bare, but the left boasted a rack of clothes organized so tidily it was mind-boggling. Shoes lined the bottom with like colors together, and the clothes were similarly sorted by color and piece.

"See anything she would have worn to a club?" Gil asked, running her hand through the outfits.

"Everything looks too conservative for the club scene," Nathanial said.

I nodded. I didn't know all that much about parties, but most of the girls I'd seen the other night had been scantily clad, which meant there was too much fabric in all these outfits.

Gil sighed and pushed the dress she was holding back into the closet. She looked around a moment then flipped through the clothes again. "Think these clothes are your size?"

"You are *not* suggesting I steal a dead woman's clothes."

She shrugged. "I can't help but notice you're wearing the same outfit you were wearing last night."

"So is Bobby."

"Actually, Bobby was wearing a dark-blue sweater yesterday," Gil said, and I noticed that Bobby's sweater was a deep green tonight.

"My clothes are clean." I pulled my coat shut. It was silly, clothing wasn't something I worried about. The last five years I'd spent minimal amounts of time each day as a human, and clothing was just something I needed to blend in. If an outfit got ruined I acquired another, but usually my clothes lasted a while.

Gil thrust a pale-blue turtleneck at me. "I don't see what you are making such a big deal about, it's not like she will miss them. Besides, you are obviously quite a thief anyway."

My jaw dropped, and I threw the shirt back at her.

"I'm not a thief. I didn't realize I had that bear in my hand when I walked out of the gift shop. It was an accident."

Gil rolled her eyes, and Nathanial put a hand on my shoulder. I rounded on him.

"I'm also not any kind of burglar, despite knowing how to pick locks."

"I was only making a play on words when I mentioned cat-burgling," he said calmly, voice smooth. The effect was like submerging my anger in cold water.

I frowned at him then turned back around.

Gil still watched me suspiciously, her scroll in hand. "I suppose you *accidentally* learned to pick locks too?"

My hand clenched into a fist, but I forced it to relax. She was sent here to study me. This was her job, and considering to whom she was reporting, I had best be sure to clear up any misunderstandings. I took a deep breath and released it before answering. "Interesting people take home stray cats. One man worked at a pop-a-lock type service. He practiced in the basement on different locks to keep his skills sharp. I paid attention, and when the house was empty, practiced."

"So then you stole the lock picks?" She kept her nose buried in her scroll, which should have lessened the sting of the continued accusation.

It still pissed me off.

"He was training his son. They had a fight. The boy threw the kit away. Trash is unwanted and fair game." Okay, maybe I sounded a little defensive. I didn't care. "Are we ready to go?"

Gil looked up, her gaze flickering over my face, never making eye contact. Her lips twisted, but she nodded and, after adding another line or two, vanished her scroll. "We've learned all we can here."

She swept by, the hem of her coat brushing mine, and she didn't even cringe. Well, that was a first. I hoped it was a good sign. I was long overdue for good news.

෧ • ෯

Gil lead the way out of the condo, setting a quick pace. As soon as the door closed behind me, another clicked open.

The neighbor we had spoken to earlier peeked into the hallway, and then shut the door again. Metal dragged across metal as he released the security locks. He stepped into the hall, his hand clutching his doorknob like a lifeline back into the safety of his condo.

"You are investigators, right?"

Whatever Gil had done to him earlier must have been wearing off. She stepped up, likely to give him another dose, but Nathanial held up a hand.

132

"Yes, but we are not affiliated with the police. We were given the assignment by a private party."

The man chewed on this information, eyes roaming over us, and then he nodded. "I overheard the family mention hiring private investigators."

"Had you been acquainted with Ms. Lamar long?" Nathanial asked.

That sounded like a reasonably legitimate question to me, and I silently applauded him. Of course, all I knew about investigating and questioning witnesses could fit in a thimble with room to spare.

"I hadn't known her long. She'd only been living next door a couple of months before she . . . " He seemed at loss as to how to end the sentence.

Was savagely murdered, I supplied for him mentally

Nathanial gave him a compassionate smile and quietly said, "Passed away."

The man nodded. "Yes, before she passed away."

"Do you know if she had any enemies?" Bobby asked, and my silent clapping continued.

"Like I told the police, she acted like a nice-enough person. She said hello in the halls, held the elevator if she saw me coming, went to the community meetings, and was a quiet neighbor. No one around here had any problems with her that I ever heard." He paused as if debating the next sentence. Apparently he decided to share, because he continued, "She was in the process of a divorce. She left her husband for a woman. That had to cause some bad feelings."

"This woman, was Phyllis still seeing her at the time of her death?" Gil asked.

"Jessica. And they were living together. I helped her move some things out a couple weeks ago. She couldn't bear reentering the condo. She was the one who found Phyllis." He paused and looked away. His hand moved to his mouth and he chewed at a nail. All his nails were gnawed to the quick. "Do you think the person who did this . . . ? Will he come back? I've been thinking about moving . . . but if the . . . killer was her ex, he wouldn't have any reason to come after me, right?"

"Do you think it was her ex?" I asked, and hoped I sounded half as smart as the others had.

"Well, I mean, she left him for a woman, and I'd heard they weren't on good terms. Messy divorce." His hand fell to his side. "How would he have gotten the dog into the building though?"

Bobby raised his eyebrows. "Dog?"

"Well yeah. Jessica was beating on my door in hysterics, and I couldn't make heads or tails of what was going on, so I went to check it out. I've never seen . . . it was . . . " He was at a loss again, and we gave him a moment to collect himself. "It was brutal. A human couldn't have done that kind of damage. Had to be a trained attack dog. She looked like a bear had torn into her." He turned pale. "I ran back here and called the police."

"Did Ms. Lamar or her girlfriend ever go to club parties?" Gil asked after the man stopped looking faint.

"Parties?"

"The kind some people call 'raves,'" she said.

"Oh, no, not that I know of. Aside from their relationship, Phyllis and Jessica were both very conservative people. Professionals. Their idea of cutting loose was showing up with funny hats and having a second glass of wine during the Halloween party at our community center." He almost smiled, then a sick look crossed over him again. "Is the guy who did this . . . is he the same one that I've been reading about in the papers?"

Nathanial and Gil exchanged glances. Apparently Bobby and I were not invited into their silent communication.

"We believe that he is," Gil finally said, and the man blanched again.

The next question, *Do you think you will catch him?* was written all over his face. I took the initiative before he could ask. "This is our top priority. We will find this guy."

"Well, we must be going," Nathanial announced. "You have been very helpful, Mr . . . ?"

"Jefferies. Thomas Jefferies."

"Yes, Mr. Jefferies. If we need anything else, we'll contact you." The man took Nathanial's statement as the dismissal it was. Jeffries said nothing else as we made our way to the stairwell. I glanced over my shoulder and saw him staring after us before the door shut behind me.

"So Phyllis Lamar does not fit our pattern," Nathanial said once we were back on the street.

I needed to hold onto the one connection we had made. "Her neighbor admitted to not knowing her well, maybe he didn't know she went to raves."

Gil blew on her hands, rubbing them together for warmth. "Without any clothes suitable for such things?"

"Maybe her girlfriend went to them," Bobby said.

I smiled, grabbing that thread of possibility. "Yes, if this Jessica girl went to raves, and brought someone home, that could explain how the rogue met Phyllis."

"I think we need to look into the other known victims before we decide that's a likely avenue. The party connection between the two could be coincidence," Gil said, jotting something in her scroll.

"Shouldn't we check into the ex-husband?" I asked.

Gil vanished her scroll. "Not unless you think he was married to all the victims."

"Well, he could be picking up girls at parties now, but maybe Phyllis was personal? He could have gone to confront her and simply lost control."

She dismissed the idea with a wave of her hand. I turned to Nathanial for support.

He shook his head. "The ex-husband would have been high on the police's suspect list. I am sure they cleared him, or he would be in jail awaiting trial. If we run out of leads we can check into him, but I think looking for a common connection between all the victims should come first." He pulled the list Gil had given him earlier from his pocket, and after a cursory scan, glanced up at the street. A bus chugged around the corner, and Nathanial pointed to the bench marking the stop. "Our chariot awaits."

Goodie.

Chapter 12

I let the door to the apartment building swing shut behind me. Counting Phyllis and Lorna's places, this was the sixth scene we'd checked since splitting up, and it had been a complete waste of time. Like two of the others, this scene had been cleaned, recarpeted, repainted, and was ready to be put back on the market. Not a trace of evidence was left behind, but at least it hadn't been like the duplex we'd checked—that one had already been rented out again.

Hopefully the guys were having better luck. Since we were supposed to meet Candice in less than an hour, we'd had to split up to cover enough of the locations. Bobby and I were the noses for either group, but it had come down to a coin toss on the bus to determine whether I went with Gil or Nathanial. I might have fudged the toss a little.

"Where is the next one?" I asked, looking at Gil.

She pulled out her scroll. "1322 Longstreet."

We walked in silence, and I mentally counted the blocks. Three women had been murdered on this street, each in a different location. I studied the buildings we passed. None were as dilapidated as Lorna's complex, but they were a far cry from Phyllis's expensive condo. So what brought the rogue back to this street multiple times? Or was that the wrong question? Maybe I needed to know what the women in this neighborhood had in common that would draw the attention of the rogue.

"That should be it." Gil pointed to a building across the street on the next block. The three-story complex looked as run down as the one we'd just left.

We stepped into the street, and the wind shifted. I froze, throwing my arm out to stop Gil.

She turned, her eyebrow lifting. "Let me guess. Shifter, and probably a hunter after us?"

I nodded, then tilted my head back and breathed deeply. Definitely male, and wolf—which made the skin along my spine crawl. His scent was vaguely familiar, but I couldn't put my finger on it. Was it someone I recognized from Evan's memories? I breathed in again, hoping for better information. Nothing. Damn, I was already losing the scent, but judging by the direction of the wind, he was somewhere near the next crime scene on the list, where we were supposed to meet Nathanial and Bobby. I glanced around. The street was empty, no sign of the hunter.

Where was he? Had he caught my scent already? Actually, it wasn't my scent, it was Evan's. If I recognized the hunter's scent from Evan's memories, maybe the hunter had recognized Evan's scent and moved on. A nice thought, but I wasn't going to depend on that possibility.

An alley carved a path between the building beside us and the one we'd just passed. I doubled back, ducking into it.

Gil followed, her small mouth twisting. "What are we doing?"

I pointed across the street. "Hiding. We're downwind of the hunter, but we can see the entrance to the building." I didn't add the fact that the sickly sweet smell of the overflowing dumpster at the mouth of the alley would help mask my scent. I rubbed my nose at the stench—now would be a good time for the old olfactory to give out. "When Bobby and Nathanial arrive, go meet them."

She frowned, but nodded. Now all we had to do was wait. I leaned against the brick, my hands in my pockets.

The trash bags piled beside the dumpster rustled. Gil grimaced, pressing herself against the opposite wall. I didn't pay the rustling any attention. More than once I'd been desperate enough to dig through trash for food as a cat.

The top trash bag tumbled down the pile, followed by two more. Okay. That was less common.

I pushed away from the wall as a man emerged from behind the mountain of black bags.

He tilted his head, doffing an imaginary hat. "Welcome to my parlor."

Crap. Evan's memory hadn't recognized the shifter's scent. The memory was mine, from when I'd been attacked outside the rave, in a drugged haze. But how had the stray gotten here from . . . ? I glanced over his shoulder, across the street to where his scent had been broadcast, where he should have been.

A puzzle for later.

The stray strode toward us, a lopsided smile spreading across his face. I blinked. *Was the darkness playing tricks on my eyes?* No. His smile truly was lopsided, but not naturally so. A thick network of silver scars traced his left cheek. A double row of slashed scars marred the finer pattern, but not enough that I didn't recognize the mark that the older, deeper scars formed.

An extra stab of panic cut into my chest as I stared at the very intentionally carved scars branding his face. He wasn't just a stray like me, he was . . .

"Clanless." The bitter term dropped from my lips before I could catch it, and his lopsided smile turned to a sneer.

I glanced at Gil. Her eyes bulged wide, all color absent in her face. *Moon-cursed.* That was what I was. Totally moon-cursed.

I stepped in front of Gil, blocking her from the encroaching clanless. If it were a hunter advancing on us, she would have been fine—run off, but unharmed. But the clanless were the outlaws of Firth. They were dangerous. Untrustworthy. Serious crimes typically resulted in death, but on rare occasions, a shifter was branded and exiled from their clan. Most shifters I knew claimed death would be safer for all concerned. The clanless roamed the neutral territories in Firth, but I'd never seen one. What one was doing on this side of the gate was beyond me.

I balled my fists, balanced my weight and lowered my center of gravity. I'd held my own in our last fight, and I'd been drugged then. I could do it again.

He stopped several steps out of arms reach. He was favoring one leg—I'd apparently scored a solid blow with my claws last time we fought. I waited, ready for his advance, but he crouched in a position mirroring mine. Reaching into his pocket, he pulled out a glinting silver chain and stretched it between his gloved hands.

His gaze drilled into mine, but cats don't lose staring contests. I held his gaze, watching for him to betray his next move.

Behind me, Gil yelled something, her hands flashing in my peripheral. A purple haze sprung up between us and the clanless. It was my turn to smile as I recognized it as the same sort of barrier the judge had trapped me in. And here I'd thought Gil was useless.

The clanless stray's eyes widened. He reached out a hand, encountered the barrier, and tumbled back a step. Then he turned and ran.

What? I surged forward, encountering the edge of the haze. The barrier stretched across the alley, effectively trapping us but leaving the clanless free to flee.

I whirled on Gil. "He's getting away."

"Mab's bloody frozen tears!" She jerked her hands through the air, but the purple haze grew blindingly bright.

I threw my arms over my eyes, shielding them. A force slammed into me; magic crashed against me, and my feet left the ground. My back hit the pavement several yards later. Stars filled my vision. Gil yelped as she hit the ground seconds after me.

Hands hauled me to my feet, and I blinked at Nathanial. *Where the hell had he come from?* I shook my head.

"A clanless," I gasped, pointing toward the mouth of the alley.

He frowned, and I pushed past him. Running, I burst from the alley but skidded to a halt in the center of the sidewalk. The only movement in the street was Bobby, who was hauling ass in my direction. I scanned all directions, searching the shadows. No clanless. I tilted my head back. Only the scent of decomposing garbage soured the air. Not that I could count on my nose.

Damn it.

I met Bobby halfway. "Did you see where the clanless went?"

His brows knit together as he shook his head. His nostrils flared. "Kita, no other shifters have been here."

"I saw him, damn it. I almost fought him again. Ask Gil." I pointed to Gil, who had emerged from the alley, her face nearly crimson.

She dropped her gaze when she saw me pointing to her, and her hand moved to cover a raw scrape decorating her chin.

"Tell him," I said, marching up to her. "Tell him about the clanless."

Her eyes remained affixed to her rain boots. "I saw a shifter. I don't know what a clanless is."

She didn't ask questions, or magic her scroll to appear. Had she hit her head when her barrier exploded?

I paced between Bobby and Gil. "I saw the scars. He was a clanless. I don't know why he didn't leave a trail unless . . ."

He had a gift. I hadn't seen a necklace, but he was wearing winter gear. It could have been covered. If he had a talent which allowed him to manipulate his scent, it could explain why his scent had come from the wrong direction. Why it was missing now. The ground suddenly felt more solid under my tennis shoes. A gift like that could explain a lot.

I stopped. "Picture a clanless wandering stray in the human world who can manipulate his scent. Now put him in a city that has a rogue who's eluding a dozen well-trained hunters. Is anything clicking for anyone else?" I looked between my companions.

Gil gnawed at her bottom lip, but finally looked up. "That doesn't prove—"

"It's a hell of a lot better explanation than you thinking *I* created the rogue." I was yelling. I didn't care. "If the clanless tagged some human, or if the clanless is an insane murderer himself, there would be bodies aplenty. Bodies that aren't my fault."

Nathanial moved to my side and laid a hand on my shoulder. I shrugged him off.

Gil tugged on her sleeves. "Your fault or not, you made your deal with the judge already. You agreed to bring him the rogue. If that means we find this *clanless*, fine. But you still have to capture the rogue. A good theory won't stay the judge's hand if you don't complete your end of the bargain."

And it always came back to that. I sighed, sagging. The clanless might have turned rogue, or tagged the rogue, but it wasn't his scent I'd caught at Lorna's or Phyllis's house. There was a city-shifter somewhere in Haven, and he was definitely rogue. "We should check that last apartment."

"Nathanial and I already did." Bobby winced as he spoke, which meant he didn't have good news. "Clean."

Nathanial nodded. "I suggest we meet with your bookstore friend before she gives up on our arrival."

I wanted to argue, to track down the clanless. But I couldn't hunt the clanless *and* the rogue city-shifter, not with only a night and a half left before the judge executed me, Nathanial and Bobby. Begrudgingly, I trudged behind Nathanial as he led us to the subway.

ೊ • ೄ

We were nearly an hour late, and there was no telling if Candice and her friend were still inside, so I was more than a little irritated at the delay caused by the large bouncer barring my way.

He held out a meaty hand. "ID, please."

"I don't have it on me," I said between gritted teeth.

The bouncer crossed his arms over his chest, his looming bulk blocking the bar entrance. He hadn't asked anyone else for an ID, letting them by with a slight nod, but the oversized gorilla had stepped right into my path.

Nathanial turned, frowning at the bouncer's back. "She is of age."

The bouncer grunted. "She looks nineteen to me, and she's not coming in unless she has some ID to prove otherwise."

"Uh, Gil . . . " I said.

She tugged at her sleeves without looking up. She hadn't said two words since we'd left the alley.

"A little help here?" I stage-whispered.

The bouncer turned to look at her.

She bit her lip, then lifted her hand like she would hand him something. The bouncer held his palm out, and she placed two fingers against his skin. A soft *zing* of magic touched the air.

"She's over twenty one. Let us pass, please."

Her whispered words were so quiet, I was afraid he hadn't heard. But, he nodded and sat down in his stool. I hurried up the steps before he could change his mind.

The inside of the bar was smaller than I'd anticipated and far more packed. A fog of smoke hung in the air so thick the dim lamps were surrounded by small halos of reflected light. Gil waved a hand in front of her face like the action would somehow create a patch of clean air. Bobby squinted and coughed. Nathanial didn't seem to mind the conditions, but then again, he'd said vampire's lungs were vestigial, so maybe the smoke didn't bother him. Except for the smell, it didn't bother me.

People clustered around the polished oak bar, leaving only standing room available. Three bartenders scurried back and forth, filling pint glasses and tumblers and then passing them to eager hands. I tried to peer through the crowd for a familiar face, but snippets of conversation distracted me. It took concentration to zone out the individual conversations and reduce the sound of the crowd to a dull roar. A glance at Bobby confirmed he was having equal difficulty. Probably more than me, because his senses didn't wane with every passing hour as mine did.

"Do you see the girl we're supposed to be meeting?" Gil asked, still trying to fan away the smoke.

Nathanial shook his head and led us along the outskirts of the crowd. I angled my shoulders to brush the wall to avoid running into the people we passed. Once beyond the crowd, the bar opened into a larger room dotted with several black, lacquered tables. The smoke hung a little less heavily in the larger area, and the wall buffered a lot of the noise from the patrons in the front half of the bar.

Candice stood up on the rungs of her chair and waved as we entered. She'd changed since work and now wore a short, pleated skirt and a low-cut sweater. Because of the clingy knit of the sweater, I was forced to notice she was rather amply endowed for someone of her slight build.

Jealous much, me? Nah, but it didn't seem fair. And speaking of fair, how had she gotten in? She couldn't have been more than sixteen.

"I was starting to worry," she said, fishing for the cherry at the bottom of her drink. "Have trouble finding the place?"

"It took longer than expected," Nathanial said, flashing her a smile of perfectly straight and flat—no fangs on him at the moment—teeth.

"Oh, sorry 'bout that. This is my friend Jace. He's a DJ." She nodded to the man on her right.

Jace was a skinny guy with disheveled blond hair and a straggly goatee. He'd been drumming his thumbs on the table, but he stopped long enough to extend his hand toward me. "You must be Kita. Candi says you have a wicked dye job. You gonna let down your hair so I can see?"

I shook my head, ignoring his hand, and Nathanial hurriedly introduced himself.

Jace tried to get Nathanial into a strange handshake that included a lot of slapping and snapped fingers. After a moment, he pulled his hand back and laughed. "It's okay man, you're just not smooth. So you guys wanted to talk to me about spinning?"

"Jace . . . let them get their drinks first," Candice chided.

"I don't think we'll be staying that long," Gil said.

Candice's attention turned to Gil for the first time, and her smile faded a notch. "You brought an extra friend."

"Candice, meet Gil," I said. I could do polite.

Sort of.

Okay, maybe not.

The table was a seat short and Bobby and Gil had already each claimed one. That left only one other chair, and Nathanial stood closest to it. *Great.* I glanced around, looking for one I could steal from another table. Nathanial pulled out the chair and gestured for me to sit. Then he walked a couple tables over and returned with another chair, before scooting in next to Candice.

She turned toward him, and her cleavage puffed up a little more.

"How old are you?" I asked, no longer able to keep the question silent

Candice blushed, her eyes darting from Bobby to Nathanial. "I'll be eighteen next month."

"The bouncer . . ."

She shot a hand into her clutch purse and pulled out a small, plastic ID card. "Best fifty bucks I ever spent." She tucked it back in its place. "So you guys should stay for at least one drink. I did drag Jace out here just for you."

I was about to protest, but Nathanial held up a hand.

"As the lady wishes, one drink," he said amiably.

Candice managed to spread her smile even wider and giggled. Okay, if she did that again, I was slapping both her *and* Nathanial.

"So, are there any parties in the area tonight?" I asked, trying to sound pleasant.

Everyone turned to look at me. Apparently, I'd failed.

Nathanial cleared his throat. "Kita, come with me to get the drinks." It wasn't a request. As soon as we were away from the table he pulled me close to the wall. "You are daughter to the *Torin*, surely you have played politics before?"

"Hello. Stray, remember? I ran away from that game. Sucked at it before that."

"Of course." He smiled, clearly amused, which so wasn't my intention. He leaned closer, his voice dropping conspiratorially low, as if he were sharing a secret. "I am a bit rusty, but here is the rule I remember. If you need to use someone for information, make them feel like they will receive something in return, or they will not help you in the future. So, be nice when we get back." He tugged my hat off gently, his fingers trailing over my cheek with the movement. "And take off your coat."

I could feel blood rushing to fill the path his fingers had taken. Snatching my hat from him, I focused on shoving it in my pocket. "Why should I lose the coat?"

"Look around. Everyone else has, so it must be warm in here. You have to pay attention to the humans around you. Take your cues from them. Now, wait here while I get the drinks." He pushed away from the wall and wove his way between the people at the bar.

I watched him disappear into the mass, and then looked around the room. It didn't feel any warmer or cooler than outside, but coats and jackets had been thrown over the backs of chairs. I shrugged out of my coat reluctantly. It would take some getting used to for me to look to others to see what the temperature was. With a sigh, I moved to follow Nathanial to the front of the bar.

I passed the first couple of people and was consumed in the throng. With people pressed all around me, I felt heartbeats against my skin. Scents so close and strong overpowered me. More than sweat and beer, it was like I could smell them dying little by little around me. A smell like decaying garbage reached my nose. I recognized it as disease, but with so many people so close together, there was no telling to whom it belonged. My head spun with the sensory overload. I shouldered my way back out of the crowd and leaned against the wall Nathanial had originally chosen for our little talk. Maybe he'd had a reason he wanted me to wait.

He emerged a moment later, precariously balancing six tumblers. "Here, take these," he said, and I grabbed two of the glasses "Remember, only pretend to drink."

"Don't you think they'll notice?"

He smiled. "You would be surprised."

When we reached the table, he set a bright blue, fruity smelling drink in front of Candice. "Miss me?"

She gushed and thanked him, flirting with her eyes all the while.

I smiled through gritted teeth and put down the drinks I was carrying before I decided to dump them on him. I was pretty sure I'd never seen Firth's clan leaders flirt their way through politics. I plopped into my chair and focused on making noncommittal noises at the right moments and holding my smile. Conversation flowed around me until Candice pushed back her chair and announced she needed to go to the ladies' room.

"Walk with me?" she asked, looking at me.

I was inclined to say "No," but the look on Nathanial's face urged me to go.

As soon as the bathroom door closed behind us, Candice rounded on me. "Listen, are you dating Nathanial? I don't want to flirt with your man if you are, even if he's flirting back"

I gaped at her. "No. Nothing like that."

"Are you sure? You're acting really offish. I don't want to trod, you know." She turned to the mirror and ran a hand through her blond curls. When I didn't answer she flicked her eyes over to me through the mirror. "What's your relationship with him?"

Well you see, he rescued me, turned me into a blood-sucking monster, and then kidnapped me. Now I'm living with him while I try to track an insane killer so I don't get eaten by demons. Truth, but nothing she would believe. "We're just friends."

"Is he seeing anyone?"

I blinked at her. I honestly didn't know. "Not that I know of."

"How'd you meet?"

"Uh . . . " I searched my mind for something more plausible than the truth. I didn't have a lot to work with. What had he said last night? "He teaches this class at the university . . . "

"Yeah, he mentioned something about that. Some kind of paranormal research involving old myths and stuff." She squished her face in thought. I was happy to see it wasn't a cute look. "He doesn't actually believe in that stuff, does he? I mean, it's just a job, right?"

I shrugged.

She pulled out a tube of gloss, and there was a blessed moment of peace while she swiped the goopy wand over her lips. Then her eyes darted to me through the mirror again.

"I'm glad you lost the hat. I really was serious the other night about liking your hair. I want to get streaks done, but I'm scared I'll mess it up. I have this." She pulled what looked like a giant tube of mascara from her purse. Grabbing a paper towel, she slid the paper under her bangs and then swiped the bristled wand over her hair. It left streaks of red in its wake. "It washes out, but cool, huh? I want to do something permanent. Could you give me pointers on how to do your streaks?"

No, was at the tip of my tongue, but I bit it back. "Maybe a little later, our drinks are probably getting warm."

She nodded, like that was a reasonable excuse. With a hand hovering over the door handle, she paused. "So we're cool right? No, hard feelings if I go after Nathanial?"

"Are you asking my permission?"

"No, but if we started something, I'd want to be able to get along with his friends."

I gave her a forced smile and she let out a sigh as if I'd blessed her and the children such a relationship would produce. *Could a vampire have children?* I added that to my list of questions to ask if I lived past tomorrow night.

❧ • ❧

I drew swirls in the condensation on my drink glass, feeling every minute tick by. My glass appeared to have only a sip or two left, despite the fact I hadn't lifted it once. Nathanial's drink was similarly disappearing. I could only guess it was another illusion; something similar to how he'd changed our appearances. Judging by the rate the liquid had been vanishing, the glasses would be empty in another three minutes. I was counting on leaving once that happened. If Nathanial insisted on a second drink, politics and I were going to have a rather rude falling out.

Candice was laying the flirting on thick, and I found my teeth gritting as Nathanial encouraged it. My reaction pissed me off. I didn't care, really I didn't. I wiped away a sharp-edged condensation drawing.

I kept trying to fade into the background, but, unfortunately, Candice was determined to pull me into conversation, mostly with questions I couldn't answer.

What did I do for a living? *Well I used to pimp myself out as a house pet, but I was recently demoted to sucking the blood of the living.* Nope, couldn't tell her that.

Candice swirled her drink. "So where did you go to school, Kita?"

"Uh, I was home schooled." Which was almost the truth. "No university."

She frowned. "Didn't you meet Nathanial in his class?"

Crap, I'd forgotten I told her that.

Nathanial lifted an eyebrow but came to my rescue. "She dropped out mid-semester," he said, then whispered loud enough for everyone at the table to hear, "It is a touchy subject. She does not like talking about it."

"Oh. Sorry." Candice gave me a meek smile. For the first time, silence at the table went unfilled, and of course, it was too good to last. She looked between Nathanial and me and said, "You guys need a new drink. Want me to run over to the bar and order for you?"

"Actually we will need to leave soon," Nathanial said, and Candice looked miffed.

"Yeah," Jace said, pushing back his chair. "It's been real, but I've gotta fly."

"Before you go, would you tell us about local raves coming up soon?" Nathanial asked smoothly, before I had the chance to blunder the same question.

Jace smoothed his goatee into a point. "Right, right, I forgot. I'll be spinning again two months from now. Date and location not set yet, but just check back with Candi. She'll let you know." He turned to leave.

I was on my feet in a heartbeat. "How about any parties with other DJs? Sooner, preferably?"

"Now why would you want to hear anyone but me? I'm hurt." He pressed his hand over his heart, but smiled. "All right, let's see . . . local, you're looking at the middle of next month. Surrounding area, next week, a field party in a little town about two hours south of here. No big names spinning there. Well, I'm out." He turned and disappeared around the wall.

Any pretense of a smile I'd managed thus far sputtered and died. Our lead was officially at a standstill. I blinked, the room suddenly appearing darker, the smoky air heavy. I sank into my chair. *Now what?*

"Hey, you okay?" Candice reached across the table to touch my hand.

The muscles in my arm tightened, but I didn't jerk away. Flashing teeth was the best I could do as I said, "Yeah, I'm just . . . tired."

Nathanial nodded. "We do need to head out. Early day tomorrow."

"Awww, are you sure you can't stay for one more drink?" Candice made a hideously adorable pouting face, but she stood, grabbing her purse. She pulled out her lip liner and wrote something on a cocktail napkin. "My cell. Give me a call sometime." She held it out to Nathanial, but nodded to the rest of us. "Share it."

Nathanial took the napkin and folded it into equal quarters before tucking it into his shirt pocket.

When he looked back at her, Candice blushed but asked, "So can I get your number?"

He took her hand and brushed a quick kiss over her knuckles. "Next time," he said, and then turned and strolled away.

Her eyes were bright, her smile nearly breaking her face as she watched him go. I waved, but I doubted she noticed any of the rest of us leave.

I stared a hole into the back of Nathanial's head as I followed him out. I seriously didn't want him to follow through on his 'next time' promise, and the sinking feeling when I thought about that possibility irritated the hell out of me.

❧ • ❧

I stared at the sky, searching for stars as my thoughts settled. *What now?*

The night was cloudy and reflected the city lights in a sickly orange glow. That didn't help my mood.

"Should we go to the next crime scene?" Gil asked as she stepped out of the club.

I sighed. Was this how I was going to spend my last nights of life? Breaking into cleaned crime scenes and chasing my own damn tail?

"Why bother?" It was pointless. It had been from the beginning.

Nathanial wrapped an arm around my shoulders. "We will find him," he whispered, low enough that the words were only for me.

The weight of Nathanial's arm was real, tangible, and so unlike the weight of the sky pressing down on me or time beating against me. Who was I kidding, thinking I could track down a rogue? Two days ago I would have walked past a tagged city-shifter on the street and never thought anything other than he was a strange-smelling human. What else didn't I know? Who else was I endangering?

I shrugged out from under Nathanial's arm and turned to Bobby. "How much authority will a dead *Dyre* wield?"

Tight lines etched themselves across his face, but he didn't answer. A bitter laugh lifted in my chest, but it caught in my throat like a sob, burning me. I swallowed it back down.

"Take me to the hunters."

Bobby shook his head in sharp, jerking movements. "The hunters will—"

"The hunters are better equipped to find a rogue!" I didn't realize I was screaming, until a couple leaving the bar stopped and stared at me. I took a deep breath and wrapped my arms around myself so tight my ribs hurt.

Nathanial reached for me again, but I stepped away from him. He dropped his arm. "They have not found him yet."

The words draped over me like chains. No, the hunters hadn't found the rogue yet either. Or the clanless. What could I bring them they didn't already know? They were already hunting. They couldn't do anything more simply because I showed up on their doorstep. They might do even less if they truly believed I was responsible.

I looked from Nathanial to Bobby. I looked away. "You know that hypothetical question about having only one day to live?" I let the slightly manic laugh bubble over this time, spilling it from my lungs. "Go. Live. While you still can. Maybe I can give you longer."

Then I turned and ran.

"Shouldn't we—" Gil began as Bobby yelled, "Kitten—"

I didn't stay to listen. Would the judge really track Bobby and Nathanial down if I failed? His mark gave him a line to me, but if they weren't with me . . . distance was best. Maybe they would live if we weren't together.

I ran hard, using their surprise to build a lead. Buildings were a blur as I pounded past. I waited for the pain in my chest, the burn and exhaustion that would release endorphins and take me to a zone where I stopped caring, but oblivion eluded me. I would never feel that release again. Not because the judge was going to kill me, but because I wasn't a shifter anymore. Even if I were, I couldn't outrun the judge's threat of death clinging to my tail.

When I finally stopped, I wasn't winded or tired. The only change was my location and the slight chill sinking into my bones. My mind still whirled with purpose and urgency.

Great. Despite my big talk about trying to pack some life into our last hours, all I could think about was finding the shifter who created the rogue or who *was* the rogue. Now what? The clanless was my best lead, but I didn't even know how to get back to the area of town where I'd encountered him. A prick of fear lifted the skin on my neck and phantom pain radiated from my knee at the idea of facing the clanless stray again. I flexed the knee, reassuring it that it hadn't been torn—or at least, not for long. I didn't know if the clanless was involved with the rogue or just hiding in the human world—a stray like me, someone who couldn't bear Firth and its prejudices and expectations anymore. But he was an anomaly in the rogue equation, and as such, worth finding.

I followed the sound of trickling water to a gated courtyard. I wanted solitude. I needed time to think, to plan. The wrought-iron gate was a cinch to scale. Someone had taken pains to clear the snow from a stone path, so I followed it to a fountain in the center of the garden. Steam rose off the water as it ran down several tiers, splashing gently as it hit the basin. I would have liked it if flowers were around, but everything was dead and covered in a heavy layer of snow.

If you were going to be killed for no good reason, it ought to at least be in springtime.

I took my coat off and laid it on the cleared path before leaping up to balance on the ledge of the fountain's basin. Small lions guarded four points of the fountain, water jetting from their roaring mouths. I stroked the cement mane of the statue closest to me. One of my brothers was a lion. He'd been fourteen when I left Firth. Now I'd never see him again.

I hit the statue as hard as I could, and its face shattered. Water spurted out in all directions, drenching my sweater. I cringed and crossed to the other side of the fountain so I couldn't see the damage I'd done. My hand felt numb, and I stared at the shredded skin over my knuckles. They were a pale, pinkish-white; the nerves still in shock at what had happened to them. Slowly, deep red blood surfaced and brought with it a stinging pain that ran up my arm. Apparently being super-strong didn't make me any more impervious to damage.

Snow crunched behind me, and I whirled around. I expected Nathanial or maybe Bobby to have followed me, most likely Nathanial, but a mastiff crouched behind me. Animals tended to have one of three reactions to shifters: most ran away, recognizing us as a large predator; a small few loved and adored us; and a handful decided we were potential rivals to be eliminated or dominated. Unfortunately, the mastiff was not inclined to love me nor make a run for it. He dropped lower, raised his hackles, and let out a tremendous growl.

I froze. He was between me and the gate. The rest of the courtyard was surrounded by an unbroken ring of buildings. No trees and no high places. A shrub would be no protection from this animal's attack.

The dog took a step forward, testing me.

Old instincts took over. Speed had always been my defense. I ran. No thought, I just ran. I reached the wall of a building.

Nowhere to go except up.

I tried to climb the brick. A powerful force slammed into me, knocking me flat against the building. Pain ripped through my upper arm, and I landed on my back in the snow.

The dog planted its front feet on me and lowered its head, teeth bared in my face. A glop of saliva landed on my cheek.

"Missy, down!"

The large dog closed its mouth, then lay down, pinning me below its weight. Footsteps ran toward me. Words drifting to my ears as the man approached.

"No, I'm all right. I need to report an intruder. Yeah I need a police officer at . . . " A gristly old guy looked down at me. "Cancel that. It was a false alarm. Sorry . . . yes, I know . . . Sorry again . . . uh-huh . . . have a nice night." He snapped the cell phone shut. "What have you caught, Missy? All right, all right. Off, girl. Off."

As soon as the dog lifted its massive weight from my body, I backpedaled. My right arm gave out under me. *Crap.*

The mastiff growled.

The old man grabbed her collar. "Quiet, Missy." He regarded me skeptically. One hand remained behind his back, even as he buried the other in the mastiff's coat. "You all right there, girl?"

A shuttering, but thankfully silent, sob racked my body, shaking me. I couldn't speak, so I nodded.

"Well, you need to get outta here. You got no business here. This is private property. Courtyard's owned by these condos. No trespassing. And you need to get that arm looked at."

Again I nodded, and scrubbed my eyes with my left hand. It came away streaked with thin, red liquid. Taking a deep breath to steady myself, I pushed off the ground. My right arm throbbed in a way I knew meant it was hurt, seriously hurt. I walked backward, keeping the dog in view. My coat was still by the fountain. I grabbed it as I passed.

Scaling the gate took longer this time. I accidentally caught myself with my bad arm coming down, and a jolt of pain shot through me. I hissed, clutching my bicep. My sweater was tattered; the bite had torn deep into the muscle.

"That was foolish," Nathanial said, a breath behind me.

I spun around. "Have you been here the whole time?"

"I followed you, yes."

"Then why didn't you help me?"

"You needed no help. You could have snapped that dog's neck without a second thought." He lifted my arm and shook his head. "Why didn't you?"

"I'm afraid of dogs, all right?"

He looked unimpressed with my great revelation.

I huffed, clutching my hurt arm. "I'm a cat. Dogs kill cats. Like, throw-them-up-in-the-air-and-rip-them-to-shreds-like-a-doll kill cats. It's a rational fear."

"Rational fear perhaps, but irrational reaction. You are not a cat anymore." He ripped the sweater at the shoulder seam and gently pulled the entire sleeve from my arm. The yarn clung to the wound, the pain making my eyes sting despite his care. Once my arm was bare, he examined the wound more closely. "The bleeding has already stopped. I can—" He looked at my face, and whatever he saw there made him pause. Frowning, he took a handkerchief from his pocket and looped it around the wound. "It will fully heal by next nightfall. Come. We know where we should go next."

Chapter 13

"Why are we here?" I asked as we hung in mid-air several hundred feet over the campus of Haven University.

Far below, the odd-shaped buildings squatted like islands in gleaming lakes of snow. Narrow cobblestone streets cut maze-like paths around the buildings; the occasional blacktop visible where newer streets had been added. Despite the late hour, groups of college kids traveled the sidewalks in noisy packs. I clung tighter to Nathanial with my good arm. *What if one of them glanced up?*

Nathanial didn't seem disturbed by that possibility, and he didn't answer my question. He hadn't said a word the entire trip. I was worried about that fact. And ticked off at the worry.

A blob of pastel pink moving out of the subway caught my attention. Who but Gil would wear an Easter-egg pink coat? Nathanial began our descent without warning, and the ground leapt toward me. I squeezed my eyes shut—the whole free-fall feeling of landing was definitely not my favorite part of flying. The wind rushing under me died as my feet touched the pavement. I staggered away from Nathanial, my heart racing. Flying was a rush—I had to give it that. At Nathanial's frown I tried to slow my heartbeat, tried not to waste Evan's gift of blood.

Gil jumped as I stumbled into her path, and then two thick arms wrapped around me. Bobby dragged me into a hug like I'd been gone for several years instead of half an hour. He crushed me against his chest, and I yelped as a fresh wave of pain shot down my arm.

He pulled back, his face drawn in concern. I'd put my coat on, so the fact my arm had been gnawed on wasn't visible, but the smell of blood clung to me.

Bobby's eyes narrowed and he glared at Nathanial. "What did you do to her?"

Nathanial removed his glasses and silently cleaned them.

I pushed away from Bobby. "He didn't do anything."

Stepping back allowed me to meet Bobby's eyes without craning my neck. I'd meant to stare him into not asking how I'd hurt myself, but his right eye was swollen and purple. "What happened to you?"

Bobby didn't answer. He just continued to glare at Nathanial.

I rounded on the vampire, driving my finger into his chest. "What did you do?"

Nathanial stopped cleaning his glasses long enough to meet Bobby's eyes. It was a quick glance, but whatever moved between them was dark. "Bobby would not listen when I told him not to chase after you." He slipped his glasses back on and shrugged. "Searching crime scenes was leading us nowhere. I am hoping we will have more luck using technology."

I wasn't that easily distracted. "What happened to Bobby?"

He backed away and ignored my question. "We will use the computers at the library." He strode up the sidewalk without a backward glance.

I opened my mouth to call him back, but Bobby put a hand on my shoulder and shook his head. "Don't worry about it. Okay?"

It wasn't okay, but I clenched my jaw and followed Nathanial. Bobby fell in step beside me, Gil following behind us.

The library was quiet, disturbed only by a slight hum from the computers and the occasional turn of pages by nightowl studiers. Nathanial paused at the elevator, then indicated the stairwell. We traveled three flights down. The abandoned floor on which we emerged was dim and slightly claustrophobic, with towers of books surrounding us on all sides. Judging by the smell, the books were old, and I hoped the scent of mold was only from the walls.

Nathanial guided us in a weaving line through the stacks until we reached a door on the far wall. He unlocked the door and ushered us in. "We can search the periodicals here."

He turned on the screen closest to him and pulled up the program we'd be using. Nathanial gave us a basic tutorial on searching the periodicals. At first Gil hung back around the door, but by the time he finished, she was leaning forward and watching him carefully. Bobby paced the length of the room, staring at his feet more than the computers.

"Is everything clear?" Nathanial asked once he finished his demonstration.

Both Gil and I nodded then I slipped into a chair in front of a cream colored machine. Queuing the archives back three months, I searched forward. Bobby paced behind me.

"This will go faster if everyone helps," Nathanial said after another failed attempt to get Bobby in front of a computer.

I glanced over my shoulder. Bobby was sweating, but Gil hadn't given any indication the room was overly warm. I frowned. Bobby hadn't had the tutors I'd had growing up.

"Can we access audio or video news feeds here?" I asked, looking at Nathanial. He shook his head. I turned back to my computer. "Let Bobby pace."

I scanned the archives as fast as I could, but Gil found the first and second relevant article. I was sifting through the local paper's archives, and the first two murders, the victims in Demur, weren't mentioned. We were searching different papers, so maybe the murders were featured in hers? Even if they weren't, she had the advantage of two hands—my right arm was painfully useless because of the dog bite, so I had to control the mouse with my left hand and hen peck commands on the keyboard. I collected my first article from the printer and glanced at the one she was printing; they weren't that different.

I passed Bobby on my way back from the printer. He was standing by the far wall with a thick, red marker in his hand. I stopped. He'd drawn a crude symbol a good five times lifesize on a dry erase board. Crude, and wrong.

"You have the lines backward."

Bobby nodded, erasing and redrawing the mark.

Gil, also returning from the printer, peered over his shoulder. Her scroll appeared in hand. "What does it mean?"

Well, at least she was enthusiastic again. She'd basically been a walking catatonic since her spell exploded. I wasn't sure the mages deserved to learn even more about shifters, but she *had* been helping me.

I traced the symbol Bobby had drawn. "It's the mark of the clanless. The top curving line that looks like a backward S runs from the corner of the eye to the ear. It represents water. The bottom line that looks like an upside-down V runs from the corner of the mouth to the edge of the jaw. It represents a mountain. 'On land and sea they are known.' Or some say, 'On land and sea, a face only a fool would trust.'"

Gil scribbled in her scroll then looked up, pursing her lips. "So the clanless are all criminals?"

I walked back to my computer. "Yes, but they are rare. The one in the alley is the only one I've ever seen in person."

"He had a necklace like yours." Gil shivered. "Shifters are barbaric, chopping up infants to make jewelry and scarring criminals."

I looked up from the screen. "You saw a necklace on the clanless?"

She nodded. "It was like yours, with bunches of bones."

Bunches? If the stray wore more than two, he had to have been *Dyre* or *Torin* before he was branded clanless. My hand moved instinctively to my throat and traced the tiny bones. I didn't remember them being harvested, I was too young at the time, but I'd seen it happen to my brothers, and to Bobby. Before I'd lived among humans, I wouldn't have thought there was anything strange about the custom. It was a great honor for the elders to agree to make a necklace for someone who wasn't in line to be *Torin.* Now I had to agree it was a bit of a bloody practice, but . . . "The necklaces are special. They allow us to do . . . things we wouldn't otherwise be capable of."

Gil's eyebrow arched. "Such as?"

Heat gathered in my cheeks. "Mine isn't very impressive. I can— could shift with my clothing."

"Sounds useful."

"Here maybe. Clothes don't count for much in Firth. Being able control your scent—like that clanless can do—*that* is an impressive gift."

Gil glanced at Bobby and his necklace with only two bones on it. He didn't volunteer its use, and I was glad she didn't ask. Bobby's necklace was something most shifters considered a fluke. A natural shifter, a shifter born of non-shifter parents, with a necklace was almost unheard of. But as teenagers we'd traveled to the Elders' mountain together. It had taken two weeks and not a little pleading, but the elders had agreed to make the necklace for him. He wouldn't have been here now if they hadn't. Bobcat was his natural form, and without the necklace he was able to shift only as far as mid-form, never reaching true human form. Only pureblood shifters fully mastered both human and animal forms.

Gil jotted a couple more notes in her scroll. "You were right. This isn't in my books. I can't wait to turn in my report! They might publish

my paper. Maybe they will even teach a class about my study here."
Her smile spread across her face, her eyes going distant.

Uh, delusions of grandeur, anyone?

"The articles we're interested in?" I reminded her.

Gil's eyes snapped back in focus. We compared highlights from
the articles as we found them. Most of the information was the same,
but occasionally a line here or there shed extra light, though most went
back to rave references.

The earliest victims in Haven, the girl at the rave and the one
found in the park, were the most brutalized—the reporter's word, not
mine. I had the feeling the word he'd been looking for was 'eaten,' but
I couldn't be sure. The first few articles indicated the police were
checking the local zoo to see if any large predators had escaped. Of
course, that search turned up nothing, and one article suggested the
police had yet to identify the species of animal used in the attack.
Frighteningly enough, one or two of the 'letters to the editor' claimed
werewolves were responsible. Luckily, those writers were regarded as
crazy.

One of the letters pushing werewolf involvement referenced a
recently discovered body which the writer believed was a werewolf.
With trepidation, I searched for an article on the body. All I found was
a brief blurb about a badly decomposed body found in the woods
south of Demur. I frowned. That city just kept coming up.

Queuing up the Internet, I tapped in "Demur" and a couple
keywords from the blurb into the search engine. Most of the results
were unrelated, but a few proved to be about the mysterious body.
Investigators reported the body to be male, but cause of death hadn't
been determined. Scavengers had scattered the body, and many of the
bones bore claw or tooth marks, some gnawed until barely
recognizable. The links leading to cryptologist sites speculated
werewolves based on fur found under the torso saturated with
decomposing fat. They also stated not all of the bones found were
human or identifiable as a known animal. The links to the skeptics
countered that the fur might have been from a coat, and pointed out
that unrecognizable bones were not good for identification purposes.
Others surmised that the body might have been dumped or dragged to
the same area as a dead animal, explaining both the fur and the
mingled bones.

I printed the reports, though even I couldn't tell if someone had
stumbled on a shifter body or not. If they had, someone in the

supernatural community had probably already destroyed the physical evidence collected from the scene. I gathered my pages and then pulled the periodicals back up.

There had been eleven attacks total, increasing in frequency at an alarming rate. Some of the articles included photos of the women— alive, of course. Most looked like they'd been pulled from a high school yearbook or a Glamour Shots session, but a couple were more natural. One victim toasted the camera, the black-on-white highlights in her hair matching her powdered skin and heavy eyeliner.

Why had the rogue relocated? None of the articles gave me a clue. The paper revealed very few details—police reports would have helped more—but reading between the lines, I gathered the murders in Haven were not immediately connected to the two in Demur. Something about the level of violence.

The final article I printed was about the attack on Lorna, though they didn't mention her by name. I was up-to-date on articles and I still didn't know where to look for the rogue. Now what? I pulled up the local weather station's website to look for a lunar chart to cross-reference the attacks with moon phases. Only a tagged shifter's first shift was tied to the moon, and there were too many to think the rogue had simply gone crazy when the gate to Firth opened each month, but maybe I'd find some other pattern.

I drummed my fingers on the table, waiting for the page to load. Gil had a dozen scrolls around her, presumably comparing the information from Sabin with the articles she'd printed. Nathanial's chair squeaked as he leaned forward.

I glanced at his screen. He wasn't reading a periodical. "What are you doing?"

He frowned, still scanning the document on his computer. "My students had a major report due last week. Several attempted to prove the recent attacks supported the existence of werewolves. I seem to remember one mentioning a survivor." He closed the document and pulled up another one.

"I thought Lorna was the only survivor," I said, abandoning my computer to read over Nathanial's shoulder.

"She is," Gil said without looking up. She set her scroll aside to scribble a note on a print out.

"Perhaps." Nathanial's finger paused on the mouse's scrollwheel. "But perhaps she was not the first. According to this paper, a student from Haven University was attacked, but did not report the incident to the police."

Gil dropped her print out and joined us at Nathanial's computer. Her lips moved silently as she read. The student who wrote the paper heard about the survivor from a friend, who then put them in contact for a short interview, but the paper writer only included the survivor's description of her attacker.

Misshapen, with fur and teeth and claws. She was quoted as saying. *It could have been costume makeup, but at the time . . . I don't know what I saw.*

"That's it?" I asked, scanning over the two paragraphs dealing with the survivor. It could have been a false claim, or exaggerated by the writer, but . . . "Should we track her down?"

Gil chewed her bottom lip. "The investigators from Sabin have nothing about this, but the writer has most of her facts straight in other parts of the paper, so this survivor may be genuine. How could the investigators have missed something this big?"

I tuned her out and leaned closer to the screen. "Did the student provide the survivor's name?"

"Of course. I do not allow unattributed evidence." Nathanial scrolled down to the bibliography and footnotes.

Sharon Hogue was our survivor's name. Nathanial copy-pasted the name then closed the document and logged into a secure page on the university's website. Several clicks later, we were staring at Sharon's personal information in the school's database.

"The address is not far," Nathanial said, shutting the machine down. "but we will have to move quickly. Dawn is only a couple of hours away."

My heartbeat doubled its rhythm, pounding in my ears. This was the break we needed. A witness who'd seen the rogue. Now we just had to hope she could identify her attacker.

Chapter 14

We emerged from the subway on a street crowded with tenement houses. The discolored brick walls sported fading graffiti, and heavy iron bars lined more windows than not. No one had cleared the sidewalk, so we trudged through icy slush, the moisture soaking into the legs of my jeans. I almost cheered when Nathanial pointed to Sharon Hogue's complex.

The security door hung ajar, the deadbolt housing rusted out. A web of fine cracks feathered through the door's thick glass, two bullet-sized holes in the center. Nice neighborhood. Well, at least we didn't have to worry about how to get in the building. Nathanial's ascent of the stoop was more glide than climb as he moved to hold the door for the rest of us.

"Kita and I will need an invitation to enter Sharon's home," he said as we stepped into the dim hall.

"I thought you said there was no truth to that myth."

He smiled at me. "I said you watched too many movies. I did not say they were wrong."

What a distinction.

Uneven yellow paper peeled from the lobby walls, the color likely created by years of cigarette smoke and not by design. Someone had tried to make the lobby more inviting by adding a small potted plant—the dried stem was home to a large spider web. The dimly lit stairwell creaked with each step we took, creating a symphony of groaning wood which played for all seven flights to Sharon's apartment. Opening the door to her floor disturbed a nest of cockroaches. They scurried across the landing, and Gil yelped, jumping backward. The middle of her foot caught on a step. She teetered on the edge of the stair, her arms windmilling.

I grabbed her, dragging her back onto the landing by her arm. She stared at me, wide-eyed. Then she turned and blinked at the narrow flights we'd climbed. Her gulp was audible and her trembling obvious.

I left her in the stairwell.

Sharon's apartment was easy to find; it was one of the few doors still numbered. A winter wreath of twisted brown limbs and white mistletoe berries hung on the painted wood, and a *Welcome* mat with happy faeries sat slightly askew in her doorway

Nathanial pointed to the mat. "We have now been invited inside."

I frowned at him. "What?"

"The mat welcomes all who wish to enter. The very reason I do not own one."

Good to know. I looked down the hall and saw three or four more mats. What would humans think if they knew their friendly footwipes gave monsters an invitation to invade their homes?

The stairwell door creaked as Gil joined us in the hall. She had a drop more color than when I'd left her, but her gaze dragged the ground. "Is someone going to knock?"

She looked up at me. I deferred to Bobby and Nathanial. No one moved. It was too late for visitors, or too early, depending on your perspective. What were we supposed to say to Sharon? Of course, we had Gil. She had a way of making people cooperative.

Still, no one moved. We looked like conspirators huddling around the door.

"Fine, I'll do it." I rapped on the wood.

Silence answered me.

"Maybe she's asleep and couldn't hear you," Bobby said.

I knocked on the door a little harder. A little too hard—the wood splintered under my knuckles. *Crap.* I'd forgotten how strong I now was, and that my knuckles were already paying for my carelessness with the fountain lion. They throbbed with the new insult.

We waited. Not a sound from inside.

I shuffled my feet. "Well that should have woken the dead. Maybe she isn't home."

"Or maybe she was attacked by a psycho and is terrified of strangers, especially when they are literally breaking down her door," Gil said with a sting in her voice.

I frowned at her. Okay, yeah, I should have been more careful, but really, the wood was probably cheap.

Nathanial waved a hand to indicate the hall. "I doubt anyone would open their door to strangers in this neighborhood."

Great. "So what, we walk away?"

"Can you pick the lock?" Bobby asked, looking at me.

I had my doubts. I'd looked at my arm on the subway, and while the wound was pink with healing skin, it still hurt too much to move. Not to mention the fact that if Sharon was inside, she might call the cops. Getting charged with breaking and entering was not on my to-do list. I said as much.

"I can probably keep her calm," Gil said, but she sounded hesitant, unsure.

I glanced from her to Nathanial. He shrugged. What other choice did we have? I dropped to my knees and attempted to pick the lock, but my hurt arm was useless. It just wasn't possible to put pressure on the tension wrench and manipulate the pins in the lock with only one hand. Looking up at my companions, I shook my head. No way could I pick it like this.

Gil tugged on her sleeves. "I'll do it."

She tapped the lock with her finger. Magic coursed through the air, and the lock sizzled. *That didn't sound good.* Oblivious and smiling, Gil grabbed the doorknob. Then she yelped, jerking her hand back.

"Mab's tears." She waved her hand in the air as a red welt rose on her palm. My knuckles and arm throbbed in sympathy.

I glanced at the knob. Whatever she'd done, the keyhole was now melted.

Nathanial sighed. "I will have to buy her a new lock." Ignoring what had to be scalding metal, he twisted the knob, and the locking mechanism popped.

I jumped at the sound and shot a quick glance down the hall. Between me breaking the wood, Gil's cries, and the lock snapping, we had to have awakened the whole complex. When no one emerged from the other apartments, I let out the breath I'd been holding. It was past time to get out of the hall. Nathanial smiled and ushered us inside.

The dark apartment was a mess. Shoes had been kicked off haphazardly by the door, and several articles of clothing had been thrown over the arm of the couch. The coffee table was piled with magazines, newspapers, and old mail, some of which had toppled to the floor below. What really made me hesitate was the smell. Mold for starters, though that was bad throughout the building, but also a smell of decay, like someone had left food out and forgot about it for a week. I glanced in the kitchen. It was surprisingly clean, with nothing decomposing on the counter and only a dish or two in the sink. Sharon wasn't a slob, but she wasn't exactly obsessively tidy either.

I went back into the living room and walked a circuit. Worn paperbacks covered every surface, sharing space with tossed-about clothing. Small, stuffed bears sat half buried on the loveseat, and little porcelain figurines of dancing faeries and cupids looked out of every nook and cranny in the makeshift entertainment stand and bookcases.

Gil padded down the hallway. I followed, though if we hadn't woken Sharon with all the noise we'd made entering, I doubted we could. *Maybe she worked nights?* Bobby or Gil would have to wait for her to come home.

Gil was still several feet ahead of me when she opened the bedroom door. She stiffened, her hand flying to her mouth to hold in a scream. With the door open, the awful smell permeating the apartment washed over me in a new wave of intensity. I ran the last few steps to the doorway.

In the middle of the room, a woman hung suspended from the ceiling fan by a belt noose. I turned away, but the smell made the image of her hanging corpse linger in my mind. I held my breath, then stopped breathing. Apparently I truly could do that. Not smelling the death in the air helped me think clearer. I turned back around and crept into the room. Bobby and Nathanial followed me. Gil still stood frozen in the doorway, wide-eyed. Her face had color now—green.

For all I knew, I was a paler shade of green. My tongue felt too large for my mouth, and I swallowed hard, forcing myself to look at the hanging figure. I assumed she was Sharon. She wore a short nightgown, but she hadn't killed herself tonight, that much was obvious. A large bug crawled over her swollen face, and I looked away.

The room wasn't large, only enough room for her bed and dresser. The edge of the bed was mere inches from where her purple feet dangled. She could have reached it to save herself. Of course, the foot of the bed was probably the platform she'd stepped from after tying the noose to the fan. I circled the body twice before exiting the room.

What were we supposed to do now? Our new lead was literally dead. A thought that wasn't completely mine but triggered from Evan's memories reminded me that we needed to dispose of the body. It couldn't be left for the police to find. They would autopsy it. Science and shifters did not mix. If she'd been tagged, and I had the feeling she had, she would have shifted with the last full moon. Her body wouldn't be completely human anymore so we had to . . . I didn't know how hunters disposed of a body, Evan's memories just insisted that we dispose of it. I frowned.

"What do we do with her?" I had to breathe to speak. I nearly choked before the question was out of my mouth.

Bobby's lips twisted, but he jutted out his chin. "I'll take care of her."

"Do you need help getting her out of the building?" Nathanial asked, but Bobby shook his head. "Well then, unless someone has any last ideas for the night . . . ?" He paused, waiting for answers that didn't come. Epiphanies were scarce standing in the room with a dead woman. "Then I will take Kita home."

His house wasn't my home, but now wasn't the time to point that out. Protecting my hurt arm by anchoring it to my chest, I nodded at Sharon's body. "Shouldn't we try to find out more about her? How the rogue found her and such?"

"We have those answers. There are glow sticks in the trashcan, and there are plenty of clothes that would fit in at a rave." Nathanial pointed to a pile of dirty clothes. "This looks like another party connection."

"She refused to go to the police. Think she left a journal or something with information about the attack? Maybe we should dig around a little more." With each word Gil's face turned progressively greener.

We made a quick search of the house. My mind kept circling back to the dead woman. She'd been attacked twelve days ago, but the only mark on her body was a long scar running the length of her arm. The silver tissue looked long-healed, which would only have happened if she'd been tagged by the rogue. When the gate opened and she shifted for the first time, her healing would have been accelerated. The last full moon, and thus last gate to Firth, had been a week and a half ago. That was more than enough time for a shifter to heal and a scar to fade to barely noticeable. I sifted through the piles of books and clothes on the couch. What would Sharon have been able to tell us?

There was nothing here. I dropped the clothes. I'd been avoiding the bedroom, but it was time to suck it up and venture in again. Apparently I wasn't the only one avoiding the room; we all ended up back at the doorway at the same time.

"Let's get this over with," Bobby said, and headed into the room.

Holding my breath, I followed him. Searching with Sharon literally right over my shoulder was hard, too hard. So, I wandered off into the attached bathroom. It had a cute motif of yellow ducks. The soap dispenser, the toothbrush holder, and the hand towel were all duck-shaped. I opened the medical cabinet over the sink and discovered several boxes of hair dye in blinding shades of orange and green. The woman in the bedroom didn't have dyed hair, but that wasn't surprising considering she'd been tagged. Shifting had a way of purifying the body and returning it to its natural state. I shut the cabinet. The duck motif continued on the shower curtain. Even the clay trashcan had little ducks painted on it. I peeked inside the trash and frowned. Picking up the clay can, I carried it back into the bedroom.

"What do you make of this?" I asked no one in particular.

Everyone wandered over, glad for the distraction.

"She burned a lot of paper," Nathanial said, his eyes sliding up to the body dangling from the fan. "Probably anything we needed was in there."

"Well that's that." Gil walked out of the room.

I handed Nathanial the trashcan and followed Gil out. I found her beyond the door, taking quick shallow breaths. She'd hyperventilate if she kept that up.

"You okay?"

Gil nodded slowly. "I've never seen a dead body before."

"I have, but never like this. People die, but this wasn't natural. Or recent."

She looked at me, and I had the distinct feeling she was reevaluating what kind of monster I was. I hoped the scale tipped in my favor. Neither of us spoke as Nathanial and Bobby filed out of the bedroom.

"I think the night is over. We will meet at the bookstore again? Same time?" Nathanial asked, and waited for nods before leading me out of the hallway.

I glanced back as we reached the door. Gil was already gone; I assumed back to her world by magic. She wouldn't have willingly reentered the bedroom. I felt bad about leaving Bobby alone to get rid of the body. I mean, how weird and creepy was that job? But he was the one who volunteered to be a hunter.

I caught up with Nathanial and followed him out of the complex. We walked to the small alley between the buildings, and he motioned me closer to him.

"Aren't you afraid someone will see us?" I asked looking around. Already lights glinted through some windows. People were starting their day.

"Did anyone notice we were not drinking earlier tonight?" He didn't wait for me to shake my head. "Trust me. I am an illusionist, and this is my best trick."

Reluctantly I stepped forward and wrapped my uninjured arm around his shoulders. His hands slid around my middle and pulled me closer. Then, as if taking a step up, we were in the air. We soared over the city, then over the suburbs. I bathed in the rush of the wind, in the weightless, haphazard feeling. A smile spread across my face as we dipped over the tree tops. After all, the real reason cats watched birds was because they envied their ability to fly. Okay, so maybe they made a fun catch and a tasty meal too, but flight, that was something special.

Chapter 15

Nathanial set me down on his porch steps and opened his kitchen door. Regan lumbered into the room, ready to welcome his master, and an involuntary shudder ran through me. I hesitated outside the door, listening as Nathanial poured kibble into a metal food bowl. *Nothing sinister about that.* Nathanial had said the dog was a big baby. I could walk past him easily, he'd be eating. The large dog plodded over to sniff his food. I took a step back, and snow crunched under my sneakers.

Regan looked up at the sound. Our eyes met for a brief second and I saw, not his apathetic face, but the snarling threat of the mastiff. Fear crashed into me, pushing me toward the perilous edge where rational thought fled.

I closed my eyes, forced a deep breath into my lungs. Had Sharon felt the same wave of fear while facing the beast who'd tagged her? The image of her rotting face filled my mind; her dangling feet swaying behind my eyelids. I choked on the breath I'd drawn. My legs jerked into motion, my sneakers digging into the snow as I ran.

I couldn't get the sight of Sharon out of my mind. Had she thought she was a monster when she shifted? That she was like her attacker? Had she killed anyone? The woods sprang up around me. I ducked under branches weighted with ice. How long after she shifted had she decided death was the only way out? I reached a clearing and stopped, looking at the sky. I wanted to see it filled with stars, or see the moon, but it was covered in clouds. At least the taint from the city didn't reach here. The air and the night were clean.

Nathanial emerged from the trees behind me. "What are you doing? It will be dawn soon."

"Good, I want to see the sunrise."

"It will kill you."

"That's what you've told me." I didn't want to die, but I didn't want to be a monster either. Was that how Sharon had felt? Would I have had the courage to loop the noose, or to take that step off the bed?

I lay flat on my back in the snow. It crunched as it took my weight, feeling like rough glass but not cold. "I think, if I'm going to die anyway, I would like it to be while doing something I like. I've always liked sunrises."

Nathanial sighed and sat down near my shoulders. "We had this conversation a couple hours ago, did we not? You are a melodramatic little thing."

I ignored him and tried to will the clouds to part.

He studied me for awhile before finally saying, "You will pass out before dawn. You do realize I will take you inside once that happens."

I bolted upright. "Why would you do that? I have the right to make this choice!"

"Says who?"

"It's my life."

"Actually," Nathanial said slowly, "More than half of it is mine. I had to give you a large chunk of myself to make you a vampire. It is a feat I may never be able to accomplish again. I used everything I had on you, and I will not see you burn in the sun."

"You think I should be grateful for this?" My voice bounced off the trees around us. "I didn't ask to be an undead, blood-drinking monster! Do I even have a soul anymore?"

"You are defending it from being eaten by demons, are you not? And I have told you several times, you are not a monster. Now, calm down. You will become weak in a few minutes and pass out long before dawn. You cannot play chicken with the sun. There will be no time to run then, or to talk sense into yourself. I will not allow you to burn, and I doubt you want me to."

I blinked at him.

"I hate you." I whispered. "I hate this city. I never should have come here. And I hate this judge guy who thinks he has some right to police supernaturals. And I hate . . . "

"You hate yourself for running away," Nathanial said, his voice too calm, too reasonable. "You ran away from Firth, and you have just kept running. If something scares you, if you get bored, if you become attached or find yourself beginning to trust anyone, you run away."

"You don't know me. Yes, I ran away from Firth, and maybe I've been looking over my shoulder a lot, but I *am* being hunted. I moved from home to home so no one would find me."

"Do not lie to yourself. I cannot count how many hearts you must have broken. You presented yourself as a loveable pet, and of course people wanted you. When you began to care about your surrogate families, you left. Did you ever think about the poor children who came home, expecting you to be waiting for them, and you were not there? How that made them feel? You are so worried about getting your heart trampled again, that you do not notice you trod all over anyone who is kind to you."

"So, what, the judge's death sentence is payback for my heartless crimes and I deserve to die?"

"We are trying to prevent that. As for fault, your arm can be blamed on your running earlier tonight. If you had not run, you never would have met that dog. It will be healed by evening. Can you say the same about any of the other consequences from running?"

I stared at the snow, and he slid closer.

"You have to stop running, especially now, when running is the equivalent of surrender."

"I'm not surrendering, I'm . . . I'm . . . " My good fist clenched, released, and clenched again. I turned my gaze back to the sky. Why weren't there any stars? Not even a single glimmer in the dark sky. I looked down.

Nathanial's hand slid over mine. "You think the judge will ignore Bobby and me if you die before the time limit passes."

"Bobby needs to go home. He needs to be there when his cubs are born. He deserves that." Leaving had always been the only thing I could do for him. I drew my legs to my chest. "I'm already dead anyway. No big loss."

Nathanial's sigh tumbled over the snow, and he gripped my shoulder, turning me toward him. His eyes were tight, his mouth drawn. Emotion washed across his face: anger, frustration, sorrow. I had the feeling it was the first time he'd fully dropped his mask around me. How could gray eyes be so cold and so hot as they swept over my face? His gaze dug under my skin, his lips tugging the world down with them.

"I cannot undo what I did, Kita. You are a vampire. You will always be one. I have apologized, but you know what? I would do it again. So there is the truth. For purely selfish reasons, if I knew then what I know now, I would still do it. You are so full of passion and rage that being in your mind woke me up. I feel again, after more than a century, and it is amazing, so I would do it all again, just for that."

My jaw clenched. He would do it again? To *feel*? Well, I had feelings too. Granted, rather conflicted ones.

We stared at each other, and the darkness hung around us, waiting. He'd ripped away the life I'd known as completely as the rogue had taken Sharon's. She'd killed herself rather than live as a monster. I clenched my fist. It was ironic, her believing she was a monster. Had I known her in life, she would have judged me one as well.

My fist uncurled and dropped to my side. Nathanial's gaze moved to my hand then back up to my eyes. *He* didn't act like a monster, and out of the two of us, I was the only one who considered what I'd become *monstrous*. Still, he'd had no right to change me into this . . . I sagged as I let out a breath I'd barely been aware I was holding.

Whatever he saw in my face made his expression soften. He slid closer then reached out and snatched my hat from my head. I jerked backward, but he followed, keeping me close. One of his hands wrapped around my waist, locking me in place, the other gently loosed my hair from the bun. With deliberate movements, his fingers combed through my hair.

"Stop it."

I tried to stand, but his hand was still locked around my waist. My struggle to get my feet under me gave him enough space to slide around me. Then he tugged me into his lap. His laughter caressed my back as he drew me closer. I squirmed, but he held me tight.

"Listen to the forest," he whispered.

I didn't want to. I wanted to move. To leave.

He didn't let me.

Dragging in a frustrated breath, I closed my eyes and listened. Stillness filled the air, some of it the quiet of winter, but mostly it was the silence of pre-dawn.

It had been a long time since I'd been in a forest. Over the last few years I'd traveled to large cities where it was easy to find lodging and transportation. I'd missed the forest. In the distance, a nocturnal animal routed for food hidden under the snow, and further away, an animal revealed itself with the snapping of a frozen twig. A gentle wind made limbs far above us creak. Icicles rattled.

I relaxed, nestling against Nathanial's chest. The rhythmic thud of his heartbeat pressed into my back, and the forest whispered around me, as if we had become nature's pulse. Nathanial's fingers trailed through my hair again, swiping stray strands across my temple, behind my ear. It was a very nice sensation when I wasn't pulling away.

Slowly, he scooted backward, putting space between our bodies. The loss of contact stung. A sliver of panic wedged itself into the space where he'd been. I started to stand, but Nathanial's hands moved to my hair again. He brushed aside the panic with his fingers as he gently worked at the tangles in my hair. After finger-combing it, he began weaving my hair into a French braid.

Silent moments passed, then his fingers hesitated and he leaned forward. "We will find the rogue tomorrow. We will figure out a way. I will do everything within my power. I was empty before, but now I am happy to have you, Kitten." As he spoke, his lips brushed my ear, sending a ticklish sensation down my spine.

"I'm not a pet, you know. You don't own me," I murmured, but there wasn't much heat behind the words.

"Really? I was under the impression you were *frequently* a pet." His voice held a hint of humor. He avoided the subject of ownership.

What did that mean? He couldn't expect to claim possession of me just because he'd turned me into a vampire.

"Cats aren't pets. They don't have owners, just people they choose to let take care of them."

He tugged me closer to him. His heat pressed into my back, his words sliding over my skin. "Then let us say that I choose to care for you."

The ticklish feeling traveled down my spine again, pooling in my middle. It was distracting, and I was sick of fighting. We could fight again tomorrow. Besides, I didn't want him to stop playing with my hair. Drowsiness, the new herald of dawn, weighed heavily on me, and I surrendered to the lulling and rhythmic movements of Nathanial's fingers. Even my arm hurt less. Above me, a pinprick of starlight escaped from between the clouds. It lasted only a single heartbeat before the sky swallowed it again.

Nathanial leaned into me, the heat of his cheek touching mine. "What are you thinking?"

I turned and lifted heavy eyelids so I could see him. We were so close, his breath tickled my skin. I smiled, but I couldn't help saying, "that the next time you get bored, you should probably buy a TV or something, and leave me the hell alone."

Nathanial chuckled and dropped the braid he'd completed. It had been a long time since anyone had braided my hair. I'd cut it to my shoulders after leaving Firth, so I was surprised that now, braided, my hair hung to my waist.

I stared at the length of braid. Tears rose unbidden to my eyes. I blinked them away. "Nathanial, what if it was me?"

"What if what was you, Kitten?"

I looped the braid around my wrist. Now that I'd broached the subject, I didn't know what else to say. The hush of the forest deepened, as if the snow laden trees were straining to hear me. It couldn't have been me but . . . "Three months ago I was attacked by a gang of street thugs. They were only human, but I was outnumbered. I panicked. It was the first time my claws extended." There. I'd said it.

"I know."

The air in my lungs turned solid, heavy, and I coughed. Twisting, I stared at Nathanial. "You didn't say anything."

He smiled, a smile that hid secrets—my secrets and what else? He gazed at me through hooded eyes, his expression unconcerned, untouched. Didn't he understand what I'd said? What it could mean?

"If my claws can make . . . If I tagged one of those guys, then I might be guilty of . . . And you. If . . . You might shift when the gate to Firth opens."

"Personally, I think it would be quite interesting if you tagged me."

I cringed. The pre-dawn no longer felt calm—too many thoughts swirled in my head. When Bobby and I had visited the elders, they'd had a giant mosaic of a gate illuminated in moonlight. Images of hundreds of spirits swept out of the pale beams marking the gate,, each spirit searching for a kindred soul to share a body with. If Nathanial . . . what type of spirit would claim him?

I banished the thought.

"Someone would have told me," I whispered. "Wouldn't they? My father would have warned me if claws . . . "

"Of course." Nathanial dropped a light brush of his lips on the top of my head. "Let's get back to the house." He stood and pulled me up. "I think I can make one wish come true."

It took me a second to run that through my addled brain, which was getting thick with the coming dawn. He lifted me high enough I could rest my cheek against his neck instead of his shoulders. As he stepped up and took to the air, I marveled at how warm his skin felt. How could I feel the warmth of his flesh but not all the cold snow around me?

It took me a moment to remember he'd said something and then another to puzzle out what it meant. "Which wish? You're hiding a cure for vampirism, or you know how to acquire demon's bane?"

We landed on the back porch, but he didn't put me down. "I was actually thinking about when you said you wanted to wake up in the same place you went to sleep. But, I think it is perhaps too late for that."

I thought I felt the warmth of lips brush over mine, but it might have been a dream, because the world filled with darkness.

Chapter 16

"Kita?"

I slid under the water, ignoring the alarm in Nathanial's voice. He'd gone who-knew-where before I woke up and left me here to wait for him; he could wait while I enjoyed my bath.

Nathanial flung open the bathroom door.

I sat up, sputtering. I should have known he wouldn't knock. "A little privacy, please."

I sank further into the black swimming pool he called a tub. He turned away gallantly, but not before I saw first relief and then irritation flicker across his face.

"I apologize, but I was worried. Regan was wandering around outside, and you did not answer when I called."

I shrugged, which he couldn't see. I was pretty damn proud of myself for letting the dog out to relieve himself. Okay, so I'd run in the kitchen and propped open the door hoping Regan would let himself out so I could explore the house in Nathanial's absence. But, it was still an accomplishment. Sort of.

Clearing my throat, I said, "Unlike some people, I can't fly off. Where did you think I would go?" I didn't wait for him to answer. He probably would have commented on our little detour into the woods last night. "Let me finish my bath. It may be my first and my last."

Nathanial didn't leave. Instead, he walked in, carrying packages, and sat on the edge of the tub. I glared at him and pulled my knees up so I was somewhat covered.

"I bought you new outfits." He set three bags beside the tub. "If you do not like something, do not take the tags off. You can go with me to exchange it tomorrow. Oh, I got you this too." He pulled something small out of his breast pocket and held it out to me.

It was a driver's license with my picture on it. I studied the image. My eyes didn't quite focus. Did he take the picture while I was sleeping?

I read the name on the ID. "Katrina Deaton?"

"I am sorry I had to change your first name, but 'Kita' sounds like a nickname."

"Right . . . I read the name aloud again. I'd never had a last name before. I was identified by my clan, Nekai, but human last names weren't the same. "Why Deaton?"

"That is the last name I am currently using."

I didn't even want to know what that implied.

"Um . . . thanks?" I handed the license back to him, and he placed it in one of the bags.

I waited, hugging my knees, but he didn't leave.

"How did this happen?" He reached into the water to touch a spot on my ribcage I knew wasn't visible from where he sat. "It is the only scar on your body, so logic would demand strong memories tied to it, but I cannot summon a memory of it occurring."

My jaw clenched though I wasn't sure if I was angrier he knew my body well enough to know I only had the one scar, or that he thought I should fill in the gaps of what he hadn't managed to steal when he was in my mind. He met my eyes patiently, waiting. I sighed.

Without thinking about it, I dropped one hand to my side and touched the slick scar tissue. "I don't remember it happening."

The answer didn't appease him. "But surely you know what happened." He frowned at me. "There are so many blank spots. Your memories and thoughts are not completely . . .human." He cocked his head to the side. "I suppose that should not be such a surprise." The smile that touched his lips was distant and not directed at me.

It was my turn to frown, and he reached down toward the ring of pale scars. I batted his hand away.

"If shifters heal so well, what would cause a scar like that?"

"A rogue," I whispered.

He blinked.

I stared at my knees. Shifting healed almost everything. Even severed limbs would move across a room to rejoin the body. Only two things I knew of left scars: wounds inflicted by silver or by the teeth or claws of another shifter in mid-form.

"A wolf from the Risly clan went rogue. I was only a child, and I was in my cat form at the time. Her mate should have dealt with her before someone was hurt, or his second should have."

"Second?"

"Elected at the time she was tagged, in case emotions got in the way of what needed to be done."

"It was his job to kill her if she went insane?"

I nodded. "But he hesitated. He thought she could get better." I rubbed at the long-healed scars—jagged tooth marks that had nearly killed me. "You don't get better from insanity."

We sat in silence for a breath, and then Nathanial said, "that is why you are so afraid of dogs."

My head shot up.

"I told you. I don't remember it happening, and what I have is a healthy respect for dogs."

Nathanial's smile touched only the edges of his mouth. He leaned downed and brushed his lips feather-light across my forehead. I jerked back, but he was already standing.

"Do not soak too long. You still need to feed before we meet with Bobby and Gil. You must be weak after healing that arm." He strolled out of the room.

I rubbed the spot on my forehead where his lips had touched. Why had he done that?

While the tub drained, I poked through the bags he'd brought and was pleasantly surprised by the clothes he'd picked out. In the past, I'd acquired clothes from items thrown away or donated to the poor—I figured I counted as poor, right? So aside from the outfit Nathanial had given me the other night, I'd never owned new clothes. He'd bought me new sneakers as well as a pair of pale boots with fluffy trim; two skirts, one long and the other short and pleated; a new pair of jeans; and a handful of sweaters—but no underwear, again. Was it polite to ask for some? Probably not. Besides, if he wanted to buy me stuff that was one thing, but I didn't want to ask, then I would be even more indebted to him. I fingered the shorter skirt. I'd never owned one before, but without underwear, it was out of the question. I slid into the jeans and then grabbed a sweater at random, pulling it over my head.

I found Nathanial waiting for me in the kitchen. His eyes took me in as he held open the door, his gaze sliding down my body. Heat rushed to my cheeks, and I nearly tripped over my sneakers. That made my face really burn. *Stupid vampire—making me feel all twisty.* I swept past him.

"I expected you to pick the skirt," he said as he stepped out onto the porch with me.

I shrugged. "I'm not into exhibitionism."

His brows knit together, not following, and then his eyes flew wide. His gaze shot down my body again.

I tugged my coat closed over my clothes. "Are we going?"

Without a word, he stepped forward, wrapping me in his arms. Then we were in the air.

Chapter 17

Bobby waved at me from the café. I trudged through the aisles and plopped down in the chair across from him.

The flight into town had been amazing, but then Nathanial and I had gotten into another fight. He'd thought my not protesting his comment about feeding meant I was ready to hunt with him. Not likely. To make the night even better, it was cloudy again and snow had started falling as I reached the bookstore. And just to add insult to injury, Bobby's food smelled delicious, and I resented the fact I couldn't try a bite of it. So yes, I was grumpy and planning on taking everyone else down with me.

Bobby smiled, one of his big, genuine smiles spreading all the way to his brilliant green eyes. He was happy to see me, obvious bad mood or not. I wished I could dislike him for it, but a smile like that was contagious.

"I have a plan," he announced.

I tried not to show my surprise, really I did. Bobby typically wasn't a planner. I was saved from embarrassing either of us by Gil's arrival.

She slid into the chair between us. "What kind of plan?"

Bobby leaned forward and lowered his voice. "There was another attack. Don't know the girl's name, but she is at Saint Mary's hospital in the ICU."

That was great, in a morbid, it-could-help-us kind of way. At least it gave us direction. Gil shook her head.

"I haven't heard anything about a new attack." She wrung her hands together. "The investigators would have told me."

"It was on the news." Bobby's chin lifted a notch. I knew him well enough to recognize the hint of defiance in his tone. He'd discovered a clue; he'd defend it.

"It's worth checking out." My chair scraped along the floor as I stood. "Let's go."

Gil rose, but looked around, not moving. "Where is Nathanial?"

"Hunting. We don't have to wait." My words, not his. Actually, the last thing Nathanial had said had to do with 'stubborn companions.' I headed for the front door, trusting Gil and Bobby would follow. I wasn't disappointed.

"What is the fastest way to the hospi—" A warm weight landed across my shoulders, interrupting me. I frowned at Nathanial, who had materialized out of nowhere. He'd returned awfully quick, but he'd definitely hunted. His skin had more color, and while his features were still chiseled, they looked fuller than on the flight over. Even his gray eyes were brighter, almost a pale blue.

"Leaving without me?" He whispered the question into my hair, his breath trailing over my skin.

I shrugged out from under his arm. "We're going to the hospital. There was another attack."

"I learned that," Bobby said, stepping between Nathanial and me even as he claimed credit for his clue.

Nathanial gave him a tight-lipped smile. "Then we should take the subway. It is not far."

He pointed, and I started down the sidewalk. Snow fell in dizzy flurries, dancing under the streetlamps as we passed. Nathanial handed me my hat, and I tugged it on as the wind picked up and pelted the street with snowflakes, obscuring the road ahead of us.

Behind me, Gil's teeth chattered loudly, her boots crunching in new layer of snow covering the cement. Bobby trudged beside me, looking straight ahead. His breaths fogged the air in front of him, but Nathanial's and mine didn't. *Weird.* I puffed out a lungful of air. It didn't condense. Well, if anyone was really paying attention that might tip them off I wasn't fully alive.

"What are you doing?" Nathanial asked, sliding an arm through mine.

"Nothing." I pulled away, but I was stuck between the two men. What happened to my personal space bubble?

I decided Bobby was the lesser of two evils and walked closer to him. He was trembling, but clearly trying to hide the fact. Shifters don't do well in the cold, or at least I hadn't. Where Bobby and I were born it never got cold enough to freeze. In fact, I'd never been anywhere in Firth that wasn't a temperate climate. I pulled off my scarf and hat and shoved them at Bobby as we walked.

He shook his head. "You need those."

"I can't feel the cold."

"You're trembling."

I looked at my hands. He was right, they were shaking.

"She would not be cold if she would feed," Nathanial said from my other side, and Bobby's eyes pinched.

"Kitten, I told you if you need—"

"Don't you start." I tossed the scarf and hat at him and then altered my pace so I was walking beside Gil. Her lips were tinted blue. I still didn't see a subway opening. "Are we almost there?"

"We were. Now we have passed it." Nathanial whispered the words.

"We what?"

He glanced at me over his shoulder. His expressionless mask had slammed into place sometime after I'd dropped back to walk with Gil. "Shhh. Listen." But he didn't say anything.

Probably because words weren't what he wanted me to hear. Two pairs of footsteps sounded on the sidewalk behind us.

"How long have they been back there?" I whispered, trusting Nathanial would hear me.

He did.

"In this weather? Too long for us not to be suspicious."

"What's g-going on?" Gil asked, her words choppy as she trembled.

I shook my head and motioned her silent. The need to look back itched at my neck, but I ignored it. Whoever was behind us, the wind and the snow were in their favor as it beat down hard against us, preventing any chance of catching their scent. Nathanial made a small hand motion at the next street and we turned. Three more right turns and we'd circled the block. The footsteps were still behind us.

"Okay, so we're being followed," Bobby said. *Like I hadn't figured that out.* "And because of this brilliant let's-go-right-until-we-make-a-circle plan, they have to know we're on to them," his voice dripped with sarcasm.

Nathanial scoffed and motioned for us to turn again. Bobby was right, we'd just made a full circle in the middle of a small blizzard—whoever they were, they knew we knew they were following. I gave in to the urge to look over my shoulder. Less than a block behind us were two figures striding through the snow. I wanted to say a man and a woman, due to the size difference, but I couldn't tell the gender under all the winter gear they were wearing. A woman wouldn't be a hunter, so who were they? We'd been downwind for that last street, and I hadn't picked up any unusual scents. Of course, as Nathanial kept pointing out, I hadn't fed. My nose wouldn't be working up to par.

"Hunters?" Gil asked, also glancing over her shoulder.

Nathanial's hand clenched at his side. "Let us hope so."

Bobby shook his head. "I don't think so."

Gil looked between them. "What's the alternative?"

"Nothing I want to consider," Nathanial all but whispered, then indicated us to turn down another street.

The footsteps paused, then turned and continued to follow. "Where are we going?" Bobby asked moments before I did.

"Somewhere public to confront them, and away from our destination so that they will not know what it is. We . . ." Nathanial stole a quick glance over his shoulder. "They stopped following us."

"Think it's a trick?" I asked, turning to double check that our tail was well and truly gone. What was the likelihood someone who hadn't been following us would have walked in the same circle we had? I was guessing pretty damn slim.

"It is probably safer to assume so." Nathanial motioned for us to turn up another street.

My sense of direction was completely screwed by this point, so it surprised me when we turned onto a busy road. The sidewalks were barren, but the street teemed with vehicles. The citizens of Haven had forgotten how to drive since it started snowing: half the cars inched along at a terribly slow and careful pace and the other half drove super fast as if to get out of the snow as quickly as possible. The result was a lot of horns blaring, screeching brakes, and dangerous lane changes. All and all, I was happy to be on the deserted sidewalk. Gil and Bobby did not look like they agreed with me.

"Can't we get out of this weather? We're not being followed anymore."

Nathanial shook his head. "I want to make sure that is true. We need . . . " He stopped and looked at the face of the building next to us. "This could work for us."

Tacky sign boards and brightly lit posters lined the walls of the building. *A theatre?* I raised an eyebrow at Nathanial, but he walked inside before I could say anything. Bobby and Gil followed quickly, most likely happy to go somewhere, anywhere, warm. Not that I blamed them. I wished it would have helped me warm up too.

I caught up with Nathanial. "Why are we here?"

"Give it a couple of minutes. There is an arcade. Let's wait in there." He led us into the arcade.

Several games featured large guns mounted in front of screens, others had floor pads with buttons players stepped on, and one had an entire fake motorcycle that simulated riding. Everything flashed, or buzzed, or called for players. Gil paused in front of a screen featuring a medieval wizard flinging fireballs at zombie knights.

I put my hands on my hips. "We're wasting time."

"A minute or two more. Here, play a game." Nathanial dropped a couple quarters in my hand. I rolled my eyes but took the money.

I chose a game with an animated dancing girl and a real microphone. The objective was to sing along with popular songs and earn points. Halfway through the first song, the in-game audience started booing and hissing at me and my character blinked bright red. I kicked it up a notch because, obviously, louder meant better where singing was concerned.

Bobby grabbed the microphone from me. "For the love of the moon! Please, Kita. I think they're going to kick us out."

He put the mike back on its holder, and the game cried out as the animated dancer crumpled. *You Fail* scrolled across the screen in large, red letters. Well, that was nothing new. I sighed and glanced at Nathanial.

"Almost time." He motioned us to where the mouth of the arcade met the theatre lobby.

Gil, still watching the demo wizard, didn't notice. I tapped her on the shoulder, and she pressed her lips together—they were almost pink again.

"Back into the storm?"

I looked to Nathanial for the answer. He only indicated we should hurry, but held up an arm before we could enter the lobby.

"Wait for it," he whispered.

A door opened, and an excited murmuring bubbled into the theatre hall. People poured into the lobby: couples, people alone, small groups, and all of them rushing for the exit. Nathanial nodded after the first handful passed us, and we joined the larger mass. At the main doors, people ran for taxies lining the sidewalk. On a night like this there were more people than cabs. Someone elbowed by me, determined to claim a cab. I glared at his back, but didn't dare stop— I'd have been trampled. Nathanial wrenched open a cab door and shoved me inside before another small group could claim it. Bobby slid in after me, and Nathanial after him. Gil took the front passenger seat.

The group from whom we'd snatched the taxi cursed, but the cabbie ignored them. "Where too?" he asked in a gruff voice and hit the button to start his meter.

Nathanial made a vague motion to the street. "Merge into traffic and head north."

The cabbie pursed his lips, frowning. Then he merged into traffic one-handed while he bumped a cigarette out of a pack with the other. Red lights flashed in front of us, and the cabbie slammed on brakes. Only the seatbelt kept me from flying out of my seat. With a curse, the cabbie jerked the wheel. I toppled into Bobby as the cab nosed into the next lane. A chorus of horns sounded.

"So, you folks from around here?" the cabbie asked, as he slammed on brakes again and executed another death-defying cut in traffic on icy streets.

My head bounced off the back of his seat. "Please, watch the road and don't kill us."

The cabbie grunted.

Nathanial reached over to squeeze my shoulder. To do this he had to put an arm around Bobby, who was sitting between us. Bobby stiffened and gave Nathanial a glare that could have burnt through metal. Nathanial ignored him.

"Calm down," he whispered. "Getting all worked up is not good for your . . . blood pressure." He shot a meaningful glance at the cabbie.

I nodded, but couldn't pry my fingers from the armrest.

"This is good," Nathanial said suddenly. "Pull over anywhere here."

The cabbie's eyes flicked to the meter; it wasn't at ten dollars yet. He made a sour face, but zipped out of traffic to idle by the sidewalk. I jumped out of the car as soon as it stopped, with Bobby at my heels.

"I'm never, ever, getting in one of those again," Bobby said, as the taxi merged back into traffic and disappeared.

Gil huddled under her coat. She nodded at Nathanial. "It was a good plan. No one could have followed us through that."

Nathanial didn't say anything, but he smiled as he led us to the subway.

I settled on a bench while waiting for our train. I'd intended to sit alone, but somehow I ended up in the middle of the boys again. I had Nathanial, who sat so still I wasn't sure he was breathing, on one side, and Bobby, who trembled violently, on the other. It was a disturbing mix. Gil was off to the side, leaning on a support column. She had the right idea. I wriggled free of the bench and picked my own lonely column.

"Maybe you should change, Bobby. You're soaking wet and—" I stopped, my mouth hanging open.

Nathanial stood. "What is it?"

Two people I hadn't heard enter the station huddled near the entrance, pretending like they weren't watching me. We hadn't been able to see that spot from the bench, but because of the angle, they would have been able to tell if we boarded a train. It couldn't be our followers from earlier, could it? There were definite similarities. For starters, there were two of them, one tall and one short, though it was the woman who was tall, more than six feet, and the man who was short, only around five-five. The woman smiled at me like she'd only now noticed me gaping at her. They crossed the station.

"Why Nathanial, it has been a long time," the man said, smiling, but the smile didn't reach his brown eyes.

He was stocky, with a military buzz cut. Young, maybe nineteen. Was he one of Nathanial's students?

"I suppose it has," Nathanial said, his voice indifferent, verging on bored. I glanced at him—the empty but calm mask was back. Bad sign. A very bad sign.

The woman shot a look over Bobby, dismissed him with her eyes, and then glanced at Gil. She dismissed her just as quickly. Then her dark, piercing gaze turned on me again. She stepped closer. If the column hadn't been behind me, I would have backed up. It must have shown in my face because she let out a throaty laugh.

"You have such lovely new companion." Her accent was heavy and rough. Russian? German?

Nathanial stepped between us. "Yes, I do."

I glanced at Bobby. He had stopped shivering, adrenaline having warmed him, but he looked like he wasn't sure if we were in danger or not. I was equally confused. My body wanted to fall into a defensive stance, but I forced myself to look relaxed. The tension in the air held a hint of carefully restrained violence, but everyone was still talking.

"We were heading out on the town," the man said. He smiled, but his tone wasn't friendly. "You two should join us."

Well, I had an easy answer. *No way.*. Who were these people?

"That sounds . . . entertaining." Nathanial said, and my jaw dropped.

"Then we should head out right away," the woman said.

"Yes, I insist. It would be like a double date." The man shot a look at Bobby and Gil. "Your friends won't mind, right? Six is a gang, not an outing."

Bobby's jaw clenched and Gil said, "We are—"

Nathanial held up a hand. "We would be delighted to join you. It so happens my friends have other plans." He turned toward Bobby and Gil. "We will meet you at Mary's later."

"We're running out of time," Gil said.

I nodded in agreement.

"We had plans. I'm rather fond of them." I shrugged at the couple, trying to appear nonchalant. "Maybe some other night?"

"Kita." Nathanial used my name like a warning. Irritating, but it meant he had some reason to go along with this. He leaned against me and his words were barely a hiss in my ear. "Please do not be stubborn right now. This is important."

Nothing could be more important than our date with death later tonight. Unless, of course, it was a date with death right now. I looked over the pair. The woman, while tall, was a skinny little wisp of nothing. The man was wider, but neither looked like they would have been a problem. Unless . . . I looked over them again and they regarded me with calm, insincere smiles.

"No. You must not refuse," the woman said when she saw me studying her. "Our Nathanial is Hermit. This is very rare treat."

Crap. Mama Neda had called him Hermit too.

"Oh, I'm sure it'll get the blood racing." I showed some teeth, then turned to Bobby. "See you at Mary's then?"

Gil jerked at her sleeves. "But . . . oh." Her hand flew to her mouth, and she studied our 'new friends' more closely. *Could she be any more obvious?*

Unfortunately, Bobby still didn't get it. "Kita?" Concern plastered his face. Or maybe he did get it. Years ago I would have said you could always take him at face value. I'd changed my mind about that, but sometimes it was still painfully true.

"I'll be fine. We won't be gone too long, will we?" I turned to Nathanial.

The look he gave me wasn't encouraging. He turned to Bobby. "If we do not meet you at Mary's by morning, we will not be coming."

The concern etched deeper into Bobby's face, and his eyes narrowed to slits. He was about to make a bad situation worse.

"Please, just meet us there?" I asked.

He looked away. "Fine, but don't take too long."

"Great!" The man added a fake chuckle to compliment the phony smile. "You know, I don't think this train is ever going to come. Why don't we four take a cab?"

Chapter 18

Besides Nathanial, Mama Neda was the only vampire I'd met, and she'd been insane. Unfortunately, my new 'friends' seemed sharp. They dropped the false-friendly demeanor as soon as we hit the street. They also made no move to hail a cab—not that I was complaining. We walked in tense silence. Our guides—or guards, I wasn't sure which—kept their eyes on Nathanial, tracking his every move. He appeared unconcerned, as if he were out on a casual stroll instead of being led who-knew-where by people I assumed were the vampire equivalent to hunters. I saw Nathanial's apathetic act for what it was—cover—while his mind worked at finding a way through whatever mess we were in. He'd warned me that I needed to see the vampire council. Maybe I should have spared a little time for what was obviously going to be more than a social call.

"Any chance the council will help us find the rogue?" I asked, walking closer to Nathanial. I was taking for granted I'd survive the meeting, but I couldn't consider the alternative.

He glanced down at me then back into the distance. "Unlikely. Their idea of help would be to lock you somewhere they assumed the judge could not find you. We would do best not to mention it."

I cringed. According to Gil, when my time limit ran out, the judge would be able to find me by his mark. He had that whole appearing-out-of-nowhere thing going on, and I did *not* want to be locked away someplace I couldn't get *out*. That just wasn't an option.

We left the retail section of town and trudged into the tenements again. Were we near Sharon's apartment? I wasn't familiar enough with Haven to know, but the complexes looked just as decrepit. As we passed a small side street, something caught my attention. I ground to a halt, breathing deeply. That increasingly familiar animal-but-different scent tainted the air. Nathanial turned, the edges of his eyes pinched. I crept closer to the opening of the street.

"I caught the city-shifter's scent," I whispered. *Finally, something useful.* Now, had the rogue been coming or going? I filled my lungs, hoping I had enough nose to sift through the scents of people who had passed this way.

The woman cleared her throat. "There is problem?"

"Yes. So sorry, but we will have to visit with you guys some other time." I tossed a tight smile over my shoulder and tried to roll the scent through my senses. Damn it. I was already losing it. The falling snow wasn't helping my weaker olfactory.

Nathanial's hand landed on my shoulder. His fingers convulsed, his grip painful. "We will come back to it," he whispered.

"But—"

He didn't let me finish, but turned toward the couple. They were closer now, and not even pretending to smile.

"Could we take a faster route?" Nathanial asked. "We are in a bit of a hurry."

The woman arched a plucked eyebrow. "Anxious to learn fate, Hermit? Fine by me."

She marched us down the sidewalk. I dragged my feet, buying time to decipher as much of the scent as I could before any more snow fell. Time didn't help. The scent had faded, or my weak nose had lost it.

The couple stopped in a dark patch between two buildings. "We see you there. Do not try to slip away." She grabbed the man's shoulder and vanished.

Nathanial wrapped his arms around me without a word, and I clung to him as we took to the air. The flight was quick, over almost as soon as it started. We landed in front of a large brick building trimmed with black lights.

"A nightclub?" We were being politely threatened by vampires because they wanted us to visit a nightclub?

"This club is known as Death's Angel. It is easily justified in being open all night. What, did you expect the vampires to gather at a gas station?"

I blinked at him, and he gave me a tight smile. Okay, so I'd never thought about it. But a vampire nightclub?

We circled the side of the building. The couple waited near the front entrance, the man tapping his wrist impatiently.

"You took your time," he said, and then led us to the door. The bouncer let us in without blinking.

Electronic music pulsed through the club. A woman carrying a tray of Bloody Marys sashayed past us wearing black-feathered wings, a couple of strategically placed leather straps, and little else. Leather was definitely in abundance among the patrons, as were corsets, wings and a lot of silver. Fog machines poured gray vapor over a dance floor that took up a full half of the room. A polished bar dominated one corner. The other corner was set off from the dance floor by a partial wall that insulated the overstuffed leather couches. Every area smelled of smoke, alcohol, sweat, and bodies. The club was packed. All around me hearts beat in discordant rhythms. The rush of pulsing blood roared in my ears. The smell of it, trapped under thin layers of skin, called to me.

I was starving.

My fangs extended and I threw a hand over my mouth. Nathanial turned me around and pulled me against him so his shoulder hid my face.

"I told you to feed," he whispered as he stroked my hair. To anyone who didn't know, it probably looked like we were hugging, or that I was crying.

I pressed myself against his chest and let his warmth envelop me. I breathed deeply, drinking down his spicy, masculine scent. Despite the fact I could feel his heartbeat through his coat, it didn't incite my hunger—my instincts didn't register him as prey. But even with my face buried against him, I couldn't block out the scents of the humans around us, and they were definitely what my new nature considered choice food.

"Get me out of here," I whispered into the collar of his shirt.

"Another problem?" the man asked, standing far too close to my back for comfort.

No problem at all , I might accidentally eat somebody, but really, not a problem. I suppressed a shiver and stopped breathing. Now that I knew I could, it wasn't hard to do. It helped a little not to be able to smell the people. I could still feel them around me. They pulsed with life. Slowly my fangs retreated, and I turned back around. Keeping my eyes to the ground, I shook my head.

"Good," the man said, and continued weaving his way through the crowd.

I followed his shoes with Nathanial at my side.

"Who are they?" I whispered, as we eased around the people surrounding the bar.

"Anaya, and her companion, Clive."

Clive the vampire? Well, why not?

The bar area was packed, and at times we had to shoulder our way through the crowd. The cacophony of heartbeats around me pounded in my ears louder the music blaring over the speakers. Every time someone brushed by, their warmth seeped over my skin and my body cried out with desires I didn't want to explore. I shoved my hands into my pockets to keep from accidentally grabbing someone.

It only took a couple of minutes to navigate around the large bar, but it felt like a lifetime. Between the bar and the area with couches was a small hallway with a sign reading *Restrooms* above it. We followed it to an *Employees Only* door. As soon as the door separated us from the masses of humanity, my hunger stopped fighting me. I let out the air I'd been holding. Now maybe I could think again.

We turned down two more halls then stopped in front of another bouncer. A bouncer *inside* the club? He glanced over Nathanial and me before opening the door and stepping aside.

Large, flat-paneled television screens covered the wall opposite the door. The area between was decorated rather haphazardly with couches and piles of pillows scattered at apparent random. Dozens of people sprawled about, more than could possibly work at the club. This must be the VIP room.

The speakers moaned, and my gaze flicked to the images on the screens. *What were they . . .? Oh.* On the screen, the actress moaned again as her costar's mouth dipped lower on her exposed body. I dropped my gaze. Only then did I notice the uncomfortably intimate positions of the people in the room—and the lack of clothing. Couples were locked together on couches, and whole groups intertwined amid mounds of pillows. Heat crawled to my cheeks.

Our guides stopped to survey the room, smiling. My face burned hotter. Why had they brought us here? I tried to look away, but everywhere my eyes landed people touched and panted over each other. My gaze passed over one couple as the woman pulled back her head, and I caught a glimpse of fangs before she buried them in her lover's neck. He moaned, giving one last thrust of his hips before collapsing on top of her. Revulsion surged through me as my fangs slid out of their own accord.

I concentrated on my shoes. "Please, please, let's get out of here."

Was this what the other vampires were like? No wonder Nathanial had become a hermit.

"I think you are supposed to be taking us somewhere," Nathanial said to our hosts.

Anaya and Clive frowned at us like they'd forgotten we were there, but, thank the moon, they led us through and out of the room. The next corridor was small and empty, with only enough room for yet another door to swing open. Clive punched in a code, then pressed his thumb against a panel beside the door. A small, green light flashed, and a series of clicks sounded as the door unlocked. Okay, obviously a restricted area. Good. Hopefully we were finally getting somewhere, and not just to another sex room. The passage revealed a large, descending staircase. Anaya strolled down it as the man held the door.

The stairs were wooden, but as I descended I could feel a slight give at the edge of half the steps. It felt like the original staircase was cut from uneven stone and the wood had been added atop it later to fix the problem. The effect was precarious, as if any moment the wooden panels would tilt and dump me down the rest of the stairs. I was happy to reach the room below and happier still to find everyone fully dressed.

Two large couches took up most of the space in the small room. Fabric draped the walls, creating the effect of a room closed off with curtains. Five people milled around. Vampires? Probably, but I wasn't sure. All shifters carried some of their animal characteristic with them, usually in hair or eye coloring, but the vampires looked indistinguishable from the human race. *Well, not completely indistinguishable,* I thought, remembering how my skin was now poreless. Of course, since I wasn't hypersensitive right now, I'd have to be way too close to see a detail like that.

"Stay here." Anaya commanded. She pulled aside some of the fabric and disappeared through a door with Clive.

I stared at the other people in the room. My hunger remained quiet and docile. My instincts weren't identifying anyone as food—a strong indication that everyone present could sprout fangs. To be sure, I leaned closer to Nathanial and asked.

"Yes." Nathanial's voice held an undercurrent of tension. "And don't bother whispering. They can hear you."

I glanced up and flinched. They were staring at me. All five of them. I felt like the newest exhibit at a zoo—one everyone was interested in but weren't convinced actually appealed to them.

I shuffled from foot to foot. An awkward heartbeat passed. Two. Three. A woman stepped forward and smiled.

"Nerve-racking being the youngest, isn't it?" She placed a hand on my shoulder. "I'm Samantha. Don't mind everyone. We don't see many new faces down here."

I managed a weak smile. The stillness of the room unnerved me. I found a marble in my pocket and rolled it through my finger tips. Samantha paused, obviously waiting for me to add something personal to the conversation, but I didn't trust my voice not to shake.

Thankfully, Nathanial filled the silence. "You look lovely as usual, Samantha." His hand indicated her blonde hair. "Are you Marilyn tonight?"

"Oh no, I'm the original blond bombshell, the exquisite Ms. Harlow." She swished her platinum tresses and planted her finger playfully into Nathanial's chest. "I know you dislike pop culture, Hermit, but this is history by now. You really should look it up."

"I apologize," he said, but all he really sounded was bored.

Samantha ignored him and turned back to me. "Take your coat off, deary. Might as well look comfortable."

As I slid out of my coat, the tension in the room broke, and the other vampires went back to their conversations. I caught several curious glances from the corner of my eye, but at least everyone had stopped staring. Samantha led me to the couch and motioned me to sit beside her. She pulled my hands into hers as soon as I was settled. I fought not to jerk them away. Her smile looked genuine enough, and I tried to smile a welcome back, but my lips refused to lie. Nathanial leaned passively against the wall. It appeared I was on my own.

"So," Samantha said after a long moment. "What's your name?"

"Kita." I didn't volunteer more information.

She waited, her smile dropping a notch. Finally she said, "So, you caught the Hermit? Not a shabby start for a new life." When I just stared at her, she went on, "I admit, when I first got out on my own I tried to get his attention, but he never noticed me."

I blinked. What the hell was she talking about?

Her smile dropped a bit more. "I mean, he's easy on the eyes, that much is obvious, but beyond that he could have quite a bit of pull in our society if he bothered to play the game. You've chosen your alliance well."

"Nathanial and I aren't . . . together," I said, frowning. "We will be going our separate ways after tonight."

Samantha's smile fell completely as her green eyes flew wide. She dropped my hands, the room deadly silent. "He didn't turn you?"

The other vampires were suddenly in a semicircle around the couch. I hadn't noticed them move. Hadn't heard them.

I climbed to my feet. The air in the room changed, promising the sharp possibility of violence. Samantha stood, watching me cautiously. She didn't seem like much of an ally now.

"You are without a master?" The question came from one of the male vampires.

My attention snapped to him. He looked middle-aged and more dignified than handsome. His eyes slid over the others before settling back on me. I wasn't sure what was going on, but I had the feeling I wouldn't like it. Were we going to fight? His fangs slid out. I dropped to a defensive stance, shifting my weight to my back leg.

That was all the time I had to prepare.

Lightening quick, his hand snapped out, closing around my throat. The speed caught me off guard. He lifted me into the air. My feet thrashed above the ground. I tried to scream, but his grip on my throat strangled the sound.

I angled a kick at his groin, but he caught my foot with his other hand. Any refinement he'd previously possessed was lost from his face as he hoisted me toward his gleaming fangs.

The jerk was going to bite me. What the hell? I ripped at the hand on my throat and wished more than anything for my claws.

A familiar arm slid around my middle from behind. Something snapped three times in quick succession, and the man grasping my throat screamed. He reeled back, letting go of me in the process. Nathanial's arm around my waist kept me from falling. He pulled me in so my back was cradled against his chest. My feet still weren't on the ground.

I chanced a look at Nathanial. His fangs were out, but his face was calm as he regarded the other vampires still in a semi-circle around us, like he silently dared anyone to challenge him. For their part, the vampires shuffled uneasily, their fangs still extended, but no one advanced. It reminded me of animals fighting over a piece of meat. That was an act of dominance I would have understood and expected in Firth, but not here, not from beings I thought so close to human in their behaviors. In Firth I would have backed away. Everyone was bigger and stronger than me, and my choices were to challenge or slink away and hope there would be something left of the meat later. But now, here, I was the 'meat' and had no idea what was expected of me. So I waited.

"I turned her. She is mine," Nathanial hissed. I shivered, and he held me tighter. "Touch her and you deal with *me*."

One by one the other vampires straightened, their fangs disappearing. They smiled like bloodshed hadn't just barely been avoided. Samantha and another woman sat back on the couch, pictures of refinement once again. The vampire who had accosted me smoothed down his jacket with his left hand. His right arm hung funny, broken in several places. He glowered at me, then jerked aside the curtain and fought to hold it aside one-handed as he opened the door. No one said a thing as he disappeared into the hall beyond.

Slowly, the tension in Nathanial's arm relaxed. I glanced up and was relieved to see his fangs had disappeared; his face once again possessed by the passive mask of which he was fond. When he saw me studying him, his eyes narrowed. His arm fell from my waist like he'd forgotten he was clutching me.

I stepped away but didn't have anywhere to go. I felt eyes on me, but everywhere I looked vampires appeared to be deeply involved in what they were doing. Still, the feeling didn't resolve. *Great. How did I get into situations like this?*

Samantha waved for me to join her and the other woman on the couch again. Apparently I was supposed to forgive and forget I'd been attacked moments before. Either that or hide behind Nathanial. I might have, if I hadn't been a shifter before Nathanial turned me. My instincts wouldn't let me show fear. Fear betrayed prey—meat. I didn't like being meat.

I lifted my chin, flashing teeth.

Samantha smiled as I sat down, the vampire I didn't know scooting over so I could sit between them. I could pretend for a little while that these women hadn't looked at me like a prize to be won.

"Kita, this is Magritte," Samantha said, casually laying a hand on my shoulder.

I looked at Magritte, and her smile widened. With her bright blue eyes and blond hair she looked more like a beauty contestant than a vampire. I could easily imagine her with a gaudy tiara on her head saying all she wanted was world peace. I'd seen her with her fangs out, so the illusion wasn't as perfect as it would be for the uninitiated.

"Wonderful to meet you, lovey," she said, and reached out to grab a lock of my hair. "Beautiful job with this. Unusual. I bet you're glad you had it touched up recently. Wouldn't want to go through eternity with your roots showing." Her hand fell from my hair to rest on my knee.

These vampires touched entirely too much.

Would it cause another scene to tell them to back off? Probably. I crossed my legs then reached down to tug on the cuff of my jeans. The movement effectively dislodged both women's hands in what I hoped was a tactful way. I looked up at Nathanial, expecting a look of approval, or displeasure if I hadn't succeeded as well as I thought. He stared blankly in another direction. Why did that disappoint me?

My willingness to ignore the undercurrents in the room faded, curiosity pushing through.

"So, what just happened?" I asked.

Both women's smiles failed. Samantha recovered first.

"It isn't the wisest idea to disclaim your master, especially when you are still fresh enough to have sun on your nose," she said in a tight voice.

"Would he have killed me?" I nodded to indicate the hidden door and the man who'd gone through it.

"Kill you? No. He planned to bind you to him," Magritte said. I waited for her to explain, but apparently she thought I should know what she meant.

"Bind me?"

Eyes were on me again, making my skin crawl. I ignored them.

"Of course. You can't go walking around without a master, now can you?" Samantha sounded bored, and yet anxiety laced her words.

The upstairs door clicked opened, and then slammed shut. No footfalls sounded on the stairs. I turned as a woman stumbled silently into the room. I recognized her immediately. It was the vampire I'd seen drink from her lover.

"Lookie! New gurl," she said when she saw me. Heat crawled to my face, and I looked away. She didn't take the hint. Instead she swayed across the room and plopped down on the couch beside me. "Saw you upstairs. Cutie, aren't you."

I tensed as she reached out to touch my face. She missed and poked Magritte in the eye.

"Ow!" Magritte batted the vampire's hand away. "How much have you had tonight, Jezebel?"

"Not enough," Jezebel slurred out.

I looked between the three women, and then up at Nathanial.

"We can drink?"

He shook his head, and Jezebel gave out a little drunken giggle.

"Nah, I have to filter my alcohol through someone else's bloodstream now. Makes for too much blood in my alcohol system, but it's better than being dry." She wrapped her arms around my shoulders and nuzzled her forehead into my neck. I stiffened, but short of ripping her arms away, I didn't know how to make her stop.

"You still smell like the sunshine," she told my shoulder.

I looked at Nathanial for help, but it was Samantha who came to my rescue.

"Come over here, Jezey dear. I think you're scaring Kita." She pulled the drunken vampire off me.

"You look so drained, kiddo," Jezebel said, and this time when she reached out she managed to grab a lock of my hair, twirling it between her fingers. "Once the council gives you hunting rights, you should come upstairs and feed."

"I don't think I could be a part of . . . ." I didn't know what to say without being offensive, so I made a wide gesture to include the upstairs area.

"Oh, you will get over that soon enough," Samantha said. "You have to feed to survive. It's safer here than on the streets, and the humans wake up thinking they had a good night, but with a huge hangover."

"And great sex, don't forget that." Jezebel tucked my hair behind my ear. "They wake up remembering great sex."

"Not all of us sleep with our food," Magritte whispered.

Jezebel ignored her.

The door on the right side of the room opened, and everyone fell silent. All the vampires held their unnecessary breaths. For my own part, I responded to the abrupt tension in the room with relief. Anaya waltzed out. Her eyes searched the room until they landed on Nathanial. She smiled, and the expression reminded me of a happy crocodile. Clive followed her, looking smug. They didn't say anything, but both sneered at Nathanial before heading up the stairs.

I glanced at Nathanial, but his expression told me nothing. The other vampires looked at each other, and then back at the door. The room's mood hung a moment in uncertain silence. I wasn't sure why everyone else was here. Nathanial and I were obviously in some sort of trouble, but I doubted the others were here for grins and giggles. There was too much apprehension in the room for a social gathering.

Jezebel laughed, breaking the tension. I suspected dear Jezey was frequently in trouble.

The door opened again.

In the hallway beyond stood a tall woman with skin so pale it glowed, even when compared to her white dress. In contrast, her dark hair spread around her like a void absorbing the light. Her eyes were little more than black orbs floating in the pearlescent glow, and her lips a slash of painted red across her face. In a way, she was beautiful, but more than anything, she looked like a specter drawn in black and white with a touch of blood on her mouth. Her dark gaze swept over the room, landing on Nathanial. She nodded, then turned and let the drapes fall back over the doorway.

Nathanial didn't say anything. He came to me, dropped a hand on my shoulder and squeezed gently. The smallest tremble passed from his fingers into my skin. I swallowed hard. Still, he didn't say anything; he just turned and walked to the door. If he was trying to reassure *me*, he'd failed. Was he trying to brace me for what was to come or to buck me up in his absence?

I really didn't want to be locked in a room with all these vampires.

I stood and fell in step behind him.

He hesitated before pulling the drapes aside. "Kita, please behave in here," he whispered so faintly I scarcely believed I heard him. I thought I'd been behaving rather well so far, all things considered, but I held my tongue and practiced being insignificant.

The woman led us down a long hallway. We might as well have been following a ghost, for all the sound she made. I felt loud and clumsy as my footsteps echoed in the stone space. There wasn't a single lighting fixture in the entire corridor. Didn't vampires know that light prompted the brain to produce happy chemicals? On the heels of that thought I considered the possibility that these vampires knew exactly how walking this hallway affected a person, and that anything I saw or experienced from this moment forward was carefully crafted and not at all left to chance. We rounded a corner, and our guide paused in front of two large double doors.

"The council will see you in a moment," she said. Then she waited.

I wasn't sure what to expect. I'd been before the elders in Firth twice, and it wasn't something I would want to do often. The first time I saw the elders in council was during a pan-clan meeting. Most of the clans' *Torins* and *Stregas*, witches, had gathered at the elders' request, an event that occurred once a decade. As *Dyre*, theoretically the future *Torin* for my clan, my father had taken me along, but I was mostly ignored. The second time journeyed to the elders mountain had been with Bobby, but I addressed the elders alone. That had been for Bobby's necklace. I'd been very lucky. My actions had inspired everything from anger to amusement among the elders, but in the end, I won his right to a necklace.

Today's wait felt a lot like those two visits to the elders. I watched our guide but never saw or heard the signal for her to admit us. She simply opened the door in that spooky, ghost-vampire style.

"Council will meet with you now," she said, and stepped aside to let us pass.

My steps were heavy as I followed Nathanial into the room, butterflies lifting my stomach until it pressed against my lungs. Seven or eight men and women stood along the wall to my left, including the vampire who had attacked me earlier. I assumed they were all vampires. They studied us with looks ranging from uncertain curiosity to cautious disdain. I frowned at them as a whole, then let my gaze sweep over the rest of the room. At least there was light, though it came from a dozen or more candelabras located around the room. Like the outer waiting room, the walls were draped with layers of fabric that could have concealed anything.

Four vampires seated around an ornate dark wood table studied us from the very center of the room. Presumably they were the council. Their location screamed dominance. I was surprised to see Mama Neda seated on the right side of the table, her hair looking just as disheveled as the first time I'd met her. She still wore the hideous bracelet Nathanial had given her. Her bloodless lips cracked into a smile when she saw me looking at her, and she fingered one of the orange beads. The man sitting beside her was a couple years past his prime, with thinning red hair combed over his balding crown. He wore a terrible tweed jacket, but at least he looked saner than Mama Neda.

Well . . . who wouldn't? The woman next to him regarded us with copper-colored eyes surrounded by long, dark braids. I did a double-take. No, not woman. She couldn't have been more than twelve or thirteen. What was such a young girl doing at the council's table?

I glanced back to the vampires at the wall. Maybe I had been mistaken? But no, the people at the table had an air of authority and the people on the wall a hint of fear. I returned my attention to the table and studied the final council member. He sat at the head of the table, his chair tilted back, his booted feet propped on the table's polished wood. He looked like he belonged there even less than the girl. I wasn't certain if he was mocking the older council members or not. His hair was dyed bright green and styled into a dozen small spikes around his head. Several shiny piercings decorated his face, and, I realized, his nipples as well, which were visible under his mesh shirt.

I stopped, and Nathanial turned toward me. His expression held a worried warning.

I ignored it. "This is the council?"

"Yes." Nathanial grabbed my hand and pulled me forward. "Show some respect."

"But . . . one of them is a kid and the other . . . " I didn't even have words to describe the green haired vampire.

Someone along the wall made a shocked sound. Okay, so the green-haired guy looked a couple years older than me, but I'd been expecting *elders*. Mama Neda and the man in tweed were one thing, but a pre-teen and a goth-punker were so *not* what I'd been anticipating.

Nathanial's grip on my hand turned painful. "Tatius is an ancient. Now be quiet and come on." He gave me another tug.

I fell in step behind him, wondering how long it took Tatius to do his hair every night. He hadn't been turned with that hair, and from what Mama Neda said, we were stuck in the form we owned when we died.

The vampires to my left murmured among themselves. My hearing must have been suffering from the fact I hadn't fed because the vampires' voices were too quiet for me to pick out any comments in particular, but the general feeling that washed over me was shocked dismay. As we approached, the ancient punk with green hair wore an amused expression. He'd heard everything I'd said. He lifted his feet from the table and stood. The shiny plastic of his pants made strange squeaking noises as he cruised toward us. I was proud I didn't roll my eyes.

"So, the Hermit decided to come out and play with the rest of us vampires," he said, coming to a halt directly in front of Nathanial. Tatius was taller and bulkier, his build more like Bobby's. He looked Nathanial over, head to toe, and somehow managed to loom over us all, despite his relaxed posture. "Not that you play well with others. You're here less than an hour and already causing trouble. Alistair has petitioned the council for charges against you. Said you made that mess of his arm."

"He threatened what is mine," Nathanial said. His voice was calm, but his hand tightened over mine.

"Yes, well, technically not. You didn't have permission to make a vampire."

"It was an emergency. She would have died had I not changed her."

The teen girl lifted her chin. "You should have come straight here after you changed her, and presented her to us," she said from her spot at the table.

"I have just now gotten the chance."

The vampire in the tweed suit leaned forward, his elbows propped on the table. "How long has it been?"

Nathanial hesitated.

"This little chicky was just turned," Mama Neda said brightly. "Mama Neda tended her and left her and the Hermit to adjust not long ago. Surprised she is out and about already. Was afraid she wasn't going to make it, last I saw her."

"And how long ago was that?" Tatius asked, annoyance in his voice. "Tonight, yesterday, last week, last year?"

"Can't say. Time means nothing to Mama Neda. But look at the little chicky, she's so pale; she probably hasn't even fed yet. Mama Neda gave her some cat's blood, but she wouldn't drink much of it. Can't have been long ago." Mama Neda smiled, her dark eyes gleaming.

Tatius frowned. Then his attention landed like a physical weight on me. His eyes were brilliant green and far too old for his face. I looked away. Nathanial drew me behind him as Tatius stepped closer, but after a look from the bigger man, Nathanial dropped my hand. He moved aside.

My gut twisted. *He's backing off? Just from a look?* This would not end well. I glanced back the way we'd come. Vampires stood between me and the door.

Crap.

I stared at the floor.

Tatius's hand closed under my chin and tipped my head back so I was forced to meet those intense green eyes. "So you are what all the fuss is about tonight. What's your name?"

"Kita."

"Kita." He repeated my name as if testing it on his tongue, then he let go of my chin and circled me. "Not as pretty as most of us require, though I'd be disappointed if the Hermit chose as the rest of us would. He'd pick a girl on personality. No, wait, brains. Even worse." My cheeks burned, and he laughed. "See, this would have gone much better if he had asked first, or brought you here, but you both had to be dragged in front of the council."

I hadn't thought there was much dragging involved in getting us here, but I kept my mouth shut.

His eyes slid over me again. Then he chuckled and reached out. "Not much of a chest on you, is there." His hand groped my right breast.

Without thinking, I kneed him in the groin as hard as I could. In hind sight, it probably wasn't the smartest action I could have made, but it felt damn good to see him double over. Unfortunately, instead of moans of pain, laughter escape him. He straightened, those intense eyes locking on me.

Crap. Never invite an alpha to notice you. I knew better.

I had only a second of panic before his hand closed on my throat. The room rushed past me. The draped fabric did little to cushion my head as it slammed painfully into the stone wall. White lights sparkled through my vision.

His grip shifted, his thumb digging under my collarbone as he dragged me up the wall with one hand. Pain throbbed through my shoulder, down my torso. He held me suspended high enough that he could look me eye to eye. Then he leaned in, pressing our bodies together.

"I do like you, lots of spirit. Unfortunately, I can't allow the lack of respect your master showed by turning you." In a quick movement his fangs tore into my throat.

He was being intentionally vicious, and it hurt, but then my body betrayed me, and the pain became pleasure. His lips were like a miniature fire on my throat, warmth pulsing from his touch, filling my body. I trembled as he swallowed, the heat flooding the base of my stomach, traveling lower. Places deep inside me tightened. I really didn't want to respond, but I didn't have much say in my treacherous body's reaction. I quivered, gasping. The fear didn't dissipate, though. Despite the waves of sensation, I was terrified.

His jaw convulsed, and he drew back, releasing me. I slid down the wall to crumple on the floor. I tried to get my feet under me, but the world wasn't quite real enough. Or my bones had liquefied. Blood slipped from the wound in my neck, trickling down into my ruined sweater collar.

Tatius looked over his shoulder. "Everyone out but council members. You stay too, Nathanial."

The council members stood, and the tension reached new heights. None moved closer.

After the room cleared, Tatius said, "She is either completely delusional . . . or she was never human to begin with."

He helped me up. I couldn't have stood if I wanted to, so he had to be satisfied with forcing me to my knees and holding me there. "What are you?"

"Really, really pissed off."

"She was a shapeshifter," Nathanial said.

Tatius lifted me a little higher. "I do like your spirit," he said, then leaned into my neck again.

I waited for his teeth to sink in, but instead felt something warm and wet digging into the wound. The last vestige of pain vanished. He pulled back. *Thank the moon.*

The thought was premature. He hauled me up to meet his mouth. I stiffened in shock as he forced his tongue between my lips, bringing with it the taste of my own blood. My fangs extended as my hunger demanded I find blood, take blood, but the rest of me fought against the kiss. He let me go before I was forced to find out which half of me would win. Lifting his own wrist to his mouth, he bit down. He coaxed a languid drop of blood from the wound.

"Drink and seal the wound," he commanded, pressing his wrist to my mouth.

He didn't have to tell me twice, though part of me screamed in revulsion as my lips closed over the small holes. I drew hard.

No more than a drop or two made its way from his vein.

"Bite me and I will kill you," he whispered.

I pulled back.

He held his wrist in front of me again. "Seal it."

I did. That small sip of blood made me feel stronger despite all I had lost. My hunger faded to a small discomfort. If Tatius had let go of me, I probably could have stood on my own. I glanced at Nathanial.

He stared at Tatius, his face pale, tight. His fangs were out, and he looked dangerous, crazy. He'd been angry earlier, when Alistair attacked me, but that didn't come close to the amount of naked rage his face betrayed now. Tatius followed my gaze and laughed.

"You have quickened our Hermit," he said, scooping me into his arms. He carried me across the distance between him and Nathanial. "How does it feel, Hermit, to rage, to hate, to be jealous, and to have desire? Are you savoring these emotions? Are they stronger than you remember, or are your memories of emotions just dim shadows?"

Nathanial didn't answer. He continued to glare.

"Your proof, Hermit, for all you have believed," Tatius said in a more serious tone and dropped me unceremoniously into Nathanial's arms.

Nathanial lowered me to my feet, never taking his eyes off Tatius. He clutched me tightly, pressing my face to his chest like he was afraid I would be snatched back away from him, or maybe, that I would leave willingly. If I'd been human, he would have smothered me without realizing it. He trembled, his whole body responding to his fury, but as he held me, the tremors ceased until he stood stock still.

"I can keep her then?" he finally asked, and I knew his fangs were out by the slight lisp in his voice.

"For now. I might take her from you in the future, but for now she is yours. Of course, my generosity will come at a cost," Tatius said.

Nathanial tensed again. "What cost?"

I pushed against his chest, trying to get him to let me go so I could see. He clung to me even tighter.

"I want you on my council, and I want both of you active in our community. I have allowed you to slide through the cracks too long, Hermit. You will come when I summon you and you will meet with the other council members a minimum of twice a week."

"You know I have no interest in being part of your puppet council."

"These are the conditions. Accept them, or forfeit her life and yours."

Nathanial's hand moved up to stroke my hair.

"Fine," he whispered, and I shivered. I was being used as leverage. I didn't like it.

"Let her go, Hermit."

Nathanial's muscles tightened for a heartbeat before his arms slackened. I'd wanted him to release me earlier, but now that Tatius was demanding I stand alone, I would have rather stayed pressed against Nathanial's chest. I turned and stared at the piercing in Tatius's eyebrow instead of his eyes.

"You will still owe me a favor, Kita. A very large one."

I wanted to argue about owing someone a favor just to live, but bit my tongue. Bite me once shame on you. Bite me twice? Not happening.

Tatius looked at me strangely, then laughed. "You know, I once ate a schizophrenic who tasted like you. Go away, now. I grant you hunting rights. Go feed. I will expect you both to return here in three nights."

Tatius turned his back on us. We were dismissed, if not forgotten. Nathanial grabbed my upper arm and led me out of the room as if tarrying even a second might change our fate. In the hallway, the ghost-like vampire watched us with quizzical black eyes, but she said nothing as we passed her.

There were now a dozen vampires in the room with the stairs. They studied us with varying degrees of veiled shock as we entered. Alistair stood in the center of the group. He had probably shared everything he'd seen in the council's chambers. Of course, he'd missed a crucial segment. He glared at Nathanial and me as we entered.

"Kita, dear, are you all right?" Samantha asked, looking me over. It was my neck she focused on. I ignored her gaze.

"Fine," I mumbled, trying to navigate around the vampires without looking hurried.

"You got your hunting rights?" Jezebel asked from her spot on the couch.

"Yes."

"Then we need to get you cleaned up and take you upstairs to feed." Magritte touched the torn neck of my sweater.

I glanced at Nathanial for help, but he remained silent. He still hadn't managed to put his neutral mask back on, and his gaze looked dangerous as it slid over the vampires in the room. He wrapped an arm around my shoulders, pulling me away from Magritte's attention. He took a step forward, and the vampires shuffled out of his way. No one said anything until we reached the bottom step. Then Alistair moved into our wake, but he hung back, out of reach.

"You should both be dead."

I glared at him. "Yeah well, you are either wrong, or we scared the whole vampiric council, and that's why they're not chasing us down right now."

A collective gasp followed my words. That shut Alistair up, for the moment, but I could tell he was straining his little mind for something else to say.

"Enough, Kita." Nathanial heaved the door open before my tongue got me in any more trouble.

Chapter 19

"The trail in the alley first?" Nathanial asked as we wove through the restricted area of club.

I frowned. Every second the falling snow could be obliterating the trail, or it might have already. I'd lost the scent when it was relatively fresh. How long had it been since then?

I shook my head, even with the taste of Tatius' blood improving my senses, I couldn't follow a cold trail the way Bobby could. "We need Bobby."

Nathanial scowled. He hadn't regained control of his emotions yet. Dark hostility shadowed his crystal eyes, a possibility of violence turning his mouth hard. I looked away. The man gazing at me from behind those eyes wasn't the same man I'd known the last few nights. The urge to say something that would make his lips twitch into a lazy smile crept over me, but I pushed it aside.

Music poured through the club. I kept my head down as we passed through the crowded rooms, but my hunger didn't surface as it had earlier. Not that I was complaining, but it struck me as strange. Apparently Tatius's blood was potent. All it had taken was a drop or two. Amazing.

"I think I'll start dinning on vampires," I said once we were outside the club.

Nathanial's gaze cut into me. "Do not drink other vampires' blood. Particularly if they have recently taken yours. If they are powerful, and you get enough of their blood in you, they can bind you."

I'd been joking, but . . . Magritte had said something about binding. And about masters. "You have given me *your* blood."

He frowned and tugged me into his arms. Wind roared by my ears as he took to the air. I scrambled for a better hold on him. He was avoiding the subject He touched down in an alley across from the hospital, but he didn't release me.

"You were bound to me when I turned you." His lips pressed the words into my hair. "That is the nature of a master and companion bond, but Tatius is old enough and strong enough to break our bond and bind you to himself."

A chill crawled down my spine. I shook my head. I had too much to worry about tonight without considering vampiric bonds. I backed out of his arms.

"Speaking of Tatius . . .I noticed you didn't exactly jump to my defense when he tried to kill me."

"He could not have killed you simply by draining your blood. He would have used the dagger on his thigh."

I hadn't noticed the dagger. "And would you have stood there and watched that too?"

"No, Kitten. Then I would have fought him, and you and I would both have died."

"Oh." I looked away. What was I supposed to say to that? *Thanks* didn't cover it. "We should find Bobby and Gil."

I started for the street, but he stopped me with a hand on my shoulder. I hated that I was getting used to him doing that, as if his touch were somehow expected. I turned. His eyes were still shadowed, his expression slightly raw, but his emotions were more hidden than before. A stranger might not even notice. But I wasn't a stranger anymore.

"We're on a tight schedule, remember?" I tried to step out of his grasp.

He didn't let go.

"You told Samantha you anticipate us going separate ways after tonight."

I shrugged. "We have to live through tonight first."

"You cannot leave alone. If you did not notice, a young vampire without a master is anyone's meat. Every inch of known land is charted as territory for some vampire somewhere. There is nowhere you can run or hide. You are mine, I will watch over you until you are stronger, but you cannot run off."

"I'm not a possession, nor am I your mate. You hold no claim over me."

"Kita, I am trying to protect you. Not date you. I have seen your disregard for other's hearts. I would not choose to trust you with mine."

His hand dropped, releasing me, and he swept out of the alley.

I watched his retreating back. He wouldn't choose . . . Why did those words make my stomach hurt? I opened my mouth to call him back, but my tongue felt heavy, clumsy. My jaw snapped closed. He was almost across the street already.

I ran to catch up, reaching him as the doors to the hospital lobby slid open.

Bobby sat alone on a bench by the door. He jumped to his feet as we entered, relief spilling over his face. The relief slipped away just as quickly, his eyes narrowing, his gaze fixed on my neck. I touched the badly torn collar of my turtle neck. I'd forgotten about it. I pushed the collar back in place and the shoulder Tatius had gripped protested the movement with a surge of pain. Bobby didn't miss my grimace. He glared at Nathanial.

"Why is she hurt?"

"She is fine," Nathanial said before I could answer.

I shot him a dirty look.

Bobby's concerned eyes narrowed, and he reached for my collar. After the night I'd had, with everyone going for my throat, I wasn't up for anyone reaching for me. I stepped back, pulling down the collar in the process. I had the distinct feeling there were no marks left, but I wasn't positive until the confusion flowed across Bobby's face. He leaned in to study my neck like I was somehow hiding the wound.

"We had a bit of a run in with some vampires. I'm fine." I looked around the lobby. "Where is Gil?"

"She said she had an idea and then disappeared."

"Did you two see the victim first?"

He shook his head, and my stomach twisted. How were we supposed to get into the ICU without Gil doing the magic thing on the receptionist? Nathanial seemed to realize the problem at the same time.

"I can hide us behind an illusion," he said, nodding us toward the stairwell. "Bobby, you will need to cause a distraction so Kita and I can see the victim."

"No way." Bobby glared at Nathanial's back. "Kita comes back injured every time you leave me behind."

Nathanial ignored that statement, but I had to admit there was some truth in it. Though, if I were being fair, I got myself into trouble that couldn't be laid at Nathanial's feet. We exited the stairs on the same floor Gil had taken us to a couple nights prior.

Despite his protests, Bobby followed. Nathanial hesitated at the door of the ICU and glanced down the hall. It was empty. Even so, he kept his voice low. "Creating a moving illusion to cover all three of us is not feasible. Besides, we will need the ICU door open. If I open it, people will notice and focus on that spot. The attention might break through my illusion. If you open the door, which gives them something different as their focus, Kita and I will be able to slip by unnoticed."

Bobby didn't like being left out, that much was obvious, but he would resign himself to being a decoy if he thought it was truly important. "What do I have to do?"

Nathanial explained his plan. He and I would disappear, Bobby would lead us into the waiting room then create the distraction and open the ICU door. We'd come back to get him after we'd talked to the victim. Easy. With my luck, too easy to actually work. I sighed.

Nathanial motioned me closer. When I wrapped my arms around his neck, my shoulder cried out and I fought not to wince again. Nathanial scooped me up so one arm was under my knees and the other around my back. The movement caused my shoulder to shift again, and I sucked in a pained breath.

Bobby scowled, then suddenly he blinked, squinted, and scanned the hall. "Amazing. I guess you weren't lying. I'm going to open the door now, so if you are in the way . . ." He carefully opened the door as if he were afraid he would hit us with it.

I cringed. If he didn't act more natural than this, we weren't going to make it into the ICU—he was going to get himself locked up in the loony bin before he made it across the waiting room.

Nathanial carried me out of the hall quickly, but Bobby kept standing there, holding the door. Finally he stepped through the threshold. At least he didn't announce he was going to shut the door. Maybe we would make it.

The same red head sat behind the counter as the last time we were here. She looked up at Bobby, her gaze passing through Nathanial and me, then her attention slid back to her computer. If she recognized Bobby, her dismissal gave no indication of it.

Bobby made a beeline for the ICU door. He ignored the receptionist as he rushed around her desk, and then he gave the door a good push. It creaked, but didn't budge. The receptionist looked away from the data on her screen and scowled at him.

"The next visiting hour isn't until nine a.m. I'm sorry, you'll have to wait."

Bobby frowned at the air about three feet to my right and gave it a questioning look. I glanced at Nathanial. He shrugged. Nothing we could do but wait it out. Bobby finally stopped trying to communicate with the empty space to our right and gave the receptionist a sly smile.

I'd never seen Bobby flirt before, but he laid it on thick. Within a couple of minutes he had her blushing and giggling. He leaned onto her desk, and 'accidentally' hit the button that caused the doors to slide open. Of course he made no move to walk through them, so she had no problem with this.

Nathanial and I slipped through the gaping doors completely undetected.

෨ • ෬

We hadn't considered that we'd have to find the right room, or at least, I hadn't. Theoretically this shouldn't have been a problem, I mean, how many mauling victims could the city have? But most of the doors were shut, and opening them would have made us visible. Luckily the charts were on the outsides of the rooms.

I ignored the rooms with thick charts; the patient we were looking for hadn't been here long, hopefully her chart would be relatively thin. Of course, depending on how much surgery she'd needed, I could have been way off base. I saw Lorna's name on one of the charts. Good to know she was still alive, even if alive in critical condition.

Nathanial went rigid a few doors from Lorna's room. I had to crane my head around to read the chart he was staring at. *Candice Mathews* was printed in small letters across the top. There could have been hundreds of Candices in Haven, and this particular one could be an old lady with heart failure, but a sinking feeling in the pit of my stomach told me that wasn't the case. Nathanial glanced up and down the hall, readjusted his hold on me, then pushed through the door.

He lowered me to the floor as soon as the door shut behind us. The patient was hidden behind a privacy curtain, but the beeping of monitors and the whooshing of a breathing machine permeated the room. Nathanial stepped around the curtain instead of pulling it back, and I followed him. On the other side, a round, bruised face with a little, turned-up nose and blond curls slept fitfully on an uncomfortable-looking pillow.

Candice had been kind to me, had tried to befriend me, even if she had been after Nathanial. I stared in sick shock at all the little tubes leading into her. She looked so small and helpless, not at all like the exuberant girl we'd left at the bar last night. That thought brought me up short. We *had* left her in the bar last night, all alone and working on drunk, but at a bar and not a rave. The rogue had been picking up women at raves. Why had his pattern changed?

Because he knew what we'd learned only last night, from Candice's DJ. That there were no raves right now, or in the near future.

A bar or club was a good alternate spot to find people of impaired judgment. He must have picked up Candice after we left. Guilt settled in my gut. If we hadn't asked to meet her friend, she wouldn't have been in the bar in the first place.

I approached the side of the bed. The red streaks she'd swiped into her bangs hung over her swollen eyes, a strange contrast to her bruised face. Why that bar? Why had the rogue picked *her*? I reached out to wipe the bangs aside so they wouldn't cover her eyes when she opened them, but Nathanial's arms wrapped around my waist, drawing me back.

"Wha—"

He pressed two fingers over my mouth as the door to the room opened. I went so still I stopped breathing. *Crap.* We were stuck between the bed and the curtain. Nathanial dragged me closer to the wall as a young nurse in salmon-colored scrubs rounded the curtain. She didn't scream, so apparently we were invisible again. She hummed as she checked Candice's vitals and wrote the results in her chart.

"Keep fighting," she whispered to Candice's prone figure.

How bad was she? How close to not making it? The need to ask burned my throat, and I bit my lips.

I looked up at Nathanial. He wasn't watching the nurse, but staring at Candice, his face lacking even a speck of legible emotion. I'd expected sorrow or anger, but he stared at Candice and there was nothing. His face was blank, his eyes cold, empty. He noticed me watching him, and turning, studied my face like I would quiz him on it later. Tension crept over his features. The rawness I'd seen when we left the council claimed his face again as the emptiness slipped away. It hurt to look at, but the only other thing to focus on was Candice's broken body.

The nurse wouldn't leave. She kept humming. Seconds dragged by. Nathanial's fingers dug into my waist. I closed my eyes to escape what I saw in his eyes. The nurse reached for one of the machines near the head of the bed, her heat filling the space between her arm and my face. I leaned against Nathanial's chest, creating an extra inch of space between the nurse and me.

As I settled against him, Nathanial's near painful grip on my waist slackened, some of the rigidity flowing out of him. *Curious.* I slid my hands under his coat, wrapping my arms around his waist. A breath slipped from his lips, dancing through my hair and tickling my ear. He relaxed against me.

I was torn between the desire to push away and the need to say something, though I wasn't sure what. The nurse's presence prevented either action.

Through slitted eyes I saw her disappear around the curtain, then the door opened and shut with a quiet swish. I dropped my arms, but Nathanial didn't move. I pushed back, pressing myself against the wall so I could look at him. There was nothing cold about his gray eyes now. One of his hands left my waist. It hung an inch from my face, then, feather-light, his fingers trailed along my jaw. My heart slammed against my chest. His lips parted, but he said nothing as he leaned closer. I didn't dare breathe. I wasn't sure what I wanted or why. Then his body suddenly wasn't there anymore.

I blinked at the empty space in front of me. Nathanial was on the other side of the bed, his back toward me as he peered out the window. Too many of my racing heartbeats flew by as I stood there, my legs unsteady beneath me. Heat rushed to my cheeks.

When Nathanial turned back around, he didn't look at me, but studied Candice's broken form again. His face was calm now, completely in control, with none of the heat it held a moment before or the empty blankness from earlier.

I took a couple of deep breaths and tried to feel half as calm as he looked, but I'd never been good at being calm. I wrapped my arms across my chest and paced at the edge of the curtain. "She's drugged. Heavily. Now what?"

"We fish for information." He sat down on the edge of Candice's bed and lifted the hand that wasn't sealed in a cast. "See how her eyes are rolling under their lids, and how she keeps twitching. She must be dreaming."

I watched for a moment, confused, until I realized his intent. "You can't be serious. She's three inches from death. You'll kill her."

"She will survive this, hopefully it will not take much, but if we do not find some clue about the rogue, the rest of us will not survive the night." He turned her hand over so her palm was facing up, then he sank his fangs into her wrist.

I watched in disgusted fascination, my own fangs extending. The moment Nathanial's fangs pierced her flesh, she stilled, her nightmares ceasing. I waited. I tried not to count the heartbeats that passed. Seconds dragged on. The machine beside Candice's head lost its steady beep.

Crap . . . I shook Nathanial's shoulder. He didn't respond. Aside from his throat convulsing as he swallowed, and the rigidity of his posture, he could have been asleep. "Nathanial."

Not even a twitch.

He'd stop, wouldn't he? That first night, he'd said the drugs in my system had confused him—Candice had way more drugs in her body than I'd had.

The mechanical beeping became more erratic. What had he done to make me stop? Pressed on my eyes. Closed off my throat. I ran behind him, but as I grabbed for his face, his hands locked around my arms.

I froze.

Candice's hand fell to the bed, but Nathanial didn't release me. I couldn't see his face, and his vice like grip on my arms kept me locked behind him. His lips slid over my right palm and up to my wrist. His fangs pressed against my flesh, and I winced, waiting to feel the sting as they pieced my skin.

They didn't. Nathanial's breath beat against my wrist, quick, short breaths. Strange for someone who didn't need to breathe. His grip pinched, but wasn't truly painful.

My heart raced, but I forced my body to remain still. I didn't know about vampires, but scared and injured shifters breathed in the scent of mates, siblings, friends—anyone who could help them calm themselves, to keep control. Nathanial's breathing slowed, and his fingers lifted one at a time from my arms like he was prying himself off. He didn't move as I backed away. I circled the bed, putting it between us.

Nathanial's irises were black with only the palest sliver of gray around the rims. He didn't look at me, but stared at his own hands. I looked away, letting him deal with whatever emotions gripped him.

I needed something else to look at. Had Nathanial remembered to close the bite on Candice's wrist? I searched out her hand on the blanket. Not only were there no fang punctures, but some of the scrapes and lacerations in the area had disappeared as well.

"Can we heal any wound?" I asked, staring at her arm.

Nathanial didn't answer. He blinked rapidly, like he was trying to wake himself. His hands trembled, and he nearly fell when he tried to stand. Over his base scent, he smelled of Candice, including the acrid scent of drugs. He took an unsteady step forward and ended up leaning against the wall.

"Are you all right?"

He nodded. "Give me a moment to work the drugs in her system out of mine."

I circled the room, trying not to act too anxious. "Did you find anything?"

Nathanial nodded. "A face, no name. I will show you outside." He stumbled around the curtain, then paused and leaned heavily on the door.

He closed his eyes. When he opened them again, his pupils were closer to normal size. He took a step toward me, and it was steady. He scooped me into his arms, and I yelped in surprise, my shoulder protesting. He frowned but didn't say anything as he carried me across the room.

"How are we going to get the main door open again?" I asked. His frown grew and he turned, scanning the room. I followed his gaze to the window. "Are you thinking what I think you are?"

He dropped me gently to my feet and walked to the window. It wasn't meant to be opened. He snapped the locked latch that secured it, then stood there, silently assessing.

"The window is too small for me to carry you out. We will have to deal with the chance of being seen," he finally said.

I moved closer and peered out. We were about eight floors up, above a black-topped parking lot.

"There's a ledge. I could climb out first and wait for you." I pointed to the narrow lip under the window.

"It is too dangerous. What if you slipped and I could not catch you fast enough? Your body can heal a lot, but a fall like that could kill you."

"I'm a cat. Do you have any idea how many windowsills I've slept on? I won't slip."

Nathanial frowned at me, weighing the options. He turned back to the window and stared at it for a long time before nodding.

"Fine, but I will go first." He popped the screen off and pushed it to the side. The wind caught it and it sailed out of sight. Nathanial grimaced and faced me once more. "Count to ten before following me out."

I nodded impatiently and he vanished. One minute he was right in front of me, and the next he was gone. Now I knew how Bobby felt. I suppressed a shudder and started counting. I'd reached four when the door opened. I froze. The curtain hid me from sight, but not for long. I all but jumped though the window.

Wind and snow ripped into me. My right foot lost its purchase. I hadn't anticipated the ledge being covered in ice. Grabbing the frame, I held myself steady. My shoulder cried out, and I bit my lip and swallowed a scream.

The nurse in salmon scrubs was rounding the curtain. If she looked up she would see me on the ledge. I looked around. There was no sign of Nathanial, though that didn't surprise me. I glanced back at the nurse; she rubbed her arms against the chill, but she hadn't noticed the open window.

Something rushed into me, and my feet lifted off the ledge. I clung to Nathanial's now visible shoulders and twisted my head so I could see into the hospital room. The nurse finally noticed the window and walked up to it. She stuck her head out and glanced around. Even though I was sure we were invisible, I still cringed as her eyes passed over me, but she looked right though us. Clearly confused, she tugged the window closed. She stared at Candice's unconscious form then back at the window.

Shaking her head, the nurse retrieved her stethoscope from where she'd forgotten it during her first visit. She shot one more skeptical look at the window, then walked out. I breathed again for what felt like the first time in an hour. I was still clinging tightly to Nathanial, but we weren't moving. He was watching me.

"What?" I asked, trying to loosen my grip without actually endangering my hold.

"Some cat-like balance you demonstrated back there."

"Hey, the ledge was frozen." I wasn't being defensive, really. "Let's get out of here."

Laughter rumbled silently in Nathanial's chest as we floated to the ground.

భ • ఎం

Once away from the window, it was a simple thing to fly down and reenter the hospital. We found Bobby still chatting up the very happy-looking receptionist and reclaimed him with a nod. The look of relief on his face as he turned his back on the redhead and left her was so genuine that I nearly laughed.

"Tell me you guys learned something useful," Bobby said wearily, as we walked out of the room.

"We discovered that you flirt. Where did you pick that up?"

Bobby shrugged. "Daytime television. I mentioned TV was an addictive thing, didn't I?"

"We may have found something very useful," Nathanial said, his voice oddly guarded. "Kita has met the guy who attacked Candice."

"I have?"

Bobby arched a brow. "Candice. The girl from last night?"

Nathanial nodded and grabbed my elbow, forcing me to continue walking. "I ran across the same face in your memory, Kita. Brief, but recent."

I tried to remember having ever picked up the scent of a city-shifter before, but I'd only learned what to look for the night before. If I'd run across it before then, the scent hadn't been significant enough to remember.

"Well, what did he look like?"

Nathanial shook his head. "Wait until we get outside. I will pass the image to you."

Bobby stopped and regarded Nathanial with another raised eyebrow. "How?"

"Outside." Nathanial said, then wouldn't say anything more until the hospital door closed behind us.

Chapter 20

"You've got to be kidding me."

Nathanial shook his head, a frown tugging his lips down. I paced in front of him. He wanted me to release my fangs? I rolled a marble between my fingers. I was pretty sure my fangs had a mind of their own. I paced the width of the alley. The tall buildings huddled close around us, providing little protection from the snow, and judging by the smell, someone had used this alley as their personal portable potty recently. It wasn't a place I wanted to linger. And it definitely wasn't a place I wanted to do anything that involved my fangs. Especially not in front of Bobby. Or ever, but I was running out of options.

I stopped in front of Nathanial. He stood there with his hand extended but made no other move. Reluctantly, I took his hand. He squeezed my fingers gently before pulling me forward. His other arm wrapped around my waist, dragging me closer. My heart thudded in my chest, only partially from nerves over the blood thing. Phantom fingers traced my jaw, the memory making my face burn.

"Let your fangs out," Nathanial whispered.

"I can't."

"Then we must excite your hunger."

Nathanial lifted his hand toward his mouth, but I caught it halfway and glanced over my shoulder at Bobby. I really didn't want Bobby to see me bite anyone. His opinion of my feeding off Evan was based solely on the result, not on having to witness the event.

Nathanial's eyes followed my gaze. "Bobby, could you keep watch at the mouth of the alley? If anyone seems too interested, give us a warning."

Bobby crossed his arms over his chest. "I think I'll stay here."

Nathanial shrugged, then bit into the meaty part of his hand. I tried to turn away, but his arm around my waist stopped me. He shoved the bleeding hand in my face. Pressure built in the roof of my mouth as my fangs slid downward. He might not normally trigger my prey instincts, but blood was blood. I grabbed his hand, sucking down the slowly pooling heat.

"You need to bite me," he whispered. "Your fangs have to be inside someone to access their memories."

His arm circled tighter around me, drawing me fully against his body. I readjusted my grip on his hand, looking for a better angle, and my fangs brushed his flesh. His breath hitched. I rolled my eyes up so I could see his face, and pressed my fangs against his skin. His heart raced, the beat pounding a rhythm in both our bodies. I slid my fangs into his flesh. He shivered, the movement running through his body and into mine. His head rested against the brick wall, his eyes fluttering closed.

Then his memories crashed down on me.

Over three centuries of random moments in his life bombarded me, but the image he wanted me to find, a memory that wasn't his, pushed through the others. A man offering to drive a very drunk Candice home, that image came whole and complete. The details flooded my mind too quickly for me to analyze them individually, but I had them all. He must have been concentrating on them. I hadn't known it worked that way.

I pulled back as soon as I had the whole memory. My body didn't want to; Nathanial's blood sent warmth rushing through me, but my head hurt from trying to cope with not just Candice's memory but also the great weight of Nathanial's memories, the fragments that did sneak through. I barely remembered to lick the wound closed before untangling myself from his arm and stepping backward. Nathanial's eyes fluttered, and when he finally managed to open them, they were glazed.

Bobby shuffled behind me and I twisted around. I'd forgotten he was still watching. I cringed, expecting Bobby to be staring at me in horror. He wasn't. His face held unbridled fury, all of it aimed at Nathanial.

"You didn't tell me it was like that," he whispered. Rage washed out of him in waves. No fear, just prickly anger.

I rocked back on my heels, rubbing my arms against the sensation. "Like what?"

"He looked like . . ." His hands balled into fists, and he paced across the alley.

Each of his footsteps echoed loud in my head, stomped down my spine. *He looked like what?* I glanced at Nathanial. He'd snapped out of his daze, but his pale skin was slightly flushed, his lips parted. He watched me with warm, gray eyes, and for half-a-heartbeat I thought he would reach for me, but he crossed his arms behind his back, trapped them against the wall.

I looked back at Bobby.

"He reacted like you two were *mating*," he whispered. "Is it always like that?"

Heat rushed to my cheeks. All and all, that had probably been rather tame for taking blood. Nothing compared to what I'd seen Jezebel do, or even as intimate as I'd done to Evan. I wanted to tell him *No*, but the true answer was *Yes,* and sometimes it was worse, or maybe better, depending on your perspective. For some psychotic reason it felt really, *really*, good when a vampire bit you. Finally I didn't answer at all, and maybe that was answer enough, because Bobby looked away from me.

"Kita," Nathanial began. "The man with Candice."

I nodded and forced myself to mentally replay the memory.

I'd drunk too much. My head felt heavy. A guy had been buying me drinks, too many of them.

He wasn't my type. His hair was shaved, only fuzz covered his scalp and he had an awful goatee, but nice body. Ripped. He was funny.

It was late. My eyes were heavy. My stomach burned. I stumbled on the stairs. Yes, a ride home would be good. The room spun. He helped me into a car.

Where was I? Everything was fuzzy, unconnected. I struggled as a hand reached out. My arm snapped. Pain shot through me, made me gag. But no, I couldn't gag, cloth was in my mouth. Tears burned my raw eyes. I'd been crying a long time. New pain ripped along my thigh, like being flayed.

A face in front of me wasn't human. I screamed into the gag. Fur, I felt fur, and it confused me.

No, it confused Candice. I understood the fur quite well. I resurfaced from her memory, shaking. I sank into the snow, phantom pain shooting through my body. The memory swept over me again.

I begged her to fight, but the *me*, the memory, that was Candice couldn't. I lay powerless. Drugged. Bound.

I shook my head, pushing away the memories. It wasn't me. I could still fight. I would still fight. I would find the rogue. But who was he?

"I don't recognize the face." My voice trembled. Had I made the alley stink of fear?

Bobby was beside me, his face drawn with worry.

"Try again." Nathanial crouched on my other side. "I know I caught a glimpse of him in your memories. You were in a crowded room. It was dark, noisy. I remember you were uncomfortable, and there was something about his breath you found offensive."

Sharing memories was unnerving, and that he recalled mine with greater skill than I did irritated me, but I tried to think back. I had to have seen him in the city, and obviously before I met Nathanial. Staring at my fingers, I ran Candice's memory through my mind again. It was a little fuzzier than the first time, with a couple of things happening in a slightly different sequence. The man was talking to someone before he'd approached her, but Candice hadn't been paying attention, and I couldn't pull up any thoughts or descriptions of the other person.

I was alone at the table when he brought me a drink. Don't take it. I accepted. He slid off his leather jacket. Nice tattoo . . . but damaged. The huge dragon with its tail wrapping around the guy's wrist had three white scars bisecting it.

I pushed Candice's memories away. Suddenly sick.

That dragon I recognized. The last time I'd seen it, my claws were ripping through it. Five guys had attacked me. I defended myself.

It was the first time my claws had extended.

I swallowed hard. This—all of this—really *was* my fault. I stared at nothing in space, my stomach twisting into a numb knot. No Clanless stray to blame.

The rogue was my mistake.

Candice made, what? Thirteen victims? The weight of that number pressed down on me. Hot tears threatened to cloud my vision. I blinked them back.

Focus. I needed to focus. I pushed out of the snow.

The attack couldn't have been the memory Nathanial recalled. He'd said I'd seen the man recently. Nathanial found me just after the rave. I tried to remember everyone I'd seen inside the party, but most of them dissolved into a blur. The man in Candice's memory definitely wasn't the man I talked to, and he didn't look like anyone who had asked me to dance. Suddenly it hit me, he had been wearing a hat, and he'd offered to sell me some sort of drugs. Damn it. That didn't tell me anything else about him. He went to raves—knew that already. He sold drugs, which made drugging victims a very short leap of logic.

I had his face. I had his scent. And I still didn't know a damn thing about him. My nails bit half moons into my palms as I related this to Nathanial and Bobby. Their faces fell. It wasn't good news. It wasn't helpful.

"So what now?" Bobby asked.

"I told you about the trail I stumbled over earlier? The storm has probably covered it by now, but it might be the only lead we have left."

Nathanial led us to the subway. When we exited the train, we were back in the tenements. The snowstorm had abated, and a grim silence hovered around us as we made our way to the side street where I'd caught the city-shifter's scent earlier. The rundown buildings we passed all looked alike to me, and I hadn't seen street signs earlier, so I had to trust Nathanial that this was the spot I'd picked up the scent. Now there was no trace of it.

Mostly the street smelled of the small fires that several slumped figures were huddled around and the overflowing dumpster hugging the wall of the building to our right. Bobby and I both searched, but neither of us could pick up a trail to follow. It occurred to me as we doggedly walked and rewalked the street that Bobby might not know what he was searching for. I knew from Evan's memories that new hunters spent several months shadowing experienced ones to learn about the human world and how to identify a city-shifter, but Bobby had become a hunter specifically to find me. If he couldn't recognize the trail if he tripped over it, then it was up to me to find it, but my nose wasn't half as good as it had been earlier, and I was fighting several hours of snow. I stopped in front of the huge metal dumpster and slammed my fist into it.

"Damn, damn, damn!" I shouted each word louder and hit the dumpster as hard and fast as I could. With the final 'damn,' my fist burst through the rusting metal, and the jagged edges tore a gash across my hand. I stared at the blood in shock, but lifted my fist to swing again. Nathanial caught my arm before the blow landed.

"Please *do* say 'Damn,' again, Kita. I think it is helping."

Despite his harsh words, his fingers were gentle as they examined my wound. He lifted my hand to his mouth, and I felt his tongue slide into the gash. I tried to jerk away, but he held me firm. *Never waste blood,* he'd told me, and clearly he didn't plan to. I wanted to scream, or hit something, or cry. I'd already done the first two, and they hadn't helped. I doubted the last would either—it never had before.

When Nathanial released my hand, I marveled at the healing pink edges around the wound. Bobby hovered around my back, and I turned so that I could speak to both of them without the homeless at the top of the street overhearing. The bums were already staring after my violent outburst.

"I'm out of plans; we're almost out of time, so please tell me one of you has some brilliant idea. I am willing to do *anything* at this point."

Bobby leaned against the wall. He closed his eyes, and his head hung low, weighted. Even Nathanial's face was drawn. He took off his glasses and rubbed his eyes. Several strands of dark hair had escaped his hair tie. They hung limp, defeated, around his shoulders.

No, giving up wasn't an option. I'd worked too hard and put up with too much over the last few nights to quit now. I didn't want to die, but more than that, I didn't want to be responsible for Bobby or Nathanial's death. Whatever awaited me in the afterlife, I didn't want to carry their deaths with me. I was already carrying too many deaths.

Candice's terror flashed through me again. eleven victims dead. Two more in ICU. I had to find the rogue. I had to stop him. I had— an idea.

"The guy I was talking to at the rave, Bryant something. The rogue spoke to him, called him by name. They acted like they knew each other," I said. "If we can find Bryant, he might know where to find the rogue."

"Do you know where he lives?" Nathanial's frown deepened when I shook my head. "Then I suppose you are hoping he is listed in the phonebook as Bryant Something?"

I crossed my arms over my chest. "You have a better plan?"

"No, that is the problem." He sighed and slipped his glasses back in place.

Damn it. We knew the city-shifter whose scent had been at two of the crime scenes—no doubt the rogue—had been on this street a handful of hours ago. He could have been anywhere, headed anywhere. He could live close by, or work around here. He could have been headed to the subway, or caught a taxi and be anywhere. He could have been headed to someone's house, or he could even have been trolling bars.

He'd attacked Candice just last night. Would he be looking for another victim again so soon? The attacks *had* been increasing in frequency.

I marched up to the men huddled around a fire they'd built inside a fifty-gallon can. Their eyes flashed wide at my approach. I looked at each in turn.

"Where are the closest bars?"

They glanced at each other. No one answered.

Finally, a hunched-over man with a bloated red nose pursed his lips. "What's it worth to you?"

My fists clenched, and I looked back at the street intersection. "Nathanial!"

Forty dollars later, we had the name of three bars within the surrounding blocks. The rogue had found Candice at a bar, so there was always a chance . . .

We walked in grim silence.

"Here," Nathanial said, jerking open the door to the first bar the man had named. The door rattled, a hinge snapping.

I grimaced, but Nathanial stormed into the building without checking the damage. Luckily the country-western music blaring inside the bar hid the sound from the patrons.

Three women sat in front of a scarred bar, brightly colored drinks in their hands. They watched a cluster of men surrounding a faded and patched pool table. I studied each man's face, but none matched either my nor Candice's memory of the rogue. No other patrons. No scent of a city-shifter.

One down, two to hope on.

We walked back out, the door creaking behind us. It hung crooked off the frame and didn't shut. Nathanial turned without a word and headed for the next location.

Bobby checked every alley we passed. I caught up with Nathanial. "I don't know you that well, but you've been the epitome of patience in the past nights. In the last couple hours you changed."

"It is easy to be patient when you are immortal, but tonight I feel death reaching for me." His fingers trailed through my hair. I jerked back, and he dropped his hand without changing his pace. "Also, *you* are not patient, and I have your memories running around my head."

"As well as everyone else's you have ever fed from."

Nathanial shook his head. "It is not the same. A human can be drained of blood in a matter of minutes. That is not enough time to absorb a lifetime of thoughts and memories. It took over three hours to turn you. I relived your memories with you dozens of times. In a way, I know you almost as well as I know myself. What are we but a collection of our experiences? Add in that I can feel a hint of your emotions through the blood bond we share, and sometimes when things happen I react more like you would."

"That's really scary."

"Yes, it is."

Silence pressed down on us again. I hadn't known he could feel my emotions. The knowledge hit a whole new level of privacy invasion, but I'd have to worry about the fact he held my emotional barometer later. We reached the second bar.

Another bust.

Only one left. *I could really use some lucky stars.* I looked up. I was more likely to get snowflakes.

Nathanial's pace picked up. I was already taking three steps for every one of his. I would be jogging soon at this rate.

"You have changed too," he said, glancing over his shoulder and fixing me with gray eyes. "Ever since Candice's memory. I feel your guilt, but you are also more determined."

Heat flooded my face, but I forced myself to hold his eyes. "Stay out of my head."

He stopped, and Bobby nearly slammed into his back before Nathanial stepped out of his way. "Is the rogue one of the men who attacked you? One you used your claws on?" Nathanial asked.

I tripped over my feet. He *did* know.

"What is he talking about?" Bobby asked.

I opened my mouth, but no words emerged from my constricted throat. No confession.

"Attackers?" Bobby watched me, seeing more than I wanted him to see in my expression. "If you defended yourself and your claws came out . . . But you didn't shift?"

I shook my head without looking up.

Bobby was silent for a long moment. "You're sure you tagged the rogue?"

I nodded, one sharp jerk of my head. Unless another person with the exact same tattoo just happened to get tagged—doubtful—the rogue was my mistake. My problem. I had to stop walking. I couldn't see past the tears swimming in my vision. I squeezed my eyes shut. I felt Bobby's gaze on me, but I knew tears would spill out if I opened my eyes. I didn't want to see his reaction anyway—I was too afraid I'd see disgust written on his face.

A large hand landed on my shoulder, and I jumped.

"I'll be your second," Bobby whispered. "You defended yourself. End of story."

I shrugged him off. "You can't be my second. Do you think a cry of self-defense would appease my father, or the elders? I created . . . " I couldn't say it. I was *Dyre*, and I'd broken one of our most sacred laws.

Sure, tagging the rogue had been an accident, but my accident had killed humans. Like I hadn't been enough of an embarrassment to my father before. "I'm declaring myself clanless. I'll not lay this shame at the Nekai clan's feet."

Bobby hissed. "I didn't hear that. I'm your second."

"No."

"I—" Nathanial started but Bobby cut him off with a growled warning.

"I'm your second," he stated again. "And when we get back to Firth, we will face the elders together."

I shook my head, but the motion was lost in the general trembling of my body. I wasn't going back to Firth. I wasn't a shifter. I wasn't clan. Not anymore. Even if I lived through the night.

I marched up the sidewalk. "Aren't you leading the way?" I asked as I passed Nathanial.

He glided into motion again. "You knew there was a possibility your claws tagged the rogue. Why does knowing it is true change anything?"

Because before I could lie to myself. But now I knew. It wasn't the clanless. It wasn't some random stray. It was me.

"Because, judge or no judge, the rogue is my responsibility, and I have to kill him."

Chapter 21

"This is it," Nathanial said, reaching for the bar door.

I grabbed his hand, stalling him. He lifted an eyebrow. I ignored him.

This was the last bar on the list. If this one fell through, we were back to nothing. I needed to hold onto hope one more second. Steeling my will, I pulled open the door.

Jazz music floated softly in the dim bar. A woman sat at a high table, absorbed in the glow of her laptop. Two men sat several stools apart at the bar, each accompanied only by their tumblers. A couple cuddled in a back booth. The bartender watched a silent television screen. No one else. No rogue.

I crumpled against the wall, all my energy draining into the uneven floor boards. This was it, then. My throat burned. Now what?

I pushed off the wall and sucked down a deep breath. Under the smell of stale cigarettes and old beer was a faint scent.

"He's been here."

Bobby, who'd been half out the door already, whirled around. "You're sure?"

I nodded. My nose wasn't good for much but this scent was seared in my brain. The rogue had definitely been here.

Nathanial stepped around me and strolled up to the bar. When the bartender didn't look away from his sports game, Nathanial rapped on the dull wood with his knuckles. That got the bartender's attention, but judging by the way his lips twisted, not his favor. The middle-aged man took his time, grabbing a gray towel as he walked over.

"What can I get you?" He picked up a pint glass, wiping it as he spoke. The towel left greasy smears on the glass.

"Information," Nathanial said flashing a dazzling smile. "We are looking for a man in his late twenties, with buzzed blond hair and a long goatee. He was probably here earlier tonight. Have you seen him?"

No *probably* about it. He'd been here. I held my tongue. The bartender's eyes slid over us. I showed some teeth.

His gaze floated back to Nathanial, and he shrugged. "Lots of people come and go here."

I seriously doubted that. Bobby grunted under his breath, clearly in agreement about the mostly empty bar. Nathanial pushed several bills across the counter. The bartender glanced at them, and then made the bills disappear in a practiced motion as he wiped the bar with his dingy cloth.

"Yeah, maybe I remember seeing a guy who looked like that. He came in around eight. Stayed an hour or two. Paid cash."

Finally. A real lead. I leaned across the bar. "Did he leave with anyone? A woman he met here, most likely?"

The bartender pursed his lips and wiped another pint glass. "You a jealous ex or something?"

"No. Nothing like . . ." *Crap.* Why had I opened my mouth in the first place? I looked at Nathanial.

He laid another bill on the table. The bartender made it disappear.

"Yeah, he picked up a girl. Not like she came here to meet him or anything. She's a regular. Nice girl. Good tipper."

"She have a name?" Bobby asked.

"Yeah, she's got one." But the bartender didn't give it to us.

"Is she local?" I asked.

The bartender snorted. "You don't come to a hell hole like the south end of Haven unless you're local."

"How much for the name?" Nathanial asked, pulling out his wallet.

Three-hundred dollars later, we had a name: Katie Jones.

Once outside the bar, I looked from Bobby to Nathanial. "Either of you have a cell phone, preferably one with internet?"

I didn't have a lot of hope Bobby would, unless they were handing phones to hunters as soon as they stepped through the gate, so it wasn't a big surprise when he shook his head. I was sort of expecting Nathanial to have a phone, so his frown caught me off guard.

"I am over four hundred years old and this is the first occasion I recall needing one." He adjusted his glasses, and started up the street. "We will have to do this the old fashioned way."

We stopped at a diner for a phonebook. There was no guarantee the bartender had given us the real name of the girl the rogue picked up, but I could only hope he had. There were five K. Jones listed for the southside tenement area. Any one of them could be her. According to Nathanial, two listings were within easy walking distance of the bar. Those seemed the most likely choices.

"We should fly," Nathanial said, reaching for me.

I stepped away from him. "What about Bobby?"

Nathanial frowned.

Bobby crossed his arms over his chest. "You're not leaving me behind. You'll need my help with the rogue."

Nathanial had to look up to meet Bobby's eyes, and his frown carved a deeper ravine across his face. "I can't carry both of you."

"Then we better start walking." I set a brisk pace down the sidewalk, Bobby at my side. Nathanial caught up quickly then took the lead.

I rubbed the small of my back. My skin was still smooth, but I swore I could now feel the judge's coiled mark slithering along my flesh. Warning of my diminishing time. Hurrying my steps.

We were six blocks past the bar when I ground to a halt, my head tilting back. "Bobby, quick, it's a trail." Faint, but a trail.

Bobby stopped and breathed deeply. His nostrils flared several time before he gave me a puzzled look. "I don't—"

He couldn't pick it up, and I was already losing it.

"Please, try again. The rogue's never been to Firth, so it's not like a normal shifter scent, but there is still animal musk to it. Try, you can find it."

He paced in circles, tilting his head back and searching. Every heartbeat that passed I grew more frantic, I barely noticed as Bobby became less frantic.

"I've got it." He took off at a run.

I'd lost the scent completely, so I had to trust Bobby had truly found it. We cut through side streets, running the opposite direction we'd been headed. The tenements faded to larger but equally rundown highrise apartments. As we burst from a sidestreet, Bobby grabbed me by the shoulders and pulled me back into the shadow of a nearby building.

"Damn," he whispered.

"What?"

"Hunter."

I tilted my head back. Any Firth scent should have been a hunter, but I recognized this one. "Not a hunter. The *clanless*. Ignore him. Focus on the rogue's scent."

Bobby nodded, but as he led Nathanial and I out of the shadows, his pace was more cautious than before. I tried not to think about what we were up against if the clanless and the rogue were allied in some way.

"Hurry," I urged him.

Bobby shot a frown at me, and then paused and backtracked a couple yards. He glanced at the building beside us. He circled the front of it again before stopping at the base of the building's stoop. "This is it."

I jogged up the three cement steps and pulled the door open with a small feeling of triumph.

Green light flashed behind me. "You have failed, Kita of Firth."

Chapter 22

I whirled around. The judge stood in his perfectly tailored suit at the bottom of the steps. Somehow he still appeared to look down at me despite the fact I was standing several feet above him. A brilliant flash of green and his three demons appeared behind him. They slid toward me with outstretched talons.

"The night isn't over yet!"

"You have had your two nights. Now receive your judgment with dignity."

Nathanial stepped in front of me. "We are very close. If you kill her now, you will not learn everything we have found, and you will not stop the rogue from killing more innocent people. Surely you do not want more blood on your hands?"

The judge made a sign, and the demons stopped gliding forward. *Smart vampire.* According to Gil, the judge was trying to clean up his karma. Killing innocents wouldn't help him much. I held my breath while he deliberated. His face betrayed nothing of his thoughts, but finally he nodded.

"If you are indeed so close, I'll grant you a little extra time." He looked at me like I was a bug to be squashed at his leisure. "You have fifteen more minutes, and then no pleading in the world will save you."

"It took you three months to find me, and you're giving me two nights and fifteen minutes to track down a deranged rogue?"

Nathanial sent me a look that clearly told me to shut up.

The judge smiled, flashing perfectly straight teeth. "Would you like to continue wasting time? Or bring me the rogue? Your choice, of course."

My heart jumped to my throat. Turning, I flung open the door.

"These two I will keep," the judge said. I flipped around in time to see him make a grabbing motion into the air. Nathanial and Bobby jerked backward as if tied to invisible strings. "Insurance that you will try your hardest. Time is ticking."

"You want me to take on a rogue alone?"

"You can come down here and join them, if you are giving up."

"Kita, go," Bobby yelled.

I hesitated less than a second, then ran inside the building.

I didn't have much of a plan, or really any plan. I needed Bobby. The building was huge. How was I supposed to find the rogue without Bobby's nose? No time to worry. Worrying would only get in the way.

I stopped in the center of the lobby and breathed deeply. I caught a hint of the rogue's scent. Katie might live on this floor, but even if she didn't they would have had to pass through the lobby to get upstairs.

I flung open the door to the stairwell but it didn't hold the rogue's scent. Okay, the first floor then. Time to start knocking on doors. I was trying to decide which was the most likely door when the elevator chimed. A young couple walked into the lobby and headed out the front exit without glancing my way.

Cautiously I crept over and hit the 'up' button. The double doors slid open again and all but poured the rogue's scent on me. I stepped inside. Okay, so he took the elevator up, but to which floor? I hit the second floor button and the doors slid shut, trapping me inside. My stomach flipped as the elevator lurched into motion. The overhead light flickered erratically. *The judge won't get the chance to kill me if the elevator does it first.* I didn't wait for the door to completely open, but slid out as soon as I could see the hall between them. The second floor didn't have a trace of the rogue's scent. I ran to the stairs and dashed up, skipping every other step.

I checked each floor as I went. The building didn't have a thirteenth floor, but skipped right to the fourteenth. As soon as I walked into the hall on that floor, I caught the rogue's scent. Okay, now which door? I was two-thirds down the hall, and ready to pull out my hair, when I caught the sound of whimpering.

I stopped and pressed my ear to the wall.

Definitely whimpering. It could be an abused dog, but it was the best clue I had.

Now what?

I stared at the door. I could break it down, but I'd still need an invitation to enter. *Damn.*

I raised my fist to knock, and the stairwell door banged open. The scent of wolf, of hunter, permeated the hall. No, not hunter—the clanless. I whirled around.

He stopped when he saw me, his nose flaring. He didn't tip his imaginary hat this time. "You again," he whispered, pulling a silver chain out of his pocket.

Crap. I really need some gloves and one of those things.

The clanless had the advantage of range with the chain. I dropped my weight evenly between my legs, but held back. I couldn't afford the noise of a fight—it would attract the attention of the rogue, and I couldn't take on both the clanless *and* the rogue.

The clanless had no reason to be here. He hadn't tagged the rogue, I had. Had they teamed up at some point? Or, was this a territory dispute? Was that why he'd attacked her in the alley?

"I'm hunting the rogue. Are you with him?" I kept my voice quiet, hoping the city-shifter inside the apartment wouldn't hear.

The clanless's jaw clenched. "There are no female hunters." His eyes flickered toward the door and then back to me. "The thing behind that door is an abomination. And yet here you are. All alone."

I didn't have time for this. Sidling cautiously along the wall, I moved further from the apartment so the rogue was less likely to hear me. I kept my voice low, but heat still bled into my words, burning my throat as I whispered. "You're no hunter, either. I found you skulking around one of the rogue's haunts, and now I find you here. With him. I have as much reason to distrust you. More. You are clanless."

"That I am." He titled his head as if I could have missed his scars. "But I'd never side with a rogue or tolerate the trouble he brings. I don't like my territory overrun with hunters. As for you, you would have me believe we share a common goal? I found you first a cat who had been in close-enough proximity of the rogue for his scent to be on her. Then I found you a wolf in one of the rogue's haunts. Now I find you not a shifter at all, here, where he is within reach. How could I believe you are hunting him?"

I had to admit, when put that way, I sounded pretty damn suspicious. Didn't make me trust *him* any more, though. If we walked into that apartment together and he turned out to be working with the rogue, I'd be sorely outnumbered. But neither could I stand in the hall all night playing this game of words. I told the truth.

"I have about eight more minutes to find and capture the rogue, or the *mage* I'm hunting for will kill me. I'll make you a deal. Come back in fifteen minutes. If the rogue is still around, he's all yours."

He stared at me, his mouth stretching into a lopsided frown. "Three nights ago I'd have thought you were pulling my tail, but since then I've been over-powered by a non-shifter, held at bay by purple light, and met a shifter whose beast changes and disappears. Perhaps your *mage* exists." He backed up.

I waited, ready for him to charge. To betray his retreat as fake. He didn't.

He backed all the way to the stairwell, never taking his eyes off me. Once he reached the door, he nudged it open with his foot, and, stepping half inside, pantomimed tipping a hat at me. "You have your fifteen minutes, little *Dyre* enigma. I'll finish the job if you don't."

I waited until I heard his footsteps take him down at least one flight of stairs, and then I ran back to the rogue's door. The clanless might have given me fifteen minutes, but I only had about seven left before the judge called *time*.

I pounded on the door.

It took an eternity before I heard footsteps moving in the apartment. *What would I say when it opened?* I needed to get the rogue downstairs without causing any kind of disturbance a human would notice. I could tell him my car broke down, but why would I have come to the fourteenth floor? The footsteps drew nearer. There was no logical reason I would walk up to this floor and ask him to leave the building with me. The doorknob turned, hinges creaked.

"Sorry, was the TV too loud . . ." said the man I recognized from Candice's memory. His face made her terror rush through me again, and I flinched. He looked surprised when his brown eyes landed on me. Then he smirked. His hand shot out, snatched a lock of my hair. "I wondered when I'd get your attention. Should I call you Mom?"

He laughed, and I gaped at him. I hadn't anticipated him recognizing me. There went the element of surprise. He knew what I was. Well, actually, he knew what I used to be. At least I didn't have to come up with an excuse to be there.

I flashed teeth at him. "Come downstairs."

"No. You should come inside." He held open the door.

Down the hall, a door opened. A man in a robe walked out with a small, yippy dog. He stood in the hall, waiting on the elevator.

Crap. What choice did I have but go inside? I couldn't just grab the rogue and drag him down the stairs. He'd wake the whole complex. I stepped through the doorway. The threshold resisted, but didn't stop me.

The rogue slammed the door behind me, bolt locking it. Oh good, the shifter who preyed on women now had me locked in the apartment. He might find me a little harder to take than Lorna or Candice though.

With the door shut, the room fell into near darkness. The city lights bled through the windows. Their pale orange glow threw strange shadows across the room. When whimpering sounded deep in the apartment, I cringed. Katie Jones, I was betting.

How was I going to get the rogue out? Time ticked against me.

"You can drop your coat anywhere," the rogue said. He tried to step behind me, take my coat, but I wasn't about to give him my back. He smiled. "Please, get comfortable. I've been waiting for you. Dreaming about you."

Okay, that was more than just creepy. I needed to distract him. I could probably knock him unconscious. Then I could drag him downstairs. But I needed a clear shot first. If he shifted, I'd be in trouble. I was stronger as a vampire, but new, untested. Playing along was the best way to get his defenses down. I shrugged out of my coat and laid it over the corner of the couch.

His nostrils flared. "You don't smell like I thought you would."

I almost laughed. I bet I didn't. I'd sucked on two male vamps tonight. "Reality tends to screw you that way."

He nodded, his goatee twitching with the movement. "I'm Tyler. Remember that. I want to hear you screaming it in your last breath." His gaze lingered on my torn turtle neck. "Someone else started my party, I see."

The time for playing along had passed. I dropped my weight to my back leg. His heartbeat sped up, loud in the silence of the apartment, but not from fear. His hand dropped to the front of his jeans, his thumb running down the bulge by his zipper.

He was turned on by the fact we were going to fight? Well I hoped he had a damn fine time while I beat his lights out.

Actually, maybe his excitement could turn the tables in my favor. If I could make that mesmerizing thing work, the way I'd turned Evan's excitement against him, I could get Tyler to follow me down the stairs and into the hands of the judge. The problem, of course, was that I didn't know how to do it.

Could I rile up my hunger and get it to do whatever it had done before?

I took a step closer to him and his eyes widened, his thumb stroking faster. He liked aggressive, I could do that.

I lunged. I was fast, but so was he. My fist glanced off his upper arm, but his punch slammed into the shoulder Tatius had ripped into earlier.

Pain surged through me and I backpedaled. Not fast enough. A back-handed hit sent me sprawling to the carpet. He followed me down, ripping at his jeans at the same time his knee landed a blow in my stomach.

I swung. My fist connected with his nose in a sickening crunch. Blood spurted from his nostrils. That was exactly what I needed. My fangs extended. I lunged for his throat. He pushed himself backward, but not far enough. My fangs sank in deep.

The world held its breath for one incredible moment, then his memories plowed into my mind like a tornado. Bits and pieces of his life filtered into me. He was despicable long before he became a shifter: a rapist, mugger, gang banger, and overall tormentor of those weaker than himself. I felt his beast burgeoning beneath his skin. *Wolf*. Even caught in his mind, I shivered.

I saw clips and pieces of his thoughts and memories of different victims both from before and after he changed. The small part of me that could still tell the difference between my thoughts and his fought the connection. Tried to keep us separate.

I became him, became Tyler as he shifted for the first time in the middle of a crowd. *The party*. Jason changed beside me. *Our form solidified and the fresh born spirit looked out of new eyes*. Jason also solidified, but he wasn't a predator. Small antlers sprouted from his head. *Food*. Like any prey that discovers a predator close by, Jason ran. *This excited us, excited our new beast. We gave chase, tearing through the crowd in our way. We raced after the shifter, until we pounced on him in the center of the woods. Flesh split under our teeth. We howled, triumphant, even as the blood of our friend poured into the dirt at our feet*.

Disgusted, I pushed the memory away and fell into a new one.

I caught an image myself, Kita, not as Tyler saw me now, but several months ago, before he'd been tagged. I had looked easy, but had turned out to be a hell cat. He'd enjoyed it until I tore through his arm. I saw the night Sharon had escaped. After that, he made sure every girl was too drugged to run. It took some of the fun away, he liked it when they screamed and fought him. *That's why they were surviving now, it wasn't as much fun when they couldn't run and fight*. Some of the girls I recognized from the paper, some I didn't. They all had streaked hair. It reminded him of me. I saw a single horrifying image of Lorna, then his mind flashed to Candice.

She kept trying to scream. It was delicious. We touched her, bringing more muffled screams. Her flesh ripped apart. Her bones snapped. We loved it. She cried for us.

I pulled away from him so fast my fangs tore chunks of flesh from his throat.

I was on the floor, Tyler convulsing on top of me with his jeans unbuckled, but thankfully, still on. I pushed him off and rolled away. I clutched my trembling knees to my chest and rocked myself while I watched him bleed onto the moldy carpet.

I should kill him now.

I didn't want to touch him again.

His eyes stared at nothing, completely glazed over. I dragged in another gulp of air. Every breath was tainted with his scent. My mouth tasted of his blood.

I spit, the red glob landing on Tyler's bare arm. He didn't blink, and it didn't rid me of the feeling of filth sinking under my skin.

Deep breaths.

Could a vampire hyperventilate?

Somewhere deep in the apartment the whimpering had turned to soft crying, and I cursed under my breath. How much time had I lost already? It was impossible to tell.

I glanced down the hall. I only needed the rogue. I could send back help but I couldn't turn back the clock and save Bobby or Nathanial if I was late to the judge.

I turned to go. Another muffled scream tore through the air, cut through my skin. The memory of Candice's fear flashed through me, nearly bringing me to my knees.

I couldn't leave her. I only needed seconds to reassure her.

Cursing again, I stood up and walked to Tyler. "Don't move until I come back for you."

His eyes stared at nothing. No acknowledgement, but no movement either. *Had the mesmerizing thing worked?* I prayed it had. I also prayed Nathanial could feel my success, could tell the judge things were going well.

Creeping down the hall, I followed the muffled cries to a door deep in the back of the apartment. I pushed it open, cringing as the hinges squealed.

A woman in a short skirt and torn blouse lay bound and gagged in the middle of the floor. Fear pulsed off her in tangible waves as I stepped into the room.

Blood. I froze.

It wasn't a lot of blood, but she was injured. Was it enough for her to have been tagged? Black mascara tears trailed down her cheeks, soaking into the torn rag gagging her.

"I'll come back," I whispered.

Her eyes squeezed shut.

Not acknowledgement. Resignation. No. *Despair.*

I darted across the room and knelt by her side. I reached for the bindings on her wrists, but her eyes flew open and she screamed into the gag, thrashing.

"Stay still. I'm a friend," I whispered.

She jerked in the bindings, her head whipping to the side. She screamed again, her eyes rolling to focus on mine and then beyond me.

A footstep creaked behind me.

I went still. There were two scents in the room, and two racing heartbeats. I should have paid more attention. The girl wasn't senseless, she was trying to warn me.

I shot up, whirling around. It wasn't Tyler. Overgrown dark brown hair hung at his ears. Had I'd tagged all the men who had attacked me? Were they *all* in this apartment? No. One was dead. Jason was dead.

This man had already changed forms, though it was hardly a shift at all. Tagged shifters rarely managed to shift far. Even an advanced mid-form was out of their ability. That was certainly true for this rogue. His face had rounded out and his nose and jaw extended to give him the smallest bit of a muzzle. Too many sharp teeth were crammed into that small, almost human mouth, and his ears had reshaped so that they pointed at the ends. A sprinkling of fur covered him. The most dangerous part of his change though, were the curved claws extending from his fingernail beds. As far as shifting went, it was a baby of a change, but still deadly if he knew how to use the claws.

I crouched defensively. If I were still a shifter, he'd over power me in a heartbeat. But now? I wouldn't know until he attacked.

I waited, but this new rogue watched me. He seemed to be expecting some reaction I wasn't giving him. Terror? That would be a human reaction, but I wasn't human.

His eyes narrowed, sweeping over me. He took another step forward and suddenly, the human face came into focus in my mind.

"Bryant? So this is what you planned when you drugged my drink?"

He smiled, his canines flashing. "You don't find my appearance monstrous? Should I turn on a light so you can see clearer?" He took a step closer, and laughed, a sound half animal, half scream.

The hairs on the back of my neck stood up. He had been in the closet, and I was between him and the door. Not that it looked like he had any intention of leaving the room, but I had to be running out of time by now. Perhaps I could drain his blood until he lost consciousness and drag him down the stairs. If anyone asked, he was drunk.

I closed the space between us in a single heartbeat. He tried to backpedal, but I grabbed him.

My fangs betrayed me, remaining hidden. I didn't need the blood. Didn't want it. But, I did need him unconscious. Bryant recovered from his surprise, and dug his claws deep into my arm. Flesh and muscle ripped to the bone.

I swallowed my scream. My fangs burst through at the first searing pain, and I plunged them into Bryant's neck.

His memories flooded over me. His beast, a hyena, had manifested itself the first time when Bryant was at a party, in a makeout room.

The pain. What is happening? The girl. She keeps screaming, trying to leave. They always leave me. I reach for her. Make her stay. But her flesh rips under my hands. Claws? Why do I have claws?

The girl is really screaming now. I have to shut her up. My claws sink into her neck. Her eyes bulge, begin to fade, but she is oh so quiet. She can't leave now.

Someone is coming. The freak who sliced up the crowd last month. He smiles as he sees the girl.

He's like me. A monster.

I reeled back, letting Bryant fall. His memories still danced behind my eyes. Tyler had found him, filled his head with nonsense about monsters and power, and encouraged the madness tagged shifters fight. Bryant and his beast had become twisted, depraved.

Bryant was why the murders were in Haven now. Tyler had found him here, and rape and torture was more fun with a friend.

I took a step back and forced my eyes to focus through the assault of memories which still clawed at my mind. Bryant sprawled against the wall, he was only dazed. He wouldn't be down long.

Footsteps thudded near the door. I spun around. A figure stooped in the doorway and my heart missed a beat. Tyler's piercing gaze fixed on me. His hand dropped from his throat, blood dripping from his finger tips.

Crap.

The energy in the room built to an unbearable tension. Tyler doubled forward, his skin splitting down his back.

Double crap.

I glanced at Bryant. He was already recovering. He rolled away, pushing himself up on his elbows. I hadn't taken near enough to weaken him.

Great, so I was going to have to fight both of them somehow. The only good thing was, their blood had made me stronger and more alert, while weakening them. If there was an advantage to being a human-shaped tick, that was it. I glanced from one to the other, Tyler's skin was slipping off, but the change wasn't progressing very quickly. Evan's memory reminded me that tagged shifters could take minutes to initiate a full change.

Okay, so I had a little extra time; I needed to use it to incapacitate Bryant before Tyler finished his change. But how? I cursed and kicked Bryant hard. He gave a grunt, but it only broke his daze faster.

My foot shot out for a second kick, but the blow went wild as pain twisted deep in my stomach. I doubled over, my fists bunching in my middle. I expected blood, expected something had ripped into my abdomen, but my skin was whole, unbroken. *What the hell?*

The pain crawled outward, spreading through my body like fire through my veins. It traveled down my arm, and the skin on my hand burst open. Then blood flew across the room to join the lurching mass of Tyler's changing form. I blinked, shock buffering the pain for a single heartbeat. Shifters heal. Even severed limbs would rejoin the body. And apparently, stolen blood.

I needed to get away. Far enough that the blood couldn't be called back to Tyler as he healed. There wasn't time. I had only enough time to realize how screwed I was. Then veins all over my body split open. I screamed as the blood ripped forcefully out of me.

I should have known better.

I collapsed, not even wasting energy on breathing. My own blood, the little blood I had left that hadn't mixed with Tyler's, dripped from my ruined veins, spilling my strength onto the carpet.

I was going to die. Two deranged tagged shifters were going to kill me. My eyes drifted closed, but on the back of my lids a terrible scene of demons closing in on Bobby and Nathanial played, and I opened them again. Not just me. If these rogues killed me, we were all doomed.

I wasn't dead yet. If my body wasn't smart enough to shut up and die, then my mind wasn't going to give up first.

A body can only take so much pain. I'd apparently hit that threshold because the pain faded to numbness. I pushed off the floor.

Bryant eyes flew wide as I climbed to my feet, his gaze pure fear and frantic. I lunged at him, my fangs already bared.

He was ready for me. He grimaced, but caught my throat in one large hand, and his thumb claw slipped through my ruined flesh and into my air pipe.

Damn!

I tried to jerk away, but he gripped my throat tighter. Unable to pull back, I pressed forward, driving his thumb deeper into my flesh. His elbow bent, but I was still too far away to use my fangs or score a decent punch. My scream of rage and frustration gurgled in my throat. *I'm a cat, dammit!*

My hand shot out, pure instinct, and claws burst from my fingertips. Bryant had been prepared for my teeth—not my claws. With one great slash, the skin in his stomach parted. He released me, falling to his knees as he tried to hold his entrails inside.

Grabbing a handful of his hair, I wrench his head to the side. My claws arched towards his throat. Before the blow landed, weight crashed into me.

I slammed against the closet door. The world flashed red.

I flipped around in time for the thing to crash into me again. A monstrous, brown-furred form charged, and I backpedaled, my claws flashing. Tyler had completed his change.

Wolf!

I pressed my back hard against the closet.

Wolf.

No tagged shifter should have transformed so far. I still bore the scars from the only other one I knew who had. Tyler had retained just enough of his human self to be lankier and larger than a true wolf. His brown eyes had remained the same, and he looked from Bryant's panicked form back to me. It was only a moment's distraction but I used it.

Now!

My brain and body didn't agree, and I caught tuffs of fur at his throat, nothing else.

Don't get cornered. I pushed away from the closet door.

Tyler threw his superior weight into me again and I fell off balance. I landed on my back, and he was on top of me in a moment. Teeth gnashed in my face, and he let out a deep rumbling growl. Fear seized me. I couldn't think. Couldn't plan.

Wolf, run!

No. Fight it!

I thrashed underneath him. His teeth ripped into my shoulder, pinning me to the ground. My knee slammed between his legs. Yelping, he jumped back, releasing me.

Up, get up!

I was on my feet and running without realizing it. I wasn't looking where I was going, all I could think about were those growling teeth over me.

Tyler crashed into my back, and the world broke around me.

No, not the world. A window.

I fell with the snow at a dizzying speed toward the ground below. Tyler howled, his teeth gnashing for me even as we fell. I lashed out with my claws, catching him on the muzzle. The blood shot straight up, our heavier masses falling faster than liquid.

Tyler yelped, his eyes rolling wide as he looked down. He whipped his spine around, trying to get his feet under him. Landing on his feet wouldn't help. We had fallen out of a fourteenth story window. Neither of us would survive.

Far below, rushing closer every moment, I could see the judge. Bobby and Nathanial were also there, not yet demon food.

Had I pulled it off?

Well, I'd be making it back within my time limit. Granted, not exactly the way I'd imagined, but I was bringing the rogue with me. They would live.

I did it.

The cement jumped closer and closer.

I cringed, closing my eyes. I could only hope it would be fast and painless.

Chapter 23

It was fast. A sudden jarring stop, quite painful, but the fact that I felt the pain meant I wasn't dead.

I chanced opening my eyes and found myself wrapped in Nathanial's arms, still several stories up. We hung in mid-air. Ever so slowly, we drifted down.

My heart was trying to race, trying to process the emotion of being alive, but there was no blood left for it to pump. I hurt everywhere. If I could have gotten sick, I would have. *Falling to my death would have been preferable.* I caught sight of the dirty-looking smear on the pavement below us and changed my mind.

"Drink from me, Kitten, you are dying," Nathanial whispered.

I shook my head and tried to speak, but only a gurgling sound issued from my throat.

"Please. You survived the fight, you cannot die like this now." He was trying to touch me so carefully and yet hold me tight at the same time.

Maybe it was the plea in his voice that got through to me, though I would like to blame it on vampiric instinct and not emotional attachment. He exposed his throat and I sank my fangs in. I expected an assault of memories, but as his mind opened to me it was different, controlled. Nathanial's memories did flood over me, but he was holding them back. I saw myself through his eyes, and was terrified by the fact that not a visible inch of smooth skin was left on my body. In fact, I appeared to be nothing more than so much raw meat with teeth and claws. I understood then the look of horror in Bryant's eyes.

I was a thing of nightmares.

But, horror wasn't what Nathanial's mind conveyed to me. His dread was in the idea that this might be too much damage for my body to heal.

I suddenly felt ashamed, like a Peeping Tom. These were the emotions Nathanial hid behind his mask, and I was snooping through them like I belonged. I drew back, closing the wound carefully.

"You need more."

I tried to answer, but my words rasped out in gurgles again. Nathanial's frown deepened. He shifted me slightly and lifted his hand to my throat. His fingers explored the damage until he found where Bryant's claw had poked through my windpipe. Nathanial's thumb slid over the hole. That hurt, but my whimper actually had a sound aside from gurgling.

"Try to speak," he said.

"My body is wasting the blood," I gasped out. I had to breathe to speak, and the most terrible whistling and sucking sounds escaped around his thumb when I tried. I pulled away so he could see what I could already feel. All down the front of my body, fresh blood—Nathanial's blood—dripped. Now that I had more, apparently I was trying to send it around, and the tracks weren't there.

"Your body is healing. You need more blood. You are right though, more now would be wasted. In a couple of minutes." I didn't have the energy to fight with him, so I leaned into his chest and closed my eyes. "Do not sleep yet, Kitten. We must still talk with the judge."

I fought against my heavy eyelids. It was a close battle. We were on the sidewalk before I was sure my eyes were really open.

Nathanial lowered me to my feet, but my knees gave out. He kept an arm around me, supporting my weight. As Bobby and the judge made their way to us, Nathanial ripped off his coat, tore it in two, and wrapped my hands in it.

What was he doing? He didn't have enough clothing to bind my whole body. *Wait, my hands . . .* he was trying to sheath my claws. *Right, claws created crazy rogue shifters, which was a very bad thing.* I tried to retract my claws, but the effort made me dizzy without affecting my hands.

Bobby ran ahead of the judge. "Kita, what happened?" He reached out a hand but dropped it without making contact. He looked concerned, but once he stopped gawking, he stared a couple inches to my left and not directly at me. Guess I was a hard thing to behold. His eyes glanced for a brief moment at where Nathanial was tying my hands, and then slid away again. He whispered, "Your claws extended?"

I gurgled a little, nodding, and Bobby frowned. He didn't say anything more.

"You went over your time limit," the judge said.

"She disposed of the rogue shifter," Bobby retorted. "Isn't that what you wanted her to do?"

"Yes, she did, but in a most excessive way. Look at this mess. Do you understand the work it will take to cover this up?"

My eyes tried to snap to the judge, but they were following my commands sluggishly. Finally I found him standing several paces away from the rest of us. He didn't look as suave as normal. I stared, and he glanced away. Sweat clung to his brow, tension between his eyes. *Revulsion? No, pain.*

A smile touched what was left of my lips. Gil had said the mark he'd left on me had costs, and that if I died while I had it, the judge would suffer with me. I guess I had taken more damage than most, and still hadn't died. He was getting the backlash.

Nathanial confirmed my thoughts in a whisper. "He was in the process of telling us time had run out when he turned pale and looked up at the building."

I reached for my throat to mimic how Nathanial had plugged the hole and let me speak, but my hands were wrapped and of no use. Nathanial's hand closed around my throat and I whimpered again.

"We had a deal." I gasped out.

"Yes." The judge gestured into the air and pulled a book out of nowhere. "I did not realize you were a vampire and a shifter when I made that deal. You are an abomination, and it has already been proven you are unreliable. We can't have you wandering around the human world, and you are no longer suited to be returned to Firth."

I gaped at him. So he had planned to banish me to Firth even if I found the rogue? Not terribly unexpected, but claiming I shouldn't exist? Okay, so I might have had similar thoughts over the last couple nights, but I'd made it through too much to give up now.

"You have no right," I whispered, anger lending me strength.

"A child's argument. I sentence you to death for being an abomination to nature. I sentence the hermit Nathanial to death as well, for creating such a creature."

Bobby stepped in front of me. "You can't do that. You made the agreement with her after she became a vampire. She earned her freedom."

I cringed. Bobby had ended up with his skull cracked last time he yelled at the judge. This time the judge merely stretched his thin lips into a frown.

"You don't seem to understand," the judge said without looking up from the book into which he was jotting his judgment. "She should not exist. We have no idea what will happen when she feeds her blood lust. What if she tags every person she drinks from? The city will be crawling with shifters in a few short months."

Nathanial held me closer. "But you do not know that will happen." His voice was strained, unsure.

The judge snapped his book closed. "It is not worth the chance."

Of course, no one knew. It could very well be true. I closed my eyes. I was so heavy, so tired.

Someone cleared her throat, and my eyes fluttered open again. Gil shuffled from foot to foot, and wrung her hands together. The movement crinkled the scroll in her trembling fingers. Biting her lip, she wiped the length of the scroll, trying to repair the damage.

"I'm s-sorry to interrupt," she stammered.

"What is it scholar? Gildamina, is it?" The judge asked, idly beckoning her forward with a manicured hand.

Gildamina? No wonder she had us call her Gil.

"Yes, Sir. I . . ." She tripped over her feet, and straightened quickly with a blush staining her cheeks. "I have a document for you, signed by four of the High Assembly members." She held out the scroll. It shook visibly.

The judge grabbed the scroll and snapped the seal. As his eyes scanned it, outrage touched his expression. His jaw clenched, but he rerolled the scroll in a slow, meticulous movement. "I cannot accept this."

"The High Assembly anticipates your appeal, sir." Gil's eyes darted over the judge. She leaned away from him, putting as much distance between his anger and her as possible without actually stepping backward.

"Fine." The judge flashed teeth, but not in anything resembling a smile.

I exchanged a questioning look with Nathanial, but he shrugged, shaking his head. He didn't know anything more than I did. Even Bobby chanced a look back at me with the same question in his eyes. The judge lifted the scroll, and it disappeared in a green flash. He turned to me. If he was still feeling my pain, he was hiding it well, or perhaps his anger had made him forget.

"You have gotten off lightly for now," he said, and I blinked at him. "Until I can get this matter taken care of, I will be watching you very closely, and watching the victims you feed from. One mistake, even the smallest hint I can take to the Assembly, and you will be mine." He turned, and with a wave of his hand, banished the demons.

He walked toward the dark mess on the concrete that had formerly been Tyler. Halfway there he turned back. "And seeing as I am not yet free to dispose of you, expect me to call on you again. You have proven yourself to be a useful, if chaotic, tool."

"But—" Bobby started.

The judge's eyes flared. "That was our agreement. When first we met, the vampire claimed she would be more useful than my demons in finding the rogue. That, at least, has proven to be true. Now be silent. I have to clean up her mess."

"There is another shifter upstairs." I croaked out, my throat fighting me. "A woman too. Hurt, but alive."

An irritated expression etched itself into the judge's face. He glanced over his shoulder. "Gildamina, make yourself useful as more than a messenger."

She cringed. "Yes sir." Her gaze remained passively on the ground as she marched toward the back door of the building. Nathanial called out to her, and she jumped.

"What was on that paper?" Nathanial asked.

"Oh, Kita is being protected as a rare species to be studied unless proven too dangerous." She shrugged. Her glance fell over me. It must have been the first time she'd looked at me fully since arriving on the scene, because she grimaced and covered her mouth with trembling fingers. Her eyes snapped back to Nathanial, and she lowered her voice to a whisper. "It occurred to me that we might be able to sidestep the judge. There have been only three other documented attempts to turn a shifter into a vampire, and all of them failed. The Assembly is reluctant to destroy such a rare specimen." She smiled, forgetting for a moment and glancing at me before snapping her eyes away again. Her voice lifted to her normal chirpy level. "So, I will be doing my grand thesis on her. My name will be in all kinds of history books!"

Some distance behind us, the judge grunted.

"Congratulations," I mumbled, oddly sincere, but she ignored me and made her way into the building.

"Kitten, is there anything I can do for you?" Bobby asked.

I could tell he was trying to look at me without showing horror on his face. He failed. Miserably.

"My coat . . ." I glanced at the building, and Bobby nodded. He all but ran to catch up with Gil.

Nathanial chuckled lightly. "You know, that coat is better at surviving than you are. Perhaps the next time you feel the need to remove it in a dangerous situation, you should take it as a hint to leave."

I started to laugh but it turned into more of a convulsion.

Nathanial cradled me to his chest. "It is okay, Kitten. It is over now. You can sleep. I will get you home." He lifted me off my feet.

The movement sent fresh pain rushing through me, and I choked back a scream. The last of my energy was vanishing; my world becoming one large, blaring, red sensation of pain. Sleep sounded like a good plan. Even Nathanial's home sounded good. I closed my eyes and let the blackness of blessed unconsciousness take me.

Chapter 24

I sat on Nathanial's front porch in the dark and watched the snow fall. I'd slept fitfully for the first two nights after my encounter with the rogue shifters. Tonight, the third night, was the first time I'd ventured from bed for any amount of time. Nathanial didn't want me up yet. He'd bought half a dozen paperbacks to keep me busy, but I was sick of his dark room.

Like some freakish tattoo, my skin still showed the traces of carnage where my flesh had been ripped apart from the inside out. My throat finally had a thin membrane over it so I could speak, but my shoulder still had scabbed wounds in the shape of Tyler's teeth, and my right arm was nearly useless where Bryant's claws had ripped through it. I guess I had pushed the extent of what my new vampiric healing abilities could handle. Nathanial assured me there wouldn't be a single scar left eventually. I wasn't as sure, but I hoped he was right.

Every time I'd woken on those first two terrible nights, Nathanial had been there in the room waiting; sometimes reading, but many times staring into space. He'd fed me from his own vein to help me heal, and now I had even more fragments of his memories swirling around my mind. It gave me a lot to think about as I sat alone, watching the snow.

I'd refused Nathanial's blood tonight. If I was strong enough to be up and about, it was time for me to get my own dinner. Bobby was staying with us, which had been a total surprise when I'd walked into the front study and found him asleep on the couch. He'd checked out the woods around Nathanial's house. They were full of snow hares, deer, and several other animals of prey. The selection sounded good to me. If it was possible for me to survive on the blood of animals, that was definitely my goal. With me taking the blood and Bobby the meat, there wasn't a chance in the world of me accidentally creating another rogue. Besides, I'd had enough of a peek into the minds of men for one lifetime.

Gil had stopped by to check on me. Apparently she'd dropped in a couple of times while I was sleeping, but I was only awake for her latest visit. Friend or researcher? I still wasn't sure about her. I'd never wondered what a lab rat felt like, but lucky me, I got to find out anyway. She had a theory; something about my cat going into shock when I became a vampire. She was planning a meditation regimen she wanted me to try which she hoped would help me reconnect. My claws had retracted during the first day, and thus far I hadn't been able to summon them again. Still, claws were a pretty damn good sign that I might shift again one day. I was willing to give Gil's program a try.

I rolled a blue marble across my palm, then tried to slide it into my pocket before remembering I was only in one of Nathanial's white shirts. I'd tried to get more fully dressed, but anything else felt like salt on my wounds. I had debated not wearing anything, but I didn't think Nathanial would be happy to find me wandering outside naked. He'd finally bought me some underwear, not that the stringy garments covered anything. We were scheduled to go shopping as soon as I stopped looking like road kill.

Regan walked up to the door and stuck his big head out. He stared at me and made a pitiful whining sound. I cringed and gently but firmly pushed the door shut again. Hopefully all he'd been trying to tell me was that he didn't approve of my letting the cold air in. He might have been wondering when Nathanial would return. I know I was.

I stared at the sky, but couldn't make out anything but the snow falling from the low-hanging clouds. Even if the sky had been clear, I wouldn't have seen much. Nathanial would be using his illusion trick, thus making himself invisible, and it was the night of the new moon, so she wouldn't be visible tonight either. Even though I knew it was hopeless, I continued watching the sky for some sign Nathanial was coming home.

It had surprised me when Nathanial agreed to fly Bobby to the city and back, but I guess there wasn't any other practical way to get to and from Nathanial's house. Both of them had business in the city tonight, so it had made sense at the time, but I was frightfully lonely.

I'd clearly become too accustomed to company.

Bobby had needed to meet with the other hunters to arrange Lorna and Candice's abduction from the hospital before the full moon. Katie, too. She had to be monitored. If any of the girls shifted, it would be disastrous if the shift happened in public. Of course, if they didn't shift, and Candice or Lorna were still in critical condition, removing them from the hospital might mean their death.

I wasn't sure what the percentage of people who survived a shifter attack were tagged. No matter what, I felt responsible for their conditions, and it ate at my conscience. At the same time, I had the poisonous thoughts of the rogues fluttering around in my mind. They had enjoyed the torment they'd caused. I was a little afraid I might start to think like Tyler one day. I felt him lurking in the back of my mind, but Nathanial claimed the memories would fade. That really didn't alleviate the fear.

Didn't matter. I had lots to fear. Like the full moon, two weeks from now. .

Bobby still insisted that I return to Firth. He'd pointed out that going back would solve my hunter problem. That would be good, but how could I face my father and tell him what I'd become? Nathanial enthusiastically encouraged the trip, in fact, he wanted to go as well. A prospect both Bobby and I firmly rejected. Of course, I'd dug my claws and teeth into Nathanial several times, so there was a chance he'd been tagged. I shivered. There were two more weeks to fret over it still, and there were other things to worry about before then.

The vampires expected me to make an appearance at their council in the coming nights. I was exempt tonight only because of my recent injury. Before I returned to Death's Angel, I needed to have a serious talk with Nathanial about what to expect, and what I really shouldn't do if I didn't want to end up in a fight. Not that, even knowing what not to do, I could always hold my tongue.

I rubbed my lower back through the shirt. I still bore the judge's mark. I'd hoped it would disappear, but I'd watched the snakes slither over each other for a long time in Nathanial's bedroom mirror earlier. I had to admit it was beautiful, if terribly creepy, but the mark wasn't fading away, so the judge was probably serious when he threatened to call on me again. I only hoped that if he showed up again, it would be with a job assignment for me, and not because he'd gotten my protected status revoked.

I sighed and pushed off the porch. As long as I didn't do anything stupid, and the judge didn't win his appeal, I was immortal, but unlike Nathanial, that prospect didn't make me any more patient.

There was an itch in me that wanted to move on, to leave this city behind. Not just because I wanted to forget about being a vampire, or the rogues either. Perhaps Nathanial was right, maybe I was afraid to trust or need other people. But here I was, waiting anxiously for others to return.

I paced a trench in front of Nathanial's porch. The snow crunched under my bare feet. It would have been easy, with everyone gone, to run into the woods and disappear. I glanced across the snowy plain to the woods beyond. They crooned a song of freedom. I breathed in the sappy scent of the evergreens, listened for the sound of nocturnal life. I could just walk away.

Not tonight. Maybe tomorrow night, or the one after. I sighed. A catnap by the fire would be nice, at least until the guys returned.

After all, it had been a while since I'd had a home.

Kita's Nine Lives Continue
Twice Dead
Paperback and Ebook
Now Available

Born to rule the realm of shapeshifters.
Forced to serve in the realm of vampires.

Tatius wrapped his arm around my waist, and he turned me, tucking me against his hip so we were standing side by side. "You'll be on *my* arm tonight, Kita. Hermit, are you coming? We have an appointment with the Collector."

I'd seen Nathanial in a rage once before, and it had been a terrifying thing to behold. It was no less frightening to see now. "Get a hold of yourself," Tatius chided. "We will present a unified front, with all of my council backing the fact my companion had nothing to do with the albino's demise."

"Your companion?" Nathanial's words were hardly more than a broken scratching sound issuing from his throat. He looked at Tatius.

The rage had thinned in his face, a sharp edge of fear taking its place. I'd seen similar expressions on animals before. The question in their eyes wasn't an indication they were beaten—it was the panic of being backed into a corner. A cornered animal was deadly.

Tatius stroked my hair. "Yes, *my* companion." A statement. No question. No room to argue.

I tried to push free. "No."

The master vampire cocked a dyed eyebrow. "No? My dear, you get no say in this matter. You are a novelty, a child, a commodity. And now, you are mine."

Chapter One

I propped my elbows on the balcony rail that hung over the Death's Angel dance floor. Below me, industrial music pounded against scantily-clad bodies contorting to the beat. A man in a wolf mask and tight pleather pants ground against a girl wearing a tattered red cloak and strategically placed electrical tape. A zombie in more chains than clothes shambled past the couple, headed for a coven of dominatrix witches. Fictional characters and sexualized movie monsters milled everywhere. What most of the clubbers didn't realize was that among the costumed masses were real monsters—and I was one of them.

I glanced at the man beside me. Well, not a *man* exactly, more like vampire. Nathanial leaned against the wooden balcony rail, his back to the club and dancers. A white opera mask covered half his face, but unlike the famous mask of the fictional phantom, the thin porcelain didn't cover deformity or ugliness—far from it. Nathanial's features were as sharp and perfect as if they'd been carved by an artist. They were also currently set in an expression of annoyed arrogance that was as fake as the mask. He'd held that exact expression since we arrived at the club an hour ago.

"We showed up. We've been seen. Can we go now?" I asked, swirling the contents of my untouched Bloody Mary.

"Kita."

My name. Just my name, without any inflection. I took his meaning as 'No' or maybe that I already knew the answer. And I did. Tatius, the big bad vampire king of Haven, had summoned us to his little party for a visiting master vamp. So here we were. I balanced the acidic smelling drink on the rail. *And here we'll stay until we're dismissed.*

So far, my introduction into eternity as a vampire sucked—and not just blood. Sighing, I shoved the untouched alcohol aside. The bartender, dressed as, shock of all shocks, a vampire—complete with genuine fangs—retrieved the precariously balanced glass before moving on to a customer whose drinking habits required a lower iron content.

Without the glass, I had nothing to fidget with, and my attention returned to the writhing bodies on the dance floor. So many people. So many hearts racing and crashing below thin skin. So many heartbeats drowning out the blaring music. Pressure built in the roof of my mouth, turning to pain as my fangs descended.

A warm hand landed on my shoulder, and I tore my gaze from the dancers. Nathanial watched me, his fingers sliding from my shoulder, down my arm, to my hand. My knuckles were white where I gripped the balcony rail.

I pried my fingers from the wood. Nathanial's crystal gray gaze flicked to the movement, then back to my mouth.

"It's nothing," I whispered, trying to keep my lips pressed over my fangs as I spoke.

Not that it mattered.

"Perhaps we should mingle." His expression didn't change. Not a feature twitched, despite the fact I knew he had no interest in talking to anyone in the balcony crowd.

The balcony was VIP only. Or really, VIV—Very Important Vampire. Some humans were present, as snacks. Thankfully, I hadn't noticed any public bloodletting. *Yet.* But, as vamps didn't trigger my prey instinct, mingling with them was less likely to result in my accidentally eating someone. On the other hand, it also meant I had to talk to the other vamps—which was way more dangerous, in my opinion.

It wasn't an option I was eager to embrace. "I just need some air."

The edge of Nathanial's lips tugged downward. A small motion, barely noticeable. It was his first slip all night—and it wasn't approval. We disagreed on my eating habits, or more accurately, the fact I was subsisting on only animal blood. He was of the opinion that I needed human blood. I was of the opinion that it was his fault I was on a liquid diet in the first place, and he better put up with my sustenance of choice. I sighed, blowing a lock of my tri-colored hair out of my face and intentionally misinterpreting his look.

"I know, I know. Vampire. I don't *need* to breathe," I whispered in an exaggerated huff. "But I can't change twenty-four years of expressions just because I recently woke up slightly less than alive."

Nathanial shook his head, but a smile touched the edge of his mouth. "Walk with me."

His fingers slid through mine and tugged me from the balcony rail. Reluctantly, I followed him into the crowd of vampires.

The costumes on this level were more diverse than those on the dance floor below. True masquerade outfits, elegant dresses, velvet top coats, and jewel-encrusted masks made the balcony crowd colorful. But for every Victorian dress or harlequin was a vampire wearing only leather straps across strategic body parts. I couldn't recognize the native Haven vamps by sight, but considering my previous experience with the local vamps, and the fact Death's Angel was operated by them, I suspected the visitors weren't the ones in bondage gear.

Nathanial conformed to neither group. His porcelain mask was plain, unadorned, and his black hair hung in a long ponytail trailing down the center of his back, blending with the lush fabric of his opera coat. His costume defined elegance in simple stark black and white.

In contrast, my costume was garishly bright. Black and orange tiger stripes decorated my skin-tight unitard. Faux fur rimmed my white gloves and fuzzy white boots. A striped mask completed the outfit. My mess of calico locks—my hair's natural color and a reminder of what I had been until a couple weeks ago—almost matched the costume. Almost. Nathanial had asked me if I could be anything, what I would be.

I glared at the stripes. Tiger stripes. Like my father's. *Me and my big mouth.*

"Hermit, it has been a long time," a male voice said.

I cringed. Only vamps called Nathanial 'Hermit.'

Nathanial turned toward the voice, moving me with him, and I looked up, and then up some more. The speaker towered over us, and while I was on the short side, Nathanial wasn't. The man wore a fitted crushed velvet maroon frock coat I could have used as a dress. Falls of lace escaped from his cuffs and collar, and a gold mask set with rubies obscured wide features. He was so massive, it took me a moment to notice the small woman at his side. She was his exact opposite. Where he was all blunt edges she was sharp, petite. She was my height, but beside him she looked like a fragile doll in her frilled dress and silver mask.

"Three hundred years, I believe, Traveler," Nathanial said, his voice polite but disinterested.

"At least." The giant's gaze moved from Nathanial to me and then back. "A lot has changed in that time."

I groaned silently—or perhaps not all that silently, as all eyes moved to me. *Oops.* Still, I didn't want to listen as they hashed out three hundred years of vampire history as small talk. I glanced around.

There was an empty spot on a couch in the far corner of the balcony.

"I think I'll just . . . " I pointed at the couch.

Nathanial's eyes frowned at me. Not his mouth, or his expression, I'd just come to know those eyes, to know *him*, well enough over the last few weeks to see the fact he didn't think it was a good idea.

"It's just right there," I said, backing away as I spoke.

He didn't stop me, so I turned tail, all but running for the sanctuary of the couch.

Most of the seating on the balcony was filled—vamps tended to sprawl, but the couch I claimed had only one other person sitting rigidly at the other end. She wore a simple, black–and-white, harlequin jumper with an elaborate, full-faced mask, a large feathered hat, and brown curls that looked so synthetic they had to be a wig.

She didn't move as I collapsed onto the far cushion, and I let out a relieved breath. *At least I won't be expected to socialize.* I refilled my lungs—the habits of the living die hard—and that was a mistake.

The cloying scent of blood rolled over my tongue, caught in the back of my throat, filled my senses. The scent was cold, bitter, not all that appetizing, but it was very close and thus, tempting. Oh, so close. My fangs burst free in a flash of hunger, and I slid across the cushion without consciously deciding to move.

The woman didn't react or look up as I sidled up next to her. There was something *off* about the scent of her blood. But that didn't matter. Not right now. All that mattered was the smell of it.

My fingers brushed her shoulder.

The mask tumbled forward.

The hat and wig followed, the wig's synthetic curls flying.

I jumped to my feet. Above the frill of her collar was a stubby, raw neck. No head.

A fake mannequin head *plunked* against the floor. Rolled. It stopped finally, settling three feet from the couch. I backed away, aware of the heavy silence suddenly coalescing on the balcony. Industrial music still pounded below me, but the vampires had gone deadly still.

A large hand closed around my arm. The grip tight. Painful.

"What did you do?" A rough voice whispered the question behind my ear.

"I, uh . . . " I gulped and made a wild, floundering motion from the head to the body. "Her head just fell off?"

A woman in a gold-trimmed gown stepped forward and knelt to

study the fake head. Un-seeing glass eyes stared out of it. As if all tied to one string, every vampire in the room shifted their gaze from the head, to me, and then to the body, which was still perched primly on the couch. Her hands were in her lap, one gripping a glass balanced on her thigh, but she was definitely *not* a mannequin. The smell of blood aside, I could see the white of her exposed spine among the pinker flesh of her throat.

"What is the meaning of this?" demanded the woman in the gold trimmed gown. "Where is her head?"

I thought, at first, that the woman was asking *me*. As if I had any idea. Then I realized her glare went over my shoulder, to the man still gripping my arm. I glanced back, but didn't recognize the vamp holding me. Based on the leather pants loaded with silver studded straps, and the electric blue hair that fell to his chin in jagged tapered tips, I guessed he was one of the local vamps. Then I noticed his eyes: green and old, with a gaze that landed like a physical weight on my skin.

Tatius.

I swallowed hard. Oh crap, a decapitated body *and* the attention of the king of Haven. Did I know how to break up a party or *what?*

Chapter Two

"What happened?" Tatius demanded, his glare boring into me.

I looked around. Nathanial was several feet away, standing at the edge of the semi-circle that had opened around me. His posture was aloof, uninterested, but he watched me without blinking. He tapped two long fingers on his full bottom lip, as if idly contemplating an obscure thought, but again, his gaze didn't waver. *Something about my mouth?* I pressed my lips together.

Crap. My fangs were still out.

I willed the damn things to retract, and Tatius's grip on my arm tightened. He shook me.

"I said, what happened?"

"I touched her shoulder, that was all."

"Should we guess why?" A chime-like voice spoke from somewhere in the mass of vampires.

I gritted my teeth and resisted the urge to press my hand over my mouth. My fangs weren't visible anymore, I knew that, but it was no great mystery to anyone on the balcony what had been motivating me. "She smelled like blood," I muttered under my breath.

I should have known better. Vampire hearing was exquisite.

The woman in the gold-trimmed dress lifted an arched eyebrow dotted with rhinestones. "In this crowd, I should think more than a reckless *child* "—she dismissed me with the insult—"would have noticed blood. Unless there was some trick involved." She stared at the posed figure again. There was no blood on the collar of the outfit—there wasn't even blood around the cleanly severed stub of neck. The woman turned back to Tatius. "What have you to say of this, Puppet Master?"

"My apologies, Collector. I assure you, I intend to get to the bottom of it." Tatius's gruff voice crackled down my back.

Collector? Great. The Collector was the big bad star of this party. The guest of honor. I *so* needed to get out of here. In my old life I'd learned better than to pull an alpha cat's tail—though knowing better didn't mean it didn't happen anyway, sometimes. But I totally hadn't meant to land in the center of this attention.

"Nuri," Tatius said, turning toward the crowd. The mass of vampires who—now that the initial shock of the body's discovery had worn off—were murmuring among themselves, parted to allow a preteen girl through.

As the girl, Nuri, approached, Tatius released my arm. *Thank the moon.* I moved to step aside, but his hand slid around the back of my neck. The touch wasn't restraining, but it was overly personal, his fingers coming to a rest in the hollow between my collarbone and throat. *Oh hell no.* The last time I met Tatius, he'd considered killing me. Then he'd forced his blood in me. I did *not* want anything else to do with the vamp.

I tried to shrug him away, but his fingers flexed in response, his nails biting against my skin. Okay, so apparently I was going to have to make a scene—another scene—or stay put. I erred on the side of caution, for once.

Nuri, dressed as an ancient Egyptian queen with a large snake peeking out beneath her dark dreadlocks, knelt beside the harlequin. As I watched her lift the dead woman's hand, I realized where I'd seen Nuri before. She'd sat at the council table the first time I was brought before the vampires, which meant she must be a lot older than she looked.

After a moment of poking at the body, she stood and turned to Tatius. "Rigor mortis has only begun to set, so I'd guess she's been dead no more than four hours. There is no tearing of the flesh, so she was decapitated by a sharp instrument. The lack of blood suggests she was drained before death. I'll report more when I find it." The words were too old, too serious for her thin, girlish voice. Not that anyone else appeared to notice. She stepped aside and nodded to two pleather-clad vampires, who rushed forward to lift the body and carry it toward a private elevator in the corner. The fake head still lay on the floor, ignored.

The Collector stepped forward, over the forgotten head, until the train of her dress engulfed it. "You have your Truthseeker looking into things, and while I'm sure she will be very thorough"—the way she said it made it clear she was *not* certain of any such thing—"I offer the assistance of one of my vampires." Without waiting for an answer, she lifted her hand. "Elizabeth, attend us."

Tatius's fingers flexed against my skin. *Agitation? Anger?* But he didn't say anything as the small, doll-like woman I'd seen earlier in the night on the giant's arm stepped forward.

"I will be happy to assist," the woman said, curtsying to the Collector. Then she turned and her icy eyes caught on mine. "At least we know the harlequin wasn't this fledgling's *snack*."

Tatius's fingers flexed again, harder this time. "Hermit, find her someone to eat." He shoved me toward Nathanial, and I gladly retreated from the center of attention.

Nathanial's arm slipped around my waist as I reached him, and he wove us through the crowd, away from the couches. We passed the two vampires waiting for the elevator with the body, and I breathed deeply, rolling the decapitated woman's scent through my senses. The sweet tang of blood reached for me, made the roof of my mouth burn, but I focused on committing her scent to memory.

Nathanial didn't fail to notice my signs of hunger. "I am taking you home."

Home. It was a nice thought. I'd had enough with vampires. Enough of their double-tongued political games. And enough headless bodies. But . . .

I glanced back at the vamps loading the corpse into the elevator, but it wasn't her harlequin costume I saw. My mind replaced her with the image of another body, one bloated from several days of death. A human body that had been, in part, my fault, because I'd accidentally created the shifter who'd killed her. I'd tracked the murderer, stopped him, but the weight of his victims wore on me.

Nathanial studied me with eyes that saw too much. Eyes that stripped away my secrets. He shook his head, a small smile tipping the edge of his lips. It wasn't a happy smile. I looked away, and he drew me closer to the side of his body without breaking stride toward the stairs.

"I will take you to the hospital," he said. "You can visit them."

Two weeks ago, I would have avoided hospitals at all costs. But then, two weeks ago, I'd still had to breathe to live, I'd spent most of my time as a six-pound calico kitten, and I hadn't yet known I'd created a rogue who'd gone on a killing spree. A rogue whose victim count totaled fourteen women.

The only two survivors were currently in medically-induced comas at Saint Mary's Hospital. Two weeks ago it would have been easier to walk away from a headless body. To trust that someone *else* would deal with it. A lot can change in two weeks.

I glanced back at the gathered vampires. All the vampires in Haven were on this balcony. The harlequin had been drained of blood.

If the killer was a vampire, he was here. *It has nothing to do with me. This murder isn't my responsibility. It isn't.*

I let Nathanial lead me out of the club. But damn, guilt was a bitch.

☙ • ❧

Two hours later, I walked into Nathanial's kitchen. Without Nathanial. After all, we hadn't been formally dismissed by Tatius, so he had to return to Death's Angel after our visit to the hospital. I was still flushed from the flight home as I followed the sounds of the television into the front den. Even after dozens of airborne trips with Nathanial, I still couldn't get enough of the wind in my face and watching the world slip by below us. I could only hope the ability to fly would be a vampire trick I'd learn one day.

I pushed open the den door. "You up for a hunt?"

Bobby, a shifter from my home world of Firth, and once the big love of my life, was currently a couch-crasher in Nathanial's cabin and would continue to be until the gate to Firth reopened and he could return to his pregnant mate. He looked up as I entered. Our relationship was complicated, and awkward, but we were working it out. Mostly. When he wasn't threatening to drag me back to Firth with him, that is.

He hit a button on the remote, muting the brightly animated cartoon on the screen. Then he lifted his feet from the arm of the couch. I slid into the free spot.

"So, hunting?"

"Still hungry? We caught dinner before you left." He frowned, his brow creasing, and he rolled to a sitting position. "Did something happen at that vamp club?"

"It, no, well . . . " I grabbed one of the hunter green throw pillows and dragged it into my lap. "I'm just hungry."

Bobby slid closer, moving into my personal space. "You're starting to smell like a frightened rabbit."

Okay, this was what I meant by awkward.

I jumped to my feet. "I'll just go by myself."

"Kitten . . . "

"Forget I asked." I headed for the door. Bobby was right. We'd already hunted tonight. Even with the heightened metabolism of a shapeshifter, Bobby was only one person and his other form was a bobcat—he didn't need two rabbits in one night. Hell, in Firth, he wouldn't have eaten more than three or four rabbits a week. It was wasteful to kill more tonight.

He caught up with me at the front door and pulled his sweater off despite the blanket of snow spreading out around the cabin. He had to shift if he intended to hunt.

I took the front steps two at a time. "I said to forget it."

He jutted his chin and continued to disrobe. "We'll freeze the extra meat." His fingers moved to the button of his jeans. "You hunting like that?"

I glanced down. I was still wearing the ridiculous tiger suit, but unlike Bobby, my clothes didn't matter. He'd lose a lot of mass once he shifted, and a thirty-pound bobcat couldn't exactly wear a two-hundred-pound man's jeans and sweater. Technically, whenever I shifted, my clothing disappeared. That was my gift. Or it had been, before I became a vampire. Now I was stuck in one form. My claws had extended, once, when I'd been in a fight for my life against the rogues. But since then, my cat had remained locked in the cold coil inside me. Dead.

I kicked off my party boots. "Let's hunt."

❧ • ❧

A Note From Kalayna Price

My name is on the cover of this book, but I didn't get here alone. Many people helped me reach this point, so I'd like thank everyone as a whole (you know who you are), and mention several people in particular.

A tremendous amount of thanks goes to my wonderful editors, Debra Dixon and Deborah Smith, who saw the potential in *Once Bitten* and helped me polish it to the state it is now. Many thanks to the ladies in my critique group, the Modern Myth Makers, and to my beta readers Michelle and Megan—you saw things I was far too deep in the story to see. Special thanks to my parents who put up with me all these years, and who encouraged and supported me in my dreams.

Thanks Abi, for too many things to mention. A very special thanks to my husband who understands that talking about people who only exist in my head and on my computer does not make me crazy, and who never questioned my need to spend massive amounts of time pounding out words on my keyboard. I'd also like to thank Chris, Erin, and all the folks over in the Office of Letters and Light who run National Novel Writing Month every year. NaNoWriMo taught me to write with abandon. I don't think the first draft of this book would have ever been completed if I hadn't learned that. Thank you everyone.

And, thank you, the person holding this book and reading this acknowledgment. I hope you enjoy the read!

Visit Kalayna at www.kalaynanicoleprice.com